...is an exquisite ...l mashup permeated with action ...ance! This book had my heart thundering ...y chest on so many levels! One of the many things I love about MacTague's writing is her ability to create strong, complex and "real" characters and the wonderful dynamic she develops between them. This book is no exception! All great steampunk features wonderful gadgets and contraptions and this novel is rife with such inventions as multifunctional goggles, powerful jump suits enabling the scaling of tall buildings and, of course, the new horseless carriage. My favourite aspect is how MacTague adds her own flair to these gadgets in terms of how they are powered. I also love how she brilliantly captures the atmosphere; the romance, etiquette and manners of the Victorian era and then pumps it full of grotesque imps and demons! However, what really draws me in to Lise's novels is her fantastic characterization. So, if you enjoy layered, well realized and imperfect but enticing characters, then this book is definitely for you!

MacTague is really suited to steampunk! She excels at writing stories with strong women and Briar and Isabella are no exception. *Demon in the Machine* is a wonderful mélange of mystery, steampunk, paranormal and romance that is appealing on so many levels!

-*The Lesbian Review*

Five Moons Rising

MacTague completely knocks it out of the park with this one, one of the best lesbian paranormals I've read. This book blew me away. Not just for the imagination MacTague demonstrated around the different creatures that haunt the darkness and the work Malice and her colleagues have to undertake to defeat the rogue ones, but also because of the underlying themes and threads that hit on so many subjects. Family, commitment, what it means to belong, what it means to trust–MacTague covers them all and in writing that's so powerful it took my breath away at times.

It's another winner from MacTague, who is rapidly becoming one of my all-time favorite lesfic authors.

-Rainbow Book Reviews

This book is absolutely brilliant. It is filled with memorable characters and a plot that will keep you coming back to it even when you know you should be working or sleeping or doing something else. MacTague really got into her head and gave us a beautiful account of what it would be like to be a werewolf. It was so wonderfully done that I now have a massive book crush.

-The Lesbian Review

Vortex of Crimson

MacTague does it again... a fantastic end to the saga that has seen Jak and Torrin fight all sorts of battles, both physical and emotional. I love how MacTague mixes in the action scenes and conspiracy theories alongside the touching and sometimes angsty romance between Jak and Torrin. Neither the action nor the romance ever takes over completely, the balance is always spot on.

-Rainbow Book Reviews

Heights of Green

What a rip-roaring sequel this is to *Depths of Blue*! There are layers within layers in this book, and the subtle ways they are revealed is brilliant in its execution. It's clear something is going on, but MacTague teases this out, strand by strand, and brings it all to a stunning ending. There's politics, intrigue, action, and lots of emotion. Both Jak and Torrin's actions and reactions are explored in just the right amount of detail alongside the story itself, and it's a fantastic blend. The book finishes on a great cliffhanger, ready for book three, and I can't wait to get started on that.

-Rainbow Book Review

The ending had me standing on my feet. Reading it had me pumped and the teaser at the end did nothing to slow my heart rate down. The way Jak's and Torrin's journeys split apart and then come back together had me turning pages so fast I got a digital paper cut and those SOBs hurt! But it was worth it.

-The Lesbian Review

Depths of Blue

I thoroughly enjoyed the story and the characters that Lise MacTague has drawn in *Depths of Blue*. The world building is top-notch and the backstories of the characters are told in such a way as to move the story along and not in a pedantic, expository way. I would recommend anyone who likes a good sci-fi book give this a try.

-Lesbian Reading Room

This is a proper sci-fi/action/adventure story with two very strong female leads and I absolutely loved it! Both Torrin and Jak are kickass women, and that was such a refreshing change—there's no tough butch here rescuing a weak femme damsel in distress. They can both look after themselves and they therefore have a lovely tension between them from the start. This is part one of a trilogy and I cannot wait to get into book two—I love MacTague's story-telling, her narrative and descriptive skills, and the universe she's created. Excellent lesbian sci-fi, of which there isn't enough, so this is a brilliant addition to that genre.

-Rainbow Book Reviews

BREAKING OUT

About the Author

Lise writes speculative and romantic lesbian fiction (sometimes in the same book). This is her first foray into contemporary romance. Previous to this, she has written space opera, steampunk, and paranormal urban fantasy. She grew up in Canada, but left Winnipeg for warmer climes. After flitting around the US, she settled in North Carolina where the winters suit her quite well, thank you very much. These days, there isn't nearly enough hockey in her life. She makes up for that lack by cramming writing in around her wife and kids, work, and building video game props in the garage, with the occasional break for D&D and podcasting. Find some free short stories and more about what she's up to at lisemactague.com.

BREAKING OUT

LISE MACTAGUE

BELLA
BOOKS

2021

Bella Books, Inc.
P.O. Box 10543
Tallahassee, FL 32302

Printed in the United States of America on acid-free paper.

First Bella Books Edition 2021

Editor: Medora MacDougall
Cover Designer: Kayla Mancuso

ISBN: 978-1-64247-182-3

Acknowledgments

Thanks as ever to those brave souls who were willing to beta read this story: Lynn, Amy, Mildred, and Tracey. Thank you especially to KD Williamson for being a sensitivity reader and keeping me from stepping in it too deeply while I was seeking to depict a Black main character. Any errors of characterization are my own.

Many thanks to my editor, Medora MacDougall, for polishing the heck out of this one. I appreciated the patience as I took a hard left away from my preferred genre.

Thank you to the Bella crew for giving lesbians their own voice in publishing, and for including mine in that chorus. Our stories deserve to be told and I'm honored to be a part of that with you.

Thank you to Kayla Mancuso for working with me on the cover. It may have taken us a few tries, but I'm proud to have a cover that represents the book and its diverse cast so well.

To my new readers: welcome! To my returning readers, thank you for coming back! I appreciate you all, and am glad you decided to take a chance on my books. The stories in my head demand to be told, but it's your reactions that keep me publishing them. Thank you for continually inspiring me to keep writing.

Finally, to my wife and kids (Lynn, Whit, and Ce), thank you for continuing to put up with me, for allowing me to hijack road trips into plotting sessions, and occasionally losing the thread of conversations to the action going on inside my head. I love you all so much, and not a day goes by when I don't count myself among the luckiest people in the world.

Dedication

For the women of the Brew City Blades. I miss playing with you, Bladies!

CHAPTER ONE

"You're pregnant?"

Shit! KJ Stennes forced a wide smile onto her face, then bent over her skate and yanked hard at the laces. "That's great!" she growled at the floor. *Crap! This is the last thing we need!*

The rest of the women in the cramped room echoed her words, though with more sincerity than KJ was feeling.

"So when do you stop playing?" KJ transferred her attention to the laces on her other skate. "Don't people play until like five, six months?"

Jamie laughed. "I'm not surprised that's the first thing you'd ask. This is my last game. My doctor said it's probably okay to play until twelve weeks or so, but with my family history..." She shrugged.

"At least we have today." KJ pulled her socks down over the tops of her skates and scooted forward off the bench. She rummaged around in her hockey bag, looking for her shin guards. They came out covered in black flakes that she absentmindedly brushed off. It was time to get a new bag. She'd get around to that one day; after all, the waterproof lining had only been flaking off since last season.

Jamie draped an arm around her shoulder when she sat back down. "Look, I know you're probably freaking out right now, but it'll be okay."

"I'm not freaking out. I'm happy for you, I really am!" And she was. The whole team knew Jamie and Joe had been trying to get pregnant for a few years, but without any luck. KJ knew how badly her best friend wanted a child. "This is everything you've wanted."

If only they'd waited another year. This would have been their year to win the league championship. The first few Bolts practices had been...well, electric. Their group had been together for seven years now, each season bringing them closer. Sure, there had been some of the turnover that was to be expected on any team, especially a rec team comprised of women who were college-age through grandmothers, but the last two had been remarkably stable. They all knew how everyone played. There was no need to think about where Jean might be. KJ knew once she'd corralled the puck behind the net that Jean would be busting her ass up the boards. If she couldn't hit her with the breakout pass, Connie or Rebecca would be curling up the center, ready to go.

The Bolts only had four women on defense. There were three forward lines each with three women, but they hadn't felt the need to run three lines on D. Jamie had been her defensive partner the whole time, and now KJ was being asked to give her up with only one game to go.

KJ's shoulders slumped. "We only have four D. What are we going to do about that?"

"I've got it covered," Jamie said. "She's great. Played defense in high school. You won't have to deal with an out-of-place center, I promise."

"You sure?" KJ glanced around the crowded room. The cinderblock walls had seen better days. Light blue paint had flaked in places to reveal bright green below it and maroon below that. The Sussburg Ice Arena was her second home; there were times she felt like it had saved her life. Windsor County boasted exactly one ice rink, and she was fortunate it was in her hometown. There weren't many in this part of Central Pennsylvania. At least she didn't have to make the drive down to Harrisburg to get her hockey fix. It was what kept her centered, and it was now in danger of falling apart around her, just when she thought things might be getting a bit better.

Her teammates had gone back to strapping on their pads or were chatting quietly enough that they couldn't be heard over the music playing on Rebecca's iPhone. Jamie's announcement seemed to have cast a bit of a pall over their normally raucous pregame preparations.

KJ loved the women on her team dearly, even the ones who drove her up the wall. Any of them would do their best if moved back on defense, but it wouldn't be the same. The centers were the most logical choice. There would be no disruption to the wing pairs, and on paper at least, centers played defense and offense. Unfortunately all the Bolts' centers were far more offensive-minded than defensive-minded. Part of that was her and Jamie's fault. They were so solid on D that the centers rarely had to drop back to help out for long.

"I'm sure," Jamie said. "Trust me. I wouldn't line you up with someone who couldn't play. Now will you stop looking like we're at a funeral?"

"Okay, you got me. I'm happy for you, but I wish you could have waited until after playoffs."

Jamie squeezed her shoulder. "There's more to life than playoffs."

"I know." KJ kept her voice soft. There was no reason for the others to hear her being crappy about Jamie's big news.

"No, you don't." Jamie gentled her tone to match KJ's. "But you will." She shook KJ playfully. "Now get your gear on so we can stomp all over those Yetis."

KJ stretched her lips into an approximation of a grin. "They won't know what hit them."

* * *

The other team had come to play. KJ plunked her butt on the bench and gulped down a cool stream of water from the waiting bottle. It soothed her throat, made raw from hauling ass up and down the rink.

"Those Yetis are running our asses off," Jamie yelled around her mouth guard.

"Are they?" KJ made a show of stretching nonchalantly. "I hadn't noticed."

Jamie swatted her with the back of her glove. "Sure you did. How many times did you have to bail me out? Two?"

"Three, but I'm not counting."

"Very funny."

"You're pinching in a little on the blue line," KJ said. "Don't go after that puck unless you know you can get it."

"I always think I can."

"No thinking." KJ rapped her glove-covered knuckle on the top of Jamie's helmet. "If you have to think, it's too late."

Even through her face shield, Jamie's eye roll was as plain as day. "Sure thing, Yoda. Not all of us came out of the womb with skates on."

"I don't think my mom would have liked that." Though it might be one explanation for why she'd left KJ behind after divorcing her dad. KJ shook her head. Now was not the time to focus on her childhood drama.

"Probably not." Jamie took one last swig from her own water bottle. "Krissy and Cam are coming."

KJ popped up and waited by the boards as the other defensive pair came skating to the bench as hard as they could. The second period was the worst for substituting in players, especially for the defense. They were so far from their bench. The shift hadn't been long, but everyone learned the hard way that in the second period, you switched out when you had the opportunity. A four-minute shift was murder on the legs, not to mention the lungs.

At the far end, women's voices raised in excitement. The Yetis had the puck and knew the Bolts' defense was changing.

"Come on, Krissy!" KJ hollered. The broad swing of her arm did nothing to get the changing defensewoman to the bench, but she felt like she was helping.

Krissy's head went down, and her arms swung as she pushed herself forward as fast as she could go. The other team's center had the puck and was streaking out of her zone, already nearly to the center line. KJ waited another half second for Krissy to get close enough so she could jump the boards without incurring a penalty for too many players on the ice.

As soon as Krissy was within ten feet, KJ planted one hand on top of the boards and vaulted onto the ice. She was moving before she landed. The center had a couple of strides on her. KJ bit her lower lip and grinned as she pushed off, her blades biting deep. The sound that accompanied that first push sent a chill down her spine. There was nothing better than a footrace.

"One on!" came the call from further down the ice as one of the center's teammates alerted her to KJ's presence.

The warning wouldn't be enough.

She shot forward, all thoughts evaporating from her mind but one: take away the other player's easy path to the net.

She was low, her skate blades digging into the ice with a forceful crunch at each step. The center had to hear her, but she didn't look back. That was too bad; it would have slowed her down a fraction, possibly enough for KJ to bust past her. She dragged a breath deep into her lungs and lunged forward, drawing abreast of the center at the top of the face-off circle. Now the woman risked a glance her way. That was all KJ needed. She flicked her wrist almost negligently, sending her stick over to collide with the other woman's. She leaned forward, giving the Yeti nowhere to go but the trajectory KJ had picked, one that curved away from the net and her goalie.

Vaughn had squared up, presenting a wall of pads and light blue athletic material to their opponent. Their hand was raised, the glove ready should the Yeti try to get a shot off. She still might attempt it, but not while she was struggling to regain control of the puck. The Yeti jabbed KJ in the side, but her elbow glanced harmlessly off KJ's chest pad.

Taking advantage of the woman's distraction from stickhandling, KJ slid her other hand down the shaft of her stick, then lifted up the Yeti's stick. The puck squirted out and away from them. KJ swiveled her hips and dug her skate blades into the ice, stopping on a dime as the Yeti kept skating forward for a moment before she realized the puck was gone. By the time she was turned around and heading for the puck again, KJ had swooped in and nabbed it, sending it toward the far boards where Michelle waited. It landed against her teammate's stick with a satisfying "thwap," and just like that, the flow of the game reversed.

She coasted past the net while she kept her eye on the action at the other end of the ice. Jamie was in the neutral zone on her way to the blue line.

"Nice work," Vaughn said. They reached out their stick to tap KJ's shin guards.

"No extra charge," KJ yelled back. The mouth guard probably swallowed half of the words, but Vaughn nodded anyway.

The Yeti center who had tried to make good on her breakaway was heading to the bench. She was definitely going to need to freshen her legs up after that little bit of excitement. KJ firmed her grip on her stick. Hopefully, she'd have another crack at her.

Her own legs had a bit of a pleasant burn to them in the thigh. She didn't need a break just yet; she'd only been on the ice about fifteen seconds. She skated up to the other team's zone to take her position opposite Jamie.

She kept a sharp eye on the action as the puck was passed around among the Bolts forwards, from center to wing and back to center. The Yeti defense was starting to drag, their reactions becoming less crisp. KJ bided her time up at the line. The play wasn't coming her way quite yet. Across the way, Jamie was displaying similar patience but was also tormenting the Yeti left wing who was trying to cover her. Jamie kept sidling in front of her and the Yeti would respond by trying to move forward. KJ grinned. Jamie loved to screw with the other teams' forwards. Maybe that was why they made such a good pair.

The puck popped out from behind the net and up the boards. The forward on KJ couldn't take it any longer. She darted down to try to corral the loose puck, but Connie beat her to it.

"Open!" KJ thundered from the top of the face-off circle. She raised her stick, telegraphing the slapshot she was about to take from the perfect pass Connie sent her way. A defender threw her body between KJ and the net. The goalie went down to her knees to stop the shot she knew was coming.

KJ angled her body and sent the puck along to Jamie, who was no longer covered as the opposing forward dashed to get to the center of the ice.

"Yes!" she yelled as Jamie caught her pass, then swiveled to the net and let fly.

It was a perfect shot, skimming barely inside the right post above the goalie's hastily stuck out mitt.

The ref whistled, pointing at the back of the net, indicating the goal was good. KJ didn't need the confirmation. Elation bubbled in her chest as she skated across the ice to grab Jamie up in a celebratory hug.

"Nice shot!" she crowed, squeezing her partner tightly around the rib cage.

"Nicer pass!" Jamie said. "It's good to go out on a bang."

KJ squeezed her again, then ducked out as the rest of her teammates skated up to pound her partner on the shoulders and helmet.

Jamie was leaving. She'd managed to forget that for a few shifts.

CHAPTER TWO

Adrienne Pierce inhaled deeply, pulling the scent of the rink through her nostrils. Her body was practically vibrating with excitement. It remembered the smell and what it promised: the joy of competition, the camaraderie, the disappointment of defeat, and beneath it all the thrum of adrenaline. The chance to be part of something bigger than she was by herself and coming out knowing she'd given it everything she had. Even losses were palatable when she could look inside herself and know she had done everything in her power. And the wins…

Adrienne hadn't realized how much she missed the smell of ice tinged with sweat. It had been nine years? No, at least ten. Ten years since she last played a game. It was past time to knock the rust off her skate blades. At least she'd managed to keep herself in decent shape. The hand-me-down exercise bike in the corner of her room saw use every night almost.

The scoreboard blasted a long note to signify the end of the game. The Bolts had held onto their 1-0 lead with little more than bloody-mindedness and grit. Without some stellar play by the defense, they probably would have lost. Adrienne might not have played since high school, but she could still read a game like the back of her hand. The Yetis had wanted this one but had been stymied by the team play of the Bolts.

She smiled. This was exactly the kind of group she wanted to play with. Excitement warred with anxiety in the pit of her stomach. The level of play was pretty high, overall. There were a couple of slower women on the team, but they were more than balanced out by the top players, especially one of the defensewomen. She played like she could have taken over the game at any time but was choosing not to. Hopefully she wouldn't be partnered with her.

"What do you think, baby?" Adrienne looked down at the boy hunched over a couple of action figures he was manipulating along the seat of the bleachers behind them.

All she saw was the top of his light brown mop of loose curls. "I'm not a baby, Mom."

"No, you're not." She reached forward and ruffled his hair fondly. "Sorry, Lawrence." He had a point. It was time to come up with a better pet name for him. Adrienne waited a second, but her son had returned to the engrossing exploits of his superheroes. "So? Can you see Mom out there doing that?"

"I guess." He shrugged one shoulder.

A movement at the corner of her eye caught her attention. A woman in a Bolts jersey and full gear was standing at the edge of the bleachers and waving at her. Adrienne squinted. The player pulled off her helmet, revealing Jamie's familiar face and blond ponytail. She waved back in acknowledgment.

"It's time to go." Adrienne placed a hand on Lawrence's shoulder.

"Okay." He stashed the action figures in the pocket of his jacket.

"Don't forget Captain What's-His-Pants."

"That's Thor, Mom. Geez." Lawrence snagged the third toy from under the bleachers and stood up.

Adrienne looked over. Jamie was still at the corner, leaning on a stick and chatting with another member of the Bolts. She guided Lawrence forward with a gentle hand between the shoulder blades.

"Hi, Jamie," she said after they'd climbed down the stairs.

"Hi y'rself." Jamie grinned, her bright green mouth guard still obscuring her teeth. "Wha'd you tink of th'game?" She held up a finger. "One sec." She spat the mouth guard out into her hand, then grimaced in apology.

"No worries. You know I speak mouth guard." Adrienne grinned widely. "That was great. You guys held on to that lead with your finger and toenails, but you got it. Who got the goal?"

"I did, thanks to KJ here." Jamie bumped the woman next to her with her shoulder.

KJ spared a glance back at Adrienne but didn't say anything.

"This is who I told you about," Jamie said. "Adrienne. She agreed to fill in."

"You play?" KJ slowly turned to regard her. Her words were a little clearer through her mouth guard. It was more fitted than the clunky piece of plastic Jamie wore.

Adrienne understood the look far better than the words. She'd gotten it all the time in high school when people found out she played hockey. She knew what people saw when they looked at her, and it wasn't someone who fit white people's idea of an athlete, on or off the ice. She was too Black, too curvaceous, her black hair too kinky and untamed. Like having darker skin and eyes the color of onyx made her somehow less-suited to athletic competition. Apparently ovaries and curves meant she shouldn't be interested in physical contests.

KJ's eyes cut down to Lawrence and a little crease appeared between her eyebrows before smoothing out quickly. Maybe to cover up her annoyance, KJ pulled off her helmet. Her hair was on the long side of short. It looked like it hadn't been cut in a long time. Sweat plastered it to her head, but when dry it would have fallen into her face. The blond hue was a bit too close to that of Lawrence's father for Adrienne's comfort, though it lacked her son's curls. Her narrowed eyes were light brown, which was good or they would have gotten lost in a face the color of raw biscuit dough.

"Yeah, I play," Adrienne said.

"Mom, do you have all that gear?" Lawrence chose that point to pipe up. The crease reappeared on KJ's face.

"Yes, sweet-pea, I do."

He gave her a sideways look at the new nickname, but didn't mention it. "Where is it?" he asked instead.

"It's at Gramma's house."

"We played against each other in high school," Jamie said. She shot KJ an annoyed look. "Adrienne knows her way around the ice."

"Then it's been a while?" KJ asked casually. "What did you play?"

"A little bit. I'm sure it'll be fine." Adrienne took a quick breath to calm the irritation rising in her breast at the third degree. "I played defense."

"What side?"

"Does it matter for D? I don't really care. I'm used to slotting in wherever my partner isn't."

KJ nodded slowly. "I'm sweaty and gross and getting cold. I'll see you in the locker room." She jerked her head awkwardly toward Adrienne, then took off toward the bowels of the rink.

Jamie stared after KJ for a moment, then turned back to Adrienne. "Sorry about her. She can be intense. The game didn't go like she expected, and with my news… Well, she isn't always this much of a jerk. Usually she's a lot of fun."

"Mm-hmm. A laugh and a half, I bet." The excitement in her belly was curdling into anxiety. "She's really good."

"She is, but she works it so the team benefits, not her, you know?"

"Yeah." Adrienne sighed. "I saw."

"You can keep up with her. I do, and you more than kept up with me in high school."

"I don't remember it quite that way." They'd been pretty evenly matched. Every time they'd played Jamie's team, she'd had to skate her rump off to keep the woman covered.

"I do. You were a royal pain in my ass."

Lawrence looked up, his eyes round at the word. "We don't say ass," he announced. "We say butt."

"Lawrence, what did I say about correcting other people?" Adrienne tried to keep the exasperation from her tone. Her son was usually sweet, but he certainly liked to hew to the rules and hadn't yet figured out that he did himself no favors by expecting others to be as diligent.

Jamie laughed. "It's all right. I forgot to get into teacher mode." She squatted down to his level. "Sorry, buddy. It's true though. Your mom would be all over my butt whenever we played her team. She never let me get away with anything. She was hard-core."

"Okay." Lawrence wasn't impressed with the reassurance. "Mom, can we go? I'm cold." He reached up and took her hand. Sure enough, his fingers were like little chunks of ice.

"Why didn't you wear your mittens like I said?" Adrienne asked.

"I couldn't see my action figures."

"Gotcha." Adrienne looked back at Jamie. "I bet you're getting cold too."

"It's all right. So are you in?"

Adrienne hesitated. If she'd been asked before meeting KJ, her answer would have been a resounding "Hell, yeah!" but after the interaction there was a serious crimp in her excitement.

"Come on," Jamie said. "I swear she'll be better. Today wasn't a good day for her. She's had some troubles lately. Besides, it's not like you sign a contract. If you don't like it, you can stop playing. You're taking my slot, and I've already paid for it, so you won't even be out the money."

"I said I'd cover the rest of the season."

"And if you don't play, there's not much point." Jamie shook her head. "I already paid the fees, so it's not like it's more money out of my pocket. It'll be fine. You'll be fine, but if you're not, that's okay too." She paused, waiting for Adrienne to say something, then continued when the silence stretched too long. "There's a practice Thursday night. Come out to that. It'll be here at seven thirty."

"Okay." Adrienne took a deep breath. "I think I can get my gear by then."

"Mo-om…" Lawrence tugged at her hand.

"It was good to meet you, Lawrence." Jamie waved to him. "And good to see you out at a rink," she said to Adrienne. "Hopefully we'll be seeing way more of you here."

"You bet." Adrienne stretched her mouth into a smile she mostly felt as she allowed Lawrence to pull her toward the door. "See you at school!"

Jamie beamed at them. "Later!"

They stood by the doors to let a couple of young figure skaters in sparkly uniforms into the rink, then passed through the lobby to the parking lot. Adrienne's remaining excitement quickly ebbed when she lost the smell of the ice. A warm autumn wind ushered a string of leaves across the pavement, sweeping the scent from her nose. She fought an urge to head back in and inhale deeply one last time.

"Are you really going to play, Mom?"

"I think so. I'm going to try, anyway."

"You should always try."

"Very true." And she would. Hopefully Jamie was right about KJ, but she'd seen that look too often to believe everything would be sunshine and roses based just because Jamie wanted everything to work out.

CHAPTER THREE

KJ slowly stripped herself of her gear. The locker room had returned to its usual rowdy state, especially given the win. The din of women chatting was occasionally punctured by the sound of a can being opened. Officially, the rink frowned upon the consumption of alcohol in the locker rooms, but they chose to ignore it as long as there wasn't a trash bin full of empties that needed to be disposed of before the next Mites game. The figure skaters were on the ice next, so no one would need the space and her teammates were taking full advantage.

Someone tried to press a can into her hands, but she waved them off. Normally she'd stick around and shoot the shit, but she wasn't feeling it, not that the reason why was any big secret.

"Nice pass, KJ," someone hollered from across the way.

"Thanks." She grinned, but she knew it had probably come off a bit strangely. She ran a hand through her hair, ungluing strands that were getting too long. The celebration flowed along around her.

"What were you thinking?" Jamie tossed her helmet and gloves into her open bag, then plopped down on the bench.

"What do you mean?" KJ blinked over at her D partner.

"You were kind of an ass to her."

"What? No, I wasn't."

"Yeah. You were."

"Oh, come on. I had a terrible game, you saw that. Do you really expect me to be all smiles after that shit show?"

Jamie shook her head. "Your game was fine. We won, and you know that's not the point."

"We should have killed them, instead we barely eked out a one-point win." KJ yanked off her shin pads and threw them into her bag. "I played like crap. The only person I set up all game was you."

"No one cares if we ran up the score or not." Jamie poked her in the shoulder. "This is about you being pissed off that I'm leaving. I knew you were going to be sad, but I didn't expect you to be a giant baby about it."

"Baby? I'm not being a baby!" The words came out louder than KJ expected. The locker room went quiet around them.

"Everything okay over there?" Connie poked her head around the corner to get an eye on them. She took her position as team captain too seriously sometimes.

"Everything's fine, Connie," KJ said. "Relax, okay?"

"If you say so." Connie eyed them dubiously. KJ waved her off. It took her a couple of seconds, but Connie left them to their own devices.

"It's not fine, and you know it," Jamie hissed as soon as they were no longer being babysat. "Are you going to be cool about this, or are you going to keep sulking?"

"I'll be cool." KJ rolled her eyes.

"Yeah, right." Jamie's shoulders drooped. "Look, be mad at me all you want, but you didn't have to take it out on Adrienne. You're going to be lucky if she decides to play for us. So maybe she hasn't played much recently, but she was hell on skates back in high school. You don't lose that kind of hockey sense." Jamie shook her head, a half-smile on her face. "I hated playing her team because I knew she was going to be all over me. Did you know I was a wing in high school?"

"You said something about that a while back. At least you eventually ended up where you were supposed to be."

"And Adrienne was better at D back then than I am now. Give her a chance. Besides, you know what it means if she doesn't wind up playing. Do you really want to have a rotating cast of centers back with you?"

"You know I don't."

"Good." Jamie stared at her for a few more seconds. The noise level in the room started to head back to its typical celebratory volume.

KJ stared back at her, not sure what to say that would keep her from getting yelled at some more. "I'm sorry?" she finally ventured.

"I'm not the one you should be apologizing to." Jamie rummaged through the canvas satchel she used as a purse for a bit before pulling out her cell phone. "I'm sending you her number. Give her a call and welcome her to the team before she decides she's better off playing with the boys."

From the pocket of the pants on the bench behind her, KJ's phone gave a sullen buzz.

"Okay, I'll text her. Will that make you happy?"

"It's a start. A call would be better."

KJ nodded, then got down to stripping off the last of her gear. "I have a shift tonight. I gotta head out."

"Tonight?" Jamie frowned. "You don't usually take the evening shift."

"Carlos needed someone to fill in. At least tips should be better at night."

"If you say so." She watched KJ closely for a few moments. "It really is going to be okay."

"I know." KJ laughed. "Kind of dumb to get so worked up over something that's not really that big a deal in the grand scheme of things." *Except it is a big deal. You know how bad you want this.* She grinned up at Jamie and tried to quash the inner voice squawking its disapproval of her cavalier attitude.

Jamie flashed her a relieved smile. "I'm glad to hear it."

"I'll see you around." KJ finished pulling on her clothes, trying not to look at her teammate. *This is it. The last time.*

Jamie stood and pulled her into a sweaty hug. "You know you will. You can't get rid of me that easy. We'll have you over for dinner soon."

"It's a deal." KJ squeezed her for a second, then let go. Her eyes prickled alarmingly.

"Good game, everyone!" she called out to the locker room at large, then waved off the chorus she received in return. She didn't deserve the accolades. Her head hadn't been in this game, no matter what Jamie had said. She was right about one thing, though: they'd held on to the win. KJ allowed herself a small grin. It had been fun running down the center who'd thought she was on a breakaway.

She pushed open the locker room door and maneuvered her hockey bag through the doorway. It wasn't as large as the bags some of the other women had, and she would be damned if she broke down and got a wheeled one. The day she couldn't carry her own gear was the day she hung up her skates. Judging by some of her teammates, she had a good thirty or more years before that was an issue.

Rays of light struck her in the eyes as she stepped out into the parking lot. The day was unseasonably warm, but the angle of the sun told her they were deep in the throes of fall. It wasn't cool enough yet that she'd be able to get away with leaving her bag in the trunk and not end up with her gear full of sweat stench, but she had plenty of time to lay it out at home. There was no evening shift at the bar. Her normal day shift hadn't changed. Carlos was on board with her being his daytime bartender, and while he did occasionally ask if she was available to cover a later shift, it was a rarity.

Why did you lie to Jamie? That was a good question. There were no answers in her trunk, but she stared into it too long before climbing into the driver's seat. It wasn't much of a secret. She was upset with Jamie for leaving her, that was evident, but *why* was she so pissed about it? KJ slammed the car into reverse, then took a deep breath before easing out of her parking space and toward the road.

The pregnancy wasn't a surprise. She'd known Jamie was trying. Playoffs could still happen. There was a lot of hockey ahead of them. If this Adrienne could skate as well as Jamie claimed, then there was every chance they'd be able to get to that championship. As long as they meshed on the ice.

KJ nodded to herself as she pulled into the driveway leading up past the side of the narrow Victorian house she called home. She parked the car in front of a garage that was only listing a little bit to one side, then grabbed her gear and headed for the back steps.

If Adrienne wasn't up to snuff, then KJ would have to take it on herself to get her there.

She pulled up on the doorknob while turning the key. The bolt stuck for a moment, then gave. The house beyond was dark and empty. Well, mostly empty. The click of hard nails on linoleum preceded the small brown and white dog with the wire-haired muzzle as he bounced through the kitchen. He watched her from the top of the stairs.

"Hi, Chester," KJ said.

Chester barked once in response, then skittered in a frantic little circle.

"Is it time to go?"

He barked again, twice this time, then trotted back through the kitchen toward the front door.

"Give me a second to get my gear drying," she called after him, as if he would be more patient. She made her way down the basement stairs. The rhythmic thumping of Chester's tail on the floor in the entryway accompanied her.

"Damn dog." KJ shook her head. She hadn't pegged herself as the kind of person who would talk to an animal as if it was a person, but the house had gotten so empty since Dad passed. Chester had been his, but there had been no question of who would hold on to him after Dad died. Her brother hadn't even raised taking Chester as an option.

She maneuvered her way past a pile of cardboard boxes, each carefully labeled in her handwriting. Erik might not think she was working her way through Dad's stuff quickly enough, but she was making progress. She didn't see him offering to help. *That's not really fair,* she chided herself. *He is nearly three hours away, after all.* The trek from Philadelphia to Sussburg wasn't easy, especially when he had his young daughters in tow. They were very distracting, and KJ was more than willing to be pulled off task by her nieces.

She dropped her gear bag in front of the drying rack her father had constructed for her almost twenty years ago. The main structure was from the first hockey stick she'd broken. With holes drilled through the shaft for dowels of varying lengths, she could set all of her pads out to dry. It kept a serious case of hockey stench at bay. For the most part.

Gear sorted, she headed back upstairs, with a quick side trip to drop her undergear in the washing machine. There wasn't enough yet for a load, but there would be soon.

"Okay, stinker," KJ called as she emerged into the kitchen. "I hope you're ready for a good long run."

Chester barked in reply. The sounds of his nails against the wood of the front door rattled through the living room and dining room.

"Keep your pants on." She jogged through the first floor, then unwound his leash from around the doorknob.

Chester spun in ever-tightening circles as she tried to clip the lead onto his collar. Finally, she grabbed it and held him still enough to get him secured. He pulled against her grip, scratching at the door again.

KJ pulled open the front door and he shot through the gap as soon as it was wide enough for his body. She didn't bother with her keys; she grabbed a couple of plastic poop bags and yanked the door closed behind her. There was no point in locking up, not when she would be gone for maybe twenty minutes. The streetlights were starting to come on, bathing the changing leaves in harsh white light. Chester strained ahead of her.

She checked her phone. Jamie's text glowed accusingly up at her from the lock screen. There was no message aside from the ten digits that made up Adrienne's phone number. Where was the area code from? The local code was 717. There were a smattering of others from nearby in Pennsylvania, none of which were 315. She couldn't place Adrienne's. It didn't matter. She would text her when she got home.

KJ broke into a jog, letting her father's dog lead the way, hoping the exertion would wash away the day's annoyances.

CHAPTER FOUR

"Hi, Ma." Adrienne tried to squeeze the phone between her shoulder and face while pouring a bowl of beaten eggs into the casserole dish on the counter. Across the kitchen, Lawrence sat at a small metal table with a chipped Formica top. He was scribbling intently on a piece of paper.

"Hey, baby!" Her ma's voice bubbled through the line. As always, she sounded like they hadn't talked in months and she couldn't wait to catch up. Adrienne talked to her ma at least twice a week, but it was nice to have someone always so excited to hear from her. "How are things going?"

"Pretty well, I guess." Adrienne shook the bowl to get the last drips of egg into the dish.

"Just pretty well?" Her mom's frown leached through the phone.

"Sorry, I'm pulling together dinner and trying to talk at the same time." Adrienne sprinkled the top of the egg and tater tot concoction with shredded cheese. "Things here are good. Work is going well. I'm meeting people and the teachers have been nice. Lawrence is settling in and has a couple of other kids to talk superheroes with."

His head popped up at the sound of his name. "Hi, Gramma!" he called, then went back to his paper.

"Hi, baby boy," Adrienne's ma responded, knowing he likely couldn't hear her. "Is he in a place to talk?" she asked Adrienne.

"He's always happy to talk to you. I'll pass you over in a second, but first…" She took a deep breath. "Do you still have my gear?"

"Your gear?" Her ma paused. "Do you mean your hockey gear?"

"Yeah, that's it."

"Of course we do. It's buried in the basement, but I'm sure your daddy can dig it out. Are you playing again?"

Adrienne sighed in relief. "Maybe. The local women's team is short a player, and I've been asked to fill in."

"That's great! It's been so long since you played, and you loved it so much." Her ma's voice was warm with approval. "I'm glad you're doing something for yourself."

"Well, we'll have to see. I'm still not sure of my…fit with the team."

"Oh?" The single syllable brought to mind storm clouds gathering on the horizon. "Did they give you a hard time?"

"No? I mean not really?" Adrienne shook her head. "I'm not sure. It was a weird interaction."

"Mm-hmm," her ma said. "There's no point playing with people who are going to undervalue you."

"Believe me, Ma, I know. I won't let that happen, but I'm also not going to pass up a free season of hockey because one chick wasn't all warm and fuzzy."

"Okay…"

"When was the last time I let someone walk all over me?"

"That husband of yours comes to mind."

Adrienne closed her eyes. "Ex-husband, and you know what was going—" She snapped her mouth closed on the rest of what she was going to say. Lawrence hadn't looked up, but the pace of his drawing had slowed. "Ma, it's not up for discussion. We've talked about this."

"I know, but I wish you'd held him to a little more. He could be paying twice what he is in child support."

"And he's been great at co-parenting Lawrence, so it's really a moot point."

"Well, it's more than he was doing when you were still together."

Adrienne tilted her head back to stare at the ceiling. The corner held a water stain that had been inexpertly patched and painted over in a shade of white that didn't quite match the rest. If she looked at it from certain angles, it looked like the Loch Ness monster. She focused on Nessie and took a deep breath in, then let it out slowly through her nose.

"Still not up for discussion." Adrienne kept talking over her ma's sharp inhale to begin her retort. "I'd like to come and get my stuff on Tuesday, if that's okay. We have a half day, so I should have the time. As long as it still fits pretty well, all I'll need is a sharp on my skates."

There was a long pause before her mom answered. "Your sticks will need a new tape job. We'll get you some new rolls. Is there anything else you'll need?"

"I don't think so." Adrienne mentally ran through the contents of what her bag should have contained. "I've got a shirt to wear under. I'll probably need a new Jill."

"What about a helmet? I doubt that's held up well over ten plus years."

"Oh yeah." Adrienne's heart sank. Good helmets were spendy, and a bad one wasn't really worth the waste of money. "If the padding is all there, I guess I'll stick with it until I can save up some money for a new one. Maybe I'll get a tax refund."

"If you're sure."

"I'm sure." She had enough for groceries, bills, and whatever incidentals might come up for Lawrence through the end of the month. She'd already borrowed a good chunk of cash from her parents to move out here. She would simply have to be careful.

"Well, Tuesday is just fine. We'll drive down and meet you halfway. Make sure you bring my favorite grandson over when you come to get it. We can get dinner."

"He's your only grandson, Ma." Adrienne rolled her eyes, then gestured at Lawrence. "Do you want to talk to him?"

Lawrence dropped his pencil and reached out for the phone.

"I love you, Ma. Say 'love you' to Daddy, and I'll see you in a couple days." She passed the cell to her son, then turned back to dinner.

He hopped down from the chair and trotted out to the living room, chatting away as he went. "It was okay. Mom took me to a really cold place today…"

Of course that was what he'd remembered from the afternoon, not the excitement as the two teams had vied against each other. Not the freedom of long paces up and down the ice. Not the thrill of the goal. It had been a nice goal. Even knowing KJ had been the one to flawlessly set it up didn't make it less beautiful. The other team hadn't stood a chance. The rest of KJ's game hadn't been as good. She'd missed a couple of opportunities, and for how well she'd clicked with Jamie on the point, she'd seemed a half-step behind for the rest of it. Her skill had been undeniable, but something else had been going on.

Was that why she was so dismissive when Jamie had introduced her?

Well, it doesn't matter, Adrienne decided as she covered the casserole dish with aluminum foil. She would play with the Bolts as long as it was fun. If KJ was the one who got in the way of her enjoyment, then she would stop, that's all there was to it.

The oven blasted her face with heat when she opened it. She slid the dish inside, then closed it with a firm thud that set the pans on top of the stove to rattling.

When Lawrence was off the phone with her ma, she would call her ex and make sure her weekends would still be open. Despite what her ma kept insinuating, Kaz wasn't a deadbeat dad. They actually had a very amicable relationship, now that they were no longer married. She didn't have any say over his life anymore, and that was how he seemed to prefer it.

She surveyed the tiny apartment kitchen with its cheap trim and dented cabinet doors. Of course, all she had to do was look around to remember. Her job paid pretty well, even if it was slightly lower than the entry-level wages she could have commanded if she'd been able to find a school counselor position in an urban center. Cost of living was lower here, but her student loans didn't care about that. Grad school wasn't cheap, especially not these days. Those payments chewed massive holes through her monthly budget. Without Kaz's child support, there would have been less than nothing in her bank account come payday. She was coming to grips with being a single mother, for all intents and purposes, but she still very much missed the life she'd built with Kaz. Well, parts of it.

Missing that life was the only reason she hadn't called him to talk about the issue with KJ and joining the team. Like his son, he saw through the crap and chaos of a situation and had a way of picking up on exactly what was bothering her. She leaned on him too much already. Their marriage hadn't worked out in the end, but she still missed his steadying presence. She missed being part of a team.

CHAPTER FIVE

Adrienne hesitated at the door to the locker room. The weight of the bag on her shoulder was familiar, but unaccustomed. She'd gotten out to the rink the night before to take a quick turn on her skates. She wasn't as crisp on them as she'd been, but she wasn't a complete disaster either. Not that she'd been able to skate for very long. Lawrence had allowed himself to be cajoled into coming onto the ice in a pair of rental skates. He'd been game for a while but had announced he was done after fifteen minutes. She'd gotten another ten minutes while he played on one of the benches.

Her thighs were sore, as were her shoulders. The stiffness would go away, that she knew from experience, but it didn't help her overall anxiety. Before last night, she'd skated ten years ago, and the stiff muscles were a reminder that she wasn't nineteen anymore.

"Clear the door," came a voice behind her.

Adrienne turned to see a tall white woman with very close-cropped dark hair and a baggy sweatshirt in eye-catching tie-dye. She carried the telltale wide stick and thick pads of a goalie.

"Oh, sorry!" She scooted out of the way of the door.

The woman turned to push the door open with her back. "You're the new one, right?"

"Uh, yeah." Adrienne followed in behind her.

"I'm Vaughn. I use they/them pronouns." Vaughn grinned at her. "I'm happy to meet my new D. It's hard to lose Jamie, but she insists you're up to it."

"Adrienne, she/her. And I hope so. I do have a bit of rust to knock off the blades, though." The smell of locker room hit her nostrils and Adrienne couldn't help but wrinkle her nose. The smell of the ice had brought back memories, but she'd somehow forgotten the unique stench of the locker room.

"We've all been there," Vaughn said. "Except KJ. I'm sure you'll be fine." They wandered over to a spot and dumped their gear on the floor with an unceremonious thud, then indicated the bench next to them.

Adrienne had gotten there early, hoping not to entertain too much of an audience while she remembered the best order in which to don her pads. There were only a couple of other women in the locker room, but one of them already had music going. They glanced up and nodded to her, one of them smiling and waving, the other turning right back to her gear.

Adrienne took the spot next to Vaughn and opened her bag. Start with the undergear, that much she remembered.

"I'm not great about covering the puck," Vaughn was saying as they stripped down. "I'll usually bury it in the corners, so remember that."

"Okay." The locker room was warm. It felt fine now, but she was sure it would feel oppressively hot when they got back after practice.

"And I'm going to holler at you to move if you're screening me. I'll also holler if something is going on behind you that you can't see." Vaughn grinned. "I do a lot of hollering."

Adrienne nodded. "Good to know. I'll try to listen, but if I've already decided what I'm going to do, I might not be able to change it up on a dime."

"You'll need to work on that." KJ sat down on her other side. "Being flexible is the D's greatest asset." She opened the zip on the top of her bag and started rooting around in it without looking at Adrienne.

"I know that," Adrienne said. Her irritation was sharp in her ears, and she tried to soften her tone. "You also don't want me coming up with a new plan after I've committed to one. It won't be pretty."

"That's all right," KJ said. "We can work on it."

"Great." Adrienne pulled her socks on, then grabbed out her skates. She jammed her right foot down into the first one.

"It's fine, KJ," Vaughn said. "We only need to get used to each other's styles, that's it. It'll come."

"We're four games into the season," KJ said. "We don't have a whole lot of time to get acquainted." She looked up at Adrienne for the first time. "You'll want to come to every practice so we can get on the same page as fast as possible."

"I'll come to as many as I can make." Weeknight practices were much harder for her to make than weekend games. Kaz had already agreed as part of the divorce settlement to take Lawrence every weekend. She'd talked him into making the drive to town to pick up their son tonight, but that had taken some doing. She wasn't sure how willing he'd be to cover all the practices, not when he already lived forty-five minutes away and did most of his work in the evenings.

"It should be all of them." KJ's face was solemn. "We're on track to win it all this year, but everyone needs to be on the same page."

"Lighten up, KJ," Vaughn said. "We'll make playoffs or we won't. Either way isn't the end of the world."

"I don't want to just make playoffs," KJ said. "I want the championship. We were almost there two years ago."

"It wasn't your fault." Vaughn paused in their dressing to regard their teammate. "What happened happened. We can't change it now."

"Maybe not, but we can make sure we get another crack at it."

Adrienne concentrated on putting on her pads, settling each one in place and making sure it felt natural on her body. She had to switch out her shin guards after discovering they were on the wrong legs, but no one seemed to notice. As more women filtered in, the atmosphere was still pretty laid-back. Some of the women chatted amongst themselves as they dressed. It didn't take her as long to get geared up as she'd anticipated, so Adrienne sat around in her pads while everyone finished pulling themselves together. It looked like most of the team was there. The room was certainly stuffed to capacity.

Finally, when almost everyone was dressed, a short woman with long red hair bound up in a thick braid stood up.

"Hey, everyone," she said. "We have a new player. She's taking Jamie's spot for the season. This is Adrienne."

"Hi, Adrienne," the women said in unison. A few of them waved.

"I'm Connie," the woman said. "I'm the captain, and I play center. I use she/her pronouns." She looked around at her teammates. "Let's go around the room and introduce ourselves and our positions. It's okay if you don't remember everyone right away," she said to Adrienne, "but it's a start, and better than making us all wear tape with our names on the fronts of our helmets."

"I'd definitely forget to take it off," Adrienne said.

"You and half the folks on the team," Connie said. "Then we'd look like a team of Mini Mites, and we can't have that."

"Certainly not," Adrienne said gravely.

Connie gestured at KJ, who gave her a half wave.

"I'm KJ. She/her. I play defense, but you already knew that."

Adrienne gave her a tight smile. "Hello, KJ."

They worked their way around the room. Adrienne did her best to pay attention, but she wasn't great with names. Getting thirteen of them dumped on her at once wasn't going to stick. She decided to start with the rest of the defense, she would move on from there. The locker room was awfully white, but that was nothing new. She'd often been the only person of color on her team. There had been a Latina woman on her club team at Cornell and another Black girl on one of her teams in elementary school. At least everyone seemed open and friendly. Some of the anxiety tightening her belly started to loosen.

"All right," Connie said after they'd worked their way around the room to end with Vaughn. "Let's have a good practice out there. Coach Aaron is waiting for us on the ice."

The women got up and straggled out of the room, grabbing their sticks from the pile in the corner as they went out the door. Adrienne crammed her new helmet on her head. Her ma and daddy had surprised her with it when she'd met them to get her gear.

"Brain damage is forever," her daddy had said. "Keep that big brain of yours safe when you're out there."

"When can we watch you play?" her ma had asked.

"Soon," she'd promised them. "Let me get my feet back under me and make sure the team is right for me."

The helmet was white, like her old one had been, and it fit much better. Apparently there had been some strides in helmet technology over the last ten or so years.

She waited until the room had almost cleared out. Vaughn had been the first to leave, but KJ had hung back and was scrutinizing her.

"Do I have something on my face?" Adrienne asked.

"No, I just want to make sure you know where to go." KJ stood up.

"I'm not going to get lost between here and the ice. I passed it on the way in, and even if I hadn't, I've been in my fair share of rinks."

KJ held up gloved hands. "I'm only trying to help."

"If I need your help I'll ask for it."

"All right, all right. Geez." KJ pushed her way through the door without a second glance, leaving Adrienne to fume her way out of the locker room on her own.

Did she really think that Adrienne was too dumb to get to the ice by herself? What was she trying to prove, exactly? Adrienne could and would take care of herself. She didn't need KJ's help, not now, not ever. She stalked behind KJ, trying not to glare daggers at her back.

KJ stepped through the door in the boards and Adrienne watched her skate away. She made every move on the ice look effortless. Adrienne tried to tell herself her spike in irritation wasn't because she knew there was no way she was going to look that good. The best she could hope for was not to humiliate herself completely. She grasped her stick in both hands and stepped onto the smooth sheet of ice that still gleamed in places where a thin layer of water sat on top of the frozen surface. Her first steps were steady; her feet didn't slip out from under herself to land her on her ass by the boards. That was something. Not much, but she'd take it.

The door didn't close easily behind her, and she struggled for a bit before getting it to latch in place. Adrienne turned to take in her new teammates warming up on the ice. A group stretched in front of the benches. Past them a couple of women shot pucks into the boards. Vaughn was at the far end practicing going down then popping back up. For all that KJ had managed to get under her skin, Adrienne suddenly didn't care. Her shoulders relaxed, and she took a deep breath, savoring the smell of the ice. This was where she was supposed to be.

She skated over to the group of women by the bench and dropped to her knees. The woman nearest to her nodded. She thought it might be Rebecca, one of the centers, but Adrienne couldn't be sure. The disadvantage of everyone introducing themselves in the locker room was that they all looked different now that they were wearing helmets. Adrienne ran through her half-remembered routine of stretches. A couple of the women were in the midst of what looked like yoga poses when she finished, but most had gotten up and were peppering Vaughn with shots. That left the other half of the rink open, which was a far cry from the previous night's open skate.

Adrienne took a careful turn around the far end of the ice, trying to get a feel for edges she hadn't used in a decade. Stopping on her left side was a little weak; she'd have to work on that. Her forward crossovers were still pretty good. Though shaky at first, they firmed up after a couple of passes. She transitioned to skate backward, taking note of a bit of a wobble in her stride as she did so. That wouldn't do at all. Her backward stride was decent, though not as strong as it had been when she was in high school.

Was anything? Her backward crossovers were crap, though. They would take some major work. All in all, she wasn't doing too badly. Hopefully it was a matter of timing and it would all come back the more she skated.

The shrill of a whistle pulled her attention back over to the benches where a tall man, made even more so by his ice skates, stood. His black helmet made his skin look very pale in contrast. One hockey-gloved hand wrapped around a hockey stick, he motioned them all in with the other. This must be the Coach Aaron Connie had mentioned. Adrienne bit her lower lip as excitement surged through her. She couldn't wait to get to something resembling hockey.

CHAPTER SIX

Practice was going pretty well. KJ had decided to back off from Adrienne after getting her ears singed in the locker room. That didn't mean she hadn't been paying attention to her new teammate, though. She was doing all right. Her skating was a little hit or miss, but it had already improved from the first few strides she'd taken. While she hadn't looked like a baby deer on the ice, those first steps hadn't filled KJ with confidence. *How long has it been since Adrienne played?* She resolved to ask Jamie.

The drills had put some confidence back in Adrienne's stride. She had a heavy shot from the blue line, which KJ was happy to see, though her timing was a little off there also. After flubbing that first one timer, Adrienne had been careful to settle the puck before taking a powerful shot from the point. The delight on her face when it had connected with Vaughn's leg pads had KJ grinning alongside her, even though she was across the ice.

"It's your go." Cam prodded her in the side.

"Shoot." KJ pushed forward, angling for the pass from Aaron down at the goal line. He fired the puck hard in her direction.

KJ waited a beat, then raised her stick and let loose, intercepting the puck and sending it hurtling toward the net.

Vaughn lifted a hand, trying to snatch the hard black projectile from the air, but was too slow. The puck sailed past them and bounced off the back of the net with enough force that it almost popped out.

It was a nice shot. KJ glanced toward Adrienne to see what she thought, but to her disappointment, Adrienne was in line chatting with a woman waiting for her turn.

Figures. KJ continued her trajectory toward the net, just as she would have if the puck hadn't gone in and her goalie had given up a juicy rebound.

"Nice shot!" Vaughn called to her before turning to face the next challenger.

At least someone had noticed. Snow sheeted up from her skate blades as she came to an abrupt stop at the back of a different line than the one Adrienne was in. She tried not to watch the other woman, but her eyes kept wandering back to her. She was solid on her skates, for the most part. They hadn't done much passing, but what little KJ had seen promised a hard pass. She needed to dial in the accuracy, though.

Adrienne was up next. She took off from the blue line, cutting across the top of the face-off dot, then down the center of the ice. She swiveled to catch Aaron's pass with only the slightest wobble. The puck was steady on her stick as she skated in toward Vaughn. She drew the puck back as if to fire. Vaughn bit, dropping to her knees, but Adrienne held on. She pulled the puck to the side and tapped it in behind the goalie as they threw their body sideways in a desperate attempt to intercept her.

"Good job," Aaron called.

"That was a good job," Michelle said from behind KJ. "Maybe the new girl would like to take on wing. I'll drop back to play with you."

"I thought you hated defense," KJ said.

"It's not my favorite, but with that kind of puck movement, Adrienne would do well as a forward, don't you think?"

"I'll thank you not to poach my new partner before we've played our first game together."

"You sure she'll be on your D line? I heard Aaron saying to Connie and Jean that he was thinking of mixing up the defense. Thought getting some new blood would be the best time for it."

KJ turned to stare at her. "He said what?"

Michelle shrugged. "He was thinking about it, is all. Besides, either Cam or Krissy would be fine as your partner, and you know it."

"That's not—"

That's not the point. KJ shook her head and turned back to the drill. *What, then, is the point?* She'd played with Krissy and Cam more times than she could think of. They were both solid defensewomen, but they were very well-matched and made a formidable pair on the ice. She didn't want to break that up. Adrienne was supposed to be matched with her. That's who she had to work with.

It was her turn again. She struck off across the ice, taking a route similar to the one Adrienne had taken. Aaron held off on passing the puck to her until she was between the hash marks, too close to let a slapper go, not on her own goalie. Adrienne was her new linemate, and part of her was looking forward to the challenge of changing it up with someone new by her side. It would be exciting and different. *It's time for a change.*

The thought startled her, and she fumbled the puck badly. It dribbled off the toe of her stick. Vaughn swatted it away with an incredulous look on their face.

Aaron eyed her, then blew sharply on his whistle. "Take a drink, everyone," he called out.

That was very impressive, KJ, she mocked as she skated to the bench. *She's sure to want to be on a line with you after that performance.* She squirted the water bottle into her mouth through the bars of her helmet cage, then closed her eyes and doused her face. The water was cold, but not as refreshing as she would have liked. She made room at the boards for someone else to take a drink.

Vaughn was alone at the net, taking a drink from their water bottle. KJ skated over to join them.

"That was a weird shot at the end," Vaughn said. "You losing your edge?"

KJ forced a grin she didn't feel. "You know how it is when you try something new. Things don't always go the way you expect."

"Ain't that the truth."

Coach Aaron joined them. "We're doing a half-ice scrimmage the last fifteen minutes. You'll be on a line with Adrienne. I'll let you know when the switch is. Pass that along to her, would you?"

"Sure, Coach." KJ looked for Adrienne among the women by the bench. When she found her, she wasn't talking to anyone. She was off to one side draining the last drops from a beat-up looking water bottle. *I wonder how badly practice is kicking her ass?*

"Half-ice scrimmage, everyone," Aaron called out. "Let's start with the red line, and Cam and Krissy on defense. Blue line, with KJ and Adrienne on O."

KJ skated over to Adrienne. "Coach will call when it's time to switch up."

"Got it." The answer was curt. "Which side do you want?"

"I'll take the right."

"Okay." Adrienne skated away to take her position on the blue line next to the visitor's bench.

KJ skated across the ice and stopped near the boards. She watched as the women sorted themselves out as if the puck had been down in that end for a bit. The shrill of Aaron's whistle started everyone's feet moving, then he buried the puck deep in the zone. Cam stopped it behind the net and dumped it out to Connie, who tried to pass it over to Jean along the boards.

"It's coming your way," KJ called out.

Adrienne spared her half a glance, then stepped neatly in front of the pass. She sent the puck hard to the opposite corner where it collided with the boards with a deep boom.

Rebecca went screaming in after it, Connie on her heels. She beat Krissy to the corner and slapped the puck weakly along the boards in KJ's direction. Michelle stepped toward it but was a step off the pace as KJ hustled past her and scooped up the puck. She glanced around and noticed Jean was giving Adrienne too much room.

"Adrienne! Incoming!" She fired a pass over to her teammate, then popped back up to the blue line, not wanting to get caught down low for too long.

Adrienne stopped the puck, then bounced it off the boards around Jean to Mavis who rushed toward the net. Cam stepped up on her, trying to force her around and away from Vaughn.

"Watch the back door," KJ yelled at Krissy, who had also stepped forward, letting Rebecca post up behind her. Krissy wasn't on her side for the drill, but she hated seeing anyone get free real estate that close to the crease.

Krissy shot a startled look over her shoulder, then skated backward to cover the lurking center.

Mavis tried to muscle her way in, but Cam got her stick on the puck, knocking it away toward Adrienne. She stepped toward the puck.

"You got this!" KJ yelled.

Adrienne looked up as the puck landed on the stick blade, then tried to pivot and send the puck to KJ. That little unsteadiness on her skates chose that moment to turn into a big wobble. Adrienne's arms windmilled as she tried to keep her balance, then she toppled backward and hit the ice with a thud.

Aaron whistled long and loud.

"Oof." KJ said. "I guess you don't got this." She skated over to Adrienne. The collapse had looked awkward, and in her experience, those hurt the most.

Adrienne stared up at her, eyes wide.

"You okay?" KJ asked, bending over her partner, trying to get a good look at her eyes. "That looked like it hurt."

"Uhhh…" Adrienne looked like she was taking stock of herself. "I'm in one piece."

"You didn't hit your head?"

"No. Kept my head up, just like I was taught."

"Good." KJ pulled off her glove and reached her hand out to Adrienne. "Looks like you need my help after all."

She'd meant it as a joke, but Adrienne batted her hand away hard.

"You know what," she said as she rolled to her knees. "Fuck off, KJ." Her tone was so conversational that KJ almost didn't catch her words.

"Well...I..." How had that gone so wrong?

Adrienne snatched up her stick and headed for the door off the ice, stopping only long enough to gather her water bottle. The door thudded in place behind her with a hollow boom that echoed through the rink.

Connie skated up to stand beside her. "What did you say to her?"

"I don't know." KJ shook her head. "I made a joke, but I don't think she took it well."

"You think?" Connie skated away after Adrienne. "Let me see if I can fix your screw up."

Screw up? I didn't screw anything up. KJ chewed on her lower lip.

The whistle's shrill cut through her confusion and irritation.

"Everyone on the line," Aaron called out.

The team gave a collective groan as they made their way to the blue line. Coach didn't finish every practice with suicides. He must have thought they could use some conditioning since it was so early in the season yet. KJ took her place and got into a crouch. At least if she was exhausted, she wouldn't have to pay attention to the little voice that wondered if Connie had been right.

CHAPTER SEVEN

Adrienne shuffled handouts across the top of her small desk in her even more cramped office. It very well might have been a storage closet during the school's earlier days. The building had been built in the 1950s, long before most school districts had seen the need for a school counselor. She did have a window, small though it was. Most days, it was a source of comfort.

She tried to concentrate on the outline she'd prepared. The third grade classes were on the schedule today for her talk about bullying. One-on-one sessions were still where she was most comfortable, but the larger classes were starting to feel all right. Whoever had said "fake it till you make it" had been right in this case.

It helped that the teachers had been supportive and welcoming since the beginning. Her internship had helped prepare her, but she hadn't realized she would be left quite as much to her own devices. Then again, Vice-Principal Thomas didn't really seem to know how best to use her. Thank goodness for the Reddit school psychology thread. She spent more evenings than she cared to admit going through its subthreads. But it had kept her from feeling too out of her depth, so there was that.

When am I going to stop feeling like I'm making this up as I go along? And waiting for everyone else to realize I have no idea what I'm doing?

Her gaze strayed toward the window. There was nothing to see today except gray skies and branches largely devoid of leaves. She resisted the urge to check her phone for messages, but her resolve only lasted an instant. She turned the phone over, but there were no texts. The occasional sound of a child's voice echoed down the hall. First bell would be soon. Where were they?

She squeezed the phone, then almost dropped it as it chose that moment to buzz. A call was coming in.

"Finally." Adrienne swiped to answer it before stopping to see who it was. It could be only one person.

"I just dropped him off," Kaz said. His voice was low and mellow, even through the crappy cell connection. It had been one of the first things she'd noticed about him all those years ago. That and the smile.

"Oh good," Adrienne said. "I really appreciate you taking Lawrence on such short notice."

"It was no problem. We had a good time."

"I'm glad." Adrienne paused, groping for something to say to him. What did you say after almost a decade of marriage and a child came to nothing? "I'm glad you got him back to school in time."

"It was an early morning, but we made it." He paused for a few seconds, before continuing. "You know I love having Lawrence."

"Yes. But?"

"It's going to be hard to take him most weeknights. I have gigs in the evenings."

"Don't worry about it." Adrienne crossed her free arm across her chest while swiveling her chair around to face the window. "It's no longer an issue."

"Oh. Okay." His voice lightened in confusion. "Not because of me, I hope. You only played club your freshman year in college. It's been so long since you played, and you know it's good to have something else to do that's yours and not anyone else's."

"I do know, as a matter of fact."

"Okay."

He was using his soothing voice. Adrienne didn't like that one. She expelled a sharp breath through her nostrils. "I didn't gel with the team. I'm better off finding something else to do."

A knock on the door frame pulled her attention away from her call. She looked over her shoulder. "Someone's here. I have to go."

"Bye, Adrienne."

"Bye." Adrienne tapped the power button on the side of the phone then turned around. "Hey, Jamie. What's up?"

"I wanted to ask you to think about seeing one of my kids, if you have the time." She approached the desk with a bright blue manila folder. "He could use someone to talk to, I think."

"Of course." Adrienne took the folder. She pulled out the cover form and gave it a quick glance over. "I'm talking to the third graders today. Will tomorrow work, or does he need something sooner?"

"That should be fine." Jamie plopped herself into the adult-sized chair on the other side of her desk. "So…"

"So, what?" Adrienne turned the form over. It sounded like the little guy was having a tough time. She was glad Jamie was comfortable suggesting he talk to her.

"How was practice?"

"Oh." She slid the paper back in its folder, then carefully placed it in a tray on her desk. "Let me take a look at my calendar and we'll see when we can fit him in."

"That good?" Jamie sat up straight. "Did KJ call you? Or text you, or something?"

"No." Adrienne pinned the teacher with a sharp stare. "Why would she call me?"

"To apologize for being a pain in the ass when I introduced you last weekend. She said she would."

"Well, she didn't. I don't have anything to say to her anyway."

"Oh, no," Jamie said. "What did she do? I swear, she's always been on the dense side, but lately it's like she's in her own little world."

"It's nothing, but it proved to me that I don't have a place on your team. KJ has made it clear she doesn't think I'm an adequate replacement for you." Hearing it out loud cut deeper than it had in her head. After what KJ'd said on the ice, Adrienne had been angry, but this was pain, not rage. Damn it, she was good enough. The kinks would shake out, she knew they would. She'd been so much better by the end of practice than she'd been at the beginning. Why couldn't KJ see that?

"Allergies," she said as she reached over to snag a tissue from the box on her desk.

"That little…" Jamie pulled her phone out of her pocket. She swiped it open, then tapped furiously at the screen. She waited a second, then tapped at it again, then returned it to her pocket. "There. How long is Lawrence in After School?"

"Until 4:30." Adrienne stared at her, trying to figure out what was happening. "Why?"

"We're going to get a drink right after last bell."

"I don't think afternoon drinking will change the fact that KJ doesn't like me."

"Which is why we're going to beard the dragon in her den." Jamie looked triumphant, then wilted a bit when Adrienne still looked confused. "KJ is the dragon. She bartends at the bar on the other side of downtown. I want to hear what she has to say about this whole mess."

"You don't have to—" First bell went off. Despite its name, there was nothing remotely bell-like about it; instead a long tone rang out through the PA system. The building wasn't old enough to have an actual bell, not like the elementary school she'd attended back in Syracuse.

"I have to get to class before my students turn feral and start tearing the room apart." Jamie pushed herself up from her chair.

"Trust me," she said over her shoulder on her way out the door. "KJ needs a shake-up. That's all."

"But…" With Jamie gone, there was no one to register her complaints with, just the rising tide of high-pitched voices carrying through the halls. What was she supposed to do with all of this? It felt vaguely irresponsible to be heading off to a bar while her son hung out in the After School program. That time was for her work, so she didn't have to take it home. She preferred to use the evenings solely for the two of them, not trying to split her focus between her son and paperwork. Still, it might be worth it to watch KJ squirm.

The thought brought a small smile to her lips. Yes, she was more than petty enough to find that amusing. She would go, but only for long enough to watch KJ's discomfort. She would chalk that up as a win, then leave and never have to deal with the woman again.

CHAPTER EIGHT

The bell over the front door jingled behind one of her regulars. Dennis hung out every day from a little after one until the kids from the elementary school started walking past the window. Some days he had one or more cronies to accompany him. KJ looked at the lonely five dollar bill in her tip jar. That was not the case today.

She looked around for Carlos, then pulled a book out from under the bar and spread it open on the rail. Her boss frowned upon her reading while she was on the clock, but there were no customers. The bar didn't need another wipe-down; the glossy finish already gleamed over the dark wood top. The glasses were spotless, the liquor restocked, the lines on the taps were clean. She had nothing else to do, and her novel beckoned. Would the planet's sovereign and the badass human captain make it through the latest attack by alien invaders? KJ turned the page to find out.

"Hard at work?" Jamie's voice pulled her out of a thrilling scene where enemy troops in robotic landing crafts were making mincemeat of the defending forces.

"You're my only guest," KJ said. She dog-eared the corner of her page and looked up. Jamie stood before her, hands on her hips. Adrienne was two paces behind her, hands in her pockets and carefully studying the front windows. "Uh, guests, I mean. I guess."

"Well, you have no one to distract you, then." Jamie sat on the nearest barstool, then deposited her purse on the bar.

"I didn't think I would have." KJ sneaked a glance at Adrienne, then back to Jamie. "I thought it was just going to be you," she hissed.

"See, that's exactly why I wanted to talk to you." Her friend made no attempt to keep her voice down.

Adrienne drifted closer, then took a seat next to Jamie. "I'll have a Coke."

"Oh. Okay." Her body on automatic while she tried to figure out what Jamie had meant, she pulled a glass out from under the bar, then scooped it full of ice. "What'll you have, Jamie?"

"Well, it would be a beer, except I'm pregnant." Jamie tilted her head and smiled blandly.

"Yeah, I know," KJ said. Should have known sooner, now that she thought about it. Jamie had been finding excuses not to drink anything harder than lemonade for a few months now.

"Do you?" Jamie asked. "Because I don't think you do. If you did, you would realize I'm not coming back to play—"

"Ever?" She hadn't meant the question to be so plaintive, but there it was, quivering between the three of them like a wounded animal.

"Oh, honey." Jamie softened. "It's not forever, only until the baby is born. I'm missing one season, that's all."

"For a few years, then your kid will start hockey. Or you'll decide to have another one. Or two. You won't be playing hockey until the kids graduate high school."

"Are you bent out of shape over playoffs, or is something else going on here?"

"What do you mean?" KJ spluttered. "What could be more important than playoffs?"

"Well, aside from pretty much everything. What has you acting like a complete doorbell?" Jamie's hands were back on her hips, which was no mean feat, seated as she was on a bar stool.

"If playoffs aren't the problem, are you upset because you feel like Jamie is leaving you?" Adrienne's quiet voice pulled KJ up short as she was about to lay into Jamie for giving her such a hard time in front of someone who was essentially a stranger.

* * *

Adrienne watched with fascination as KJ's face cycled through about five different expressions in rapid succession.

"Of course not," KJ finally said.

"Huh," Adrienne said.

"Huh? What do you mean huh?" KJ looked down and realized she had Adrienne's drink in her hand. She placed it on a coaster with enough force that some of the soda slopped over the edge of the glass. She gave it a quick swipe with a rag, then passed it Adrienne's way.

Adrienne waited until she had her drink, then took a long pull. "Most people would think that being upset over playoffs would be more...how can I say this without sounding like I'm attacking you?" She paused, a small part of her delighting in how KJ was turning redder and redder, the larger part actually interested to find out why she would answer that way. "Well, selfish. It's a bit blunt, but I think we can say it's accurate here."

Jamie's mouth was round in an O of surprise, but she closed it with a snap and swiveled to look at KJ. "It's a fair question," she said. "Maybe a little harsh." She reached over the bar to pat KJ's hand.

"I'm, that is, we're— I mean..." KJ took a deep breath. "I'm not her keeper. She can get pregnant and leave the team whenever. I don't own her, so if she wants to leave, she can leave."

"You do realize she's not leaving, right?" Adrienne watched KJ closely.

"I know she's not leaving!" KJ glanced toward the back of the bar, then closed her eyes. "Look, playoffs are important to me, okay?"

"So important that you give me the cold shoulder the first time you meet me?"

KJ tilted her head to one side. "Is that what this is all about?"

"That's just where this started." Adrienne took another sip of her Coke. "What this is about is you being a total ass to me at practice. First you treat me like a newbie who doesn't know one end of the stick from the other, then you make a comment to me about needing you to help me out. I don't need that shit. It's condescending as fuck." She was proud of the way her voice held steady without wavering or raising. There was no way anyone could accuse her of being angry.

"That's not what I meant," KJ said. "I was trying to help. You have to admit that when you first took the ice, you were a little rough."

"And I got better with every stride. What happened at the end was a stupid fluke."

"Well, yeah."

Adrienne shot her a surprised look. She hadn't expected KJ to agree with her on anything.

"Hockey is all about falling," KJ said. "You just gotta get up and keep going."

"I didn't see you offering a hand up to anyone else who biffed it at practice."

"They weren't my partner." KJ sighed. "All I want is for you to be at the top of your game as soon as you can so we can kick some ass together. If you can end up where Jamie was, that championship game is ours."

"She's better than I am," Jamie said. "Or at least she was. She will be again. You're trying to force things." She glanced over her shoulder at Adrienne. "There's a reason the team hasn't voted her as Captain or Ass-Captain."

"Wait. Ass-Captain?" Adrienne asked.

"Mavis can never remember if the A stands for Assistant or Associate Captain, so she's dubbed it Ass-Captain, or Ass-Cap for short."

"Everyone knows the only difference is tenure," KJ said.

Adrienne couldn't stop the surprised laugh from escaping her. "That was funny."

"Don't act so surprised." KJ was all grumbles, but a small grin lurked at the corner of her lips. "I've got jokes."

"I bet you do."

"I definitely do. I'm a funny, funny gal."

"My dad always said looks aren't everything."

It was KJ's turn to snort in surprised laughter. "I'm not the only one with jokes."

"That one's an oldie," Adrienne said. She became aware of Jamie sitting back on her bar stool, observing them both with a considering but delighted look on her face.

KJ caught the look also. "Look, I'm really sorry I said those things. I didn't mean them to come out that way, and if I could start over, I'd be a paragon of politeness."

"And you'd text her when you said you would?" Jamie asked pointedly.

"And I'd text." KJ crossed her heart over the dark flannel she was wearing. "And I wouldn't be a condescending shit, but would welcome you to the team with open arms and delight."

"Okay, now you're laying it on a little thick," Jamie said.

"There are worse things than open arms." Adrienne snapped her mouth shut. *Oh my god, am I flirting?* No, that was preposterous. She was merely trying to lighten the mood. KJ had obviously learned her lesson. There was no point in making her grovel. "Apology accepted. I'll try to be better about letting you know what's irritating me and not just snapping your head off."

"I don't think that's going to be necessary," KJ said. "Didn't you hear? I've turned over a new leaf. I'm a reformed woman."

"I have no doubt that you're going to make me angry at some point." Adrienne held up her hand when KJ opened her mouth to protest. "And I'll tick you off too. Being partners means communicating." That was one she knew well, especially how quickly things got gummed up when communication was lacking.

"I figured that would be me yelling across the ice that I'm open." KJ was grinning widely. She didn't seem too worried about Adrienne's assertion that they were going to drive each other up the wall.

"So you're staying with the team, then?" Jamie asked. "And you're okay with it?"

Adrienne nodded. "I'll let Connie know." And she'd have to let Kaz know. That would be an awkward conversation, given that she'd told him she was done with the team earlier that same day. He was already planning on taking Lawrence pretty much every weekend, so she'd have plenty of time for games. But how was she going to swing practices?

Her son might be all right unsupervised, but anyone who knew him would associate him with her. In a small town like Sussburg, everyone knew everyone else, and while they weren't the only Black family in the area, it's not like there were a whole lot of them. She'd watched her brothers be held to a far different standard of behavior than their white peers, and that was in the relatively liberal city of Syracuse, New York. Lawrence might not look Black, but it didn't take more than a couple of glances to realize he was biracial. If she wasn't there to run interference, how might the fine folks who ran the Sussburg Ice Arena respond to him if he got even the slightest bit rowdy? No, it was better to get a feel for the town and the rink employees before letting Lawrence have the run of the place on his own.

Completely unaware of the direction of Adrienne's thoughts, KJ leaned forward. "That's great! They would probably have moved one of the centers back if you hadn't stuck around. You know how it is when forwards play back."

"Yeah, they disappear into the other team's zone and you don't see them again until you've been scored on."

"Exactly."

"I'm glad we had this talk," Adrienne said, pushing herself away from the bar. "We should make sure we keep doing it. You already have my number, so text me. I don't bite." She grinned, showing more teeth than she really needed to.

"I don't believe that for a second," KJ said under her breath. "Point taken," she said more loudly. She held up her phone.

"I'll see you Saturday," Adrienne said.

"Yes, you will."

"Okay."

"Okay."

"Okay!" Jamie scooped her purse off the bar and pulled out a few bills and plopped them on the bar. She ignored the shake of KJ's head, then made for the entryway. She held the door open for Adrienne, then walked to catch up with her outside.

"That wasn't terrible," Adrienne said after they'd walked half a block in silence.

"Way less than terrible," Jamie said.

They headed back to the school in silence, passing by the Windsor County Courthouse with its brick facade, broken up by white columns and trim. Adrienne pretended not to notice the sideways glances Jamie was giving her. Past the courthouse, and after another half a block, Jamie finally blurted: "Were you flirting with KJ?"

"Of course not," Adrienne replied calmly. "What an odd thing to say."

"Is it, though?"

"Yeah. It is. I have a kid, I just started a new job, and now I have to get back into top hockey shape so my new D partner can win a championship. Who has time for flirting?"

"But you didn't say you're not interested."

Adrienne sighed. "I'm not interested. This is exactly the wrong time for me to get in a relationship with anyone." *Let alone KJ.* There was something else going on with that insistence on winning a championship. She had a feeling some major emotional baggage came along with that one.

"Is it because KJ's female?" Jamie asked, her voice artificially light, as if she was trying to broadcast that she didn't really care about the answer.

"It's because I need to get my life back together and heading in a direction that makes sense." KJ's gender didn't bother her. Sure, she'd married Kaz, but she'd dated widely her first two years in college. There had been a couple of women in there, but once Kaz had come into the picture, they'd been exclusive. She didn't know how to think of anyone else romantically, which was still the major irony of her life.

"If you say so." Jamie sounded disappointed.

"I do say so," Adrienne responded firmly. "Let's leave it at that, okay."

"Fine. I'll stop trying to play Cupid."

"Do that, or I'm going to find a nice adult diaper and curly blond wig for you to wear."

"That sounds like a fate worse than death." Jamie held up her hands in surrender. "I'll be good."

"See that you are." Adrienne kept her face as solemn as possible for a few moments but couldn't stop the grin from creeping out.

Jamie stuck out her tongue, and Adrienne laughed back at her. They dissolved into a shared fit of giggles as they made their way down the street back to the school.

CHAPTER NINE

"Adrienne!" KJ's shout from behind the net pulled Adrienne's focus away from the red jerseys swarming their end of the ice. The opposing team's center was bearing down on their goal with laser focus. Without looking toward her, KJ banked the puck off the boards around the center.

Adrienne skated after it, her strides flagging a bit as she looked up ice to see where the forwards were. The center and the right wing had hustled back to help, but Lou was open along the far boards. Adrienne wound up and let the puck fly in her direction.

A red jersey stepped in her way, intercepting what would have been an amazing pass right before it could clear the zone.

"Oh, shit!" A pit opened in her stomach. Adrienne tore toward the hash marks, trying to get between Vaughn and the red-jerseyed forward. She lunged, stretching her stick out as far as it would reach, going so low one knee almost dragged the ice.

The forward could hear her coming. Luckily, she didn't look up to see exactly where Adrienne was and opted instead to let fly at the net. The toe of Adrienne's stick caught the puck and redirected it high over Vaughn's head and into the netting above the boards.

The refs' whistles blew in unison, and both teams turned for their respective benches.

Dammit, dammit, dammit! Adrienne glared at the ice as she chopped her way across the rink, her skate blades sounding angry even to her. *You know better than that. Never send it up the middle. Never, never, never!*

She threw herself down on the far end of the bench and wasted another second to berate herself before grabbing her water bottle. Her legs were already much steadier than they had been that first practice and her lungs felt pretty good, but the pace of the game was a little too quick for comfort yet. She still felt like she was behind the play and not seeing quite as much of the ice as she remembered being able to.

KJ slid onto the bench and bumped Adrienne with her shoulder. "What happened out there?"

"I fucked up, all right?" Adrienne squeezed another stream of water into her mouth. "That was a boneheaded move."

"It was, but you fixed it."

"I guess." Adrienne focused on the action on the ice. They'd taken the face-off in their own zone, but red had won the puck and was cycling it around from the forwards to the defense, then back again. "Why does a team called the Tigers have red jerseys anyway? That makes no sense."

"Way to focus on what's important," KJ said. She grinned, showing off her red, white, and blue mouth guard.

"You know it." Adrienne turned her attention back to the game.

The Bolts were doing a lot of scrambling, trying to keep the Tigers from getting a clear shot on the net, but with mixed results. Every time a red jersey got even a touch on the puck, they were flinging it toward the net, keeping the Bolts from being able to pull themselves together. Vaughn had to stand on their head to keep the other team from scoring. Adrienne lost track of how many times she caught her breath, convinced that this was the shot that would go in. Finally, one of the red forwards took a shot right at Vaughn's midsection. They absorbed it against their pads but couldn't corral it completely. The black disk dropped to the blue of the crease, and they lunged at it. They didn't get there in time, and the Tigers descended on the goal en masse, Cam and Krissy in the middle of the scrum. From what little Adrienne could see, they were swatting away sticks as Vaughn tried to close their glove over the puck.

The entire bench was on their feet, leaning over the boards and shouting encouragement to their teammates. On the home team's side, the Tigers were hanging way out and yelling too, though it was impossible to make out what they said.

"Come on, come on!" Adrienne yelled. She thumped her palm against the outside of the boards, adding a booming sound to the cacophony of her teammates. KJ joined her, ratcheting up the racket.

For a moment, it seemed like they had it. Vaughn brought their gloved hand down to the ice with authority, but before they could cover completely, a red-jerseyed forward poked her stick under it. The puck squirted out and rolled past Vaughn's leg pads and into the net. The goalie threw their head back in an expression of dismay that was echoed by those on the Visitor bench. Further down the boards, the Tigers erupted in celebration.

"First blood to them," KJ said. She swatted the boards with her hand one last time, then stood up. "Ready to get it back?"

"Yep." Adrienne took a last drink of water, then followed KJ over the boards. Cam and Krissy skated toward them, pictures of dejection.

KJ tapped their shin pads with her stick. "We got this," she said to them.

Maybe they did, and maybe they didn't. Adrienne didn't know that she shared KJ's confidence. She took her place a few paces above the blue line and waited impatiently for both teams to array themselves for the face-off. The Tigers were giving them a run for their money, but she knew the Bolts wanted this game as badly. KJ practically vibrated with her readiness for the puck to drop, but then she always wanted it.

Adrienne was glad they were on the same team. KJ on the line beside her was a comforting presence, now that they'd patched up their initial misunderstanding. Giving her another chance was panning out.

The referee approached the face-off dot and held out the puck. Everyone tensed, waiting for the rubber disc to hit the ice. There was still a lot of game left to go, and Adrienne would be right there until it was over.

* * *

KJ led the way across the parking lot to her car. Her breath created windy clouds in the air, as did the skin on her bare hands. She watched the vapor escape, ever bemused that she could be so warm from a game that her skin would steam. The air had gotten chillier now that it was almost November.

"Why does my bag always weigh twice as much after a game than before?" Adrienne asked from beside her. She leaned away from the weight of her hockey bag, while juggling a couple of sticks.

"Sweat?" KJ suggested. She was used to the weight of her own bag, so much so that it was almost comforting.

"You're hilarious." Adrienne hitched the bag further up her shoulder. "I'm pretty sure I didn't sweat out twenty pounds worth today."

"There's another option," KJ said gravely, "but I don't think you're going to like it."

"That I'm thirty, and not getting any younger."

"Okay, two other options."

She tried to keep a straight face when Adrienne smacked her on the arm, but failed. Biting back another snicker, she held out her free arm. "I can carry it for you if it's too much."

"Very gallant, but I think I'll soldier on, thanks anyway."

Once at the car, Adrienne waited impatiently while KJ unlocked the trunk. KJ stepped back and allowed her to cram her gear in first. She muscled her bag in next to Adrienne's, then made her way to the front seat.

"Seat warmer is down there," KJ said as she buckled her seat belt. She stabbed the little button. "I'm setting mine to toasted buns."

"Oh, I'll toast those buns," Adrienne muttered.

"You're also hilarious." KJ started the car, then headed for the road. It was going to be almost an hour and a half to drive home, and she was glad for the company.

Over the past three weeks, KJ had been getting to know Adrienne much better. This was the third away game they'd carpooled to. For someone who worked as a shrink at an elementary school, she had a raunchy sense of humor. So far, it seemed there were very few innuendos that were beyond her. Not that KJ minded, not in the least. She'd mentioned it to Jamie, who had looked at her like she'd grown another head. Apparently, Adrienne saved her humor for KJ.

She wasn't sure what to make of that. Maybe she saw KJ as someone safe? KJ was out to everyone on the team. No one had any problem with her being a lesbian, and she wasn't the only one of her teammates to swing that way. In fact, some of her teammates had dated each other. KJ had mostly abstained from that. For the longest time, she'd been the youngest one on the team. Some of the other team dykes were old enough to be her mother.

"Do you mind if I turn on the radio?" Adrienne asked.

"Not at all, but you're not going to get much more than God and country out here."

"It's too bad your car doesn't have a hookup for my phone. I've got some decent music on there."

"What kind of music do you like?"

"A bunch of stuff. It's pretty eclectic. There's some pop, alternative, Motown, the occasional metal song every now and again depending on my mood. A little gospel."

"Gospel?" KJ risked a sideways glance at her D partner, trying to see if she'd been offended by the God and country remark.

"I like the harmonies. All those voices together working toward one purpose. It's pretty great."

"You could play it anyway."

"Nah." Adrienne leaned back in her seat and braced one foot against the dashboard. "It won't do it justice at all, and then you'll think I have terrible music taste."

"I will judge you quite harshly, it's true."

"See, that's exactly what I thought. If there's one thing I know about KJ Stennes, it's that she's incredibly judgmental."

"Oh, come on," KJ said. "I apologized about that!"

"About what?" Adrienne stared at her, then her eyes opened wide when she realized what KJ was talking about. "Sorry! I wasn't thinking about that at all. I was just giving you a bit of a hard time."

"Oh, I'll give you a hard time."

Adrienne watched her, her face blank.

Oh, no! I've totally offended her. KJ swallowed hard. "That's not what I meant, I was—"

Her teammate burst out laughing. "That was great. I wish you could have seen the look on your face. You were about to poop your pants."

"No, I wasn't." KJ shook her head for emphasis. "I didn't want to come off as some perv."

"You were worried. That's adorable." She reached out and patted the side of KJ's arm reassuringly. Her skin tingled slightly at the contact. That was odd. Adrienne must have built up a bit of a static charge. "It's all right, I'm not mortally offended. I like having someone I can joke around with. There aren't as many people in my life I can do that with as I'd like."

"Oh no? Why's that? Are you having problems making friends in town?"

"It's a few things." Adrienne sighed, then stared back out the window on her side. "Joking like that with Lawrence is completely inappropriate. Doing it at school also feels kinda… squicky. My mom and dad are straight out. I used to be able to goof around like that with Kaz, but that's a massive no-go zone now. That only leaves you."

"Lucky me," KJ said, completely deadpan. "Kaz is your ex-husband?"

"Well, yeah."

"I don't think I've ever heard you say his name before. You usually just call him 'the ex.'"

"Is that right?" Adrienne asked. "I guess it must be. That's a little odd. Huh."

"I don't think it's terribly surprising. I don't know of many people who are super-thrilled with their exes."

"It's not even that. Kaz and I are still pretty tight. I talk to him at least once a week."

"It must be different when you're sharing custody of a kid."

"I'd probably call him anyway. He's decent company. We simply couldn't be married anymore."

"Oh." She hesitated, wanting to know more but unsure if Adrienne would welcome a little light prying. "So why did the two of you break up if you still get along so well. Did he cheat?"

"Oh, no. At least not that he ever admitted to." Adrienne was quiet for a long time, long enough for KJ to start worrying about offending her again. "Kaz isn't…He couldn't anymore…"

"Is he gay?"

"No. He didn't leave me for someone else. I guess you could say he left me for his career." Adrienne chewed on her lower lip. "At least that's how the relationship started to go sideways."

"What does he do?" KJ shot a glance over at her D partner, trying to figure out the strange tone in her voice.

"He's a musician."

"That's a lot of traveling, I bet."

"So much. He put in a lot of time, got in pretty tight in the music scene in Philly. He'd be gone every weekend and most nights. I was working a job I hated and was mostly a single mother for Lawrence. Even when he was around, he was exhausted from spending so much time on the road. He didn't do a whole lot to help with our son."

"That sounds really tough."

"It was." Adrienne tapped her knee with her fingertips. "I decided to go back to school, to get a master's degree in educational psychology. I was miserable both at work and at home. We sat down and talked it out and he agreed to stay home more often so I could attend classes and do my homework."

"I take it that didn't last?"

"The first month was really nice, but then there was just one more session, and then a couple on the weekend, but can't you work on your homework around that? Within three months, we were back to our old patterns, and my grades were starting to suffer. I called him out on it, and he said he would try, but…"

"That's not cool at all." KJ gripped the steering wheel hard.

"You want to know the worst part of it?"

"If you want to tell me."

"I was so mad that he couldn't make Lawrence and me a priority. After we divorced and I moved in with my parents for the rest of my degree, he got so much better with our son." Adrienne gestured both hands at the windshield. "Even now, he's gotten a part-time job at a music store in Harrisburg and only gigs on weeknights so he can take Lawrence on the weekend. He finally got his shit together, but he couldn't do it for me." She sniffled, then scrubbed at her cheeks.

"Are you crying?" KJ glanced over at her partner, but she'd turned to watch the scenery pass by. She reached out and patted Adrienne awkwardly on the shoulder. Another static discharge left her fingertips tingling. "Please don't cry. It's obvious he didn't deserve you."

"I'm not crying." Adrienne dragged her hand across her face. "Really."

"Of course not." KJ turned her attention back to the road before she killed them in a fiery wreck. "But it would be okay if you were."

"Dammit, KJ." Adrienne sniffled again. "Would you stop being so damn nice about this?"

"Okay, you asked for it. I will now cheer you up." KJ stiffened her spine, drawing herself to her full height. "Stop crying!" she mock-yelled. "There should be happiness only in this car!"

"Even though we lost our game?"

"Oh damn, now you're going to make me cry."

"It's all right to cry."

"Yes. I know."

Silence filled the car, punctuated occasionally by Adrienne's sniffles. Those grew fewer and fewer until she turned around to face the front again.

"It's hard," Adrienne said. "We were together for nearly ten years. The last few weren't great, but it was really good when we were first in love and when Lawrence was born. But the more he made a name for himself, the less time he had for us."

"That's a lot to deal with." KJ's heart ached for the pain she heard in Adrienne's voice. KJ had no problems empathizing with the lost quality to her tone, as if she was still coming to terms with the wounds of her past.

"It is. I think the hardest part is that he's so much better now. He's almost a different person."

"Do you wish you could be together again?"

"Oh no." Adrienne's head shake was emphatic. "I'd never be able to trust that he wouldn't fall back into his old patterns. No, we're done, but we can't be entirely out of each other's lives. He seems to have made his peace with it, and I guess I have too. I do miss having someone to share my day with. An adult, I mean. It's not the same with Lawrence."

"You know there's nothing wrong with wanting that, right?"

Adrienne waved a hand dismissively. "Oh yeah."

"I mean it. I can't tell if you're blowing me off or you believe it, but just in case."

Adrienne smiled. "Thanks for that. I'm really not being flippant about it. I've spent enough time of my own in therapy to come to terms with the whole mess. It's kind of an occupational hazard, as it turns out."

"Oh yeah? So have you used your psychology brain on me? Figured out what makes me tick?"

Adrienne regarded her more solemnly than KJ thought was justified for the joke. "It can be hard," she finally said. "I try not to engage that part of my training when I'm not at work, but it's so much a part of me now that I sometimes find myself analyzing others without being aware of it. Since I work with kids, you're not too hard to read."

"Was that a slam on me? Did you—" KJ flicked her eyes from the road to find Adrienne's face for a second. When she saw the big grin on her face, she shifted her attention back to driving. "You're a butt."

"My point exactly."

"I don't want to talk about this anymore," KJ said. "I'm getting beat up on seven ways to Sunday. Let's talk about something a little more important."

"Like what?"

"How about like our breakout and how you might be picking it up a bit faster if you were coming to practice."

CHAPTER TEN

"Practice?" Adrienne shifted in her seat. She'd been worried this would come up. Over the past few weeks, she and KJ had developed a rapport. It was fragile in places, but she felt like it could be the foundation for a really solid friendship. She took a deep breath, giving herself a second or two before answering.

"You know, practice: that thing we do so we get better?"

"I know what practice is."

"You've only made a couple of them. You're really shaking the rust off your skills, but it would be great if the rest of your game would come together." KJ glanced over at her. "Correct me if I'm off base. I don't want to come off like I'm telling you what to do and how to be."

Adrienne shook her head. "You're not wrong. When I passed that puck up the middle, all I saw was our wing. I didn't even notice their forward hanging out. Everything is still moving pretty quickly."

"Practice would help with that."

"I know it would, but what am I supposed to do?" Adrienne tapped the top of her leg with her fingertips. "I have Lawrence on weekdays. Sometimes Kaz can take him on a weeknight, but he works most evenings. I don't feel comfortable leaving Lawrence to run around the rink unsupervised."

"He's how old, eight?"

"He'll be ten after Christmas."

"Sounds like he's getting old enough for less supervision. Besides, from what I've seen of him, he's likely to sit quietly and draw or play with his action figures."

"Until he gets bored." Lawrence was deceptively quiet and mostly well-behaved, but he had an inquisitive mind. If he got it in his brain to check out the Zamboni, she would look up and he'd already be on it. And how would the rink staff react when they saw him up there? For sure they wouldn't be happy, but she didn't need them deciding to call the sheriff's office on him, not while she was distracted on the ice. And would she even be able to concentrate on practice while he was off doing who knew what? That would defeat the whole purpose.

"So make sure he doesn't get bored."

"That's difficult to do while playing," Adrienne said. "I'm not comfortable with the idea. I'll try to get to as many practices as I can, but my attendance is going to be spotty."

"How about a babysitter?"

"Babysitters cost money I don't have. The end of the month is already tough for me. If it's the difference between not eating for the last week and making it to practice, well, food is important."

"There has to be something we can do about it."

"I'll see what I can come up with, but it has to be free and I have to be okay with it." Her voice was firm, as she willed KJ to drop the topic. There were some things she wasn't ready to discuss with this woman who she was rapidly coming to see as a good friend.

"I get it, he's your son." KJ shrugged. "I was a latchkey kid by the time I was his age, but then I also had an older brother to come home to."

Happy for the change of subject, Adrienne leaned into the conversational shift. "Both your parents worked?"

"Dad did. He and Mom divorced when I was nine. She left. I haven't seen her since she moved out."

"That's rough." And not at all what Adrienne had expected. KJ occasionally talked about her dad, but this was the first time she'd heard anything about her mom. From what she'd said, her silence on the subject made perfect sense. Mothers didn't usually cut ties with their children.

"It wasn't fantastic. But Dad was great with us, when he got home. He never missed one of my games."

"Mine either. Ma couldn't make a lot of them, but Daddy made every single one."

"Our household lived and breathed hockey. Erik played in high school but stopped after graduation. During hockey season, the TV always had a game on. Dad would sit and point out what was happening on screen. He did that before he and Mom broke up too. She liked summers best, I think because the TV was quiet." KJ sat straight up in her seat. "Why don't we do that?"

"Do what? I lost you on the last left you took."

"Sorry." KJ reached over and tapped her excitedly on the thigh. "You should come over and we can watch hockey together. It'll help you get the feel of it back and no babysitter needed. Bring Lawrence with you. I'm sure I can find something to distract him with. If he's not into the game, that is."

KJ was definitely warming to the subject, growing more animated as she worked through her idea out loud. Adrienne was trying to deal with her own excitement, but not at the idea. No, the tension in her gut was from KJ touching her on the leg.

What's that about? Adrienne shook her head.

"Oh," KJ said, her voice low with disappointment. "Is it a bad idea?"

"What?" Adrienne asked, before realizing they were still talking about her coming over to watch hockey at KJ's house. "Oh, no, it's a great idea. I was distracted by a work thing. Very serious stuff, you know." *And definitely not the warm and fuzzy feelings you got from your teammate patting you on the leg.*

"Great! How about Monday night? The Flyers are playing the Islanders."

"Let's give me a day to convince Lawrence," Adrienne said. *And figure out what to do with this little wrinkle.* She rubbed her hands over the tops of her thighs. The left one felt a little tight.

"Tuesday?"

"That could work. Let's put a pin in it."

"I'll take care of dinner. All you need to bring is yourself. And your kid."

"If you're sure. I don't want to impose."

"Help my D partner become one of the best defensewomen in the league, and get someone to watch games with?" KJ sighed dramatically. "That is such a terrible imposition. I don't know how I'm going to manage it. First I need to clean my house from top to bottom, then get started on a five-course meal, as I'm sure you require."

"Sure, you know me and my need for fancy dinners," said the woman whose cupboard was filled with boxes of store-brand mac-n-cheese. "I do hope it shall be served on fine china and crystal and that your butler is well-informed of my food preferences."

KJ shot her a look of mock horror. "A butler! I need to hire a butler! It's a good thing you moved this event to Tuesday. Gives me time to start interviewing folks."

"Event?" Adrienne tutted at her while shaking her head. "Darling, you know an event isn't nearly fancified enough for me. I require nothing less than a soiree."

"A soiree? When do we get time to watch hockey during a soiree?"

Adrienne tapped her chin. "Tell you what," she finally said. "Instead of having it at your house, we rent out the fanciest establishment in all of Sussburg, and we have it there. You can project the game and it can be going on in the background while you and I mingle with the guests and eat canapes."

"So the Legion Hall out by the highway." If KJ's voice had been any drier it would have turned to dust and blown away.

"I suppose that's not the most posh location ever. How about something in Philly? Plenty of fancy venues there."

"Or you come over and I feed you and Lawrence spaghetti and meatballs, and we stream a game on my TV."

"I suppose it'll do in a pinch."

"Oh good." KJ elbowed her in the upper arm without taking her eyes off the road. "I'm glad you can rein in your rich girl impulses when you need to."

"Hey, right now I'm the one with the chauffeur. I'd ride in the back, but our sticks are in the way."

KJ shook her head and laughed. Adrienne couldn't help but join in. She hadn't noticed how much she liked KJ's laugh. It was warm and open. She'd have to work at hearing it more often.

CHAPTER ELEVEN

KJ glanced at the clock, its swinging tail and exaggerated feline eyes darting back and forth to mark the seconds. It was already 4:30. Why did the cat clock look so much more judgmental when she was running late?

"Crap." The sauce on the stove was bubbling merrily, sending little drops of viscous red liquid spattering every which way. She snagged a pot lid and turned down the burner before setting the timer. Adrienne and Lawrence would be by in thirty minutes or so, and she hadn't done any cleaning up.

She'd been mostly joking when she told Adrienne that she needed to clean the house from top to bottom, but it could use some tidying. Half-filled boxes lurked in the corners of pretty much every room, a natural collection area for tumbleweeds of dog fur. A quick vacuum would take care of the worst of those, and she could close up the boxes and stack them a bit more neatly. Some of them had been in their partially filled state for months. Maybe it was time to get back to packing stuff up.

Not tonight. KJ pushed the nagging thought from her mind. She had more pressing things to contend with than packing up the things her dad had thought worth saving, no matter how much Erik kept pushing.

Chester lifted his head when she made her way over to the pantry. He'd been watching her cook with his head on his paws. He was good about staying out from under foot, at least until some food hit the ground. Then he came over and quickly cleaned it up before going back to his rug and waiting patiently for the next snack opportunity.

The pantry had his treats in it, which he well knew. It also held the vacuum cleaner. He popped to his feet, then trotted over to the stairs and disappeared to the second floor so quickly he practically left a dog-shaped puff of fur in his wake. That was just as well. He either ran from the vacuum or he stood in the nearest doorway and barked at it. Apparently, he was in the mood for avoidance today.

He must have picked up that something out of the ordinary was happening, KJ thought as she fitted the wand to the vacuum's hose. She didn't often cook from scratch. Dinner was usually a frozen pizza and a smoothie. Occasionally she spruced it up with some steamed vegetables. She was an athlete, after all. She needed to keep her body in fighting trim. When she remembered.

Tidying up didn't take too long, though once the boxes were neatly arranged and the fur clumps sucked up, she could see how shabby the rest of the house looked. The glass on the front door was covered with Chester noseprints. The glass coffee table showed evidence that he'd sneezed on it at least once, though likely more than that by the number of spots. Thankfully, most of the corners on the first floor were covered with dark wood, but even that was starting to show where the dog liked to rub his face.

KJ glanced at the clock. It was almost 4:45. She dashed back to the kitchen and gave the tomato sauce a quick stir and taste, cursing when she burned her tongue. It needed a little more salt and oregano. She sprinkled in the spices and splashed the spoon around, then dropped the pot lid back on.

Nails clicked gently on wood as Chester made his slow way downstairs, eyes peeled for the hated vacuum, but she'd already stowed it. He resumed his post on the rug and had barely settled into his waiting pose when KJ strode past him to the utility room. She grabbed some glass cleaner and paper towels and hustled to the living room to take care of the door and coffee table.

Which one do I do first? KJ hesitated. *Don't think, do!* She snickered as she put the mantra she used to kick herself in the butt for hockey for housecleaning instead. The crap on top of the coffee table was swept aside. She attacked the clear surface with the glass cleaning spray, then ruthlessly eliminated Chester's sneeze spots. It didn't take long to stack the couple of hockey magazines and remotes back on the table, then she was off to the door.

"I should have done this one first," she complained to herself. The door was multiple panes of glass held together by dark wooden dividers. Each one took time to clean, so she did so as quickly as she could. She was finishing up the bottom-most panes when she looked out to see two pairs of legs at the top of the concrete front steps.

"They're here," she called out to Chester, but he was already sprinting out of the kitchen, barking his head off. He crammed his nose against a newly cleaned pane while trying to get a closer look at the interlopers to his kingdom.

"Hush, you," KJ said. She pushed Chester away from the door, then opened it. "Don't mind him," she said to Adrienne and Lawrence. "He's a bit of an idiot when people come over."

"Mom, she has a dog!" Lawrence exclaimed. He bent down to get a closer look. "What's his name?"

"This bundle of excitement is Chester. You're not scared of dogs, I take it."

"Nope." Lawrence beamed. "Can I pet him, Mom?"

"I'm not the one to ask, baby," Adrienne said. "Ask KJ."

"Can I pet your dog, Miss KJ?" Lawrence's eyes were wide with pleading anticipation.

"It's just KJ, and of course you can." She scooped Chester up in her arms to keep him from making a break for it, then pulled the door open wide. "Come on in."

They entered the house, Lawrence craning his neck to see everything he could.

"Shoes on or off?" Adrienne asked.

"On is fine," KJ said. "I don't usually kick mine off unless they're gross with snow. We don't have any of that yet." She reached out and rapped her knuckle on the nearest piece of wood molding.

KJ turned to Lawrence, keeping her grip on the bundle of squirming dog in her arms. "He's going to be a little hyper until he gets a good sniff. Are you up for that?"

He nodded emphatically, his eyes shining.

"Here goes." KJ leaned forward and placed Chester on the floor. His excited back end wiggled so much that he almost fell over before getting his feet under himself. As soon as he was steady he zoomed over to Adrienne and circled around her ankles once, giving her a cursory sniff before darting Lawrence's way.

Lawrence squatted in the hall with his hands out. Chester snuffled them closely. His tongue darted out to bathe Lawrence's fingers, sending the boy into a fit of giggles. Chester sniffed his way along the boy's arm to his chest, then stuck his nose in Lawrence's face. He whuffed a deep breath, then ran his tongue the length of the boy's face. Delighted, Lawrence wrapped his arms around the squirming dog.

"Don't squeeze him too hard," Adrienne said, her hand out.

"It's all right," KJ said. "Chester is pretty tough, and Lawrence is being gentle, despite my dog's very bad manners. He's usually a little more reserved."

"Lawrence, why don't you give me your coat, then you and the dog can…do whatever." Adrienne waited as her son squirmed his way out of his jacket without letting go of the dog.

"I have some toys in the basket over there." KJ pointed toward the corner. "He'll be your friend forever if you play tug with him."

"Okay!" Lawrence clambered to his feet. "Come on, Chester."

The little dog followed at his heels. When he realized they were heading for the toys, he started running in little circles, his back end nearly a blur from his enthusiastic wagging.

"I guess he's not my dog anymore," KJ said to Adrienne.

"I'm so sorry!" Adrienne looked mortified. "I'll have a talk with Lawrence."

"I was kidding." KJ hastened to reassure her. "I haven't seen Chester this ramped up in a long time. It'll be good for him to have someone to lavish attention on him. He was my dad's dog."

"For Lawrence too." Adrienne's face cleared in relief. "He's always so quiet and serious. It's wonderful to see him excited."

"They're good for each other."

An exuberant session of tug was taking place in the living room. Chester was stronger than he looked and managed to snatch the tug toy from Lawrence's hands a couple of times before the boy figured out that he had to really hold on to it. It wasn't easy, KJ knew from experience. Chester would lash his head back and forth. There was definitely some terrier back in his very mixed ancestry.

"Lawrence, don't lift him up," KJ called out. "It's not good for him, and he's too riled up to do the smart thing and let go."

"All right," Lawrence responded. He leaned down, allowing Chester's back legs to touch the ground instead of dangling six inches above it.

"Now that you're both here, I can put the pasta in." KJ headed back to the kitchen. "I hope you guys like spaghetti."

"Spaghetti is fine." Adrienne followed along behind her. "I wish you'd let me bring something."

"I don't mind," KJ said. "I don't get many opportunities to cook. I hate doing it for me only." She opened the lid on the sauce and took a deep sniff. It smelled perfect. "Do you like garlic bread?"

"I didn't realize you were the cooking type." Adrienne leaned in to take a look at the sauce. "That looks amazing, and it smells even better."

KJ's chest swelled with pride at Adrienne's compliment. "Dad couldn't be trusted around the stove by the time I moved back home, so it was something I had to pick up. About the garlic bread?"

"I like a good garlic bread."

"Then I'll put some in while the pasta cooks. I like it garlicky, so I always ask. In this house, either everyone has garlic bread or no one does."

"Fair enough."

KJ bustled around the kitchen preparing the rest of the meal. The sounds of a boy and a dog rumpusing around the living room occasionally percolated in to them as they chatted lightly. The sounds mainly involved thumping, so KJ wasn't too worried that she would be facing a trashed living room. Adrienne barely twitched at the noises, so she figured they must be at an expected level.

"The game doesn't start until six thirty, so we have plenty of time to eat," KJ said. "It gave me an excuse to clear off the dining room table, which I really appreciate."

"Are you one of those people who subscribes to the horizontal surface filing system?"

"Not normally, but things have gotten away from me." KJ stopped in the middle of the kitchen and gave the counters a considering once-over. The pile of mail by the toaster was taller than it should have been. Those papers stacked on top of the microwave had a purpose she'd long ago forgotten. There was so much that still needed to be done. She shook her head and got back to working on dinner.

"Your son has completely won Chester over," she said a while later.

Adrienne looked up from tossing the salad with a quizzical tilt to her head.

"I can't remember the last time I made a meal without him hanging out right there." KJ pointed to the coiled rug with the wooden spoon still red with marinara sauce. "He's like a furry Roomba when it comes to kitchen scraps."

"That sounds really handy, actually." Adrienne laughed. "Maybe I can borrow him from time to time. Lawrence is at an age where he's expected to help in the kitchen, but man does he make a mess."

"I'm sure we can come up with an arrangement. I don't think Chester would mind. Free snacks and someone to really play with him? He'll think he's gone over the rainbow bridge." As soon as the words left her mouth, KJ wished she could recall them. *Great topic of conversation*, she snarled to herself. *Let's talk a bit more about pets dying when you're trying to make nice with a new friend.*

Fortunately, Adrienne didn't seem to notice her faux pas. "I'm really glad Lawrence has something to keep him occupied. I was a little worried he'd be bored out of his mind."

"Chester to the rescue." KJ stepped back to observe the spread. Pasta and sauce each had their own bowls. Adrienne had the salad. "Garlic bread." She opened the oven door and grabbed out the tray with its savory treats, but not before wrapping a dish towel around her hand to protect it. Even so, the heat of the tray quickly permeated the towel and she had to drop it on the cooktop with a clatter.

"Are you all right?" Adrienne asked, moving up next to her and reaching out for her hand.

"I'm fine," KJ responded cheerily. She glanced at her fingers, but they weren't even red. "See?" She held out her hand to Adrienne, who grasped it and inspected her fingers carefully. Adrienne's hands were warm and soft. KJ became acutely aware of the calluses on her fingers and palms. "I'm fine, Adrienne. You don't have to be such a mom with me."

"If you say so." Adrienne let go, and KJ's fingers were immediately much lonelier. Cooler. They were definitely cooler. How could fingers be lonely?

"I don't want to have to break in a new defensive partner if you end up being out for a chunk of time with burned hands," Adrienne said.

"Very funny."

Adrienne smirked, then picked up the pasta and salad. "Lawrence, dinner," she called as she left the kitchen.

KJ was left to scoop the garlic bread into a small basket. Her hands were still cold. *I wish Adrienne had held on longer.* Not that there was any reason to. KJ was fine. There was no pain, no burn. She'd been quick to grab at KJ's hand, though. Adrienne was a mom and a good one from what she'd seen of her and Lawrence together. Mom-mode must be hard to turn off, especially with her son in the next room. Adrienne was merely being motherly, that's all there was to it. Satisfied with her line of reasoning, KJ finished filling the basket and went to join the other two in the dining room.

CHAPTER TWELVE

There was nothing nicer than a belly full from good food, Adrienne decided. She leaned back in her chair, stretching her arms way back. "My god, KJ, that was delicious."

Lawrence nodded energetically. He took another bite of his garlic bread, then his hand dipped below the table. When it came back up, it was empty.

"Lawrence, are you feeding Chester under the table?" Adrienne asked.

Her son looked down at the dog sitting next to his chair. Chester's focus never wavered.

"Maybe?"

"Please don't do that," KJ said. "I don't need a dog who is as wide as he is long. Table scraps will kill his girlish figure, not to mention give him worse habits than he already has."

"All right," Lawrence whispered, wilting a bit under KJ's words. "I'm sorry."

"Don't be." KJ leaned over to affix the dog with a mock-glare. "You're not the first person he's hoodwinked. I'm sure you won't be the last either. But now you're on to his game, and you won't let him fool you again, right?"

"Right." Lawrence straightened up in his chair.

"We can give him some T-R-E-A-T-S later."

"Why are you spelling trea—"

"Don't say it!" KJ held out her hand to stop him, but it was too late. Chester had gone from sitting and staring at Lawrence to dancing on all fours. "He knows the word and thinks it means he's going to get some right away. Someone never did learn patience. There's just one thing to do about it."

"Give him a T-R-E-A-T?"

"Nope." KJ stood up and picked up her plate and one of the serving dishes. "We're going to clear the table, then take him for a W-A-L-K." She winked at Lawrence, who nodded sagely back. "What are you grinning about over there?" she said to Adrienne.

She hadn't realized she was smiling. "I'm waiting to see how Lawrence is going to be about cleaning his spot. It's not his favorite task to do."

Why was she smiling, really? There was something so homey and comfortable about the whole scene. It verged on domestic, not a word she'd ever thought to associate with KJ. It occurred to her that she didn't know a whole lot about her partner beyond the fact that she lived, breathed, and probably bled hockey. Even the time they'd spent in the car on the way to and from games hadn't told her a whole lot beyond that.

"I can do it," Lawrence reassured KJ. "See?" He picked up his plate and glass, then realized it was still half full of milk. Carefully balancing the plate with its cutlery, Lawrence gulped the milk down.

"This way," KJ said, leading Adrienne's son into the kitchen.

Adrienne stood and stacked the remaining serving dishes. There wasn't much food left. They'd done a number on the meal. She added her plate and silverware to the pile, then joined the other two. KJ was directing Lawrence where to put his plate in the dishwasher. He complied quickly but kept sneaking glances down at Chester, who seemed determined to become Lawrence's shadow.

"You're good to go," KJ said.

"Come on, Chester," Lawrence yelled on his way out of the kitchen. He needn't have done so, the dog was already trotting along at his heels.

"Maybe I should send Chester home with you two."

Adrienne swatted KJ on the shoulder. "Don't you dare. I don't need to be responsible for another living being. Then there's the pet deposit and the added monthly rent. Do you know how much my place charges for dogs?"

"I was kidding." KJ made a show of massaging her upper arm.

"Did I hurt the big, strong defensewoman?" Adrienne affected a concerned moue. "Are you going to be able to make it to practice on Thursday?"

"I think I'll manage." KJ rolled her arm in its socket, then got to loading the rest of the dirty dishes into the dishwasher. "I'd like to take Chester for a quick walk before the game. We have about twenty minutes before the puck drops. Are you okay with me taking Lawrence along?"

"Of course. Are you okay with me joining the three of you?"

"Is there some reason I shouldn't be?"

Adrienne pretended to consider the question. "I don't think so…I'll let you know if anything comes up."

"You're smiling again."

"You're funny."

"Looks aren't everything."

"Hey, look at that, you got it. Good for you."

"It's a hell of a dad joke."

"So you're telling me you're turning into a dad?"

A spasm of what could only be pain crossed KJ's face before she smiled brightly. "There are worse things, I suppose."

"Of course." Adrienne didn't understand why her ribbing had caused the reaction it did, but she decided she didn't like it. "So, about that dog walk…Don't want to miss the start of the game."

"Right." KJ shook her head. "Chester." There was a long pause and no response from the other room. "Chester! Do you want to go for a walk?"

Scrambling erupted from the front of the house. Chester burst into the kitchen, Lawrence racing along behind him. As usual, Chester's nails weren't enough to stop him from sliding sideways on the linoleum floor. He hit the rug, did a quick 180, then shot out of the kitchen toward the front door.

"Someone is a little worked up." Adrienne looked over at her son, who responded with a shrug and a grin, then went running after the dog.

"It's all right," KJ said. "Chester needs someone to wear him out every now and again. This means I don't have to go on a five-mile run with him."

"In that case, we're happy to help." Adrienne waited for KJ to leave the room, then followed after her. She'd been looking forward to watching a game, but so far the evening had been so nice she didn't think she'd care if they didn't get to it.

* * *

The walk had been nice, if a little chaotic. KJ had allowed Lawrence control over the lead. It was clear the boy had never walked a dog before, and Chester had taken advantage of his ignorance by conveniently forgetting everything he'd ever learned about walking on one side and heeling. KJ had worked with Lawrence on how to gently correct Chester, but it had been slow going. The dog finally relieved himself, but KJ knew they'd have to go out again later.

Adrienne walked next to her as they watched Lawrence and Chester's weaving path across the narrow sidewalk and back again. The street was quiet. A breeze blew leaves from lawns onto the street. Little vegetation remained on the trees to impede the light from the street lamps. KJ didn't feel the need to make conversation. She was content to walk in companionable silence next to Adrienne, speaking only to give Lawrence advice on reining in her poorly behaved pet. They were close enough together that their hands kept brushing up against each other. She stopped apologizing after the third time. It was odd how she kept getting little tingles with every contact, even though they were wearing gloves. It didn't hurt. Quite the opposite. KJ had to stop herself from reaching over for another brush.

By the time they got back to the house, it was nearly puck drop.

"Go on in," she said to Lawrence and Adrienne. She took a detour to throw Chester's poop bag in the trash cans at the back of the house, then entered through the back door.

Adrienne was in the middle of the kitchen, staring at the cupboards.

"Do you need anything?" KJ asked.

"I thought some popcorn would be nice, but I didn't want to go rooting through your stuff." Adrienne grinned. "At least not until the second visit."

"I appreciate you being so circumspect. Not that going through my cupboards would have helped. I'm right out of popcorn, sorry. There are some chips, but I didn't think of munchies." *Good job, KJ.* "Check the pantry." She pointed at a narrow wooden door tucked at the end of the cabinets.

"No problem. I'm sure chips will be fine."

"We can throw them in here." KJ opened a cupboard and pulled out a large metal bowl.

"I'll get it, you get the game set up."

"Got it." She tossed the bowl to Adrienne, then booked it to the living room. Chester was curled up on his bed with Lawrence next to him. The last time Chester had been this knackered was when KJ had taken him on a bike ride in Fireman's Park. She snagged her laptop and hooked the HDMI cable into the TV.

Erik hadn't approved of the expense of a new television after she'd first moved back home. He thought it was a needless extravagance and that Dad wouldn't benefit, that it was only for her, and besides what was wrong with their old set, never mind that it was too old to hook up to a computer to stream games. He'd been wrong, no surprise there. Dad had loved watching games with her. Even after he'd stopped speaking, he'd had some of his most lucid moments watching sports, especially when ESPN played classic match-ups. She'd missed having someone to watch hockey with. Chester would occasionally get interested in watching the puck, but he wasn't great company when it came to breaking down the action.

KJ picked up the remote and fiddled with it. A blue screen flickered to life on screen, then the picture resolved into a long shot of a darkened rink from above. A stylized bobcat logo stared up at the camera while distant figures stood at each blue line. The familiar strains of music filled the room. Good, they were still on the national anthem. They weren't going to miss anything. She took her favorite spot on the couch's right end.

"It's almost time," KJ called as the women left the ice for their benches. The camera angle switched to a close-up on the face-off dot.

"I'm here." Adrienne plopped down on the couch next to her. "Chips?" She waved the bowl in KJ's direction.

"Not yet." KJ didn't look away from the screen. "I don't want to miss the puck drop. First face-off tells you a lot about how the game is going to go."

"Yep." Adrienne hunkered down into the couch, then crunched on a couple of chips.

"What's a face-off, Mom?" Lawrence asked from next to Chester.

"It's what's happening on the TV right now." She pointed at the screen where a ref held the puck over the ice. Two impossibly young-looking women frowned in concentration at the red face-off dot between them.

"Why are they doing that?" He sat up to get a better angle on the screen.

"It's how they start the game. Whoever is fastest—"

"Or sneakiest," KJ interjected.

"Or sneakiest," Adrienne said, "wins the puck for their team."

"Oh."

The ref let go of the puck. The center in white slapped her opponent's stick blade out of the way, then slung the puck back to her defense. Everyone scattered. KJ loved the first face-off. There was such stillness before the game started, then it was all over and everyone exploded into frenetic but focused movement. ·

"That was a nice win," KJ said.

"It was." Adrienne scooted toward KJ to make room for Lawrence, who had decided he'd rather watch from the couch than the floor. "Who are we rooting for?"

"Quinnipiac, of course."

"Oh, of course."

"I went to school there for a few years."

"Got it."

"Besides, Princeton is cocky. If someone takes them down a notch, it might as well be my girls."

"At least these Tigers have orange jerseys. That makes sense."

"And it's a terrible reason to root for them."

The Quinnipiac defense cycled the puck around and passed it up to the wing along the boards in the neutral zone. The center broke for Princeton's end, but the other forward banked it around her opponent and stick-handled it into the zone. The Quinnipiac center tried to get a skate out to touch the blue line, but her legs didn't stretch that far. The linesman's whistle split through the sounds of skates and women voices.

"Offside." KJ grinned at Adrienne when she realized they'd groaned the word at the same time.

"What's offside?" Lawrence asked.

"It's when a player goes into the other team's zone too soon. Do you see the blue line there?" KJ pointed at the bottom of the screen.

"Yes."

"It marks out each team's area. If a player goes over it before the puck does, it's called offside."

Lawrence furrowed his brow in confusion. "Why does that matter?"

"Otherwise you'd have people hanging out in front of the other team's net all the time. It would make for a pretty boring game." KJ looked over Lawrence's head at Adrienne. "Haven't you taught him anything about hockey?"

Adrienne shook her head. "We weren't a big sports household. Kaz is big into music, but not into athletics. Lawrence has inherited those particular tendencies. I think I'm the only one of us who was ever into playing, and I haven't exactly had the time the past few years to educate him." She reached over and pulled Lawrence into a loose hug. "Besides, he's never been interested before."

"Ask when something doesn't make sense," KJ said. "Your mom or I will explain it to you."

"I will," Lawrence said. "Can I have some chips?"

"And now we see his true motivation," Adrienne said. She passed the bowl over. "Help yourself, but leave some for the rest of us."

The first period went on as it had started. Lawrence had a lot of questions. As they passed the bowl of snacks around, KJ found her fingers wrapping around Adrienne's as she went in for more. At first, they were awkward, snatching their hands away from each other with muttered apologies, but as they continued watching and explaining, the contact started to feel more natural. KJ found herself watching the bowl out of the corner of her eye and reaching for it whenever Adrienne did. She liked touching Adrienne's hand. Her skin was soft, with little calluses forming on the fingers from getting back into hockey. Adrienne didn't seem to mind.

By the start of the second period, Lawrence had decided to go draw at the dining room table. Adrienne pulled a pad of paper and colored pencils out of her purse for him, then joined KJ in time for the puck to drop.

"Thanks for being so good about his questions," she said.

"It's no problem," KJ said. "It was kind of fun to explain that stuff to someone who has no idea what's going on. Did you see his face on icing?"

"I did." Adrienne laughed. "I think I felt the same way as a six-year-old."

"Is that when you started? What got you into playing? Was it a family thing, or something else?"

"That's a lot of questions," Adrienne said. "Yes, I started when I was six. It was better than soccer, which I'd played over the summer. I think it was the skating that did it. Once I had that figured out and I realized I could stop skating, but still move, I was sold. My parents were very much into us having some sort of extracurricular activity. They didn't care too much what it was, as long as we had something. One of my brothers and my sister seemed to do a new thing every year, but I stuck with hockey. How about you?"

"I think I was four. When I was three, my dad bought me a pair of white figure skates and I refused to have anything to do with them. The next year, he took them down to the community center and swapped them out for a pair of hockey skates in my size. I loved those things. He'd take me and Erik out to a frozen pond outside of town to practice on. Not long after that, he enrolled me in Mini-Mites. I never looked back."

"Why didn't you play all four years at Quinnipiac?"

KJ froze at the question. She hated this one. She should have been expecting it, but her guard had dropped. Things tended to slip when Adrienne was around. "It's a boring story," she finally said in a terrible attempt at sounding breezy.

"Not by the way you're acting." Adrienne put a hand on her arm. "If you don't want to talk about it, I won't press you."

CHAPTER THIRTEEN

At the offer to back off, KJ's shoulders loosened. Adrienne stared at the TV but was only half paying attention. Her eyes might have been facing away, but every other sense in her body was sharply attuned to her friend.

The game continued as each team strove for the upper hand. They'd each scored once during the first period. KJ's excitement at getting the first point up on the scoreboard had been dampened when it was followed quickly by a goal by a determined Princeton.

"I played for Quinnipiac," KJ abruptly said during a commercial break. "Under the same coach, even. None of the players are the same, of course."

"That must have been some high-level hockey."

KJ smiled broadly. "It was, and I loved it. The team made it to the NCAA tournament my second year. Didn't make it very far, but it was amazing. But then…" Her face grew somber and she sat back against the couch. She still watched the flickering screen, but Adrienne was pretty sure she wasn't seeing any of it.

Adrienne reached over to pat her on the forearm again. She hoped it was reassuring and not an annoyance. Not everyone liked contact when they were upset, and she couldn't yet tell if KJ was touchy-feely or not.

"Dad had been getting a little off over my last years of high school and into college. At first it was kind of funny. Erik and I would tease him about having a memory like a sieve, but then he got lost driving home from church one morning. We decided I'd put college on hold and move home to take care of him. We couldn't have him wandering the countryside or burning down the house."

"Alzheimer's?"

KJ nodded. Twin tracks glistened down her cheeks, reflecting the light of the television. "I don't know why, but I thought he would get better. I mean, I know what Alzheimer's is, I know it only gets worse, but I thought when I moved in it would help enough for Dad to be back." She sighed. "He was occasionally, but it wasn't long before he became mostly nonverbal. He forgot who I was before he forgot who Erik was."

"That must have hurt."

KJ's pained grimace confirmed Adrienne's words. "Anyway, it went about like you'd expect. He died March before last, during our league playoffs. I had to miss the championship game. We'd put him in hospice by then, and he was stable enough that I went to playoffs with the team. Erik got word to me he was declining rapidly, so I left and came home before the game. We lost."

"And you lost your daddy." Adrienne wrapped her arms around KJ. That explained her insistence on getting back to playoffs and winning the championship. Talk about some major emotional redirection.

KJ let out a sob that she tried to swallow as it came out. The result was a painful-sounding hiccup.

"I've got you." Adrienne ran her hand over the small of KJ's back in soothing circles. The movement always helped Lawrence when he needed to cry but wouldn't. It seemed KJ was no more immune to the effects of a little sympathy. She buried her face in the crook of Adrienne's shoulder and sobbed silently.

The sound of pencil on paper from the table had stopped. Adrienne turned her head and met Lawrence's wide eyes.

"It's okay," Adrienne mouthed.

He nodded and went back to his drawing, but not without sneaking the occasional concerned glance back at the couch.

The sound of a distant horn on the television heralded the scoring of another goal, but neither Adrienne nor KJ looked up. A warm wet spot was spreading across Adrienne's shoulder where KJ's tears soaked into the fabric of her shirt. She was no longer shaking with sobs, just holding onto Adrienne like she was the only thing keeping her from drowning. Adrienne kept rubbing her back in slow circles. She was prepared to hold on to KJ for as long as she needed it. How could she not? Obviously, KJ needed to let some pent-up emotions out before they strangled her.

Despite the dampness on her shoulder, holding KJ wasn't at all uncomfortable. She had a nice solidness to her, a weight Adrienne had missed. Their bodies were molded together, KJ's warmth bathing her like the sun coming out for the first time in a long while. She continued stroking KJ's back and shoulders, soothing the tension out of her partner until she was a limp ball of mostly spent emotion. She'd found she didn't mind touching KJ. Their little accidental hand-touches throughout the evening had been a nice touchstone, a physical reminder of KJ's presence. This embrace was many times more intimate than those glancing touches, but it felt natural. Like she could hold KJ forever.

She caught herself about to lay her cheek on the top of KJ's head. *We're not there*, she told herself sternly. *Yet*, a rebellious voice whispered back at her from the depths of her mind.

Feeling Adrienne stiffen, KJ relaxed her grip. "Sorry about that." She wiped her face, trying to dry off the worst of the tears, but she was only somewhat successful.

"Here." Adrienne reached out and gently dried KJ's face with the cuff of her shirt. "Better?"

"Um, yeah." She sat back with a watery chuckle. "I don't usually do that to people."

"That's a relief." Adrienne retreated back to her corner of the couch. Her body still sang at KJ's closeness, and she wasn't prepared to unpack that yet. Those thoughts needed to wait for some alone time and a glass of wine. A big one.

"Oh hey," KJ said. "We scored again."

If only. "You were a bit distracted when that happened."

"I'll get it again when they drop the game to On Demand." KJ grabbed the bowl of chips off the coffee table and popped a couple into her mouth. She crunched them down in a hurry. "I'm glad you came over. Thank you for that and for..." Her voice trailed off awkwardly.

"Thank you for having us. It's been good for both of us. We're going to have to watch Lawrence to make sure he's not smuggling Chester out under his coat."

"You two are welcome anytime."

"I don't want to impose. I think once a week for hockey games is fine." She had too much to figure out to promise more than that. "I think it's time for Lawrence and me to head out." She stood up abruptly. "Let's wrap it up, baby," she called toward the other room.

"Already?" KJ looked surprised. "There's still the third period."

"It is a school night." Adrienne crossed into the dining room, then looked down at the table. "What did you draw?"

He handed her a piece of paper adorned with colorful shapes. "It's Captain America and Black Panther," he said. "They're fighting Dr. Doom. And don't call me baby."

"It looks great, sugar bug." She carefully folded the drawing and tucked it into her purse.

"Ugh, Mom." Lawrence stared up at her. "Sugar bug?"

"Just trying it on for size." Adrienne grinned at him. "We'll strike that one off the list."

"There's a list?"

"There is now." She patted him on the shoulder. "Now get your coat and say goodbye to KJ and Chester."

"Okay."

"Is everything all right?" KJ was standing right behind her. It took everything Adrienne had not to lean back into her body heat.

"Fine. Everything's fine, I promise. I have an early day tomorrow, and so does Lawrence."

"If you say so." Disappointment lay heavy on KJ's voice, but Adrienne refused to give in to it. "Text me so I know you got home in one piece, okay?"

"Sure thing." She retrieved Lawrence, who had taken advantage of their conversation to engage in one last tussle with the dog, then headed for the door. She didn't bother buttoning up her coat, even though it was chilly out. The car was on the street not twenty feet away; she would be fine.

During the quick drive home — everything in Sussburg was a short trip away — Lawrence chattered on about how cool KJ's house was and how great it had been to play with Chester. He thought KJ was amazing, and Adrienne couldn't disagree. She'd been struck at how good KJ had been with him. Making their way through the darkened town streets was challenging for her lack of knowledge of them, so she confined herself to short answers when Lawrence sounded like he wanted one.

Getting him settled for bed was difficult. He'd finally agreed to head to the shower when Adrienne remembered her promise to KJ. She pulled out her phone and pressed her thumb down on the Message icon.

Got home OK. Trying to get L to bed. He's a little keyed up.

"I don't hear any water running," she yelled at the bathroom door.

"I'm almost ready," Lawrence called back. "I just have to…" His voice descended into mumbles.

"Just have to what? Don't make me come in there."

"Okay, Mom. Geez! I'm not a little kid, I can take a shower by myself." The sound of the shower switching on effectively ended any chance she had of responding.

Her phone buzzed in her hand. It was a message from KJ.

glad to hear it

The phone kept on vibrating as message after message came through in rapid sequence.

had fun tonight
we should do it again
thanks for letting me cry on your shoulder
sweet dreams

Adrienne kept waiting after the last one, but no more came through.

All she could think to text back was: *You too.* She cringed a bit at the impersonal reply, but her thoughts were too conflicted to do much else. The shower was still running in the bathroom, along with a vigorous undertone of splashing that Adrienne was sure was meant to convince her that Lawrence was being industrious in cleaning. She wondered how much tidying up she'd have to do around the tub once he got out.

You need to make lunches, she reminded herself. The kitchen seemed so far away, but she pushed herself away from the wall after taking one final look at her messages. There was nothing beyond the final "sweet dreams."

Her parents had given her a bottle of wine as a housewarming present, and she'd stashed it high up in a kitchen cupboard. She'd been saving it for a special occasion, but what could be more special than trying to figure out if the woman she seemed to be developing feelings for was a crush or something more? It took some digging, but she finally located the wine behind the cereal. For a moment, she contemplated drinking it straight from the bottle but decided that was a little much. A wineglass was easier to track down than the bottle opener, and by the time she had both, Lawrence was out of the shower.

"Do you want me to read you a story?" she asked him as he carefully arranged his action figures into dynamic poses on the shelf above his headboard.

"I'm gonna read a comic, then go to bed." He stretched and yawned, his jaw giving a little pop as he opened it as wide as it would go. "I'm tired."

"I bet. You and Chester had a grand old time of it."

"We did." Lawrence slid between the sheets and picked up a battered comic book from his bedside table. "Can you turn out the overhead light?"

"Of course."

"But leave the hall light on."

"All right. Is there anything else?"

"No." He yawned again. Adrienne was pretty sure the comic was going to sleep with him tonight. "Thanks, Mom."

"For what?"

"For taking me to KJ's place. I had a good day."

"Me too." Adrienne flicked off the light switch. "Good night, baby."

"G'night, Mom." He opened the comic and stared at the first page.

Adrienne shook her head and went back to the kitchen and her bottle. The silence of the apartment rang in her ears. After the chatter and general background noise of KJ's place, the quiet of her place felt like it was pressing in on her, like she was stuck at the bottom of a lake. Alone. She took a long sip of wine. She wouldn't be falling asleep as easily as Lawrence would, that was for sure.

CHAPTER FOURTEEN

The snow was starting to pile up on the road. It wasn't their first snowfall, but it was the first of the season to stick. KJ was comfortable driving about half the speed limit, though that didn't stop the occasional truck or SUV from whizzing past her on the highway.

"Four-wheel drive doesn't mean four-wheel brakes, dingleberry," she grumbled at the black pickup that blew past her. Its taillights disappeared into the flakes shrouding the landscape.

"Hopefully they make it home in one piece," Adrienne said.

"Oh, I don't know. Sometimes it would feel like there was some justice in the world to pass them in a snowbank."

"I don't like wishing ill on people. Instead, I assume there's something incredibly important they need to get to. Like maybe the driver is a lawyer whose client just got arrested for public intoxication and they need to be bailed out."

"If I were a lawyer, I'd let my client wait a little longer on a day like today." KJ leaned forward in a futile attempt to get a better view of the road. "Especially for public intoxication."

"That's because you're way smarter than the lawyer." Adrienne stared out at the snow for a few moments. "I was going to be a lawyer for a while. I was prelaw for a hot second."

"Really? Why did you decide not to pursue it?"

"I liked the idea of helping people. I thought about being a public defender or something like that. But then I realized the kind of hours public defenders have to put in if they're going to manage their caseload and actually help their clients, and I liked the idea of getting home with enough time to see my family. My mom was a lawyer, and there were a few years early in her career that we didn't see her much."

"I get that." Multiple brake lights bloomed to life down the road, like so many angry eyes. KJ tapped the brake enough to notify anyone behind them, then took her foot off the gas, trusting on the car's weight to slow them down. She knew better than to be sharp with the brakes in slick conditions like these. "How did you get into the psychology biz, then?"

"I still wanted to do something where I'd be helping people. I'd taken a couple of psych classes because I thought they'd be helpful for practicing law, and I liked them. When I switched up my major, it seemed like a logical path to take. Not that I graduated with anything that allowed me to get a job in the field. After a few years filing papers for the world's most toxic insurance firm, I knew I wanted to move on. I got interested in child psychology when I started looking at master's programs."

"Very cool." Traffic was inching along now. Red lights stretched ahead of them as far as she could see. KJ firmed her grip on the wheel.

"What was your major?"

KJ laughed. "A very useful one. I use it constantly from day to day. How does French lit sound to you?"

"Like you'd read some interesting books." Adrienne sat up straight and looked over at her. "Does that mean you speak French?"

"I read and write it better, but *un petit peu, oui*." The accent wasn't terrible for not having spoken the language much since leaving school. She wondered where her books had gotten to. Had she even unpacked them after moving back home?

"That sounded pretty legit. I know a smattering of Spanish, but that's about it."

"That's not nothing. If you want to learn more, I'm happy to try it out with you. Maybe I'll have a bit of a leg up since I already have some French."

"We'll see. I don't have much extra time in my schedule." Adrienne turned to look out the window again.

Traffic continued to crawl along for a good mile before they passed a car with its nose pointing out of the ditch between the north and southbound lanes. It would be a while before anyone would be able to get out to give them a tow. She hoped the driver and passengers were all right.

They drove in silence. Somehow, it didn't feel as companionable as it had the other night when they'd walked the dog. Something had changed, but KJ couldn't unravel what might have happened. She was pretty sure she hadn't said anything to irritate Adrienne. They hadn't spoken much beyond texting to arrange carpooling to today's game. The game had gone well, better than well, really. Adrienne had gotten a goal and KJ had set up a couple of others. They'd pounded the other team and had come out with a 5-1 win. Adrienne had looked more at home on the ice than ever. The only goal that had been scored against them had happened while Cam and Krissy had been on the ice, and it had almost been the end of the game. Vaughn had only seen a handful of shots, and KJ was certain they'd been pretty cold by then.

So do I say something? That seemed like a good way to end up in Adrienne's bad graces again. *Maybe there's a situation at work.* She didn't like this. No, she wasn't a fan at all. The drive to and from games was something she looked forward to for the chance to chat, not this vaguely tense silence.

When Adrienne's phone started playing a loud refrain, KJ nearly jumped out of her skin.

Adrienne grimaced in apology, and scrambled to pull the phone out of her purse. She thumbed it on. "What's up, Ma? Is everything okay?"

Adrienne's mom's response was barely audible. KJ could make out that she was talking, but not what was being said.

"The game was great. We won five to one. Really took it to the other team." Adrienne chuckled throatily. "They didn't know what hit them." She tilted her head to one side as she listened to her mom.

KJ stared at the road ahead, trying not to think about the interesting things her body was doing in response to Adrienne's laugh. *I need to hear that again.*

"That's really exciting! Congratulations to you and Daddy." She listened a few seconds. "Oh, no. There's no way. School is out Thursday and Friday only. I can't take the whole week."

Her mom's response was louder, but words were still undecipherable.

"I'll be okay. This is a great opportunity. You'll have so much fun." Adrienne listened on the line, then responded. "I insist. Lawrence and I will be fine. Yes, I have him for Thanksgiving this year. Kaz is going down to see his parents."

The response was more muted.

"I get it, but it really won't work, especially not my first three months on the job. You and Daddy go, have fun." She waited a moment longer, then smiled. "I love you too, Ma. I'll talk to you later." She swiped her finger across the front of the phone, then stowed it back in her purse.

"That sounded exciting," KJ said. "What was that all about?"

"It is exciting, for Ma and Daddy." Adrienne sighed. "My dad won a Thanksgiving-week ski getaway in Colorado through his office. They wanted me to come along, but there's no way I can get off work." She shrugged. "I don't know that I would have been comfortable taking Lawrence out of school for that long, so it probably wouldn't happen even if I could get the time."

"So you'll be home alone for Thanksgiving?"

Adrienne heaved another sigh. "It sure looks that way. I should probably see if Kaz will take Lawrence to his parents. There's no point in both of us missing out on it."

"Or you could come to my place." The words were out of her mouth before she had the time to consider them.

"Your place?" Adrienne lifted an eyebrow.

"Sure, my brother and his family will be there." KJ made a mental note to invite them as soon as she got home. It was past time for her to host dinner at the house. Besides, some recent positive memories might cool Erik off on his plan to sell the family homestead. Not to mention she'd get to spend more time with Adrienne. And on the holiday too!

"Are you sure we won't be imposing?"

"Of course not! You saw the size of the table. We'll have plenty of space. Lawrence can meet my nieces. They're a little younger than he is, but if they don't hit it off, there's always Chester."

"He would like that. I swear he doesn't stop talking about your dog. Worst part is his discussions of dogs are starting to shade into hinting that we should get one."

"Sorry about that. I'm happy to have him as surrogate dog parent for Chester, though." Maybe Jamie and Joe would be around. She'd crashed their small gathering on a couple of occasions. Besides, now that Jamie wasn't at hockey every weekend, she was seeing much less of her best friend. "So it's settled, then. You'll do Thanksgiving with me and the family."

Adrienne tapped the tops of her thighs with her open palms. "I guess it is. You'll have to let me contribute something this time."

"For sure. This is going to be way more complicated than our dinners on Tuesdays. What do you want to bring? You get the right of first choice."

"Do you want something sweet or savory?"

"Oo, definitely sweet!"

"A woman after my own heart."

KJ tried not to grin at the words. This was her straight friend, after all. It was on her not to do anything to make Adrienne feel like she was being creeped on by the resident lesbian, but that didn't stop a feeling of warmth from blooming in her chest.

Adrienne considered for a few seconds, turning her gaze on the snow coming at the windshield. "I have my grandma's chocolate pecan pie recipe."

"That sounds amazing." KJ grinned. "We should do that!"

"Sounds like a plan. It feels more like Thanksgiving already."

"We have a couple of weeks, so don't rush things. I have a list as long as my arm to tackle so this comes together without a hitch." Half that list was getting the boxes cleared out of the living room, dining room, and kitchen. And then there was the food. As she contemplated everything there was to do, KJ wondered if she had signed up for more than she could handle, and why precisely had she done that? It wasn't a bad plan, but it wasn't anything she'd remotely considered until Adrienne had sat looking so disconsolate in the passenger seat. Still, she seemed much cheerier now, so it was worth it. A happy Adrienne would make a happy KJ, and there was nothing wrong with wanting her D partner to be in a good mood.

Thanksgiving would be amazing. She would do everything she could to make it perfect. As she started compiling a mental list of everything she would need to accomplish, an uncomfortable swirl of butterflies fluttered to life in her abdomen.

CHAPTER FIFTEEN

Adrienne maneuvered her car carefully up the narrow lane between KJ's house and her neighbor's. The driveway might have been paved at one time, but the concrete had long since broken down. Snow and ice bridged the gaps between chunks of gravel and made for interesting footing. They hadn't been doing the coming-over-for-hockey-games thing long before KJ had instructed her not to bother parking on the street. Now, she parked next to KJ's car in front of the ancient garage. Come to think of it, she'd never seen KJ park in the dilapidated building. Was it as full of stuff as her house? Maybe she was worried about it collapsing on her and/or the vehicle.

Beside her, Lawrence held the chocolate pecan pie in his lap as if it was a precious package. To him, it probably was. After the turkey, that pie was his favorite thing about the holiday. It wasn't one of Kaz's family traditions, and she was glad Lawrence wouldn't have to miss out on it this year. The pie was assembled, but unbaked. As far as she was concerned, it was best right out of the oven.

They were a bit early, but Adrienne doubted KJ would care. Adrienne didn't, that was for certain. She'd been looking forward to the holiday for two weeks.

"I'll get the door," she said to Lawrence as they made their way up the back steps. She pulled it open without knocking. "Hello?"

"I'm in the kitchen." KJ's voice verged on panicked, which was odd. KJ usually sounded like she had everything together, even when she was the only defender against three opposing forwards. At least the smells that wafted out the back door were promising.

"We'll be right there."

Lawrence preceded her through the door, but she reclaimed the pie so he could take off his boots and coat. The dog already circled his feet, tail wagging in frantic excitement.

"Hold on." Adrienne grasped his shoulder as he tried to make a dash for the kitchen. "Put this on the counter, then you can play with Chester."

His sigh told her what he thought of the delay, but he took the pie.

"Put it down gently," she called after him.

"Okay, Mom," Lawrence said. "I get it."

Maybe he did, but she wasn't remaking the dessert if he dropped it.

"How are you doing in there?" Adrienne called as she hung her and Lawrence's coats on a hook by the back door. Seeing their jackets lined up next to KJ's made her smile.

"I'm…doing." The response was faint, as if KJ had her head in the fridge.

Or the oven. Adrienne took the opportunity as she crossed the kitchen to admire KJ's posterior. It was a nice one. Muscular, athletic, eminently squeezable. Her fingers itched to see if it felt as good as it looked. *That's more than a little inappropriate,* she told herself sternly. Still, looking couldn't hurt. She sighed. So far that was the best she'd come up with to deal with the KJ situation.

The infatuation shouldn't have been a surprise. KJ was the first adult she wasn't related to that she'd spent time with since

Kaz. The timing wasn't great. She was still getting her footing back, and anything resembling a relationship was premature in the extreme.

That didn't stop her from wanting one, and wanting it with KJ: the woman who had her back when they played, the woman who dropped by work to make sure she had leftovers after hockey-watching nights. They were partners on the ice. Was it so strange to think they could be off the ice also?

Not now, she told herself. A pit developed at the bottom of her stomach, building yet another layer around a pearl of yearning and unhappiness.

The kitchen was warm. Pots bubbled on the stovetop, and more filled the oven, at least what she could see of it past KJ's perfect rump. As KJ stood and closed the oven door, Adrienne glimpsed a truly massive turkey.

"Are you okay?" Adrienne stepped around the end of the counter. She pushed the pie away from the edge.

"I may be in a little over my head." KJ was looking a little whale-eyed. "This is…a lot."

Her normally unflappable partner was definitely frazzled. Her sleeves were rolled up, but the edges were dusted with flour. All manner of stains decorated the waist on the once-white apron she was wearing.

Adrienne nodded decisively. "Then let's do this. Where do you need me to help?"

KJ raked a wide-eyed look around the kitchen, her gaze pausing at the pans on the stove, then running over the ingredients on the counter next to a cutting board mounded high with chopped vegetables.

"I don't even know," she said faintly. Her eyes snapped to Adrienne's. "Oh god, you're here. What time is it?"

"Relax, KJ," Adrienne said. "I'm early. It's three thirty."

KJ's shoulders relaxed a bit from where they'd risen by her ears. "That's okay. I can still get this handled."

"You take care of what needs to be cooked," Adrienne said. "I'll manage everything else." She headed over to the cupboard. "How many places are we setting?"

"Okay." KJ nodded, her eyes losing some of their wild look. "Okay, yes. We can do this. We need…" She counted quickly on her fingers. "Nine places. If you could set those out, that would be great."

"I'm on it." Adrienne started pulling plates out of the upper cabinet. "Let me know if you need me to drop table setting and work on something else."

"Yeah, you know I will." KJ moved back toward the stove.

Adrienne set the table as quickly as she could while also keeping half an eye on Chester and Lawrence. The living and dining rooms had been cleared of the boxes and the floors cleaned, so they had far more space to romp in than normal. There was no trace of dust. It hadn't been this clean when they'd been by to watch hockey on Tuesday. KJ had done a lot of work in only a couple of days.

There weren't enough plates of one color, so Adrienne settled on combining a few into a pleasing combination. There were plenty of glasses, so that wasn't a problem. Silverware was a mixed bag, but Adrienne did manage to find a knife, fork, and spoon for each setting. It wasn't high tea at the palace; it would do.

"Is anyone else bringing food?" she asked when she reentered the kitchen.

"My brother is bringing green bean casserole," KJ said without looking up from the pot she was stirring. "Jamie and Joe are bringing pumpkin pie. Everything else is on me."

"On us." Adrienne sidled up next to KJ and gave her a small bump with her hip.

"Yep, on us." KJ looked up, sharing a warm smile. "I am really glad you're here. This feels so much more doable now."

"I aim to please."

"And you do."

They stood in the kitchen, eyes locked. Adrienne so wanted to reach out and run the backs of her fingers along KJ's cheekbone. She longed to lean forward and press her lips to KJ's. They looked soft, as if they were inviting her in for a kiss she'd never forget. The sounds of pots bubbling and clanking receded. Adrienne let out a long breath, trying to calm her tripping heart, but if anything, it hammered harder.

A crash from the living room shattered her rapt contemplation of KJ.

"What was that?" Adrienne said, her voice raised.

"Nothing," Lawrence yelled back.

KJ closed her eyes and bowed her head.

"I'll take care of it." Adrienne patted her on the back of the hand. A light sprinkling of goosebumps ran up KJ's arm.

"Thank you."

Adrienne paused in the living room doorway to survey the damage. Lawrence was wrestling a floor lamp taller than he was back in place. The look he gave her over his shoulder was clouded with guilt. "It's not broken."

"Are you sure about that?"

"Yes!" He looked around and spied the lampshade in the middle of the floor. It was visibly dented on one side. "Uh-oh."

"Uh-oh is right." Adrienne waited while he tried to pop the lopsided shade back into place. It almost worked, but the top ring had been deformed, and was still visibly skewed. "It looks like you owe KJ a new shade." Lucky for him, it wasn't likely to be too expensive, but Lawrence's allowance wasn't what she would call robust.

"Okay," he whispered. "Is she going to be mad at me?" Unshed tears glistened along his lower lids.

"I don't know, but you have to let her know."

"Okay," he said again, so softly she almost couldn't hear him. Chester whined from his spot at Lawrence's feet. "It's all right, Chester. It wasn't your fault."

"I'm sure Chester helped, but since he doesn't have an income stream, he doesn't get to assist with reparations." Adrienne put her hand behind her son's shoulder and gently propelled him toward the kitchen.

Lawrence dragged his feet but allowed himself to be guided along.

"My son has something to tell you," Adrienne said.

"What?" KJ turned to them from the refrigerator, a jug of milk in hand. "What happened?"

"I knocked over the lamp when I was playing with Chester." He extended the lampshade toward her. "It's all dented now."

"The lamp?" KJ crossed to the stove and dumped a quick splash into a pot.

"The shade. I'm really sorry."

KJ glanced down at the misshapen shade. "I'll get another one. They're not exactly difficult to find."

"I think Lawrence should make sure to pay you toward the purchase of a new one," Adrienne said.

"Oh, I don't—" KJ paused as she caught Adrienne's tilted head and pointed stare. "—know exactly how expensive that'll be. Let me look into it and give you an amount, all right?"

Lawrence nodded mutely.

"You can throw the shade in the trash," KJ said.

He shuffled to the corner of the kitchen. The tall garbage can was filled almost to the top, but he squished it down enough for the lid to close, then made his way back out to the living room. Chester scampered after him, but the ruckus didn't pick back up.

"Hopefully he'll be more careful in the future," Adrienne said when he was out of earshot.

"I don't mind covering the cost." KJ took a taste of something bright red and bubbling.

"It's a good lesson to learn. He can't go around breaking other people's stuff and be free of the consequences. He needs to know to hold himself to a standard where no one can accuse him of trying to get away with something."

"If you say so."

"He's my kid, and I do say so. I'm not raising him to take advantage of other people being too polite to say something when he messes up or for them to assume that he's pulling a fast one. Like it or not, he's going to be watched more closely than other kids." She didn't say the "white kids" part out loud, but at KJ's slow nod, she understood the implication.

Adrienne dusted her hands together. "So, what else do you need me to do?"

"The salad needs to be put together."

"I can do that." She walked over to the fridge to pull out vegetables for the salad. Whatever moment they'd been sharing was gone. It was probably just as well, but she couldn't help but wonder what KJ might taste like and if her lips were as soft as they looked.

She watched as KJ chopped potatoes at the cutting board. She was easy on the eyes. Her hair was shortish, but it looked like either it hadn't been cut for a while or like she was going through an ill-advised early Justin Bieber-style haircut phase. Her fingers itched to tuck errant locks of hair behind KJ's ears whenever they flopped forward to conceal those beautiful brown eyes.

Oh, and those eyes. She'd noticed a while back how light they were, right on this side of being amber. Adrienne was very fond of how the corners crinkled when she smiled and how the tops of her cheeks sometimes eclipsed her eyes when she grinned widely. She could have gazed into them for a long time. When they talked, Adrienne had to force herself to look away occasionally to keep from staring too much.

And how did KJ feel about her? It was more than a little hubris to assume that simply because she was interested that KJ must return those feelings. Should she ask? But was she really ready to take that step with someone else? Adrienne sighed as her brain chased through another turn on the well-trod circle it had already worn for itself.

"What do you need?"

KJ's voice broke Adrienne out of the battle she'd been waging with herself for a few weeks now. She was looking back at her, one eyebrow raised.

Oh no, I'm still staring at her! Adrienne turned back to the fridge. "I'm wondering what I should get out for the salad."

"And you forgot how to ask questions about vegetables?"

"Something like that."

"I trust your judgment," KJ said. "Pretty much everything I need is already out."

"I'm on it." Adrienne injected her voice with as much cheer as she could. There was no point in letting KJ know she was lusting after her, not until she decided whether or not she was ready to date.

CHAPTER SIXTEEN

KJ barely had time to think, so why was she watching Adrienne's back while she worked on the salad? It was a terrible use of her time. How long had Adrienne been staring at her like that? Adrienne had looked as though KJ was a plate of ribs and she hadn't eaten for six days.

Or maybe she was spacing out? *Lord knows you've been doing enough of that.* That was true, she did seem to be more distractible of late. There was too much to focus on, though. For the past few weeks, KJ had been feeling as if she'd woken up from a long nap. The leaves on the trees had been more vibrant than the previous fall, the first snowfall more beautiful. She was even getting crisper on the ice. She hadn't noticed how much of her edge had been gone until it had started coming back.

Grief was a hell of a thing. For the longest time, she'd thought she'd been handling Dad's death pretty well. Oh, there had been a few crying jags in the shower and the whole issue around getting his stuff packed up, but for the past little bit she felt somehow lighter. The weight she'd been lugging around for twenty months was starting to lift. She still felt it on bad days, when she came into the house and was surprised to find it dark or when Chester curled up in front of the chair that only her father had used. She still wouldn't sit in it, but many nights, Chester would lie on the rug in front of it as if he was still warming the feet of the man who had loved him, even when he no longer remembered his name.

Adrienne had her own losses, maybe that was what was behind the stare. That seemed likely. Satisfied that she'd landed on the right answer, KJ opened the oven and pulled out the turkey. She was basting it with the fat on the pan's bottom when the doorbell rang. The sound was quickly followed by Chester's mad dash to the door and excited barking.

"Can you get that?" she asked.

"Sure." Adrienne wiped her hands on some paper towels and headed toward the front of the house. A few moments later the door opened. Chester's barking stopped. KJ imagined he must have found someone who would pet him. The sound of voices drifted back to her, then the door closed.

"It's your brother," Adrienne announced.

"Hey, Erik." KJ looked up from her basting.

"Auntie KJ!" Twin squeals came from the mouths of the two young girls who hurled themselves into the kitchen at a sprint, Chester in hot pursuit.

"Whoa, there." KJ dropped the baster and stepped to intercept them before they got too close to the open oven. "Who are these two who have invaded my kitchen?" she asked.

"It's me, Emma!" said the younger girl. She'd lost her front teeth, and the new gap was giving her a bit of a lisp. She threw her arms around KJ's leg. Her head was almost up to her hip. Emma seemed to be in the midst of a growth spurt.

"You know us, Aunt KJ." Her older sister was a little slower, but she still came forward for her hug. "It's Harper," she whispered into KJ's ear when she bent down to wrap her arms around her niece. Chester danced ecstatic circles around the three of them for a few seconds, then trotted out of the kitchen.

"I know," KJ whispered back.

"Did you really forget us?" Emma's eyes were wide.

"You know KJ," Erik said from the doorway. "She'd forget her head if it wasn't nailed on."

KJ stuck her tongue out at her brother.

"Is your head really nailed on?" Emma asked.

"Nah," KJ said. "I had the nails replaced by bolts. Much sturdier."

"Like Frankenstein's monster?" Harper asked.

"Exactly like. Why do you think I wear turtlenecks so much?" She craned her head to see around the corner. "Where's Sophie?"

"She's hanging up the girls' jackets," Erik said.

"Let me guess," Adrienne said. "They magically fell off as soon as they came inside?"

Erik nodded.

"And here I thought that was a phenomenon unique to my son."

"Erik, that's Adrienne," KJ said. She let go of the girls and cleared them out with gentle shooing motions, then went back to the basting.

"Yes, she introduced herself at the door. I was a little surprised when someone else answered it. She was quick to assure us we were at the right house if we were KJ's family."

"Hi, KJ." Sophie appeared next to Erik. He wrapped an arm around her shoulders. "Thanks for having us for dinner. I can't believe this is the first time we've done it here."

"First time?" Adrienne's eyebrows went up. "With this big house? KJ, why'd you wait so long?"

KJ lifted one shoulder noncommittally. Now was not the time to dig up her grievances with her brother.

"You should meet my son," Adrienne continued when KJ didn't elaborate. "He's around here somewhere." She stuck her head out so she could see into the dining room. "Lawrence!"

It took a minute, but Lawrence squeezed himself into KJ's kitchen, which now seemed tiny with seven people in it, even if some of them were on the small side.

KJ busied herself with cooking tasks while Adrienne introduced Lawrence around. He was being quiet, but polite. She smiled at how much more reserved he was than the two girls. They immediately started peppering him with questions, starting with that concern of eternal import to kids: "How old are you?"

"Why don't you all head to the living room," Adrienne said. "I think Chester is starting to feel left out."

"Chester!" Emma yelled, then sprinted out of the kitchen, followed more slowly by Lawrence and Harper.

"Does she run everywhere?" KJ heard Lawrence ask. If the answer was anything but yes, Harper was being exceedingly generous.

"So does she?" Adrienne asked.

Erik laughed. "She sleeps."

"I don't know," Sophie said. "With the way her legs kick when she's dreaming, I think she's running there too. She takes after her aunt."

"There are worse things," KJ said.

"Are there?" Erik snickered when she wrinkled her nose at him.

"So how can we help?" Sophie asked. "I saw the table is already set."

"Adrienne's been lending a hand, and honestly, I don't think we can fit anyone else around the counter."

"Then all I need is somewhere to plug in the green bean casserole," Erik said. "I got it mostly cooked at home. Figured I'd finish it up here."

"Thank god you don't need to put it in the oven. With everything else in there, it's getting to be a tight fit."

"I'll plug it in by the sideboard, then."

"Good plan."

Erik wandered out. Sophie took the opportunity to come over and give her a much more sedate hug than her daughters had offered. "How are you holding up?"

"It's been hectic getting everything timed, but I think I'm managing. The turkey is coming along well."

"That's not what I meant." Sophie squeezed her gently, then let go.

"Oh. That." KJ gave herself a mental kick in the ass. "Better. Things are coming along."

"Good. You seem more open today."

"More stressed, you mean. How have you and Erik managed Thanksgiving all this time?"

Sophie looked over at Adrienne. "It's good to have a partner to help out."

"I couldn't ask for a better linemate," KJ said.

Adrienne gave them a small wave from her pile of vegetables. Sophie's brow furrowed in confusion.

"Adrienne is my defensive partner," KJ said. "We play hockey together."

"Oh!" Her face cleared, then turned slightly horrified. "I thought— I thought Jamie was your D partner."

"Until she went and got herself knocked up." KJ laughed. "I plan on giving her plenty of crap about that tonight."

"She's coming too?"

"And her husband." They were interrupted by an insistent knock at the front door and Chester's inevitable response to newcomers.

"And that'll be them," KJ said.

"I'll get it," Adrienne said on her way out of the kitchen.

"I'm going to make sure the girls aren't overwhelming poor Lawrence." Sophie followed along behind Adrienne.

The kitchen was finally quiet, and KJ took a deep breath. It was nice that everyone was showing up, but a little breather from the company was nice. She bent her attention back to the turkey.

She could hear the chatter of the others in the front of the house. There was a liveliness to the space that had been missing for far too long. Adrienne and Lawrence brought the same energy with them when they visited, but that was only once a week. How great would it be to get that on a regular basis?

Jamie burst into the kitchen like a whirlwind. She bustled over to the stove. KJ had enough time to close the oven door and straighten up before she was engulfed in an enthusiastic hug.

"Careful," KJ said in a strained voice as the air was pushed from her lungs.

"I'm pregnant, not dying," Jamie said.

"I meant with me." She produced a theatrical wheeze.

"Wow." Jamie eased up on the hug. "You're getting soft without me. You look good, though."

"Just what I need," KJ said. "To know that I'm slowing down, but at least I'm still cute."

"Gotta keep your options open." Jamie grinned. "So Adrienne is helping you host things? That's…interesting."

"Is it?" KJ transferred her attention to the cranberry sauce. It was starting to thicken nicely. "She's made this whole deal a whole lot easier."

"Yep. Definitely knows her way around the place." Jamie paused, waiting expectantly for a response that didn't come. "So you two aren't…Not even a bit of it?"

"The most purely platonic of defensive partners." What was she going on about? KJ fixed her former partner with an incredulous look. "Jamie, you know she has a kid. She was married to a dude."

"I know I don't have to tell you that bisexual people exist." Jamie skewered her with a penetrating stare. "You two seem… cozy."

"We play together twice a week, three times when she can make it to practice. We're used to working together. A certain level of comfort comes with that."

"If you say so."

"I do." There was no way Adrienne could be interested in KJ that way. The idea was so absurd as to be laughable. Except now she wanted to hit something.

"You giving the cook a hard time?" Adrienne asked as she entered the kitchen, Joe and Sophie in tow.

"Someone has to keep her on her toes," Jamie said.

"I work her out as hard as I can manage," Adrienne said, her voice bland.

Everyone turned to stare at her, KJ included. Adrienne blushed, her skin shading from its normal warm brown to a much redder tone. "I did not mean that the way it came out."

Jamie shot KJ a pointed look. KJ shook her head. Adrienne's sense of humor was nothing new. The day she stopped making double entendres was the day the sun rose in the west.

Sophie was the first to break the tension with a warm laugh. "On that note, how does everyone feel about me breaking out a bottle of wine?"

"Yes, please," Adrienne said in fervent agreement.

"Erik, where did the wine end up?" Sophie left the kitchen with the look of a woman on a mission.

"Hi, Joe." KJ leaned around Jamie to wave at her husband.

He was on the shorter side for a man, only an inch or two taller than his wife. A hat covered his shaved scalp, clipped short to disguise, or at least mitigate, the hairline that had receded almost to the crown of his head. He grinned, his teeth white against the olive of his skin and the five o'clock shadow so dark it looked like he was trying to grow a beard, though KJ knew for a fact that he shaved every morning.

Joe waved back. He was quiet and more likely to watch than say much, which made his well-timed zingers all the more devastating when he chose to let them fly.

"I need to get back to work," KJ said. "I'm not trying to be rude, but you all need to clear out so I can get everything on the table at around the same time."

"I can help," Joe said.

"Adrienne picked the short straw as the first to arrive, and I don't have room for anyone else back here. I'll take you up on that when it comes time to get food on the table."

"Deal." Joe snagged Jamie's hand and pulled her back into a hug.

"We can hang out at the kitchen table and chat," Jamie said.

"That's fine, just stay out of my way." KJ brandished her spoon. "Otherwise, you're going to get gravy or worse on you."

Sophie and Erik came back in with a bottle of red wine. They set up at the end of the counter and poured out glasses.

"None for you, I take it," Sophie said to Jamie.

"Not for another four months, or so," she said.

"How about you, KJ?" Sophie asked. She handed a glass off to Adrienne, who accepted it gratefully and took a quick sip.

"I'll wait," KJ said. "Let me get dinner on the table, then I'll join you lushes."

"It's not cherry liqueur," Erik said. "I'm surprised you'd want any."

KJ shuddered. "You know I can't stand the stuff after the Incident."

"Incident?" Adrienne's ears perked up almost visibly. "What's this about a cherry liqueur incident?"

Erik turned to her with a grin. "It happened when my baby sister was fourteen. She and some friends stole a bottle of cheap-as-hell kirschwasser from our dad's liquor cabinet and went out to the woods to drink it."

KJ shook her head and peeked into the oven to check on the status of the sweet potatoes. Maybe getting Adrienne in the same room as her brother was a tactical error. He loved to give her a hard time, and doing so in front of an audience would be even more delicious. Granted, she'd done the same with Sophie about Erik, but they'd been dating for a while before she could regale her with all his embarrassing moments from childhood and adolescence. She and Adrienne weren't even dating yet.

Yet? What was this yet? Hadn't she been listening when she told Sophie that Adrienne had a kid and had been married to a man? She knew better than to pine away after straight women. It never worked and led only to heartache if she never said anything or awkwardness if she did. There was no "she and Adrienne," and there wouldn't be. The faster she accepted that, the faster she could move on to…whatever. And what was whatever? The house she'd grown up in that reminded her of her dad who was never coming back? A dead-end job as a daytime bartender that she mostly kept at because there wasn't much else to do in this podunk town that would also give her the freedom she wanted to play hockey. And why did she only feel really and truly alive when she was on the ice? At twenty-seven, there should have been more to life than hockey, and yet for KJ there wasn't.

These were big life questions, ones she hadn't expected to confront while standing over a stove crammed with bubbling sauces and warming dishes while her family and friends chatted and made merry mere feet from her. Adrienne had slotted right into the little group of people KJ held closest. She chimed in without a problem and gave as good as she got. She fit in well. Maybe too well. It was becoming clearer and clearer that KJ was developing a thing for her. That was going to be a problem.

CHAPTER SEVENTEEN

They were a little squished around the table that had seemed so large when it had only been the three of them. Adrienne shifted to give Lawrence some arm room. Normally his sharp elbows weren't an issue. At home, they ate across the table from each other, and the fact that he was a lefty and she a righty wasn't a problem. Adrienne moved her fork to her left hand. The switch meant she kept brushing her arm against KJ's, not that she minded.

Somehow, dinner had come together at the last minute. There had been a bit of swearing on KJ's part, but that was tamped down hastily by a quick glare from the parents in the room. Jamie had thought that was hilarious until Erik reminded her that she'd have to watch her words after her baby was born. Jamie had laughed and reminded him that she was an elementary school teacher and quite capable of turning that off, but Joe had looked a bit panicked.

Light conversation made its way around and across the table as everyone dug in. The spread KJ had managed was nothing short of amazing. It was a full traditional Thanksgiving feast. Well, possibly a little too white-person traditional. The green bean casserole was a dish she'd thought was a stereotype until the first time she'd spent the holiday with her ex-husband's family. It had been no surprise to see it as part of the Stennes family's spread. Some mac and cheese would have been nice, especially the way her ma made it where it got rich and gooey in the middle, but the edges stayed deliciously crispy. She sighed. What she really mourned was the inclusion of dinner rolls. They smelled good enough, nice and yeasty, but they wouldn't stick to her ribs like cornbread smothered in butter would. She'd have to bring more sides next year, which would also take some of the pressure off KJ.

So far everyone was doing their best to make her feel right at home. Being the only Black person in the room was nothing new and barely registered. She'd been a little nervous about being thrown in to a group of new people who seemed to know each other pretty well. It would take a few more visits without issue for the anxiety to dissipate completely, but she hoped it would. It wasn't her family's Thanksgiving: the noise levels around the table were much too sedate. At least KJ didn't have the TV on in the other room so they could watch football while eating. That had been one of Kaz's family traditions, and it had driven her up the wall. As far as Adrienne was concerned, the distraction-box was for after dinner when everyone was in a food coma anyway.

"So what do you do for a living, Adrienne?" Erik asked.

Adrienne finished chewing her bite of turkey. "I'm a school psychologist for Sussburg Elementary."

"Really?" Sophie leaned forward. "That's fascinating. When we were going to school there, they definitely didn't have one of those. They did have a nurse and a librarian, though."

"There's still a nurse, but she splits her time between three schools in three counties. The librarian is a group of volunteers from the Parents' Association. That happened a few years ago, I think."

Jamie piped in. "We lost our librarian five years ago. He was great, but the school board decided to cut his position. This is our first year with a psychologist, though."

"That seems like an odd tradeoff," Erik said. "When I went there, Miss Chambers was one of my favorite teachers. She'd let me know which of the new books she'd gotten I might like."

"It's awful that they have to make the tradeoff at all," Adrienne said. "Obviously, I think school psychologists are important, but librarians are equally so. I would love to have someone to partner with. We'd be able to do some interesting programming for the kids, but it's so much harder with a group of volunteers who rotate through. They have a lot of enthusiasm but not a lot of...well, experience. A couple of them also have some very, shall we say, stringent ideas for what is and isn't appropriate for young kids."

"They don't like to get comic books," Lawrence said around a mouthful of mashed potatoes. "They did get me a book on how to draw them, though. I guess that's cool."

"You like to draw?" Harper asked.

Lawrence nodded, then shoveled more potatoes into his mouth.

"Chew and swallow those before you answer," Adrienne said when he took a breath to respond.

The three kids proceeded to get into a discussion on drawing, leaving the adults to continue the boring talk.

"So what do you two do?" Adrienne asked.

"I'm an IP lawyer," Erik said.

"Intellectual property," Adrienne said. "That sounds fun. It must be a very active time for you, what with technology and all."

He grinned. "That's right. I'm impressed you've heard about it."

"Adrienne was prelaw," KJ said. "She knows plenty of fancy law stuff." Her defense of Adrienne was surprisingly stringent, almost aggressive.

Adrienne patted the back of KJ's hand, and her bristling subsided a bit. While Adrienne didn't mind the backup, she didn't need someone else fighting her battles for her.

"All right then." Erik nodded to Adrienne. "I have a private consulting firm. We do pretty well for ourselves."

"I'll say," KJ said, barely loud enough for Adrienne to hear. She reached over for her wineglass. Her arm brushed against Adrienne's upper arm, sending a ripple of goosebumps down to her fingertips.

"I'm a programming director for Homeward Bound," Sophie said. "It's one of the larger nonprofits dedicated to combating homelessness in Philly. I'm lucky Erik is doing so well. His business has really taken off over the past five years. It meant I could take a pay cut to work for an organization whose mission I'm passionate about."

"That sounds really nice." Adrienne nodded. Erik and Sophie seemed like perfectly lovely people, but she couldn't help but fill in the rest of what they'd said as if they were on some HGTV home show. Surely they groomed alpacas in their free time and had a budget of $5.2 million. He liked carpet, but she wanted hardwood floors and ceramic tile. Would they be able to find a house they could both agree on? "How old are your girls?"

"Emma is five and Harper just turned eight," Sophie said.

"So kindergarten and third grade?"

"Technically, yes, but we have them in Montessori. There, Emma is preschool, and Harper is lower elementary."

"Lower el," Harper said from next to her.

"For how much longer?" Adrienne asked Harper.

"This year and next. Then I'm gonna be upper el."

"Are you looking forward to it?"

Harper nodded vigorously. "They do really cool projects."

"Harper likes the presentations the upper el kids do for them," Erik said. "I think she's looking forward to doing the presenting herself."

"It's a good skill to have," Adrienne said.

Harper nodded again, then turned back to the discussion she and Lawrence were having. Every now and again, Emma would interject something completely unrelated to the topic. Lawrence seemed to be amusing himself by interweaving her suggestions into the conversation, but Harper mostly ignored them with the long-suffering patience only an older sister could muster.

The adult conversation morphed into funny stories from the local elementary school. Adrienne didn't have as many as Jamie, and there were a lot of things she couldn't say given the nature of her interactions with the kids, but she did chime in with some of her odder experiences with group presentations. The lower grades especially had a talent for derailment. The upper grade kids had a tendency to get very giggly when she touched on topics that might be considered even remotely sexual.

KJ laughed along with the others at their tales, but Adrienne noticed that she didn't contribute much. She was a consummate host, however, making sure dishes were removed as they emptied and refilled if there was anything else still in the kitchen. The wine flowed freely, and by the end of the meal everyone except Jamie and the kids were quite lubricated.

As the main course wound down, Erik stood. He raised his wineglass and cleared his throat. The group conversation had broken down into a number of side discussions and were starting to rival the exuberance of Adrienne's family gatherings. When his gentle attempt at getting their attention failed, Erik tapped his glass with a fork.

That did it. All eyes were on him; Erik raised his glass higher.

"KJ, this was amazing. I had no idea you had this in you. You've been holding out on us! We should have gotten you to host holiday dinners years ago."

KJ gave him a tight smile and took a large sip of wine.

"Thank you for having us here, and for all the work that you did on the food and preparations. It's great to see the old homestead filled with people and cheer." He placed a hand on his chest. "From the bottom of my heart, you are the best, and I have one very important question." He raised an eyebrow at her.

"Which is?" KJ mirrored his lifted brow with her own. Adrienne was struck by how much they looked alike in that instant.

"When are you going to host us next?"

KJ laughed and mimed throwing a roll at his head. "We'll see. Thanksgiving only happened because Adrienne saved my bacon." She turned and raised her glass to her. "Thanks, partner. I couldn't have done it without you."

"Then to KJ and Adrienne," Erik said. "Thank you and happy Thanksgiving!"

"Happy Thanksgiving!" came the chorus of voices around the table. Everyone clinked their glasses together, the kids with their milk, the adults with mostly empty wineglasses.

"What is that amazing smell?" Jamie asked.

"That would be Adrienne's pie," KJ said. "It's chocolate pecan. Do you think it's ready?"

Adrienne pulled her phone from her pocket. The timer was counting down to two minutes. "It's really close. I'll check on it." She pushed her chair back from the table and made her careful way around the perimeter of the crowded dining room. KJ followed behind.

"It looks good," Adrienne said. "I'm going to pull it and let it cool a bit so we can cut and serve it."

"Sounds like a plan." KJ pulled a carton of heavy cream from the fridge. "I'd better get the best part of the pumpkin pie ready." She glanced at the counter opposite the stove which was piled high with empty serving dishes and dirty pots which overflowed from the sink. She pulled a stand mixer from a lower cabinet and set it up on the small bit of open counter next to the stove. "Will this be okay?"

"Of course." Like Adrienne was going to complain that KJ was too close. She'd enjoyed their proximity at dinner. A pleasant warmth had set up shop in her abdomen, and she was in no hurry to banish it. It might have been the effects of the wine, but Adrienne rather suspected it was a result of KJ being so near. She was relaxed enough not to worry about the implications. There would be time enough for that some other day.

CHAPTER EIGHTEEN

The television flickered, the sound low as it streamed a football game KJ had no particular interest in. Unless it was the Steelers, she wasn't that excited, and even then, it would have been better had it been hockey. She crooked a small smile. The story of her life: everything was better when it involved hockey.

Erik was ensconced in their dad's chair, the now-shadeless lamp next to him. Chester had taken up residence at his feet for a few minutes but had apparently decided it was too weird and wandered off to find Lawrence and the girls. What was his attachment to Adrienne's son? Chester was a friendly dog, but he'd taken a particular shine to Lawrence. KJ didn't mind, except that she didn't know why. Still, she got plenty of free dog-walking when he was over.

Lawrence's mom. Her gaze drifted back over to her where she was in quiet conversation with Joe and Jamie. Whatever the discussion was, it was clear by the way she was talking with her hands and leaning into the words that she was passionate about it.

"Good pass," Sophie said from the couch.

KJ took a look at the TV in time to see the replay. It had indeed been a good throw. The player in teal and white had caught the ball. And then they whistled the play dead and everyone milled around for a while. KJ sighed.

"It's not hockey," Erik said quietly.

"It really isn't." KJ shook her head. "I wish we had sports other than football to watch on the holiday."

"No one can break the NFL's stranglehold." He shrugged. "It could be worse."

"Yeah, the big sport of Thanksgiving could be golf." KJ shuddered. "Can you imagine?"

"Not in the least." Erik was quiet for a moment.

KJ waited. He had a look in his eyes like he had something else to say.

"It looks good in here," he finally said. "You can actually see the walls without all those boxes in the way."

"Yep." *Here it comes.*

"Does the rest of the house look like this?"

KJ grinned crookedly. "Where do you think the boxes went?"

His shoulders dropped. "Really, KJ? Come on. I thought maybe you were finally getting serious about cleaning the house out."

"I've been busy."

"Doing what?" Erik hissed.

"I do work, you know." KJ also kept her voice down. She had no desire to broadcast their disagreement to everyone else in the house.

"I do know. Under the table at a no-prospect job at the local pub. I'm sure you're raking it in, and putting in so many extra hours that you don't have time to do the barest minimum toward the most basic thing you need to do to get the house sold." He shook his head once, a decisive chop of denial. "If I know you, and I'm pretty sure I do, you're spending all your extra time training for a stupid game."

"It's not a stupid game." She sat forward, glaring at her brother, willing him to actually hear her for once. "I'm doing what I can. You don't understand what it's been like for me."

"You're right, I don't understand what it's like to live rent-free with someone footing all the utilities. The worst part is, you have nothing to show for it."

KJ sneered. "Nothing to show for it? What did you expect? You decided it was better to pull me out of school to take care of Dad. It's not like you were here to take care of him. To feed him. To bathe him. To wipe his ass."

"Oh, come on." Erik pushed himself back in the chair and crossed his legs, bringing his ankle up to rest on the opposite knee. "What were you going to do with a French lit degree?"

"I guess we'll never know, will we."

"You were just there to play hockey, and you know it."

"What the hell is your problem with me playing hockey?"

"You're wasting your goddamn life on it. It's not going to get you a decent job. It won't even get you to clean this damn house up so we can sell it!" He waved a hand at her. "If it could do that, I'd be happy. This house is our only inheritance from Dad. It's my kids' college fund. Are you so apathetic that you'd steal from their future?"

"For crap's sake, Erik. Don't even try to feed me that line. We both know you're not hard up for money. Your kids have a college fund whether or not the house gets sold."

"You have a duty to sell it." Erik glared at her. "As executor of Dad's estate, I could force your hand."

"I'm not ready to. I'm not ready to erase Dad from my life. And I'm not ready to give up hockey, certainly not on your say-so." KJ pushed herself up from her spot on the couch. "If you can't abide any of those things, then maybe you should leave. This is my life, Erik. Maybe I don't live it the way you want me to, but I'm going to live it my way. I spent five years living it for Dad while you got yours. You got your house and your job. You got your wife and your kids. You had the chance to find your way in the world and do something with it. I didn't. So drop it. I'll figure things out, but I don't need you sticking in your nose when I didn't ask and where I don't want it."

She finished her diatribe, chest heaving big gulps of air as she struggled to breathe. Her face was wet, the taste of salt on her lips. When had she started crying?

Erik pushed himself out of his chair, his long frame unfolding until he loomed over her. He opened his mouth, but stopped when Sophie appeared next to him, her hand on his upper arm.

"Uh, guys," Sophie said. "Maybe you should cool it in front of the guests."

Uncomfortable silence filled the room. It felt like the air had been pulled out, consumed by the heat of their argument.

"I'm sorry, everyone," KJ choked out past the massive lump in her throat. "Hang out if you want, or help yourself to leftovers if you need to go." She inhaled deeply. "I need to hit the head." She left the room, not bothering to swing wide of Erik. He twitched his shoulder back before she could bump into him. It was juvenile, KJ knew it, but she wanted him to hurt, to experience even a bare fraction of the pain she'd been holding in for so long.

Despite her excuse, the bathroom wasn't her destination. Her bedroom was dark. The sky outside still held some light, though the sun had set a little while earlier. It did nothing to dispel the deep shadows, which suited her perfectly. She lay down on the bed and curled up around one of her pillows. KJ was only vaguely aware of the sounds of soft voices and movement that drifted up the stairs and through the doorway to her bedroom. Her world narrowed until all it held was despair over a future lost and the loneliness of the long years with and without her father. The pillow soaked up her tears, and eventually she had to turn it over. Quiet clicks on the stairs heralded Chester's arrival before the bed dipped and a warm body settled against the small of her back. His presence was comforting, but for some reason she found herself crying harder, pressing her face into the bedclothes to muffle her sobs as best she could.

"KJ?" Sophie's voice drifted up the stairs. "We're heading out. The girls want to say goodbye. Can I send them up?"

KJ swallowed to dispel the bolus of grief lodged in her throat. "Give—" She cleared her throat. "Give me a second," she finally forced out loud enough to be heard down the stairs. It wasn't her nieces' fault her brother was a Grade A knob, even if he had tried to use them as leverage. She sat up and scrubbed her face dry of tear tracks, then blew her nose.

"Send them up," she said. Her voice hardly wavered, for which she was grateful.

The patter of two sets of feet changed to the scuff of small footsteps on carpet.

"Auntie KJ?" Harper asked. "Are you there?"

"One second." KJ turned on the small bedside lamp. "Here I am."

The girls rushed over to her, Emma climbing on the bed to wrap her little arms around her. Harper gave her a hug from the side of the bed.

"Did you guys have a good time?" KJ asked, wrapping them up in a snug embrace.

"The food was really good," Emma said. "I liked the pie with the chocolate."

"I had fun drawing with Lawrence," Harper said. "I'm sorry you and Daddy got mad at each other."

"Do you hate him now?" Emma asked, a wobble in her voice.

"Of course not." KJ leaned her head back to regard Emma. "Do you hate Harper when you two fight?"

"Uh-huh." Emma nodded tearfully.

"Forever after?"

"No."

"That's what it's like for your dad and me." Though their situation was rather different than a matter of who had taken whose stuffed animal and why wouldn't one share their Legos with the other. "We'll be okay." She hoped she wasn't saying that merely for the benefit of her nieces. She would make nice with Erik so she could continue to see Harper and Emma, but it would be a long time before she forgave him.

For which part? What he said tonight, or sticking you with taking care of Dad? That was something she wasn't ready to confront, so she shoved the voice into a small corner of her mind and gave the girls a last big hug.

"Head on downstairs and hug your parents for me, all right?" She squeezed them a little longer, then let go. "I love you both very much."

"I love you, Auntie KJ," they chorused back at her, then thumped down the stairs.

A few minutes later, the front door closed and an engine started up outside. KJ stretched out on her front, clutching the soggy pillow under her head. Chester stayed put beside her. When she put her hand back to pet him, his warm tongue bathed her fingers. She blinked to keep the tears from starting back up.

She wasn't sure how much time passed before she was startled by a quiet voice at her bedroom door.

"Do you mind if I come in?" Adrienne asked.

"I'm not exactly great company right now," KJ said.

"That's all right." The bed dipped under her D partner's weight.

"I thought everyone left."

"Just your brother's family. Jamie and Joe are keeping Lawrence company downstairs. I volunteered to check on you." She laid a hand on KJ's shoulder.

At the gentle contact, tears threatened to choke her again. KJ coughed twice. "I appreciate it. I'm really sorry you and Lawrence had to see that."

"I'm sorry you had to go through it. That had the sound of an argument that maybe hasn't gotten to that point before."

KJ shook her head. "It hadn't, no. Usually he pushes on why I'm not getting the house cleaned up to list, and I tell him I'll get to it and if he's so eager to get it done, then he can come up and help." She snorted. "How many times do you think that's happened?"

"By the number of boxes in the next room, I'd say not very often." Adrienne's hand rubbed soothing circles over KJ's upper back.

"You got that right." She sighed, relaxing into Adrienne's touch. "I've never told him why before. I'm not sure I even knew why."

"It sounds like you've been holding on to this for a long time. It's all right to feel grief, you know. Not only over losing you dad, but also losing the life you were building for yourself in college. You're not selfish for being glad it's over, nor are you selfish for wanting the chances your brother got that you didn't."

"Selfish." KJ choked on a sob. How could Adrienne not only know her deepest secret, but say it in such a sympathetic tone? At the end she'd been glad for Dad's death. She'd hoped for it many times as the man she'd once known had drifted further and further away from her, only to be replaced by this person who didn't know her and who she didn't recognize. Who said terrible things to her. Who dragged her down until all she could do was get through each day as it came. How did anyone deal with knowing those things about the person who was supposed to take care of you? Erik didn't understand the role hockey had in her life, but it was the thing that had saved her, that had kept her from succumbing to the darkest thoughts she had. The long stretches in the spring and fall where there was no hockey to play had been the darkest.

"It's all right. You aren't defined by your thoughts. You're defined by your actions. We all have bad thoughts, but what makes us good or bad people is whether or not we act on them."

"I suppose. I never suffocated him with his pillow." Not that she hadn't entertained the notion a few times.

"See, you're not a bad person." Adrienne patted her shoulder. Her hand lingered, then gave her a reassuring squeeze that again threatened to set KJ off into another crying jag.

"If you say so," she managed to choke out.

"I do," Adrienne said, her voice firm. "Take all the time you need. I'm going to head back downstairs and keep Jamie and Joe company. I'm not sure when they're going to leave, but they love you too. I'll be here until we can say good night properly, all right?"

"All right."

Adrienne's weight lifted off the mattress after a short while. The bed was much cooler and emptier without her there, even with Chester still glued to her hip. KJ's breathing was easier, though she'd started crying again at some point. The deep, wracking sobs were gone. Tears coursed down her face like a flood. She hated to cry, but these felt like maybe they were doing something, as if a knot was loosening inside her, one she hadn't realized was that tight until the tension gave.

CHAPTER NINETEEN

Lawrence chattered nonstop on the way home. He'd been yawning until settling into the back seat, then gained his second wind out of nowhere. Adrienne was trying to pay attention to what he was saying, but her mind kept wandering back to the moment she'd accidentally professed her love to KJ.

They love you too. She'd felt KJ's pain almost as if it had been her own and had moved to say something, anything, to alleviate it. What possessed her to use the L word? The one whose realization should have included songbirds chirping in unison and a beam of light breaking through the clouds at precisely the right point to shine down upon them both as they… As they what? The mental image was a little out of focus. What would it be like to kiss KJ?

"Mom, did you hear me?" Lawrence's voice cut through her imaginings as they veered directly into X-rated territory.

"Sorry, baby." Adrienne made brief eye contact with him through the rearview mirror. "I'm trying to drive. What did you say?"

"I said it was fun to hang out with Harper. She's really good at drawing. Can we do that again?"

"I don't know. I'm not sure the next time Harper and her family will come to visit."

"Is it because of the argument her dad had with KJ?"

She met his eyes through the mirror again, noting the sad look on his face. "Partly, but even if they hadn't, I don't know how often KJ visits with the rest of her family. Not like us with Gramma and Gramps."

"We haven't seen them much lately, either."

"That's because we live so much further away from them now. Erik and his family are also far away."

"When will we see Gramma and Gramps?"

Adrienne tilted her head as she considered the broad shapes of their holiday plans. "If we don't see them around Christmas, then probably for Easter."

"And Nana and Pop-pop?"

"You're doing the holiday with your dad this year, so I'm positive you'll see them." Kaz's parents never missed an opportunity to spoil their grandchildren rotten. Fortunately, Lawrence didn't seem to take their doting to heart. Come to think of it, KJ had taken to doting on him also. Not in the same way, to be sure. She didn't lavish him with expensive gifts, but she made sure to make time for him. Adrienne loved the way KJ stopped and explained what was going on whenever her son had questions. KJ was patient with him, which had surprised her at first, but now that she'd seen how she behaved around her nieces, it made sense. The woman might have a tough exterior, but she was soft inside as a down comforter when it came to the children in her life.

"Why were they fighting?"

"Why were who fighting?"

"KJ and her brother."

"Oh." Adrienne shook her head. She should have picked up on that. She was out of it tonight. For good reason, to be sure, but there it was.

She'd caught some of the argument, but only after it had escalated to shouted words, then suddenly KJ and Erik were standing nose to nose in the living room. "I'm not exactly certain. I think Erik wants his sister to do something she's not ready to yet. They've been discussing it for a while now."

"What does he want her to do? Is it gross?"

Adrienne laughed. Trust her son to turn a family spat into something more interesting to him. "Nothing like that. I think he wants her to get the house packed up so it can be sold. She doesn't want to." There was more to it, to be certain. There always was.

"I hope she doesn't. She should tell her brother to go shove off. That's what I'd tell my brother to do if he wanted me to move out of my house."

"First of all, you don't have a brother, and don't hold your breath waiting for one. Second, I don't think it's only her house. It's supposed to belong to both of them. Third, we don't tell adults to go shove off."

"I didn't," Lawrence said with remarkable poise. "I told my brother who I don't have to do it."

"As long as it doesn't come out to Erik."

A long silence met her directive.

"Lawrence. Promise me you won't tell KJ's brother anything like that. If you do, he probably won't be too thrilled about having his daughter spend time with you."

"She can draw anime style, Mom!" With the lightning change of topic her son excelled at, he was back to chattering about drawing.

She listened with half an ear the rest of the way home while she tried to keep her mind from wandering back to her ill-timed confession. Her cheekbones heated every time she thought about it for too long. It was a good thing it was dark so she didn't have to avoid explaining to her son why she kept blushing.

He flaked out quickly once they got home. They came to a mutual agreement that he could skip his nightly shower.

"Don't get used to it, mind," Adrienne said, but he didn't say much in return. An afternoon and evening of adventures with the dog, playing with new friends, gorging himself on delicious food, topped off with some good old-fashioned family drama had worn him out. She was worn out too.

She was brushing her teeth when she looked up into the mirror and stopped.

"Oh no!" she said to her reflection. The figure in the mirror looked as horrified as she felt, eyes and mouth round.

She'd accidentally professed her love to KJ.

KJ hadn't noticed.

CHAPTER TWENTY

Three days later, Adrienne still hadn't decided if she was upset or relieved about KJ missing her little slip. She stared at the ceiling of her bedroom, her eyes following the edge of the nearly round void in the plaster. Lawrence was somewhere in the apartment playing quietly or reading. She was retreading familiar ground, looking for something to change and not having much luck.

The holiday weekend was wide open, with nothing to distract her. There were no games scheduled. Someone had arranged a scrimmage for later that evening, but she was on the fence about going. For one thing, she had Lawrence. It still felt irresponsible to leave him with the run of the rink while she played. On the other hand, he'd come to one of her in-town games on a weekend when Kaz would normally have taken him. A gig had come up at the last minute. It was one thing to let Lawrence wander around in an ice rink with the families of those who had come to cheer them on; it was another to leave him at the bar while his dad played bass on stage with three strangers.

Fortunately, he'd been adopted for the game by the husband and small children of one of her teammates. There would likely be someone who could keep half an eye on him. Still, this wasn't even a full game. It wouldn't be as exciting as watching them play against another team. She wasn't even certain how it would work out, since the team had enough for three lines of offense and two lines of defense, and most importantly, only one goalie.

And KJ was there. Excitement warred with dread in the pit of her stomach. What would happen when KJ realized what Adrienne had said? After a few days to stew on it, Adrienne had decided it was very possible that KJ had been too wrapped up in her issues to parse out her exact words in the moment. But she might still. At that point, either KJ would be cool with it, or she'd freak and Adrienne wouldn't see her again. Or third option, she'd get awkward and stilted and the nice rapport they'd built would evaporate. She missed that sense of partnership. She kept trying to pinpoint the second things with KJ had changed, as if that would give her some insight into her situation, but she couldn't. It was a series of events, each inextricably linked with the one before it. A chain which led inevitably to her telling KJ Stennes that she loved her.

Adrienne flipped over onto her belly and stared at the pattern on her pillowcases. They had no answers for her either. On the nightstand, her phone vibrated.

She ignored it. A few minutes later it buzzed again, then kept buzzing.

KJ.

She propped herself on her elbows and watched as the phone vibrated its way merrily over to the edge of the small table. KJ was on a roll. As the phone buzzed its way off the edge, Adrienne snatched it out of the air. She couldn't afford to buy a new phone, especially not over some randomness only KJ would find amusing.

hey, the phone greeted her as she turned it over.

scrimmage tonight? Was the next message.

something going on? u been super quiet on here. hope all is OK

The next few lines looked like song lyrics. She wasn't sure what song they were from, but they were still populating as the phone continued to buzz in her hand.

Adrienne shook her head, lips curving in a smile despite herself. Either KJ still hadn't noticed what Adrienne had said, or she had and was being a butt about it. It was too bad she couldn't ask without busting herself.

Enough already, Adrienne texted. *UR blowing up my phone. What if there's an emergency?*

The reply came back almost immediately.

there is an emergency. i have no partner for scrimmage!!!

Adrienne typed out her response, then waited a minute before sending it. There was no sense in looking like she had nothing better to do than text with KJ.

That's not the traditional definition of an emergency.

KJ's reply came right back.

u going or not? i don't wanna be somebody else's partner

Adrienne stared back at the hole in the plaster. Was she going or not? What an excellent question. A week off her skates had her itching to be back on the ice. That KJ wasn't playing it cool toward her was also reassuring.

I'll be there.

sweet!

KJ's next response was a fruit salad of excited emoji. Adrienne was sure they were more a product of KJ excitedly and randomly picking them from her messaging app than some sort of pictographic secret message, but she still scrutinized them carefully.

pick u up? Came the question after the excited happy faces and explosion icons splashed across her screen.

Not this time. I have Lawrence.

OK! see you on the ice

Adrienne waited a moment to see if KJ had anything else to say for herself, but that was it.

"Lawrence, grab your sketchbook and pencils," Adrienne called out as she bounced out of bed. "We're going to the rink."

"Aw, Mom," Lawrence called back from his room. "I'm warm and cozy."

Adrienne stuck her head into his room. "Bring your hat and gloves, and you'll be warm there too." She clapped her hands together. "Let's get it going. I've got a scrimmage to get to."

"Ugh. Fine." He was much slower about getting out of bed than she had been.

"Fifteen minutes," Adrienne called out. She had to change if they were going to leave the house. Showing up to the rink in pajamas would engender all sorts of mockery that she wasn't willing to suffer at the hands of her teammates, no matter how deserved it might be. That was how nicknames started. Someone would definitely decide to call her PJ to go with KJ. A small smile quirked up the side of her mouth. It was a cute idea.

She shook her head. This was getting ridiculous. She wasn't the cutesy type, and yet the notion had a definite appeal.

At least she was going to get to see KJ again soon and without having to wait until next week. Everything was fine between them, and so long as KJ didn't put too much thought into Adrienne's words in her room, they would continue to be.

* * *

KJ took a long turn around the ice, warming up her legs for the upcoming scrimmage. It was one of her very favorite events of the season. The Bolts threw the game open to everyone who was remotely related to the team. Players who had moved on to other things and could no longer commit to full-time travel hockey would come back. Relatives of current and past players were also welcome, no matter their gender. There would be a few husbands and brothers, possibly a son or two out on the ice tonight. The tone was completely informal, though they occasionally had a ref. That would usually be someone's kid who was working on getting their certification. She hoped that would be the case tonight. Some of the guys got a little salty when she skated rings around them. KJ had gotten an elbow or two in past scrimmages when they had no one to ride herd.

Adrienne wasn't there yet, but she'd said she was coming. They'd been on almost complete radio silence since she left the house after Thanksgiving dinner blew up in her face. KJ hoped she wasn't too upset still. She totally understood if she was. The argument hadn't been something KJ wanted anyone to witness, let alone Adrienne and Lawrence. Frankly, she'd been surprised at her response to Erik's pushing. There was some resentment there, she'd known that, but she had managed to keep it under control so far. That night... Well, if it kept Erik off her back for a little longer, then it was worth it.

The doors to the lobby area opened. KJ's head snapped up, but it was only Jamie and Joe. She plastered a smile on her face and waved at them. It was too bad Jamie wasn't up to playing. She would have loved to see her D partners, current and former, going at it on the ice. When Jamie came back after having the baby, she might get to see that.

What if she wants to be your partner again? KJ stopped skating and coasted, her hands on her knees, staring at the far boards. A couple of months ago, that was all she'd wanted, but now... *Now, what?* Adrienne was Jamie's equal on the ice after a bunch of games and a few practices, but KJ was pretty sure there were depths to her game that she hadn't quite regained yet.

She skated over to the bleachers and banged on the glass to get Jamie's attention. Jamie waved and grinned cheekily, then pretended to moon her. KJ tapped the glass with her stick and shook her head in mock reproof.

Movement at the far end of the rink caught her eye. Someone was walking toward the locker rooms. By her gait and the way she held her sticks, KJ knew it was Adrienne. She cheerfully flipped Jamie off, then sprinted toward the opposite end of the ice. Most of tonight's players were still getting changed; only a handful had hit the ice early. She had a clear path to the door. She stuck her head through the opening in the boards fast enough to catch Adrienne as she made her way past.

"Hey," KJ said. "I'm glad you made it."

"I'm here."

"I see that." Adrienne looked amazing as always, her hair in the short fro that would still manage to look adorable even after being crammed under a helmet for an hour or more. "Where's Lawrence?"

"I told him to hang out in the stands and not go too wild."

"Lawrence? That doesn't sound like him."

"You haven't seen him when he gets bored." Adrienne rolled her eyes. "The scrapes that boy can get into."

"You would know. Fortunately, Jamie and Joe are here. I'm sure they'll be willing to keep an eye out for him."

"That's something, I suppose."

KJ came the rest of the way through the door to make room for a couple of players in light jerseys. "Can I talk to you for a second?"

"Isn't that what we're doing?" Adrienne hiked up her hockey bag and took a step toward the locker room.

"In private."

Adrienne blinked at her, eyes wide. She licked her lips. "I really need to get ready. You know how pokey I can be."

"I do, but I really want to talk about what happened Thursday night."

Adrienne smiled wide. "That's all right. I don't think we need to revisit anything."

KJ cocked her head. "That's not a very shrink thing to say."

"Look, KJ. I don't know what to tell you. It's fine. I need to get changed." She gave a half-smile of apology and kept on toward the locker room, then disappeared through the door without even bothering to drop her sticks off in the holder.

KJ stared after her. Adrienne was acting squirrely as all get-out tonight. She must still be pissed about Thanksgiving. How was she going to make it up to her? Whatever this was with Adrienne would blow over. Her partner was here and not avoiding her by staying home. If she wouldn't let KJ apologize, then she would simply have to win her over by being extra charming.

KJ grinned. She could do that.

CHAPTER TWENTY-ONE

The scrimmage had been fun so far. Adrienne hadn't been certain what to expect. When it had been described to her, it had sounded like a bit of a free-for-all. She'd felt sorry for their diminutive referee who looked all of twelve years old, but so far everyone had been listening to her. She certainly blew her whistle with authority. Adrienne suspected she was enjoying riding herd on a bunch of adults.

KJ was in her element tonight. Some of the players who'd come back for the evening were very good. Not as good as KJ, to be certain, but then she had no match among the women on the ice. The men were a bit of a different matter. It was clear that KJ was more skilled than they, but the advantages offered to them by their denser muscle and longer reach certainly went a long way to equalizing the competition. It had been years since Adrienne had played in a coed environment. The boys were being fairly respectful. The better ones were giving those who weren't as good a little more space with the puck before making a move on them. That courtesy didn't apply to KJ, nor apparently to Adrienne. A bit of time would have been nice, but she couldn't deny that she was working her butt off on the ice tonight.

She was glad for the opportunity to sit down. Each side was running three defense. Even with the extra people who'd come out, they were still a little short. They were running nine to a side, and as usual the defense were the first to be asked to rotate. That meant a lot of ice time, which was nice, but not something her legs were happy about.

A tall man with a bit of a paunch visible under his pads came striding up to the bench. She thought his name might be Bob. He motioned for her to hop over the boards.

Seriously? She thought. *I just now sat down. What in the hell is his ass doing over here already?* Maybe-Bob was the husband of one of her teammates, but she couldn't remember which one. She rolled her eyes, then swung a leg over the boards. The play was already coming back to their end.

"I'll head them off," KJ yelled as she blew past Adrienne. "Stay back."

She didn't need to be told twice. Her legs wouldn't have given her the burst of speed KJ's were still capable of. She skated backward toward their zone, keeping an eye on the action at center ice. KJ was everywhere, impeding the progress of the puck carrier who got tired of her interference and dumped it back toward the boards. KJ went with it, almost beating a white jersey to the puck.

Adrienne risked a look behind her at the scoreboard. Still eight minutes left to go. That meant about five shifts to play. She glanced over at the bench where Maybe-Bob was bent over and barely visible. It looked like he was sucking wind pretty hard. More like six. She could do this.

The white team's forward picked up possession of the puck half a second before KJ got there. She had enough time to pick her head up and pass the puck to a wing on the far side of the boards. Adrienne slid over, interposing her body between the other team's player and her goal.

"Screen!" shouted an unfamiliar voice from behind her.

She cringed. That was the last word you wanted to hear from your goalie. She skated up on the other player, to move herself out of the goalie's line of sight and to force them to make a move. KJ was already slotting in behind her, splitting the ice between the puck and the white team's players who were now streaming into the zone. As the wing lifted her stick, Adrienne realized it was Jean with the puck. There was no mistaking the signature windup for her slapshot. She moved her arms in front of her body and stood up straight so her pads were facing the release of the puck. If it hit her, hopefully it wouldn't find a hole in her padding, but would instead bounce harmlessly off the equipment designed for precisely this purpose.

Jean let loose, her stick hitting the ice with a crack that reverberated through the rink. The puck came off her stick low and hard, then caromed off Adrienne's shin guards, sending the puck wide of the net. She pivoted and pushed off, determined to get the corner before Jean could.

"I got it," KJ hollered behind her, skating wide to retrieve the puck from the far corner. KJ was immediately mobbed by two white jerseys but was able to trap the puck against her skate. Despite hacking at her skates and ankles with their sticks, the white players weren't able to budge it.

Adrienne hesitated. KJ needed help, but having both of them in the corner wasn't the wisest move. She looked over at the net and was relieved to see Connie had taken up a defensive position in front of their goalie.

"I'm here," Adrienne called as she skated down to support her partner.

KJ looked back over her shoulder right as the taller of the white players allowed his frustration at KJ to boil over. He stopped trying to go after the puck and grabbed his stick with both hands, using the shaft to pin KJ against the boards with enough force that side of her helmet impacted the glass.

The air exploded from KJ's lungs with an audible "Huh The puck squirted out from behind her foot and back a yard o so. The other white player went after it, while the one who ha hit KJ was still holding her up against the boards.

Before Adrienne realized she was acting on her anger, she'd gone in shoulder first on the asshole who had cross-checked her partner into the glass a second ago.

"And fuck you, dipshit," Adrienne spat out as the player went reeling away from her defense of KJ, a glove raised to the side of his head. For a second, KJ's knees seemed to wobble, but she locked them before she could hit the ice. Her head snapped around with its unerring instinct for the puck.

"What the hell?" He shook his head and glared at her through the bars of his face cage.

"You know what the hell. That was a dirty play."

"I didn't hear any whistle."

By now they were toe to toe. The players on the ice were slowing down around them as they sensed a fracas brewing.

"There's only one ref. Just because she didn't see it doesn't mean it wasn't a shitty thing to do." Adrienne sneered. "What, you afraid of a girl who can skate circles around you?"

The ref's whistle cut through the tension before either of them could take the first swing.

Adrienne looked over. The twelve-year-old ref had both arms straight up in the air. She pointed at the penalty boxes. "Both of you," she called out. "Two minutes."

"What for?" the salty dude asked.

Adrienne opened her mouth to give him even more well-deserved crap for jawing at the ref.

"Go, Mason," Lou said before Adrienne could speak. The left wing glared at the dipshit who'd cross-checked KJ. One of the team's resident lesbians, she'd warmed up to Adrienne early on. Somehow, she always seemed to end up in the thickest frays on the ice. "Come on, the ref is twelve and half the ice saw you cross-check KJ."

"And did you see her little girlfriend nail me in the head?" He sneered over at her. "What the hell you playing our sport for, anyway. Don't you have some jump-up to play?"

Adrienne froze at the pejorative nickname for basketball.

"Shut the fuck up." Lou pushed on his shoulder. "Go on. Don't make this into a thing."

Mason skated off with poor grace.

"I'm sorry, Adrienne. My little brother is an ass. He thinks being a competitive douche-canoe is an excuse to say horrid things. You have my permission to hit him harder next time. You might knock some sense into that thick head of his."

"You too, blue," the ref called out. She pointed toward the other penalty box.

Adrienne skated over to the box and hopped over the boards without bothering with the door. She was still pissed at Mason but made an effort to put his words out of her head. At least Lou hadn't tried to sugarcoat it. Her shoulder was a little sore. She'd hit him pretty hard and it was starting to sting, even through the padding.

"The things you'll do for a little time off your feet," Connie said from the other side of the boards.

"I'd do it again," Adrienne said.

"Of course you would. Gotta have your teammate's back." Connie gestured toward the scoreboard with her chin. "Ref says you can come back on the ice after the first stoppage in play in two minutes. I'm stepping into the rotation with KJ and Bob. Hurry back, I hate being stuck on D."

"I'll be out as soon as I can," Adrienne said. "You'll be fine." She sat back far enough to lean against the back wall of the small box. There was only a thin sheet of glass between her and Mason, and he seemed to be doing his best to ignore her. That was fine; she was pretty sure he'd gotten the point.

Across the ice and behind the benches, her attention was caught by waving arms. Lawrence was jumping up and down and gesturing at her. When he saw her looking his way, he grinned wide and waggled a finger at her in gleeful admonishment she could read from ninety feet away. She would be hearing about this for a while.

The sight of KJ being mashed up against the glass by a guy who outweighed her by probably forty pounds flashed behind her eyes. No, she would do it again, whether Lawrence was watching or not. She could probably spin this in a way he'd understand. His beloved superheroes stood up against bullies all the time.

She watched KJ as she skated in for the face-off, watching for any sign that she was hurt, but she seemed to be doing all right. Adrienne would keep her eye on her, nonetheless.

* * *

KJ waited in the locker room for Adrienne to join them, but she was taking her time. That was unlike her. So was almost getting into a fistfight on the ice. Not that she minded Adrienne coming to her defense; Mason had given her a pretty good hit. Nothing she couldn't handle, of course, but knowing that Adrienne would take on someone who had tried to take her out warmed her inside. Adrienne had only gotten a handful of penalties all season, usually for things like tripping when she went after a puck caught up in an opponent's skates and the other player happened to fall down afterward. She'd seen her engage in jostling for position in front of the net when Adrienne would make the crease an inhospitable area for the other team to hang out. But this…

The locker room door opened. KJ tried not to be too obvious about craning her neck to see who was coming in. She needn't have bothered. It still wasn't her D partner.

Vaughn nudged her with their elbow. "Looking for Adrienne?"

KJ shrugged.

"I think she was talking to her son." They waited for a response, but when KJ didn't have one, they continued. "That was a hell of a check she threw. Clocked Mason good. He had it coming, the way he cross-checked you. That was close to boarding."

"It didn't feel great," KJ said. "He didn't hurt me, though. Gave me a bit of a surprise, but that's it."

"Glad to hear it."

"Hear what?" Adrienne asked. She sat down on the bench and dropped her gloves and helmet between them.

"That KJ didn't get hurt from the crap Mason tried to pull."

"Good." Adrienne scrubbed a hand through her hair. The flattened curls sprang back to slightly damp life.

"I'm glad you were looking out for me."

Adrienne gave her a crooked smile. "No one picks on my partner but me."

"That's the way it should be," Vaughn said, then went back to the laborious task of removing their pads.

"So, I was thinking," KJ said.

"Uh-oh." Adrienne pulled the navy blue jersey over her head, then shucked her shoulder pads a moment later.

"Very funny." KJ carefully looked away, bending down to undo the laces of her skates. It was the age-old plight of the lesbian in the locker room. She was probably more circumspect about keeping her eyes down than the cis-het women on the team. She didn't want them to feel like she was creeping on them and especially not Adrienne.

"So what's this ominous thought of yours?" Adrienne asked.

"Oh yeah." KJ tugged at the double knot at the top of her right skate. "So our game on Saturday is in Philly, yeah?"

"That's what the schedule says."

"The Philly Belles are playing that night."

"Is that a band?"

"What?" KJ jerked her head up to stare at Adrienne. She was still fully dressed on the bottom but was down to her bra on top. The view was very nice and a bolt of heat shot through KJ's middle. "No." She went back to her skate laces, her fingers trembling a bit. "It's a dumb team name, I know. I think it's supposed to make them sound all feminine so that people don't automatically associate the players with lesbians. As if there's anything wrong with that. Just because some hockey players are dykes, doesn't mean they all are, and even if they were…"

KJ's voice trailed off when she realized she was babbling. She could feel Adrienne's stare like the hot sun on her neck. With a deep breath, she tried to keep on. "They're the local NWHL team. You know, women's pro hockey. I think it would be really fun if we went to a game while we're in town. Tickets are about twenty bucks, so not bad at all for pro hockey." She warmed to the subject. "I played hockey with or against some of those women when I was in college. It's the highest level of hockey out there below Nationals."

"Okay," Adrienne said quietly.

"The games aren't too crowded, usually. It's too bad, because it really is great hockey. They only play on weekends, which is why we haven't watched any—" Adrienne's response finally sank in. "Oh, cool," she finished. "So, yeah. I figured you won't have Lawrence, so we can take our time heading back to town. We can get a late lunch after our game, then watch that Belles play, then head home."

"Sounds like a plan." Somewhere in there, Adrienne had managed to strip off the rest of her gear. She pulled on a shirt and pants over clean underwear, then shoved her stuff in her duffel. She looked up at KJ before zipping up the bag. "You sure you feel all right?"

"Uh, yeah. Not even a headache. I might be a little stiff in the shoulders tomorrow where he hit me, but that's it." KJ grinned. "Since you have my back so well, I don't suppose I could convince you to give me a backrub if I'm sore?"

Adrienne's eyes widened. Realizing she may have miscalculated that particular joke, KJ backtracked quickly. "I'm only kidding. Unless you'd be into it, in which case I'm not."

That didn't work either. Adrienne took a long look at the ceiling above her. "Text me details about next weekend and let me know right away if you start having concussion symptoms."

"All right." KJ could feel her face heating. Charming wasn't working out like she'd hoped. She bent over her left skate. "Good night, Adrienne. Good game."

"You too, KJ." The door closed after Adrienne.

"That was real smooth," Vaughn said.

"You know me," KJ said. She willed the redness of her face to fade. "I'm the queen of smooth."

"Sure you are." Vaughn's voice was low, for which KJ was grateful. If the rest of her teammates said anything, she worried her face might self-immolate. "That sounds like a nice date you set up with Adrienne."

Shocked, KJ glared over at the goalie. "It's not a date," she hissed. "We're going to catch a game together, is all. As teammates. Friends."

"Oh great! So you don't mind if I tag along."

The pit dropped out of KJ's stomach. "N-no."

"That was convincing. Admit it, you don't want me anywhere near this." Vaughn leaned closer. "You're going on a date with Adrienne."

"Shit." KJ took a deep breath. "Shit, shit shit." This wasn't what she'd meant to happen. It had seemed like such a good idea in her head, but now that it had hit the light of day, she could see it for what it truly was: an attempt to spend some time one on one with Adrienne. Just Adrienne and her. No one else. "It is a date."

"There you go." Vaughn swung a hand over and clapped KJ on the shoulder. "If it's any consolation, she doesn't seem repelled by the idea of spending time with you."

"Vaughn, going on a date with Adrienne is a terrible idea!"

"Why?"

"Well, she's straight, for one thing! She was married. To a dude! She has a kid with him."

Vaughn sighed. "Look, maybe she is. If that's the case, you two will go out, shoot the shit, and watch some decent hockey. If she's not, or not as much as you think, well…Live a little, KJ. God knows you've been avoiding that for a while."

"What is it with everyone trying to get me to move on?" Embarrassment flashed to momentary despair which turned to anger more quickly that she could have imagined. She yanked at her laces.

"I'm not trying to do anything." Vaughn's voice was low and soothing. "I want you to be happy, and it seems like you're maybe ready to let that happen. I really don't want you to miss that."

Their calm demeanor snuffed out KJ's sudden rage. "Oh," she said. Her shoulders drooped.

"Don't take it so hard," Vaughn said. "You're a good person and you deserve some happiness. Don't forget that, and if it looks like things are headed in the right direction, don't overthink it. You know you like to complicate things."

"Hardly." KJ sniffled and laughed at the same time. She glanced around the locker room, which was mostly cleared out. That was good. If she was going to start blubbering, she didn't really want an audience.

"Hey." Vaughn patted her on the forearm. "You'll be okay. I promise. It gets better."

"If you say so." KJ closed her eyes and concentrated on her breathing. Her dad's death still had a way of sneaking up on her, and she was getting on to two years since it happened. It would have been nice if the feeling would give her warning, instead of ambushing her, but no. Grief was awfully inconsiderate. And inconvenient.

"I'll be all right," she said. The breathing helped.

"I know." Vaughn swept their pads off the bench and into their bag. "I'm around to talk about it if you need to." Vaughn's mother had passed away five or six years ago. They were one of the few on the team who had dealt with the loss of a parent while still relatively young. Some of the older women had lost their parents, but they'd been in their forties. Vaughn knew what it was like to be launching into adulthood, only to be brought up short by a parent's death. They still had their dad, which was more than KJ could say. Her mom was out there somewhere, but that was all she knew.

"I know."

"Good." Vaughn hauled their bag up to their shoulder, then hung their leg pads around their neck. "Want to get a drink?"

"You know what," KJ said. "I would love that."

"Then get your ass in gear. You're the last one in here."

"I am?" KJ looked around. The locker room was now empty except for them. "Ah hell." She popped her skates off and tossed them in her bag. "I'll meet you in the parking lot."

CHAPTER TWENTY-TWO

"That. Was. Awesome!" KJ smacked the car's steering wheel with glee. She pulled them out of their parking spot, slowing so as not to run over a player from the other team. The dejected slope of her shoulders projected her depression for all to see.

"It was amazing!" Adrienne crowed next to her. She pounded the car's ceiling. "Why do ties feel so good when you're the team to tie things up, but so bad when you're on the other end? Did you see the look on their faces? They couldn't believe what happened to them."

"I know!" KJ shot her a look, drinking in the way Adrienne's face beamed back at her. What she wouldn't give to have that look turned on her for something other than a hockey game. "It might be a tie on paper, but that was a win in my book. We really clicked out there, did you notice? I barely had to check to see where you were."

"You're pretty easy to clock on the ice," Adrienne said. "I did feel like I was keeping up with you better than usual. Maybe it's that everything was moving faster."

KJ looked both ways, then pulled out into traffic. She was so proud of how their team had played. The Philadelphia Misfits were technically one level up from the Bolts.

"We were supposed to lose that game," KJ said.

"Technically, we didn't win it."

"They're taking it like a loss." KJ grinned, then glanced at her phone in its mount on the dashboard. The map blinked on it, showing her which way to go to get to their lunch destination. A sports bar named Buzz's had seemed the best option. It was a block from the Hayne-Fisher arena. She wasn't looking forward to the drive. The arena was on the edge of downtown and Philadelphia drivers were an…interesting bunch. Sure, they might be swerving to avoid the city's admittedly massive collection of massive potholes, but too many of them thought the turn signal was an optional upgrade for their cars that they'd opted out of. Still, if it meant she got to spend more time with Adrienne on top of the drive home, she would have happily driven through Philly for hours.

"Hey, KJ?" Adrienne asked after they'd been driving for a while.

"Hmm?" KJ was watching the car next to them. She couldn't tell if they were going to come over or not. Every time she accelerated to give it some room, it sped up with her. Finally, she eased off the gas so she didn't have them building a house in her blind spot.

"What does KJ stand for?"

"Why do you want to know?"

"Ooh." Adrienne pushed herself up in her seat. "Is it something awful? Is that why you don't want to tell me?"

"Nothing like that. It's just that we've known each other for a while and you never asked. Why now?"

Adrienne shrugged. "I guess it occurred to me that most people don't have a couple of initials on their birth certificates. And then I realized there's probably another name or couple of names on it. So what is it?"

Before KJ could answer, Adrienne continued.

"Is it Kathy Jane? Kelly Joel? Krystal Janice? That has to be it. Krystal Janice. Did I get it?"

KJ laughed. "Not even close. I do have a middle name, but it doesn't start with a J. You sure you want me to tell you? You're having so much fun guessing, I don't want to bust up your little game."

"Oh fine." Adrienne stuck out her bottom lip dramatically. "You can tell me. Krystal."

"Har har." KJ risked shooting her a quick glare, then returned to watching for the other driver. "It's Kristjana."

"Christie-Anna?"

"Close, but spell it with a K and a J, and slur the first and second part together a bit more. Now you see why I go by KJ."

"You sure I can't call you Krystal?"

"Not where anyone else can hear you." KJ shuddered. "I don't need that one getting to the locker room. That's not a nickname I want." She glanced at her phone. "The turn is coming up. We should be there soon."

"That's good. I'm starving and didn't think to pack any granola bars."

KJ put on her turn signal, then gave her blind spot a quick check. It was a good thing too. The car in the other lane had apparently decided to zip past her since she was foolish enough to announce her intentions. She waited for it to clear, then merged.

"That isn't very mom-like of you. I thought moms always carried snacks in their purses."

"And I thought you were old enough not to need someone else to supply you with munchies."

"I don't get hangry, so I don't usually think about it."

"I'm glad you don't. That's not one of my superpowers."

"Uh-oh. Do I need to step on it?"

Adrienne waved a hand. "I think I'll manage. You don't irritate me as much as most people."

"Awww, that's nice of you to say." It was oddly sweet. KJ grinned. "I'm glad I'm not on the list of people who piss you off."

"It's weird," Adrienne said, her voice thoughtful. "You were number one on it for a while, but you've managed to move yourself off. That doesn't happen very often. If someone's on my list, it's usually for good reason, and they don't move off it quickly, if at all."

"So what you're saying is I've grown on you."

"Foot fungus grows on you too."

KJ cringed. "Ouch. Point taken." The happy warmth should have left her after Adrienne's sharp retort, but it made her want to laugh instead. Laugh, then lean over for a kiss. This was the kind of bantering she heard between Jamie and Joe, and they had the most solid relationship of almost anyone she knew. The sniping she'd heard between her parents had been much harder-edged. How many times had she buried her head under a pillow in a vain attempt to soften the harsh corners of their voices when they'd bickered?

They chatted about nothing in particular as they made their way closer to the arena. It was too early for event parking to be up yet, but KJ found a parking spot along a side street.

"Don't mock my parking skills," she said. "They're not stellar."

"I'm impressed you're even going to try," Adrienne said. "If it's not a space I can pull into headfirst, I'm not parking there."

"Hold your applause for the end, then." KJ started backing up slowly. "Let's see how this goes."

She only had to pull out once to take another run at the spot. Fortunately, there were no other cars on the road waiting to get past, so she didn't feel pressured to give up on the attempt and find an easier place to get into. When she turned the wheel toward the curb a final time and set the parking brake, Adrienne burst into wild applause.

"You did it! Without bumping into the car in front of you either. Now that is impressive." She undid her seat belt. "You know, if you don't nudge at least one, preferably both, you're not a real Philly driver."

"Thank you, thank you." KJ brushed imaginary dust off her shoulders. "I do what I can."

"If you're done preening, let's go. If I don't get a burger soon, I'm going to get snippy."

"Get snippy?" KJ pushed open her car door with alacrity at Adrienne's glare. "Okay, okay. Let's get you fed before you try to rip my throat out with your teeth." Her whole body caught fire at the idea of Adrienne's teeth at her neck. For once, she was happy it was brisk out.

"It's that way." KJ pointed, then started off toward the restaurant, hoping that by the time Adrienne caught up, her body would have calmed down.

CHAPTER TWENTY-THREE

"Yes!" KJ and Adrienne surged to their feet with the rest of the people in their section as the buzzer rang out long and loud. The Belles had scored from a scrum in front of the net. KJ watched the scoreboard, waiting for the replay that would show whose stick had shoved the puck across the line. It had probably been mostly luck, but the goalie hadn't been able to extend her leg all the way to the post, and it had gotten past her.

She clapped and hollered with the fans as she waited. The goal had the Belles ahead by one. She squinted at the large screen that took up the far end of the rink. It was an older one, not nearly as nice as the replays they might have seen in an NHL rink or at a men's college game, but she was able to make out what had happened.

"That was a good one!" she said to Adrienne.

"It was!" Adrienne said.

"They don't usually play in a place like this," KJ said as they were sitting back down, waiting for the puck to drop again. "Usually the venue is smaller, but this is really nice." She craned her neck to look around. "It really feels like the pros." There was a time when she would have given a lot to play in a place like this again. The arena at Quinnipiac had been about the same size. She missed the electricity that came from having fans that numbered more than a dozen or so.

"Do you miss this?" Adrienne asked. She leaned in closer so KJ could hear her. "Or close to this, anyway?"

"Are you reading my mind?"

Adrienne shook her head.

"Weird. I was just now thinking I miss playing in front of a crowd. Mostly, though, I'm glad I'm still playing at all. Coming from a town as small as Sussburg, we could easily be without anywhere to play, let alone at a decently high level."

"Does it ever bother you to hold back so much?"

KJ took her time considering the question. It was a good one and one she was never completely sure of the answer. "Sometimes," she finally said. "I love setting people up to make big plays. It's amazing when someone who doesn't score very often gets a goal. Their faces light up like nothing else."

"Yeah, but you're by far and away the best player on the team. If you wanted to, you could go end to end and score pretty much every time."

KJ shrugged. "Why, though? Winning is great and all, but if we only ever win because I'm carrying the team, we don't get better as a team." She shook her head. "Besides, it's exhausting. I don't mind putting in a little extra effort every now and again to get something going, but if I'm the only one scoring, that's no fun for anyone."

"So you'll never take over a game. Not even to win a championship?"

KJ tilted her head as she considered the question. "Playoffs are a lot of pressure, but I don't think I would even then. The Bolts aren't the only team with a mix of levels. The games we have in playoffs will be more like the one we had today." KJ grinned. "And we've shown we can hang. So far we're on course to make it through to the big tournament. This is going to be our year, I can feel it. You've been great for the team."

"So you're willing to admit you were wrong?"

KJ drew herself up in her seat. "I don't recall ever saying you were terrible or anything. I was merely cautious with an unknown quantity, which was only prudent on my part."

Adrienne swatted her on the shoulder. The contact barely registered through KJ's winter jacket. "An unknown quantity? Is that all I am to you."

"Not anymore." KJ cocked her head as she looked back at Adrienne. The corner of her mouth crept up in a crooked smile that she tried to wipe off her face before Adrienne could register it. She wanted all of Adrienne to be a known quantity, but she didn't need Adrienne to know that.

"Mm-hmm," Adrienne said. She shook her head slowly, but she was also smiling.

Someone tapped on the back of their chairs. KJ looked back to see the one of the women who'd been sitting behind them pointing toward the scoreboard.

"It's you two, look," she said.

"What?" KJ turned her head. Her heart plummeted into her stomach. The massive screen over the scoreboard had zoomed in on her and Adrienne and framed them with a massive pink heart. She watched as her mouth dropped open in a surprised O. KJ started to shake her head, but a warm finger under her chin stopped her.

With very little pressure, Adrienne turned her head. *When did she get so close?* Her pulse thundered in her ears as her heart picked up what her brain was still struggling to process. Adrienne's face filled her field of vision.

Adrienne waited a second. "Is this okay?" she asked quietly.

KJ nodded. She'd never wanted anything so much in her life.

A wide smile spread across Adrienne's face. She leaned in, her beautiful black eyes all KJ could see before she closed them. Her hand slipped around from under KJ's chin to cradle the back of her neck. She didn't need to exert any pressure to pull KJ closer. She floated forward in a daze.

Her lips were warm and soft, so much softer than KJ ever could have imagined. She gloried in the feel of their warmth against hers, their breaths mingling for the first time. She raised her hands, skimming them over Adrienne's forearms, up almost to her shoulders and holding her close, not sure if she was anchoring Adrienne or herself. It didn't matter, she decided, and held on for everything.

The soft lips moved over hers, and she responded, opening her mouth so Adrienne could venture inside, if she chose. And she did choose. The tip of her tongue slipped inside KJ's mouth, tasting her. KJ savored her back, twining their tongue tips together for a brief moment. She tightened her grip on Adrienne's arms, pulling her closer, angling her mouth over Adrienne's as she slipped an arm around the small of her back, holding her close, wishing they could be closer.

A dull roar filled her ears.

They couldn't be closer. They were still in public, no matter how fervently KJ wished they weren't. She loosened her grip and relaxed back. Adrienne let her go.

KJ rested her forehead against Adrienne's as the sounds of the crowd's approval washed over them. They were both panting as if they'd come off a long shift. Adrienne's rib cage expanded and contracted beneath KJ's hands. She was sure hers felt much the same.

"I don't want to let you go," Adrienne murmured.

"Me either." KJ licked her lips. "I think maybe we should, though."

"Maybe." Adrienne squeezed the back of her head, then lowered her hand, but not before dropping a quick kiss on her forehead. She pulled back completely, leaving KJ cold and wanting, needing more.

She turned to face the ice, noticing that the camera was only now panning away from them. The applause and hoots continued for a moment, then crested again a bit for the next couple, a man and a woman who didn't even try to top the display KJ and Adrienne had given them. He leaned over and gave her a chaste smooch on the lips.

"Oh," Adrienne said. "I suppose I could have done that."

KJ grabbed up her hand, holding it tightly. "I'm glad you didn't."

"Do you want to get out of here?" Adrienne asked.

KJ nodded fervently. The rest of the game could be damned. Would be damned. There was a promise in Adrienne's eyes that KJ longed to see delivered.

* * *

They made it back to the car without letting go of each other's hands. The walk back had taken longer than the trip there, with KJ taking every opportunity she could to steal more kisses from Adrienne. They would look around to make sure there was no one around to see them, then sneak what Adrienne always intended to be a quick smooch, but turned into a longer kiss every time. Every kiss they shared became more intense until Adrienne had to pull back with a laugh.

"We need to get back to the car before someone decides they've had enough of seeing two girls kissing," she'd said.

"Or decides they want to watch," KJ had said. They'd shared a strained laugh and shudder at the idea but had quickened their pace back to the car.

"Oh hell," KJ said as she stared out the front windshield.

"What is it?" Adrienne sat up.

"I just realized we have a three-hour drive back home." She turned to face Adrienne, then leaned in for a long, hungry kiss that shot shivers of excitement through Adrienne's core all the way to her toes. "This is going to take forever." KJ said after they came back up for air.

"Tell me about it." Adrienne sat back, hoping some distance would calm the energy coursing between them. It helped a little. "It's probably not a bad thing, though."

"What do you mean?" KJ reached over and put a hand on Adrienne's thigh. The tension at Adrienne's core wound tighter. She covered KJ's hand with her own, as much to maintain the contact as to keep her from moving higher.

"We should talk about what this means for us."

"Less talk, more kiss?" KJ said. She gave Adrienne's thigh a quick squeeze, but withdrew her hand with visible reluctance.

Adrienne chuckled. "I would love nothing better, but we really do need to take a second and clear some things up."

"I can do that." KJ sighed, then with infinite care, as if she didn't quite trust her driving skills, she eased out of the parking spot.

The inside of the car was quiet as they made their way through the fringes of downtown and back to the freeway. Feelings ran unspoken between them, filling the air with possibility and a tautness so delicious Adrienne wanted to soak it in. The strain was exquisite, but she knew that when it broke it would be beyond amazing, but she'd meant what she'd said.

"So…" Adrienne eventually ventured.

"So." KJ chuckled, her laugh ragged around the edges. "I wasn't expecting that." She looked over at Adrienne, her eyes wide with sudden concern. "I'm not complaining. Please don't think I'm bothered at all. I mean, I am, but more the hot and bothered type of bothered than the upset type of bothered."

The babbling was adorable and it surprised a throaty chuckle from Adrienne. KJ always seemed so with it and competent. The only other time Adrienne had seen her this flustered had been when she'd first arrived for Thanksgiving dinner. "You are cute as hell when you start rambling."

"I'm glad you think so." KJ ran a hand through her short mop of hair. "It seems to happen around you a lot."

"Do I make you nervous?" Adrienne leaned closer, sliding her hand down the top of KJ's thigh.

The car immediately picked up speed. "Oh god, Adrienne. If you keep doing that, I'm either going to crash the car in a fiery wreck or pull off to the side of the road and we'll…" KJ's breathing had deepened. She shot Adrienne a half-lidded glance that sent a skitter of warmth through her groin.

"Sorry, I meant to be good, but then you were so…" Adrienne waved her hand generally in KJ's direction, "…you. I'll behave, but it's so damn hard with you sitting there next to me like that."

"Like what?"

"Like…Like you." Adrienne raked KJ's frame with a hungry gaze. "I've been wanting a taste of you for a while now. All I needed was a push in the right direction." She licked her lips at the memory of their kiss in the arena. "I wish I hadn't waited so long."

KJ's laugh was breathless. "Me too. I didn't know this was possible. I thought if I said something to you about what I was feeling that I'd scare you off. All I wanted was to be around you, but I couldn't let you know how much. No one wants their lesbian friend panting after them."

"If you knew how many times I'd fantasized about you kissing me like that, you wouldn't have been scared to ask." Adrienne sighed. "I'm not straight, KJ. I'm bi. I've been getting crushes on boys and girls as long as I can remember."

"Yeah, well," KJ said. "It's a little harder when the woman you're interested in has a kid from the guy she was married to. And there was a point where I didn't know if you were sending me signals or if I just wanted you to see me that way. It was so frustrating." She groaned. "But not nearly as frustrating as this is." She reached out her hand toward Adrienne, who grasped it and held it between both of hers. "I want to be with you so badly I could scream."

"And I want to be with you." Adrienne bit her lower lip. "But to what end? I'm not a one-night-stand kind of a woman, I don't do flings, I'm not going to do the friends-with-benefits thing, and I'm no one's fuck buddy. So if that's what you're looking for with me, then this is where it ends. We don't have to move in together. I think we can keep from playing to the stereotypes too much. I'm not asking you for a declaration of undying love, but if we're going to do this," Adrienne gestured between them, "I need us to be serious about it, and take our time. It's going to be complicated enough as it is."

"Complicated?"

"It's not only me I have to think about. If it was…" She watched KJ's profile, imagining what it would be like to nibble her way along her jawbone.

KJ's hand tightened in her grip. She swallowed. "I don't get it," she said, her voice hoarse. "You kissed me, and now you're saying we can't be together?"

"Oh no, KJ." Adrienne lifted her partner's hand to her lips and dropped a gentle kiss on one knuckle. "I'm making a hash of this conversation. What I'm saying is I want to be with you, at least I'm pretty sure I do. But it's not as simple as if we were hooking up at university or something. Lawrence is in the mix, Sussburg is in the mix. We have to move slowly.."

"I understand Lawrence, but what do you mean about Sussburg?"

Adrienne took a deep breath. "Sussburg has…limitations."

When KJ cocked her head slightly in confusion, Adrienne plowed ahead.

"It's very white, and I'm obviously Black. Things haven't been terrible, not nearly as bad as I feared when I took the job offer, but it's not going to be easy for you to be with one of the few Black faces in town."

"I don't think it'll be a problem," KJ said. "And if it is, no one's going to say it twice, not to you, not to us."

"I love that you don't care, but you need to be prepared for people to possibly treat you differently. I've been through this before. Kaz lost some friends over our decision to be together." She shook her head when KJ opened her mouth to respond. "Most of all, I need you to be comfortable with standing back if someone gets ugly about who I am. It's my problem to deal with. It'll mean the world to me to have you backing me up, but I need to be the one to decide what the response will be. For me, and for Lawrence. At least until he's old enough to start pushing back on the bigots on his own." Which was a much bigger and scarier prospect than simply standing up for him on her own. They'd started having the discussion on how to behave around authority figures last year. If things with KJ were to work out, she'd have to have a similar talk with her.

KJ nodded slowly. "Okay."

"Is that all you can say?"

"No. I wanted to make sure you'd said everything you need to." KJ sat up straight. "I can't promise you forever. Not right now, anyway. But we can see how far now takes us, and I can promise to be there every step of the journey."

Adrienne cocked her head to one side. "I'm not sure what you mean."

KJ grimaced. "I'm terrible at talking about my feelings. In my family, you squash them down and everyone pretends they don't exist." She took a deep breath. "I can't know the future, but I do know this." She squeezed Adrienne's hand. "I like you. A lot. I like how we are together, before the kiss, even. That was really nice, by the way. I'd like to do it again soon, but that's not what I want with you. Or not all I want with you, even if it's hard."

"And what do you want with me? With us?"

KJ smiled. "I think it's a little early to put boundaries on this. I want to see where it goes, and I think we should explore it. I want to get to know you better. I want to see who we can be together. If our connection on the ice is any indication, it's going to be pretty great."

"I agree." Excitement bubbled up inside Adrienne. It wasn't arousal, or at least not only that. The idea of KJ being around for a long time, of getting to see her more frequently, of learning who she really was filled Adrienne with euphoria. She wanted to throw her head back and scream with glee. When was the last time she was this giddy over the idea of spending time with someone? She must have had it with Kaz at some point, but so much had happened between them. She bit her lower lip to keep herself in check; there was no point in scaring the pants off KJ while she was driving.

The silence stretched between them. She was content to let it, happy to hold KJ's hand and take in her warmth and presence.

After a while, KJ shifted in her seat.

"So what do we tell people?" she asked. "Are you cool with our teammates knowing? What about Jamie?"

Adrienne inhaled to say that of course others could know, but the reassurance stuck in her throat. She closed her mouth with a snap.

"What's wrong?" KJ asked.

"Are you going to be upset if I ask you to keep us under your hat for a while?"

A sliver of emotion Adrienne was sure was hurt flashed across KJ's face. "How long?" KJ asked.

"Not forever." Adrienne dropped her gaze to her lap. "If everyone knows, Lawrence will find out. I don't want others to know before my son does. He's been through a lot the past couple of years, and I don't want to introduce more instability to his life, not now that things are finally calming down."

KJ nodded slowly. "I see where you're coming from. I'd rather be up front about things, but I understand."

"I want to know the relationship is serious before I tell him." Adrienne reached over and took her hand. "Please be patient with me, all right?"

"All right."

"Thanks, KJ." Adrienne bent forward to kiss KJ's cheek, then sat back to await the end of the ride.

CHAPTER TWENTY-FOUR

It had been dark for an hour when the lights of KJ's house finally came into view down the block. KJ bit her lip at seeing them. The drive home had been so long, never mind that she'd managed to shave thirty minutes off the drive with a mostly unintentional lead foot. Adrienne's hand was back on her thigh, stoking the fires of her anticipation. They'd become somewhat banked after their talk, but they hadn't gone out.

KJ gasped. "Dammit, Adrienne."

"Sorry," Adrienne said. She pulled her hand back into her lap. "I got excited."

"I'm right there with you." KJ pulled into the driveway, but not without noticing the little head with floppy ears that bounced into the front window. "Oh hell." She put the car in park. "I have to take Chester out. He's been home for hours without a walk."

"Oh hell, indeed." Adrienne pushed open the door. "At least once he's walked you won't have to do it again, right?"

"He should be okay for the night. It's late enough now." KJ leaned over for a kiss, but Adrienne pulled back.

"If we start that here, we won't make it inside. I'm not going to lose my composure this close to a real bed."

"Point taken. I'll hurry." KJ shoved the door open, swung herself out, then closed it behind her in one motion.

"Good."

"Yep." KJ headed for the back door.

"KJ, the trunk," Adrienne said.

"Forget about our stuff."

"And have stinky frozen gear for tomorrow's game, I don't think so." She held her hands out for the keys. "I'll get everything set out to dry while you walk the dog. I'll still be here when you get back."

"Deal." She tossed the keys to Adrienne, then jogged into the house. Chester met her at the back door, then dogged her steps to the front. "Let's get this over with, buddy. I have plans for tonight, and you don't feature in them."

Chester gave a short, sharp bark as if agreeing, then pranced by her feet. KJ clipped the leash to his collar, then opened the door. He shot ahead, straining at the end of the lead, then stopped to water the snowbank at the end of the sidewalk. That was a good sign. Now, if he would take a poop as efficiently, they'd be back inside and KJ would be ready for the activities her body had been crying for the past three hours.

* * *

As KJ disappeared inside to take care of Chester, Adrienne stared at the bags in the trunk. Could she manage them both at the same time?

Can you manage a new relationship and getting settled in Sussburg?

The bags were a terrible metaphor. Inside each was a set of smelly equipment. She didn't really want to open either one, while she very much wanted to start something new with KJ.

I can do this. She wrestled KJ's gear out past the lip of the trunk and slung it over her shoulder. Once settled, she was able to drag her bag out. It weighed more than KJ's. At least the back door was already unlocked.

"You don't have to do both at the same time," she said aloud, her breath steaming in the cold air. *No, it's more efficient this way. I can handle it.*

The muscles in her legs wobbled under the extra weight, but she made it up the back steps, through the door, and onto the landing at the top of the basement steps. With a groan of relief, she let her bag go and watched as it tumbled end over end to the middle landing. There was nothing in there that could be damaged by a slightly rough trip down the stairs. She clumped down the steps and pushed the bag firmly around the corner with her foot.

KJ kept her drying station in the corner by the washer and dryer. Adrienne made short work of getting the gear set out on the rack to dry. She laid hers out on her open bag, then hesitated. Did she throw her undergear into the wash with KJ's?

"I can get it in the morning." Her soft words carried through the unfinished basement. *The morning.* No, this was what she wanted. But then why did it feel like they were rushing things?

She ached for KJ. Wanted to touch her, to get to know every inch of her body. The excitement at the idea of exploring this new facet of KJ couldn't quite overshadow the misgivings at the back of her mind. *What about Lawrence?*

"What about Lawrence?" Adrienne fished her gear out of the end pocket of her bag and tossed it into the washing machine. "He likes KJ."

But as a parent? What if he thinks you're trying to replace his dad?

"That's why we're taking it slow."

Sleeping with KJ a few hours after your first kiss isn't taking it slow.

"Well, shit." Adrienne sighed.

And what if she gets cold feet? Are you really prepared to devote that much time to someone all to have it come to naught. Again.

"She's not Kaz." That much she knew, but the hard knot in the bottom of her stomach was refusing to go away. As much as she wanted to ignore the little voice in her head, she knew it was right. She yearned for KJ, more than she'd yearned for anyone in years, but tonight wasn't the right time. Still, that didn't mean nothing could happen. There was room for compromise.

She headed toward the stairs. Hopefully KJ would understand.

CHAPTER TWENTY-FIVE

"Honey, I'm home," KJ called when she got back into the house, a somewhat disappointed Chester in tow. Fifteen minutes was much shorter than his usual evening walk.

"I'm right here," Adrienne replied. She shifted on the couch, into the light being cast through the door to the kitchen.

KJ unclipped Chester. "Go get some food." She pointed to the kitchen, then turned to face her partner. "Uh, hey," she said, suddenly nervous. The anticipation that had been coursing through the center of her being suddenly froze as the enormity of what she wanted to do—was about to do—confronted her.

"Hey, yourself." Adrienne patted the couch next to her.

KJ kicked off her shoes, padded across the living room, then hesitated. There was so much space on the sofa. Did she sit right next to Adrienne and risk looking overeager, or did she take a seat at the far end and imply she'd changed her mind? Flutters of anxiety clashed unpleasantly with her arousal.

"I'm not going to bite," Adrienne said. She took KJ's hand and pulled her down next to her. "Not unless you're into that."

The last was offered in a deep whisper. KJ closed her eyes as her excitement blew away the last vestiges of uncertainty. She leaned toward Adrienne, desperate to taste her again. She didn't think she'd ever get tired of kissing her partner.

Adrienne's mouth met hers, lips parted and breath hot, so very hot. KJ dipped the tip of her tongue between Adrienne's lips. When she was met in kind, she deepened the kiss. Adrienne's hand crept around the back of her neck, holding her in place. Not that KJ had plans to go anywhere. Ever. She was dimly aware of her own hand cupping Adrienne's jawline. All of it paled to the sensations that swirled within her. She moaned into Adrienne's mouth.

When they broke apart an eternity—an instant—later, both their chests were heaving.

"Oh dear," Adrienne said quietly with a soft laugh. "That wasn't quite what I meant to happen."

KJ leaned her forehead against Adrienne's. "No? Because I thought it went pretty well." She gently stroked the side of Adrienne's face, memorizing the curve of her cheekbone with her thumb.

"It definitely did. That's part of the problem." Adrienne shifted away from her so they weren't quite touching, but KJ could still feel her body heat.

"Problem." The word sharpened in KJ's mind, pulling her partway out of the fog of her arousal. "What's the problem?" The butterflies returned in a swarm.

"This is moving too fast." Adrienne took a deep breath. "We need to pump the brakes a bit."

The bottom dropped out of KJ's stomach. "Oh." She pulled away from Adrienne, tucking herself into the corner of the couch. They'd just talked about taking it slow, but KJ had thought that meant not broadcasting their attachment to everyone. She hadn't realized it meant the physical side of things also. She should have known better.

"It's not a no, sweetie." Adrienne reached over to place her hand on KJ's ankle. "It's a not-right-this-second. It's a let's-give-this-a-little-time-to-breathe and make sure it's right for us."

"It feels right to me." KJ reached out for Adrienne's hand.

Adrienne intertwined her fingers with KJ's. "It would be so easy to roll into bed with you right this second, which is exactly why we need to slow down. I want to be sure what's between us is real without complicating it with sex." She squeezed KJ's hand. "It's important to me."

"If it's important to you, then it's important to me too." KJ meant it, but that didn't do anything to calm the arousal twisting at her core. She closed her eyes and took a long breath in through her nose. "I can do this."

Adrienne's chuckle sent a throb through her groin. "It's not easy for me either. All I want is to run my hands over your skin." There was a catch in her voice.

KJ opened her eyes to see Adrienne staring at her as if she was a plate of particularly delicious-looking nachos.

"You said no sex?" KJ licked suddenly dry lips. "That doesn't mean no nothing, right?"

"It means nothing under the clothes." Adrienne leaned in toward her. "A kiss or two can't hurt."

Can't it? KJ ignored the voice and leaned forward to drink Adrienne in again. Her arousal flared so quickly it was almost painful. She sucked Adrienne's lower lip into her mouth and bit down gently on it. This time, Adrienne was the one who moaned.

She speared her fingers into KJ's hair and gripped it tightly. KJ gasped, her lips pulling free of Adrienne, who took advantage of the pause to pull KJ's head back. She nipped at the column of KJ's throat, each application of teeth leaving an expanding pool of fire on her skin. KJ grabbed on to Adrienne's shoulders and held on tight. It was all she could do not to send her fingers roaming over Adrienne's body to places that would take them past the under-the-clothes rule.

Adrienne pulled at the neck of her shirt. Cool air bathed KJ's collarbone, followed quickly by the heat of Adrienne's tongue.

"Oh god, Adrienne." KJ hesitated, torn between pulling back and pressing herself more firmly against her. She tucked her hands under her legs. She was trying so hard to be good, but Adrienne wasn't making it easy.

"KJ." The syllables were husky and filled with as much longing as she felt. Adrienne gave her neck one last nibble, then sat back, reluctance in every muscle. "This is way harder than I thought it would be."

"You're telling me."

"It's getting late. I should head home. Is it all right if I leave my gear to dry here?"

"You could stay over," KJ said. "We can be good." Even as she said it, she knew that wasn't likely.

Adrienne lifted an eyebrow in artful skepticism. "Can we, though?"

"We could try." It was a weak argument, but KJ had to make it, if it would only delay Adrienne's departure.

"It's a terrible idea, but tempting." Adrienne leaned forward. "You're tempting."

Her scent tickled KJ's nostrils. She buried her head in the crook of Adrienne's neck, trying to commit the delicious smell to memory. When her tongue flicked out to taste the dark skin behind Adrienne's ear, it wasn't a conscious move.

Adrienne groaned and shifted away again, breaking all contact this time. "So, so tempting."

KJ felt her absence like a blow to the gut. She whimpered at the loss.

"We'll be all right." Adrienne stood up. Her slight unsteadiness was a little gratifying. At least KJ wasn't the only one having trouble.

"It doesn't feel like it," KJ said.

"I know." Adrienne dropped a kiss on her forehead while being careful not to touch her anywhere else. "Now imagine how amazing this will feel when we get all the way there."

"I suppose." KJ tried not to let grumpiness bleed into her voice, but judging by Adrienne's chuckle, she'd failed miserably. God help her, but that deep little laugh did fascinating things to her insides.

"I'll be over tomorrow for my gear. Do you want to ride to the rink together?"

"Of course I do."

"I'll see you then. Sleep well."

"You too." If KJ got a lick of sleep, she would be surprised. Her body buzzed with arousal and adrenaline; the muscles of her legs twitched with a mind of their own. "I'll walk you to the car."

"How gentlemanly of you."

"Can't have you kidnapped by aliens right after we found each other, can we?" Not to mention that even a few more minutes with Adrienne was better than her being gone.

"That we can't." Adrienne shrugged on her jacket without zipping it up and didn't bother tying her boots. She led the way out the back door to her car. Her breath steamed in the cool air, wreathing her head in a pale cloud of vapor that glowed in the moonlight.

KJ was so gone. She was composing poetry to this woman in her head while freezing her butt off. She'd forgotten to grab her jacket, but at least she wasn't barefoot.

"Drive carefully," she said. *Real smooth, KJ.*

"I will." Adrienne paused with the door open. She looked KJ in the eyes for a long moment, then leaned in for a kiss.

KJ met her halfway, forgetting how cold it was. Their lips met, their tongues tangled for a brief, desperate instant before Adrienne was drawing away. KJ jammed her hands deep in her pockets to keep from holding on to her.

Then Adrienne was getting into the car and backing it down the drive to the street. She stopped before pulling out of the drive. Their eyes met. It felt like Adrienne was peering into her soul, even from twenty feet away. Adrienne looked away first, but not before blowing her a kiss. She pulled into the street, then was gone.

KJ watched after her long after the exhaust from Adrienne's car had dissipated. Her body cooled rapidly in the freezing air, which sadly did nothing to quench the fire that still raged within her core, demanding to be satisfied.

"Looks like you're going to have to be satisfied with me," KJ whispered to her outraged libido as she trudged back to the house. "Better get used to it."

CHAPTER TWENTY-SIX

As Adrienne pulled her car into the driveway to KJ's house, she saw the movement of the form in the living room window. KJ's silhouette was unmistakable. Adrienne smiled. She couldn't wait to see KJ again. Sure, they'd played a game on Sunday and had even managed to steal a kiss or two afterward, but that was two whole days ago. Her phone constantly buzzed when they were apart. It turned out KJ had a steady supply of GIFs for almost any situation. Her own library was sorely lacking, but she was squirreling some away for later.

The car crunched over the mix of ice and gravel at the back of the house, and Adrienne brought it to a stop. She took a deep breath. It was going to be so much harder to keep from touching KJ than it had been before, but with Lawrence along, they had to be good.

Too bad. The last thing she wanted was to be good. Where had her conviction from Saturday gone? The longer they spent apart, the sillier it seemed. Taking things slow had sounded so good, but the reality of it was another story altogether. She didn't like this story.

"Mom?" Lawrence asked from the back seat. "Are we going in?"

"Of course, baby." Adrienne bit the inside of her lip. *You can do this.* "I needed a couple of seconds, that's all."

"Okay." He didn't seem at all interested in her reasoning and was already pushing the door open. The lure of Chester was difficult to counteract. He trotted quickly across the cold ground. The door opened before he could lift his hand to knock.

KJ stood in the doorway, silhouetted by warm light. She said something to Lawrence, who charged into the house. Her hair looked blonder than normal in the light. The floppy locks framed high cheekbones and a curving jawline.

KJ bent down to get a better look at Adrienne through the car window. She raised her hands in question.

"Time to go," Adrienne said out loud. Her hands shook slightly when she took them off the steering wheel. Adrenaline and need made it nearly impossible to think of anything except the way KJ's lips felt or how it felt to be in her arms. "Oh hell."

Footsteps crunching across loose stone pulled her attention away from the sensations clamoring for her attention. The light knock on the window wasn't unexpected, but Adrienne still jumped. Being so keyed up was uncomfortable, but she knew it would feel so good when the tension broke.

KJ's concerned face watched her from beside the car. She tucked an errant curl behind her ear. Adrienne's fingers twitched as she wished she could have been the one to do that.

"Are you okay?" KJ mouthed at her.

"I'm fine." Adrienne pushed open the door. "I'm fine," she repeated.

"Do you want to come inside? Your car's going to cool down soon."

"Of course I want to come in." Adrienne tried not to pay attention to the double entendre. It hung between them demanding to be acknowledged. "I didn't think it was going to be so hard."

"To see me?" KJ cocked her head.

"To see you and not touch you."

"Ah." A brilliant smile lit her face. "I know what you mean. I'd rather you didn't freeze to death in my yard, though."

"Same here." Adrienne got out of the car. KJ was so close. She could have reached out and taken her hand. "Let's get inside." She hurried toward the kitchen door. It was slightly ajar, spilling light into the dark yard.

KJ's feet crunched along behind her, then up the steps.

Adrienne busied herself shucking her coat and boots. The house smelled like KJ. The realization sent another twist of longing through her.

"What's for dinner?" Adrienne asked as she hung up her coat.

"Flank steak and mashed potatoes." KJ hovered by the doorway to the kitchen. "Sounds good?"

"Sounds amazing."

"I wanted to do something a little fancier."

"No objections here." The thread of conversation dried up, leaving Adrienne staring at KJ in silence. "So..." she finally said to break the silence.

"So." KJ grinned. "It's a little weird."

Adrienne laughed. "A bit." She moved closer to KJ, keeping an eye out for Lawrence. "I really want to kiss you right now."

KJ's eyes fluttered shut for a second. "I would love that," she said, her voice hoarse.

Adrienne swallowed hard. "Not while Lawrence is around."

"I know." She moved further into the house, then stopped on the other side of the counter. A pot boiled on the stove. "Can I get you anything to drink?"

"You have a beer?"

"Not cold. I didn't think you'd want one." KJ opened the refrigerator. "I've had this Bordeaux chilling about forty minutes. It should be perfect. Would you like some?"

"You're a lifesaver." Adrienne fetched two glasses out of the cupboard. "This evening gets fancier and fancier."

"I aim to please."

"Honey, your aim is amazing so far."

A faint flush bloomed to life across KJ's cheeks. She bent to opening the wine.

"Where's Lawrence?" Adrienne asked.

"I think he's in the front room with Chester."

"They're being awfully quiet."

"Yeah, I should probably check on them, then get the steak under the broiler."

"I can take care of the mashed potatoes."

"That would be great. The potatoes will be ready in a couple of minutes, then I'll put in the broccoli."

"Sounds like a plan." Adrienne bustled into the kitchen. Now that she had something to work on, maybe she'd be able to stop thinking about how good KJ looked.

They worked in silence that was only a little strained by the glances Adrienne kept shooting KJ's way. Those little looks were intercepted more often than not. The look of yearning on KJ's face when she thought Adrienne wasn't looking resonated deep within Adrienne's belly.

By the time dinner was ready for the table, Adrienne was ready to combust. When Lawrence went into the bathroom to wash his hands, Adrienne scooted next to where KJ stood at the counter.

She was met halfway for a searing kiss. KJ's arms wrapped around her, holding her tight, and she returned the hug with the same ferocity. There was no time for gentleness, only the contact they both needed. It was too bad she couldn't focus all her attention on KJ's warmth and the pleasing way their bodies fit together. When the water flushed in the bathroom off the kitchen, she lifted her head. Their embrace had been short, but intense. KJ swallowed hard enough that Adrienne could hear it.

"Wash your hands," she called when the door opened too soon after the toilet seat clunked down.

"Aw, Mom," Lawrence said.

"Clean hands save lives."

"Ugh, fine." The sound of water in the sink filtered into the kitchen.

Adrienne shared a quick smile with KJ, then pressed a relatively chaste kiss to her lips.

"So, who's playing tonight?" she asked as she moved away from the temptation that was KJ.

"Stanford is playing USC. I thought that would be fun. We haven't watched much West Coast hockey. There's one problem, though…it won't start for an hour or so yet."

"I'm sure we can figure out something to do until then." If they'd been alone, Adrienne's efforts to keep things moving slowly would have been in vain. If they'd been alone, KJ would have been flat on her back as Adrienne kissed her way up from her belly button to her breasts. "Any ideas?"

"We could see if there's anything else on to watch. I can pull up Netflix and see what I can find."

"Can we play a game?" Lawrence asked from behind them. "I thought I saw Jenga in the cabinet that one time."

"What one time?" Adrienne asked. "If you want to go looking in the cupboards, you should ask first."

"I was closing it," Lawrence said. "Chester knocked into it and the door popped open. I saw some games and Jenga was on top."

"My nieces love that game," KJ said. "Emma's not great at it. She may think the point of the game is to knock everything over. But I'm game if you are." She raised an eyebrow at Adrienne.

"I could play." Adrienne rubbed her hands together.

Lawrence cast her a sideways glance.

"What?" Adrienne blinked at him. "It'll be fun." She could rein in her worst competitive impulses when she had to. She'd been doing it all of Lawrence's life. Most of the time.

"Sure it will," KJ said. "Dinner first, then games."

Lawrence smiled widely. He grabbed a plate and stood by the stove for his food. KJ filled his plate, then Adrienne's.

The table was back to being half covered with stuff. A few boxes were open along the wall. It seemed KJ was back to packing up her dad's stuff. Adrienne took her seat at the table.

"Wait until KJ gets here," she said to Lawrence.

Disappointment wreathed his lips, but he put down the fork and knife. He didn't have to wait long.

"You guys can start," KJ said as she entered the room, plate in hand.

Lawrence dug in before Adrienne could say anything. She let it drop this time, but she made a mental note to let KJ know that she expected him to wait until everyone was at the table before eating. Otherwise, he'd be halfway through his dinner before anyone else could get started. Table manners were important, that had been drilled into her by her parents, and she was doing her best to pass that lesson along to her son.

Dinner was less awkward than she'd expected. KJ kept up a fairly constant stream of conversation with Lawrence, peppering him with questions about school, his latest drawing projects, and the goings-on in his favorite comics. Her son was more than happy to discuss those topics. Adrienne was content to sit back and let them chat. She enjoyed watching Lawrence and KJ. On nights like this, it was easy to imagine that they could do this all the time.

CHAPTER TWENTY-SEVEN

They finished dinner and cleaned up after, with only minor prodding from Adrienne to get Lawrence to help. The promise of a game seemed to have focused him.

Adrienne and Lawrence took their places at the table again as KJ went over to the cabinet in the living room. She returned a moment later with a battered box held together by rubber bands. She cleared the placemats away from one corner of the table and dumped out the box.

Lawrence reached eagerly for the pieces and started piling them up in neat rows. KJ passed him blocks, allowing him to erect the tower. Her patience with him was one of the things that made Adrienne hopeful they all could have a future together. For someone who was so driven on the ice, KJ was pretty easygoing off it. Adrienne was glad that her way of rolling with things included her son.

Before long, a tower of wooden blocks stood on the edge of the table.

"So we all know the rules, right, Mom?" Lawrence said, looking her in the eye.

"Yes, we know the rules," Adrienne said.

KJ leaned over toward her. "Is there some reason he keeps giving you a hard time about this?"

"Mom likes to win," Lawrence said.

Adrienne opened her mouth to deny his statement, then closed it.

"I already know that," KJ said. "She gives it everything she has when we're on the ice."

"It's perfectly reasonable," Adrienne said. "You get a little passionate about winning a few times and people start to think you have problems." Which she most definitely did not. She was merely pleased when she managed to come out on top. She gave a mental groan at missing out on the chance to air that statement where KJ could hear it.

"Sometimes she cheats," Lawrence announced in a loud whisper to KJ.

"Only at solitaire." Adrienne put a hand to her chest. "I would never cheat with you." She thought about it for half a second. "Maybe against my siblings, but only because they expect it."

KJ looked back and forth between her and Lawrence, a half-smile quirking up the side of her mouth. Adrienne was nearly overtaken with the urge to kiss her, to turn that smile into a gasp or even better a moan.

She cleared her throat. "Don't worry." Adrienne placed a hand on KJ's forearm and immediately noticed how smooth and warm it was. She snatched her fingers back. "Um."

"Don't worry about what?" KJ asked.

Adrienne noticed her eyes seemed slightly unfocused. "Oh." What had she been about to say? "I would never cheat against you."

"Good to hear," KJ said slowly.

"Besides, it's Jenga. How do you even cheat at it?" She could think of a couple of ways. "You're fine. Everything's fine." Was she babbling? Oh god, she was. Adrienne tried to stop the nervous laugh before it left her mouth. It only sounded a little strangled when it came out despite her best efforts.

"Youngest goes first?" Lawrence said hopefully.

"Sounds like your mom isn't the only one who gets creative with the rules," KJ said, but she moved to let Lawrence have a clear line of attack on the stack.

He studied the tower carefully, then gingerly pushed a middle block out near the bottom. His hands hardly wavered as he stacked it neatly on top.

"You want to go next?" KJ asked.

"If you're offering." Adrienne leaned forward before KJ could change her mind. She surveyed the stacked blocks from one side, then the other. It didn't hurt that KJ was sitting on the left and she was able to get in really close to her while she pretended to look for the best option. Adrienne paused well within KJ's personal envelope, basking in her closeness, the barest hint of warmth that seemed to welcome her in, the waft of KJ's subtle scent. She took a deep breath.

"Come on, Mom," Lawrence said. "You're taking forever."

"Patience, young one," Adrienne said. KJ smelled nice tonight. Her hand trembled a bit when she reached out for her first block. *Focus, Adrienne.*

There was a split second of worry when the edge block she'd chosen got hung up between those above and below. She tried to put KJ's closeness out of her mind and, with a little finessing, wiggled the block free.

"There." Adrienne triumphantly placed the piece next to Lawrence's at the top of the tower.

"My turn." KJ rubbed her hands together, then stood next to Adrienne. Her attention appeared to be on the neat stack of blocks, but her angle on the game was a little awkward.

She wasted little time focusing on a likely candidate. Her fingers were also shaky, but she took a deep breath and held it while she slid her block out.

"That wasn't too bad," Adrienne said after KJ deposited her piece. "Good job." She patted her heartily on the shoulder.

Lawrence also stood for his turn. As he had been the first time, he was very serious about finding the best option.

The game continued in much the same way. Adrienne found it difficult to keep her hands steady. The more time she spent in KJ's presence, the higher the tension ratcheted in her belly. It wasn't unpleasant, but neither was it going away. When the tower finally fell at KJ's hands, it was almost a relief.

"I'm gonna go draw," Lawrence said. He popped up from his chair and crossed the room to where Chester was curled up. The space in front of a battered easy chair that had seen better days was his favorite spot when Lawrence was otherwise occupied.

"How long until the game starts?" Adrienne asked. Surely they'd spent a good thirty to forty minutes on that round.

KJ craned her head and squinted at the clock that was barely visible through the doorway to the kitchen. "Looks like we have forty-five or so minutes to go."

"That long?" Adrienne looked at the pile of blocks on the table. "Another go then?" She needed to keep her hands busy. If she didn't, she was going to start tracing the outlines of the muscles on KJ's forearms. That would lead to her elbow, then up to the shoulders Adrienne knew were strong with exactly the right amount of muscle. From there, it would be a struggle to decide if she should run her fingers up KJ's neck and bury them in her hair or to drag their tips across KJ's collarbone over to her sternum. She became aware that she was staring at the shadow of the bone under KJ's pale skin where the V-neck of her shirt allowed it to peek out.

"Nice shirt," Adrienne said, a tad breathlessly. "I've never seen it before."

"Oh yeah." KJ looked down at it. "It doesn't get a lot of play. I thought tonight would be a good time to bring it out."

Adrienne grinned. "KJ Stennes." She glanced over at Lawrence. He didn't seem to have noticed anything untoward about their conversation. She lowered her voice anyway. "Did you wear that shirt for me?" The idea tickled her down to her core. It had been a long time since anyone had peacocked for her. Of course, KJ's idea of showing off seemed to be skinnier-than-normal cargo pants and a V-neck, long-sleeved T-shirt that showed off a bit more extra skin than usual. Still, she made it work for her.

"Maybe." An answering smile spread over KJ's face. "I don't think I'm the only one who had that idea."

"Oh, this?" Adrienne didn't look down. She knew she looked damn good in the sweater, with its almost electric blue against the dark brown of her skin and the way it hugged every curve of her torso. The jeans were more snug than most in her wardrobe. She'd considered dropping them at the thrift store instead of packing them when they'd moved. It was a good thing she hadn't. "I have no idea what you're talking about."

"Sure you don't." KJ started stacking up the blocks again. The resulting tower wasn't nearly as tight as Lawrence had managed.

"I guess I get to go first since you knocked it down last time." Adrienne reached past KJ, lightly placing her left hand on KJ's upper arm for balance.

The muscles under her hand flexed. Adrienne smirked. She poked a middle block through to the other side.

"There we go," she said, her finger lingering in the opening left by the piece. KJ's arm twitched again. Adrienne didn't try to stop the low chuckle that bubbled up out of her chest. She trailed her fingers down KJ's arm before reluctantly giving up the contact. She picked up the block and dropped it on top, not paying too much attention to its placement. "Your turn."

KJ closed her eyes for a moment, then opened them. Despite the shaking of her hands, she was able to pry free a side block without sending the tower tumbling.

"Very nice," Adrienne breathed into KJ's ear.

The block dropped out of KJ's fingers and hit the tabletop with a clatter, bouncing once, twice, before coming to a stop against the tower.

"Is this how it's going to be?" KJ asked. She picked up the block and placed it carefully on top.

"Do you want me to stop?"

"Dear god, no." KJ shot her a half-lidded look. The naked need in the depths of her eyes rivaled what Adrienne felt.

"I'm glad to hear it." Adrienne bit her lower lip, noting with delight how KJ's nostrils flared in response. "If you'll just let me…" She trailed her hand over the KJ's upper back as she moved past her to get a different angle on the stack.

"Of course," KJ murmured.

Adrienne went for another center block about a third of the way down the tower. It had some clearance above it, and she suspected it would come out easily. She leaned forward, feeling KJ's gaze on her backside. The block moved easily at her first probing, so she kept pushing it.

A hand warmed the strip of bare skin that had been exposed when she bent forward. She started but was able to pull her hand away before it could knock into the tower. KJ removed her fingers, but Adrienne could still feel the shadow of their presence.

"You going to finish your move?" KJ asked, her eyes wide with an innocence that was belied by the smile curving the edges of her lips.

"I am." It was difficult to keep an eye on her partner and pick up the block, but Adrienne managed. She stuck it on top without checking to see if it would stay. There was no clatter of wood on wood, so she was good.

"This is way more fun," KJ said. She grinned wickedly. "I like this version."

"I'm glad to hear it." Adrienne waited until KJ was pulling her block through from the other side. She glanced over at Lawrence. All she could see was the top of his head. She ran a fingernail gently along the edge of KJ's jaw.

"What the—" KJ's arm jerked, pulling the block up and toward her. The tower came down in a cacophony of bouncing blocks.

"Huh," Adrienne said. "Guess I win again."

"Lawrence is right," KJ said. "You do cheat."

"Cheating is such an ugly word, don't you think?" Adrienne blinked in her most winsome way at her partner. "I prefer to think of it as winning unconventionally."

"You guys are terrible at that game," Lawrence called from across the room. "You knocked it down so soon?"

"Adults," KJ said. "Guess we're not as steady-handed as you are."

"Guess not," Lawrence said. "Maybe you should play a card game or something."

"I think I'm going to go again." KJ started reassembling the stack.

"Who knows," Adrienne said. "You might get lucky."

"I would love that." She stared Adrienne in the eyes. Gone were the flirtatious glances. What stared back at Adrienne was open longing. For her.

An answering pull in her chest was echoed by a twist in her core. "Me too." She placed her hand over KJ's. "Me too."

The resolution to take things slowly had seemed like such a good idea a few days ago, but the shine had quickly worn off. The reality was that she wanted KJ Stennes more than she'd wanted anything or anyone for a very long time. What would convince her head the time was right? Her body knew what it wanted, who it wanted. Logic was losing ground to passion and quickly.

She and Kaz hadn't taken things slowly. They'd dated for six months, then gotten engaged. They were married barely a year after they met. Was that what she wanted, again?

Was it really that bad? Things were really good for the first few years. The voice in her head seemed to have changed sides.

It wasn't wrong, though. They'd had some great times together, both before Lawrence came along and after. Sure, it hadn't ended up being the forever she'd wanted, the forever her parents had and that Adrienne yearned for, but she wouldn't give up those memories for anything. They were amazing in their own right, plus they'd brought her here, to this very moment, where she was playing sexy Jenga with a woman who literally took her breath away when she smiled.

Some caution was natural, and probably a good thing, but she couldn't allow it to harden into inaction. Life kept on, and she had to also, as long as it was right for her and Lawrence.

She pulled her hand away, after giving KJ's fingers a gentle squeeze. "I'll be good this time."

KJ smiled at her. "Don't you dare."

CHAPTER TWENTY-EIGHT

KJ busied herself in the kitchen. Since the previous weekend, she'd had more energy than she knew what to deal with. So far baking was helping to take off some of the edge. So was getting back to packing up her dad's things. When she didn't do something to occupy herself, her brain kept going back to thoughts of Adrienne. The way her neck curved and the eminently kissable divot at the base where it met her clavicles. The softness of her lips, how they yielded to and dominated KJ's in equal measure. The smoothness of her skin. She wanted to see more of it..

Her core spasmed deliciously, surprising a small gasp out of her, tightening her hands around the mixing bowl and spoon. KJ put down the batter for the sticky buns and closed her eyes. So much for baking taking her mind off her partner.

She glanced at the kitchen clock. It was hours until game time yet. Hours until she saw Adrienne. She wiped her hands on a kitchen towel and pulled her phone from her pocket. A swipe opened the lock screen.

Good luck today! a message from Jamie read. The date stamp was from only a few minutes previous.

thanks!!! KJ hesitated a moment before her thumb flew over the screen keyboard. *miss us yet???*

Of course I do, came the response a few seconds later. *I miss the ice like crazy.*

i miss you out there

Liar. The word was accompanied by three laughing faces. *You and Adrienne look amazing together. I knew you would.*

She and Adrienne could be even more amazing together. Her fingers paused over the screen as an image of Adrienne's neck and shoulder popped into her brain. She ached to kiss it, to feel the skin beneath her lips.

The front doorbell rang. Chester barked once, then stopped. That was odd. Usually he kept going until he could investigate who it was on her front stoop for himself.

KJ crammed her phone back into her pocket as she headed toward the front of the house. Chester sat in front of the door, his tail wagging so fast it was almost a blur. The edge of the jacket visible through the front door was a familiar blue. Her arousal spiked up another few notches. KJ hastened her steps but stopped from running to the entryway only through sheer force of will. She took a deep breath, then opened the door.

"Adrienne?" KJ looked around for Lawrence but didn't see him. "Is everything all right?"

"Not really." Adrienne chewed on her lower lip. "Do you mind if I come in?"

"Of course not." KJ stood back, letting her into the house. She closed and locked the door. "What's going on? The game isn't for hours yet."

When she turned around, Adrienne was standing right there. "I know I said we should take it slow, but…"

"But…" KJ closed the miniscule distance between them.

"God, KJ." Adrienne reached up, sliding her hands into KJ's hair, pulling her head down.

Their lips met in a collision of softness and need. Adrienne slid her arms around KJ's waist, holding her close with shared desperation. KJ inhaled sharply at the sensation, reveling in their closeness, at the way Adrienne's lips moved against hers, winding the arousal within her tighter and tighter. Adrienne moaned into her mouth and crushed KJ against her as KJ dipped her tongue into Adrienne's mouth. Was it possible to take Adrienne's breath away, the way she'd taken KJ's? She smiled. There was only one way to find out. They broke for breath, inhaling deeply in near unison.

The jacket was in her way, KJ decided, and she needed to see what lay beneath it. She bent her head to Adrienne's neck where the skin was so soft and smooth that she couldn't resist one nibble, then another. Then another. She worked her way down Adrienne's neck to her collarbone as her fingers fumbled with the offending item's zipper. Adrienne's scent filled her nose and she inhaled, pulling it into her. She smelled of warmth and the promise of spring after a long winter. Something about her scent made KJ want to weep, but not because she was sad. No, it was joy that welled up within her. She swallowed hard, pushing down a sob before it could escape and ruin the moment.

Adrienne slid her hands under KJ's shirt, running her hand over planes of muscle and flesh. Everywhere she touched warmed, awakening a trail across her body. The tension in her bones spiked up another notch. KJ sank her teeth into the large muscle where Adrienne's neck met her shoulder, reveling in the play of strength beneath her skin. Adrienne was so strong; KJ hoped she could be as strong for her.

A deep hiss and groan met her bite, and Adrienne's nails dug into her side.

"Too much?" KJ managed to ask.

"No." Adrienne eased up with her nails. "That feels…really good."

"Does it now?" KJ dropped a kiss on the spot. She would have to remember that trick. The last button gave way, and KJ tossed the sweater to one side. The shirt beneath was thin, but not thin enough. It also had to go.

"Mmmm, KJ," Adrienne sang, her voice low and resonant in her chest. She swayed against KJ for a second, then backed out of her arms.

KJ's heart dropped into her stomach with a sad thud. She opened her mouth to ask what was wrong, but Adrienne held one finger to her lips.

"It's okay." She took KJ's hand and pulled her toward the kitchen and the back stairs. "Let's head to your room."

"Oh," KJ said, then swallowed. She nodded vigorously. "Yes! Upstairs." She allowed Adrienne to draw her through the house.

Every few feet, Adrienne would look back and smile an expression equal parts delight and promise. At each knowing glance, another bolt of warmth shuddered through KJ. She barely noticed the kitchen passing by, then the stairs, until they were at the doorway to her room.

Adrienne hesitated at the threshold. "Are you okay with this?"

"More than okay," KJ said, her lips dry. She moistened them with the tip of her tongue. Adrienne's eyes lit up at the movement, so KJ tried the move again.

Adrienne pulled her into the room and around, moving her backward until KJ felt the bed frame against the back of her legs. With gentleness that did nothing to mask the urgency she felt, Adrienne wrapped an arm around KJ's waist and leaned her back against the mattress. The softness of the comforter cradled her, but it couldn't compare to the care Adrienne showed for her.

"Now where were we?" She looked down at KJ. "Oh yes."

Adrienne climbed onto the bed to straddle her hips. KJ couldn't stop the jerk of her pelvis in response to her closeness. She longed to feel her stretched against the length of her body, for their warmth to combine with no barriers between them. She grasped Adrienne's hips, pulling her against her.

"Is this good?" she asked, her voice hoarse with need.

Adrienne rocked back against her, the motion making KJ squirm in place as she tried to maximize the pressure between them. "So good. It'll be even better when there aren't so many damn layers between us." She pulled KJ's T-shirt and sweatshirt up, exposing her belly to cool air. KJ let go, lifting her arms and leaning forward so Adrienne could pull the shirts completely over her head. The bedroom's cold temperature barely registered, not over the heat of Adrienne's gaze as she drank in KJ's nearly naked torso.

"What about you?" KJ asked.

Adrienne looked down at her, smiled wickedly, then pulled her shirt off in one motion. It disappeared into a corner of the room. KJ couldn't believe her eyes. It wasn't that she hadn't seen her partner topless before. You didn't change together in locker rooms for a couple of months without catching the occasional glimpse, but she'd never seen her like this. Hadn't looked at her like this. She drank in the glory that was Adrienne, trying to memorize every curve of her body and every shadow on her skin, which glowed a beautiful brown-red in the light from the window. Adrienne reached behind herself to unhook her bra, then she was sitting atop her in all of her topless glory, her flawless breasts topped with aureoles of darkened umber. KJ lifted her hands, then paused, not daring to touch the perfection that had fallen into her lap. Adrienne reached down and covered KJ's hands, bringing them into contact with nipples that stiffened further at her touch.

"My god, Adrienne," KJ murmured. "You look..." Amazing wasn't enough. Marvelous was laughable. There were no words to describe how Adrienne looked, how she made KJ feel.

"You have a bit of an advantage." Adrienne looked down at KJ's torso with the bra that was still in the way.

"Oh no." She didn't want to let go. KJ squeezed, an experiment that was rewarded by the rock of Adrienne's hips and the closing of her eyes. She brought her thumbs up to caress the undersides of Adrienne's nipples. A guttural moan was ripped from her throat.

KJ sat up and moaned herself at the feel of so much of her bare skin against Adrienne's. She bent her head and ran the tip of her tongue around Adrienne's aureole, deliberately avoiding the proud nipple. Adrienne threw back her head and let out a strangled cry. KJ seized the opportunity to roll Adrienne over to her back and paused.

"We still okay? If anything gets out of your comfort zone, let me know, okay."

"Ditto." Adrienne's eyes slitted open to watch her.

"Good." KJ rolled to one side, then reached back and quickly undid the clasp on her bra, then dropped the piece of underwear behind her. She snapped open the button at the top of her cargo pants, then shimmied them down her legs with her boxers, cursing when she realized she hadn't taken her shoes off. They were easy enough to kick off, and then she could remove the pants the rest of the way.

Adrienne didn't miss a beat. She kicked off her own footwear, then skimmed off her jeans.

"What's with these?" KJ plucked at the edge of her underwear.

"I thought you might enjoy the final unwrapping," Adrienne said.

"You know me so well."

"Not as well as I'm about to." Adrienne chuckled low in her chest, the sound caressing KJ's insides and adding to the heat between her legs. It was like adding a match to a forest fire, but KJ felt it all the same.

KJ hooked her finger around the underwear and slid it down, watching closely as it moved over Adrienne's shapely hips, down heavily muscled thighs and calves until Adrienne could kick them off into the shadows in the corners of the room.

And with that, nothing stood between them.

"If you knew how often I've thought of this moment," Adrienne whispered. "I wasn't sure we'd ever get here." She laughed quietly. "It's been such a long week."

"I'm glad we're here." KJ slid the palms of her hand up over Adrienne's thighs, over her belly and rib cage, memorizing every dip and swell, then gently recaptured her breasts. "There is nowhere else I'd rather be." She lowered her head to Adrienne's breast again and covered a nipple with her mouth. Adrienne's hand landed on the back of her head, then tightened in her hair in clear encouragement. A shiver raced down KJ's spine.

She reached down with one hand and trailed her fingertips through the tangle of hair at the juncture of Adrienne's thighs.

Wet ringlets had formed and when KJ delved deeper, she discovered the extent of Adrienne's arousal.

"Don't stop," Adrienne panted.

KJ lingered for a moment, marveling at the feel of Adrienne's pubic hair, then slid a finger between the folds of her lips. Her finger was enfolded by wetness and heat rivaling her own.

"KJ!" Adrienne gasped when she grazed the top of her clit.

Giving a light bite to the nipple in her mouth, KJ skirted the perimeter of Adrienne's clit with her fingertips, not quite touching it, but knowing the sensation would ripple outward. Her own center tightened in sympathetic response.

She followed the trail between the folds of Adrienne's labia, down to the entrance of her most intimate place. If her arousal was anything like KJ's, she needed to be touched there. KJ shifted her weight, not wanting to crush Adrienne with her entire body weight.

The movement gave Adrienne an opening, and KJ felt her partner's fingers questing around her hip toward her center. She shifted again, opening herself to Adrienne as KJ entered her for the first time with one finger.

Adrienne welcomed her, opening her legs further, urging her deeper within her heat.

"You feel so good," KJ whispered. "So damn good."

"God, KJ. What you're doing to me…I need more."

"Your wish…" KJ slid another finger into her lover, feeling the walls of her vagina stretching to accommodate the intrusion.

A finger slipped over her mound. KJ knew what Adrienne wanted. Knew what she wanted. She moved her hips forward to intercept her. Adrienne slipped inside her, KJ's own arousal making it as easy as breathing. As necessary as breathing.

"Adrienne," KJ keened. There it was. What she'd been craving. She rocked forward, pushing into Adrienne at the same time.

"KJ," Adrienne whispered, her name half sob, half invocation. She moved with KJ as they pushed each other to new heights of shared sensation.

All that mattered was the pleasure she was giving Adrienne and receiving in return. She felt herself tightening and felt

Adrienne's body grasp her fingers deep within. It wouldn't be long now. It would be an eternity.

Something deep inside her gave, the tension of days surrendering in the space between seconds. A flash behind her eyelids was the only warning she had before she became undone. A million points of light prickled to life across her skin, then faded, taking her with them. KJ was borne aloft by them and floated for a while, before becoming slowly aware of warm arms holding her close.

It was over too soon.

She looked up into the black eyes that gazed back into hers.

Adrienne smiled, her face soft and open. "Welcome back. How was your trip?"

KJ stretched. "It was…everything."

"Everything was it? That's going to make for a difficult follow-up."

"I think you'll manage."

"I'll certainly try." Adrienne propped herself up on her elbows. "I think I'll try…now."

CHAPTER TWENTY-NINE

"How did we end up running so late?" KJ asked. She anxiously scanned traffic for an opening so she could pull into their home rink's parking lot.

"I'm pretty sure you know the answer to that question," Adrienne said. "We have twenty minutes still. We'll be fine."

"I like more time to get ready. To get in the proper head space."

"Then you shouldn't have pulled me back down on the bed for 'one last smooch.'"

KJ's wicked look rekindled the longing Adrienne had thought sated. "When you put it that way, I regret nothing." She took advantage of a gap in the stream of cars and pulled into the driveway leading to the ice, then slotted into the first open spot she saw.

Adrienne took the time to grab both sets of their sticks from the back seat, while KJ headed to the trunk for their gear. It took some juggling at the back of the car while KJ tried to hand off Adrienne's hockey bag at the same time Adrienne was giving KJ her stick. After some fumbling, they got it sorted out.

"There you are," Vaughn said as they entered the locker room. "I tried to save you two a seat, but they got snagged by the members of my defense who show up on time." Cam and Krissy waved from either side of the goalie.

KJ took a spot closer to the door. A major disadvantage of arriving so late was that Adrienne couldn't sit next to her. There weren't any spaces big enough for them both. Lou scrunched over into Rebecca's space, leaving enough of a gap for Adrienne to sit down.

"You two were running pretty late," Lou said, her voice oh-so-casual. "Did you get held up?"

"Something like that." Adrienne rummaged around in her bag for her set of undergear, then started pulling it on.

"You guys don't usually show up at the same time," Rebecca added from beyond Lou. "Don't you only carpool for away games?"

"KJ picked me up this time," Adrienne said. "My car is making a funny knocking sound."

"That sucks," Lou said.

Rebecca nodded in sympathy.

"It sure does," Adrienne said. She concentrated on getting her gear on in time to hit the ice, hoping Rebecca and Lou would take the hint.

The two forwards subsided in their interrogation. She was still pulling on the last of her pads when Coach Aaron knocked at the door for their pregame talk. She glanced over at KJ, only to discover she was already being watched. KJ's smile widened, then she turned her attention to the coach. Adrienne did her best to pay attention to what he was saying, but her thoughts kept getting interrupted by memories of KJ above her. And below her. And inside her. She inhaled deeply in an attempt to focus but was only somewhat successful.

KJ fell into step next to Adrienne as they made their way toward the door ice.

"You looked a little unfocused during coach's chalk talk," KJ said quietly. "Do I need to be worried you won't know what's going on out there?"

"Seems to me you were as distracted if you knew I was distracted," Adrienne replied. "If you really want to know I can tell you, but you'll have more than your head in the clouds."

KJ's breath caught. "It's an hour. I can last for an hour. Does Lawrence get home from his dad's today or tomorrow?"

"Tomorrow." Adrienne grinned widely. "I'm sure you'll last until then." She bumped KJ with her shoulder.

"Not that you're making it easy on me."

"I might as well get something out of keeping us a secret. Teasing the crap out of you is so much fun."

KJ sighed. "I'd rather be open about it."

Adrienne shook her head. "I want to tell people too, you know. And I will. We will. When things are sure and Lawrence knows."

"I just wish it was sooner." KJ limbered up her shoulders.

"Me too, KJ," Adrienne said. "Me too."

CHAPTER THIRTY

"Did you bring your homework?" Adrienne asked as they headed toward the back stairs to KJ's house. Her breath steamed in the chilly evening air. As if it had gotten the memo that it was winter now that it was December, the weather had decided to overcompensate for a temperate autumn.

"I don't have any tonight," Lawrence said.

"Are you sure? You know you forget sometimes."

"I don't, Mom, okay?"

His tone was exasperated, but Adrienne held her tongue. She wanted to see KJ and she wasn't going to let Lawrence's pre-dinner crankiness get under her skin. He would be fine once they ate. Chester would go a long way toward improving his mood.

The dog was already yapping at the back door, the sturdy wood doing little to muffle his barks. Lawrence reached for the door handle.

"Wait for me," Adrienne called behind him. If she didn't remind him, he would go barreling inside, leaving the door wide open. KJ wasn't trying to heat the neighborhood.

He stood impatiently on the top step, then pushed the door open as soon as her feet hit the stairs. Chester greeted him in a blur of bouncing, butt wiggles, and tight circles, barking his excitement the entire time. He wasn't at all circumspect about declaring Lawrence's status as his favorite. Adrienne was glad KJ didn't seem to harbor any resentment over losing her dog's affections to a nine-year-old boy. She smiled. KJ took it in stride and even encouraged Lawrence to spend time with Chester when she could have gotten territorial. Not for the first time, Adrienne wondered how Lawrence would react when she told him that she was with KJ. How would she even tell him? What was the right time to tell your son that you were seeing someone who wasn't his father? He hadn't said so, but she knew he harbored fond hopes that she and Kaz would patch things up and get back together.

"Hey, you two," KJ said from in front of the stove. Her grin stretched across her face and her eyes crinkled around the edges. Adrienne ached to give her a deep kiss but restrained herself.

"It smells good," Adrienne said. "What's on the menu tonight?"

"I hope you guys like enchiladas."

"Enchiladas?" Lawrence bounced on his toes in excitement. "I love enchiladas! What type are they?"

"Does chicken meet your approval?"

He nodded emphatically.

"It's going to be another twenty minutes or so." KJ said.

"Do you need someone to walk Chester?" Adrienne asked. It was a duty Lawrence had been happy to take on, and she'd gotten reasonably comfortable with him taking the dog out on his own. The first couple of times, she'd watched him from the front stoop as long as she could to make sure no one was paying him any untoward attention. No one was hanging out on the porches tonight, but on warmer evenings, she'd been happy to see him exchanging friendly waves with those of KJ's neighbors who were out and about.

"That would be a huge help," KJ said. "What do you say, Lawrence? I can have a cup of hot chocolate waiting for you when you get back."

"Yeah, okay." He headed toward the kitchen.

"Boots!" Adrienne said.

"They're only gonna get snowy again, Mom." Despite the protest, Lawrence backtracked and carefully wiped his boots on the mat.

"This way you won't track snow water across KJ's clean floors."

KJ looked up from the sink where she was filling the kettle. "Which I appreciate," she said.

"Do you want to go out, Chester?" Lawrence asked.

The little dog barked once, then tore through the house, Lawrence following along behind him. Adrienne pulled off her boots while listening to the racket of her son getting the dog's leash and trying to settle Chester long enough to clip it on his collar. She hung up her jacket and was padding into the kitchen in her stocking feet when the front door slammed shut.

KJ met her halfway, her arms open. Adrienne wrapped herself around KJ and lifted her face for a kiss. KJ's mouth lowered to hers, and Adrienne closed her eyes and lost herself in the warmth of their embrace. She relaxed into KJ's arms, teasing her partner with the tip of her tongue, then deepening the kiss when KJ moaned. Her eyelids fluttered at the sound of KJ's arousal. They wouldn't be able to do anything about it, but, oh, she wanted to.

The kiss was over too soon. They stood in the kitchen, arms wrapped tightly around each other.

"I wish…" KJ said.

"Me too." Adrienne squeezed her hard, then let go. She stepped back out of arm's reach.

KJ sighed.

"We need to keep it cool until I tell Lawrence," Adrienne said.

"I know, and I agree." KJ took a deep breath, then blew it out slowly. "It's only that I haven't seen you or really talked to you for two days. I didn't think it would be this hard to keep my hands to myself once we were together again."

"Tell me about it."

"So we'll tell Lawrence tonight?" KJ asked hopefully.

Adrienne laughed. "That seems a little premature. Four days does not a relationship make."

KJ stepped closer. "Are you sure? Because this feels right."

"It feels good," Adrienne said. She made no move to get out of the way when KJ wrapped her up again. "He's barely had time to get used to me and his dad not being together. Let's not yank the rug out from under him by telling him we're together, then breaking up over something dumb in a few weeks. I want us to be stable and know this is right for the three of us."

KJ nuzzled her face into Adrienne's hair. "I know. I even agree. Though I'm pretty sure we're not going to break up over something stupid like you not liking how I chew." She paused, but Adrienne could tell by her the tension in her body that she had more to say. "Do you think Lawrence will be upset you're dating me, a woman?"

"Wait, you're a woman?" Adrienne yanked her head back in exaggerated shock.

"Har har." KJ took a mock bite at Adrienne's neck, her teeth clacking together next to Adrienne's ear. "I'm serious," she murmured, before dropping a gentle kiss below the same ear.

"I'm not too worried about it. When he was in second grade in Philly, one of his best friends had two moms. And then in Syracuse, after I separated from Kaz, he had a classmate with two dads. There were also single moms, kids being raised by their grandparents, or a sibling. He's been exposed to lots of different families."

"That's encouraging." Adrienne felt KJ's lips stretch into a smile against the sensitive skin of her neck. "So we'll tell him next week, then."

"Unlikely. I won't drag it out forever, but you should be patient." It was tempting to go along with KJ on this one. Letting Lawrence know would mean they could spend more time over here. On the other hand, Kaz took Lawrence every weekend, so they had plenty of sleepover time. It was a lot, more than many single moms had. It didn't feel like enough. A large part of her wanted to throw caution out the window and dive headfirst into a public relationship with KJ, but the rest of her knew she and Lawrence had to get back on solid ground. Still… "What if we come over another night a week?"

"Monday or Wednesday?" KJ asked immediately.

"Good question." Adrienne stared into the darkness out the back window. "We'll get to see each other Friday night, all of Saturday, and Sunday until after dinner. Thursday is practice."

"Which you've been making more now that you're okay with Lawrence hanging out."

"Let's do Monday, then." Adrienne nodded, satisfied with the decision. "Lawrence can work on his homework here where I can make sure he isn't drawing superheroes all night instead of studying. So really, that only leaves Wednesday when we won't see each other at all."

"Wednesdays are the worst. I don't like them at all."

Adrienne laughed. "Funny, you've never had a problem with the day before."

"And I never had to go the whole day without seeing you before."

"That's plainly not true. We didn't hang out that much before this past weekend."

"But we weren't seeing each other before then. Now I hate Wednesdays."

"Fair enough. How about we Skype after Lawrence is in bed."

KJ nodded. "I can get behind that."

"Good. I'm glad we've figured this out."

"Me too."

They stood, arms around each other, trading soft kisses for a few minutes. At the first sound of the front door rattling in the frame, Adrienne sprang away from KJ. By the time her son entered the kitchen, Adrienne was cutting vegetables for a salad and KJ was grating extra cheese.

"How was he?" KJ asked.

"Good," Lawrence said. "He peed and pooped!"

"That's always good to hear," KJ said gravely.

"Who's playing tonight?" Lawrence asked.

"Tonight we have the University of Wisconsin against Bemidji State."

"Bemidji?" Lawrence snickered. "That's a strange word."

"For sure," KJ said. "It's somewhere in Minnesota."

"Can I help?" he asked.

"You can finish grating the cheese," KJ said. "I'm about to check on the enchiladas."

"Okay!"

Adrienne watched the two of them. She hoped the ease with which they interacted remained when they told him about their relationship. If they lasted long enough to tell him, that was. There was no guarantee, though seeing how good KJ continued to be with him gave her hope that they would eventually come clean. She hoped for her sake, and for his, that she wasn't wrong about KJ and what they had together.

CHAPTER THIRTY-ONE

Adrienne looked down at the display on her desk phone when it interrupted her lunch break. Thursdays weren't her day to supervise in the lunchroom or out on the playground, and she'd been looking through some files while eating her sandwich. Her and Lawrence's lunches were depressingly the same. Sure, she didn't long for the Lunchables the way he did, but she had to admit some variety would have been nice.

"Hi, Ma," Adrienne said into the phone. "What's up?"

Her ma had taken to calling her at lunch every few days to chat. She still called at home once a week, but that was mainly to catch up with Lawrence. Adrienne was glad her ma didn't call more frequently as the conversations she had with her grandson could go on for more than an hour, and it was difficult to get him back on track with his homework after that. They'd missed talking earlier this week. Her ma had called on Monday night, but she'd been over at KJ's.

"Nothing much. You never called back the other night."

"Sorry about that," Adrienne said. She kicked herself mentally. That had been a tactical error. "It's been a busy week."

"Mm-hmm." Her ma didn't say anything else after that, allowing the silence to expand between them. It grew edges the longer it went on. No one wielded silence as well as Moesha Pierce. Fortunately, part of Adrienne's therapy training had involved getting comfortable with periods of quiet. Even though the tactic no longer worked with her, it didn't stop her ma from trying.

"How has your week been?" Adrienne asked blandly.

"Pretty good, even though I missed talking to my grandson."

"Why don't we call tonight?" Adrienne asked. "It'll be after practice, though."

"I suppose that will have to do." Her ma sighed, disappointment radiating down the phone line.

"I'm glad to hear it."

"What had you so busy you couldn't pick up or call me back?"

"We're hitting the end of the semester," Adrienne said. "Things have really picked up." It wasn't even a lie, though she was still managing to get most of what she needed to done at school after the final bell.

"I guess. You're still liking the work?"

"Yes, Ma. I still like the work."

"Good." Her voice firmed up. "Now, let's talk Christmas holidays."

"No fabulous trips this time?"

"Your daddy hasn't said anything, so we'll be having it at our house, as usual."

"Sounds good." It didn't, actually. There was no way out of the holiday without telling her ma what was going on between her and KJ. In her head, Christmas had become an opportunity to spend the better part of a couple of weeks curled up with her girlfriend, a dream that was drifting away like so much smoke.

"Is Lawrence coming this year?"

"No, it's Kaz's turn to have him. We're going to open presents on the 20th, then he'll be gone with his dad until January 7th."

"Oh, then we'll have two whole weeks together." Her ma was very excited and Adrienne tried to match her joy.

"A good bit of it, anyway," she said. "I can't wait."

"A good bit? What else are you going to do?"

"Mom, I have a life here, you know." As soon as the words left her lips, Adrienne wished she could grab them back. She held up her hands as if she could, but it was too late.

"A life in Sussburg?" Her voice lowered. "Do tell? Who did you meet?"

"Does it have to be like that?"

"I don't know how else it would be?" Her mother projected the patience only a woman who'd raised five children could muster. "Why else would you decide not to spend the entire holiday with your family? The last time you did that, well, you and Kaz were married the following summer."

"You don't have to worry about that," Adrienne said firmly. "I won't be getting married next summer."

"That's good to hear, except you didn't answer the question."

Adrienne hesitated. This time it was her ma who was content to let the silence stretch between them. Apparently, training didn't trump mom tricks every time.

"I am seeing someone," she said after a long pause to gather her thoughts. Saying it out loud felt surprisingly good. It wasn't like she was keeping KJ a secret, not really, but it felt right to take a step off the cautious path she'd set for herself.

"I knew it!" Her ma's triumph came through with crystal clarity. "Who is he? What does he do? How did you meet him?"

"First off, he's not a he. He's a she."

Silence met Adrienne's pronouncement.

"Her name is KJ. I play hockey with her." Her ma still had nothing to say. "It's a new thing. A really new thing, like not even a couple of weeks, but I really like her."

"I see." Her ma's response was a little too hearty, a little too approving.

Adrienne hadn't brought anyone home until Kaz. She hadn't known how her parents would react to her girlfriends. None of them had lasted long enough to be close to serious, so she hadn't had to confront any possible pushback. It wasn't that she thought her parents were homophobic. They had a couple of male friends who were now married to each other. They'd been some of the first they'd known to get married after it had been legalized in New York State. Having queer friends was one thing, a queer child was another, and Adrienne knew her community wasn't always open to queer folk.

"It's early," she found herself saying, "but this could be the real thing. She's so good with Lawrence, Ma. You should see them together. He adores her."

"Does he know about the two of you?"

"No, we haven't told him yet. I want to make sure we're solid before opening that door."

"That's smart." Her ma paused. "Are you happy?"

"Very. I haven't felt like this in a long time."

"Good. You should bring her home for Christmas."

"Oh." The invitation was unexpected. Her parents didn't usually want to meet their kids' boyfriends and girlfriends until they'd been together a while. "I'll see. I don't know what she has planned. She has family down in Philly."

"Well, if she's free, you should bring her with you. I'd like to meet her." Her ma's voice softened. "You sound content, Adrienne. I'm so glad."

"Thanks, Ma." Adrienne glanced over at her computer and noted the time. "I should get going. I have some work to do before lunch is over. I love you, and I'll talk to you soon."

"Love you, sweetie."

Adrienne hung up her phone, a smile on her face. It faded a bit as she considered the ramifications of the call. How would KJ react after Adrienne was the one who'd said they should keep their burgeoning relationship between the two of them. Would she want to spend the holiday with Adrienne's family? Was she even free?

There was only one way to find out.

Adrienne opened her desk drawer and pulled her phone out. *What are you doing for Christmas?*

CHAPTER THIRTY-TWO

"Are you okay?" Adrienne asked.

KJ leaned forward to loosen her seat belt. "Sure. Why do you ask?"

"You're a little fidgety. Positive you aren't a bit nervous?"

"Nervous?" KJ's laugh sounded hollow, even to her. "Why would I be anxious? It's not like I'm going to meet my girlfriend's whole family for the very first time or anything."

Adrienne spared her a quick smile before turning her attention back to the drive. "You didn't have to come. No one would have been upset if you hadn't. I mean, I would have been disappointed not to spend the holiday with you, but I would have understood."

KJ shrugged, the seat belt digging into her shoulders. She ran her hands under it to shift it away from her neck. "What else was I going to do? I'm still not talking to Erik. I think he decided to take his family down to the Keys as an excuse not to spend it with me." She reached over and placed her hand on Adrienne's thigh. "Besides, I get to be with you. Our first holiday as a couple."

"I like the sound of that." Adrienne's face lit up in a huge grin. KJ could have watched her smile all day.

"So what are your parents like?"

"They're pretty cool. Ma is a judge, Daddy is in finance."

"Damn, that's impressive. Way more impressive than two electricians in the family."

"Two electricians?" Adrienne cast her a sideways glance. "Your dad was an electrician, right? Who's the other one?"

"That would be Mom. They met on the job. Windsor County doesn't employ many electricians."

"Your mom was an electrician? That's badass."

"I guess." The talk about her mother was making KJ nervous. She hadn't been comfortable with the topic for years, and beside that, she was supposed to be gathering information on the people she needed to impress in a few hours, not divulging family secrets. "Okay, tell me your siblings' names again. I don't want to mess up and call someone the wrong thing."

"Sure. There's Cedric—"

"He's the oldest one, right? Then you?"

Adrienne nodded. "Yep, then it's Tamra, Justus, and Carleton. He graduated from high school last year."

"Big family. Your parents must have been busy keeping up with all of you."

Adrienne shook her head. "I don't know how they managed it. I feel like I'm running my ass off taking care of the one."

"You're doing it mostly by yourself. Having someone else in there really helps." Things had gotten a lot harder at home after Mom had left. They hadn't seen Dad nearly as much. He'd started picking up side jobs on the evenings and weekends to make ends meet, except when she had games, of course. Fortunately, KJ had been spending most of her time at the rink, and there was always another family around to pick her up for practice. When she'd been home, Erik had usually been there too, even if he seemed to be locked up in his room studying all the time.

"If you say so." Adrienne was quiet for a bit. "There are days when I feel like a failure."

KJ sat straight up in her seat. "What? Why?"

"Everything is so much harder than I thought it would be. Juggling work and making sure Lawrence is getting to school, has three square meals, and is taking somewhat regular baths is a crappy baseline. I see parents that I used to hang out with posting all sorts of extracurricular activities with their kids. I can't swing those. The most enrichment Lawrence gets is a new comic book every week and twice-monthly trips to the library."

"He seems like a happy kid to me," KJ said. "Isn't that what counts?"

"I suppose." Adrienne sighed. "We used to do a lot more when Kaz was living with us."

"We can do more with him than stay in and watch hockey. There's all sorts of stuff that happens at the county rec center. He doesn't strike me as a sporty type, but there are art classes."

"Which all costs money."

"That part is a little harder." KJ thought about it for a moment. "I can put in a few extra shifts at the bar. On a good evening, I could make that much on tips. I'll tell Carlos to keep me in mind if he needs night coverage. Usually I turn him down, but this is important."

"I can't let you do that." Adrienne frowned out the windshield as if she was personally affronted by the passing scenery.

"Why not? I want to help, and it sounds like this is a place where I can." KJ patted Adrienne's thigh. "Let me do this, please, sweetness?"

"Sweetness?" The crease in Adrienne's brow eased and she glanced over at KJ. "That's a new one. I like it." A smile tugged at the corner of her mouth. "Just don't get yourself on the hook for too many shifts. I like our evenings together."

"It's a deal. If it makes you uncomfortable, we can call it Lawrence's birthday present from me. It's a few months away yet, but show me a kid who minds an early birthday." KJ nodded, glad that was sorted out. "Now, tell me about your brothers and sister. I need to know as much as possible going in."

Adrienne chuckled. "It's not some sort of covert operation. You'll be fine."

"I'll be fine once I've prepared. Now dish."

"Okay, okay." Adrienne thought for a bit. "Oh, this is fun. Ma must have told everyone you're coming to visit because Cedric called. He congratulated me on being so progressive as to have a girlfriend."

"That's kind of odd."

"No kidding. It's way more progressive to be married to a musician than it is to have a girlfriend. I don't know what he was thinking, but it's better than the rest of my siblings. I haven't heard word one from them."

"Will they be all right with me?" Meeting new people was always a bit of a balancing act. She never knew how they would be toward her. Only a few people had ever been crappy to her face about her being a lesbian, but it was a risk every time she came out to someone.

"I told Mom you make me happy, and that was enough for her. That's when she said I should bring you to family Christmas."

"That's a relief."

"For me too."

Now that she knew she likely wouldn't have to deal with the homophobia of her girlfriend's family, KJ was starting to relax. It helped that they were still three or more hours from Syracuse. "So, what kind of holiday traditions do you celebrate?"

"Still preparing?" Adrienne asked.

"You know it. I'll stop prepping once we get to the house, how's that?"

"I guess it'll have to do."

KJ sat back in her seat and listened as Adrienne talked about her family's Christmas, what she could expect, and things they'd done in the past. It sounded like heaven, to be honest. If the three days they were going to spend up in New York were even half as idyllic, it would still be amazing. Despite her nerves, she was starting to look forward to it.

* * *

"And here it is." There were still plenty of spots in the driveway, so Adrienne pulled her car in behind her ma's gray SUV. The sun was mostly down below the horizon and the house stood out like a beacon, outlined as it was by hundreds of tiny lights. Rows of white windows broke up the red brick facade as, also wreathed in lights, they marched with precision across the second story. The first floor windows were interrupted by a modestly colonnaded front door that was only partially visible behind a massive holiday wreath. Red and gold garland and bows decorated the dark green shutters on either side of the windows.

"Oh my god, Adrienne," KJ breathed next to her. "Your house looks like it came out of a fancy living magazine."

"You think so?" Adrienne peered at it, trying to see her childhood home through KJ's eyes. To her, it was simply the place she'd lived until she moved out for university. The place she'd had to come back to after her marriage with Kaz ended.

"Yeah. It looks like Martha Stewart designed it, then the guys from *Queer Eye* came in for a decorating blitz." KJ looked down at herself. "I should have worn something nicer."

"You're fine. I'm the one wearing jeans."

"And I'm wearing cargo pants. I didn't bring anything dressy. It's all cargo pants and flannel pajama bottoms. I have slacks at home, but I didn't think…" KJ's voice trailed off as her eyes widened into something close to panic.

"You're perfect the way you are." Adrienne leaned over and pressed a kiss to her girlfriend's cheek. "I think you look great, and no one is going to care. By this time tomorrow, if they're not still wearing pajamas, they'll be changing into them. Daddy cooks a mean turkey."

KJ claimed her mouth for a lingering kiss. "How about we stay here and make out instead," she said when they broke away from each other.

"We'll probably freeze to death."

"I'll keep you warm."

"And my mom is watching from the living room window."

"Oh god!" KJ pulled back from her in horror, almost smacking her head against the window. "I'm making a hash of this whole thing already."

"Be yourself and they'll think you're as adorable as I do." Adrienne waved at the face in the window. Her ma waved back, wearing a bright smile she could see from twenty feet away. "Come on." Adrienne pushed open her door and stepped out into the cold evening air. It wasn't too far to the house, which was good since she hadn't bothered with a hat and gloves. She grabbed her overnight bag from the back seat, then waited at the front of the car for KJ to join her. Together, they made their way up the front walk to the door, which was thrown open as soon as Adrienne's feet hit the top of the brick steps.

"Come here, you," her ma said, her arms held wide.

"Hi, Ma." Adrienne stepped into her ma's embrace. She closed her eyes as her ma's arms folded her close. "It's so good to see you." She squeezed her once more for good measure, then stepped out of the hug and all the way into the house. "Ma, this is KJ."

"KJ." Adrienne's ma stepped up to her girlfriend and gave her a very obvious once-over before stepping back and allowing her into the house.

KJ cast Adrienne a panicked look. "Uh, hello, Mrs. Pierce. It's very good to meet you." She stuck out a tall box gift-wrapped in cheerful green and silver paper. "I brought you some wine."

"Ma, stop torturing my girlfriend," Adrienne said.

Her ma's eyes glittered with amusement. "It's very good to meet you, KJ." She took the box from KJ's hands and set it on the hall table, then wrapped KJ up in a quick hug. "Welcome to our home." She let go and gestured them toward the back of the house. "You call me Moesha. Let's get you two comfortable. You're the first to arrive. You can meet the rest of the family when they get here."

"Thanks, Ma." Adrienne pulled off her coat and held her hand out for KJ's. After a moment, KJ passed it over. She looked a little forlorn without the leather jacket, as if she was missing a layer of armor. She followed Adrienne to the coat closet and waited close by as she hung up their outerwear.

"Dinner won't be for an hour or so," her ma said. "Bring KJ by to say hi to your dad. He's in the kitchen putting the finishing touches on things."

"Yes, Mama." She kicked her boots off onto the plastic tray in the closet, then held out her hand. KJ shucked her own boots, then gratefully grabbed on to her as if clutching at a lifeline.

Her eyes were wide and her head turned, trying to take in everything. As usual, Adrienne's ma had pulled out all the stops on the decorations. Garland festooned the tops of door frames and wrapped the banister. Tasteful groupings of holiday-themed decorations graced the tops of tables and mantels.

"There's mistletoe around, I'll bet you," Adrienne said. "Try and catch me under some."

"I can do that." KJ's eyes sharpened as she tried to find the plant among the decor.

Adrienne didn't know for sure that there was some this year, but there had been many previous years. The number of times she and her siblings had caught their parents under it as kids was more than she'd wanted to deal with. Her parents had found the protestations of their children hilarious and had continued to smooch in doorways whenever they'd found the chance. Come to think of it, as they'd gotten older and the protestations had become weaker, the mistletoe had stopped showing up as frequently.

She led her girlfriend past the stairs and through the dining room into the kitchen. Her daddy looked up from the tray of potatoes and vegetables he was topping with salt.

"Sweet-pea!" He wiped his hands on a small towel, then opened his arms for a hug.

Adrienne launched herself into them. He closed his arms around her and lifted her up, whirling her around in a circle before letting her feet touch the ground again. He laid a loud kiss on her cheek, then let her go.

"Dad, this is KJ."

"I'm pleased to meet you, KJ," he said, his hand outstretched.

"Me too, sir." KJ took his hand and shook it.

"Not sir," he said. "Levar, if you would. You say sir, and I start looking for my Pops, thinking I'm about to catch some trouble."

"Okay. Levar it is. I don't want to get you in trouble or anything."

"I appreciate that." He turned back to the tray of vegetables. "There's wine in the fridge. Why don't you two have a seat and tell me how the drive up went?"

"Thanks, Daddy." Adrienne snagged the bottle, then poured glasses for the three of them.

They spent their time chatting easily with her daddy as he worked on dinner, for which Adrienne was just as glad. Her ma could be very intense, and there were good reasons why she'd only brought Kaz to visit once before they got married. It felt early to be bringing KJ by, but the circumstances had lined up. Coming home felt like a long, warm hug, and it felt surprisingly natural for it to include KJ. Maybe the universe was trying to tell her something.

Her siblings arrived one by one. She would hear her ma greet them at the door, but none of them ended up in the kitchen. She suspected they'd made their way down to the family room instead. At her best count, they were only waiting on one more, though who, she didn't know.

Number five arrived. Her ma had a lengthy conversation with whoever it was. From the sound of the voices, it was one of her brothers, and he was there with a man whose voice wasn't familiar. Had one of them brought one of their cousins along? The discussion took a while, but then her ma appeared in the kitchen with Cedric and a tall man with the darkest skin she'd ever seen in tow behind her.

"There you are," her ma said brightly. "Your brother is here with his boyfriend. This is Jamal." She gave them a wide smile.

"Cedric!" Adrienne sprang off the bar stool and flew over to her brother.

He wrapped her up in an exuberant hug, then put her down carefully, leaving Adrienne only a little short of breath.

"I'm Cedric," he said, leaning around her to extend a hand to KJ.

"I gathered as much," she said, trying to hide a grin but failing miserably. "I'm KJ."

"So you're Cedric's boyfriend?" Adrienne said to the tall man standing next to her ma. "I'm so glad to meet you. Ma didn't say you were coming."

"Ma didn't know he was coming," Moesha said. "I'm very happy to have you, but I only have one room for unmarried guests."

"Ma!" The simultaneous protest came from Adrienne and Cedric.

"Come on, Ma," Cedric said. "I think we're a little old to have our partners staying down the hall instead of in our rooms."

"You know the rules," their ma said. "Unless you're married, no sleepovers."

"I thought that rule was for opposite sex boyfriends slash girlfriends," Adrienne said.

"Nice try. You know the spirit under which that rule was intended." Their ma raised her hand to forestall further interruptions. "It's not like you aren't able to get married anymore, so don't even try that one on me."

"A month is a little early, don't you think?" KJ said quietly. They all turned to stare at her, and she shrank back a bit in her chair until Levar let out a loud guffaw.

"All right, Moesha," Adrienne's dad said. "Let's not terrorize the guests too much." He came around the counter, wiping his hands on his apron. "Jamal, you said?"

"That's right," he said. The faintest trace of an accent colored his speech, but Adrienne couldn't place it.

"How long have you known my son?"

"Three years. We met in grad school."

Levar grinned. "And how long have you been dating him?"

"About two and a half years." Jamal smiled over at Cedric, his teeth startlingly white.

Now it was Cedric's turn to get stared at. He shrugged and scuffed at the floor with the sole of his foot. "I didn't know how you guys would react. When I heard Adrienne was bringing a girlfriend to Christmas, I thought that meant it was all right to bring my boyfriend."

"Oh, honey." Their ma moved up next to him and patted him on the forearm. "Of course it's all right to bring him. Next time, a little more warning would be nice. Jamal, I hope you won't mind sleeping on the air mattress in the guest room. KJ can take the bed."

"Oh, so they can stay in the same room?" Adrienne asked.

"I'm not worried about what they're going to get up to under my roof," her ma replied. Her face was serene, but Adrienne knew an appeal at this point was impossible. She'd made her judgment known, and now it was up to them to comply.

"Yes, Ma," she said. Her sigh of compliance was echoed by Cedric.

"Excellent." Gracious in victory, their ma beamed at them. "Now, let's get the table set. Everyone's here, and if we don't get food out soon, your youngest brother will start foraging."

"We can't have that." Adrienne headed for the cabinets to grab plates. "No, sweetie, you sit down," she said as KJ got up from her stool.

"Really," Moesha said. "We'll put you to work tomorrow. Today, you're a guest. You too, Jamal." She indicated that he should sit, then prodded Cedric toward the kitchen.

Adrienne hoped KJ wasn't freaking out over what she'd gotten herself into. They were a bunch of weirdos, that was for sure. But they were her weirdos, and for the most part she wouldn't have it any other way. The sleeping situations were going to need some tweaking, but if she put her head together with Cedric's she was sure they could come up with a better solution.

CHAPTER THIRTY-THREE

The smell of coffee and frying bacon woke KJ. Rays of sun streamed in through a gap in the drapes, illuminating a room as gorgeously decorated as the rest of the house had been. She lay there for a few seconds, fighting a losing battle with her bladder. Finally, the inevitable results of the previous night's wine could no longer be denied. She pushed back the covers and tried to slip out of bed but was denied by a strong arm that snugged around her waist and pulled her back.

"Don' go," Adrienne mumbled.

"I kind of have to," KJ whispered. "I'll be right back."

Adrienne's eyes popped open. "What time is it?" She lifted her head to squint at the clock on the bedside table. "Almost nine. Oh no, I was supposed to be back in my room before sunrise."

"You're not the only one who missed their cue," KJ said. She peered over the foot of the bed at the air mattress that was as empty as it had been since Adrienne had stolen into the room around midnight and told Jamal that Cedric was waiting for him. There had been a complicated plan around getting everyone back into their assigned beds, but it seemed to have been foiled by their need for sleep.

"Ma is going to kill us." Adrienne sighed. "I guess it's better than having to take on her disappointment alone."

"What's she going to do? You're both adults. It's not like she can spank you."

Adrienne shuddered theatrically. "Don't give her any ideas."

"Really?" KJ was shocked at the notion. It didn't fit at all with her understanding of the woman she'd met the night before. Granted, it was limited, but still.

"Of course not. I think the last time I was spanked was when I was three and I'd tried to stick something in one of the outlets. Ma has way more creative ways of punishing us than by hitting."

"That's good. I guess."

"Is it? At least then we'd know it was over."

"I don't know," KJ said. "This sounds worlds away from the woman I met last night."

"She's still being nice. Don't worry, at some point, I'm sure you'll end up on the wrong side of her."

"I suppose." *It's nice having a mother in your life at all.* "I really need that bathroom. If you want, I'm happy to come downstairs a few minutes after you do so it doesn't look like we spent the night in the same bed."

Adrienne flashed her a bright smile. "You're the best." She leaned forward for a kiss, which KJ was happy to grant. "I'll see you in the kitchen."

The strain on her bladder hadn't been something KJ was exaggerating, and it was no problem at all to take her time before going to breakfast. If she was going to be honest with herself, and it was difficult not to be when she was alone with no distractions, she would have to acknowledge that she was also putting it off. Christmas Day was a big deal.

She stared at herself in the bathroom mirror. *You can do this.* The grin her reflection flashed at her slid off her face. *Too cheesy.* She nodded soberly toward the mirror. *Ugh, too uptight. Why is this so hard?*

What if she doesn't like her present? Wide eyes met hers through the glass. The thought was unexpected, but no less worrisome for that. What she'd gotten wasn't much in the romance department, but Adrienne hadn't given any indication she was into that. She barely wore any jewelry. Her earrings were usually the same studs, and she only switched them out on occasion. She didn't wear rings or bracelets. Sexy lingerie might have been more romantic, but the idea of having Adrienne open a package like that in front of her family turned KJ's stomach. Besides, she was of the opinion that you wore sexy lingerie as a gift; you didn't give it. She'd wracked her brains, even going so far as to call Jamie and talk over her options, which had been difficult given that Adrienne wanted them to keep their relationship under wraps. Her friend had been very helpful, gleeful almost, which told KJ that she probably hadn't been as subtle about her line of questioning as she would have hoped.

"You only have the one present," she finally said to her concerned-looking reflection. "It's the horse you rode in on. There's no point in changing it up now." The metaphor was no less true for being so tortured. "Here goes."

She paused at the top of the stairs on her way back to the guest bedroom. Adrienne's voice floated up to her. She was chatting with one of her brothers, either Justus or Carleton. Their voices were so alike that they'd entertained the family the previous night by verbally ordering each other's phones to do things.

Their cover was intact. KJ hurried back to her room to get a sweatshirt. She slipped a large envelope from her duffel bag into her front pocket.

"Hey, sleepyhead," Moesha greeted her when she made her way into the kitchen. "Coffee? The mugs are in the cupboard above the coffee maker."

"No thanks." KJ smiled. "I'll microwave some water for tea, if that's okay."

"A tea drinker?" Adrienne's mom pulled a tin out of one of the upper cabinets. "No one in the family ever took up that one. Coffee drinkers one and all, just like Levar and me."

KJ lifted one shoulder. "I never got a taste for it. For something that smells so good, it sure tastes foul."

"Help yourself to any of the teas in there," Moesha said with a smile.

"Thank you, ma'am." KJ poked through the assemblage of tea bags until she found a nice Earl Grey that didn't look like it had been hanging out for too long.

"Ma'am, nothing." Adrienne's mom tapped the back of her hand. "Moesha is fine. We don't stand on a lot of ceremony here. I get enough honorifics at work."

"I just bet you do. Adrienne says you're a judge. That's really impressive."

It was Moesha's turn to shrug. "It is what it is. I enjoy the work, and I think I'm pretty good at it. President Obama apparently thought so too. He nominated me back in 2011."

KJ blinked. "Did you get to talk to him?"

"He called with congratulations after I was confirmed by the Senate. It was all very formal and pro forma."

"I can't even imagine what that must have been like."

"It was very exciting. I've done my best to make him proud, ever since."

"Ma, are you telling KJ about how you have an in with a former president of the United States?" Adrienne wrapped her arms around KJ's waist and deposited a gentle smooch behind her ear. KJ turned to give her a proper hug. She really wanted to give Adrienne a thorough kiss, but not with her mom standing not five feet away.

"It's nice to have someone around who hasn't heard all my stories yet." Moesha indicated the coffeemaker. "More coffee? I'm sure you're exhausted."

"I'm fine. I'm dealing with exactly the proper amount of tiredness, thank you very much." Adrienne stared at her mother, who pretended not to see it.

KJ headed over to the cabinet with the mugs. She poured herself some water while mother and daughter made pointed conversation with each other, neither of them willing to admit that they knew that the other knew.

Cedric and Jamal joined them as her water was heating. They seemed completely oblivious to the weird verbal power struggle Adrienne and Moesha were having. They served themselves coffee, then headed to the dining room for the promise of cinnamon rolls.

"That's the last of them," Moesha said. "When you're done assembling your tea, we'll adjourn to the living room."

"Is it Christmas?" Adrienne asked, her eyes shining with excitement.

"It's Christmas." Moesha leaned forward and kissed her on the cheek. "Merry Christmas, baby. Don't make us wait too long." She left the kitchen with her mug in hand. "Merry Christmas, everyone! Let's head to the tree." A stampede of feet met her pronouncement as the family in the dining room decamped en masse to the living room.

"Have I told you how adorable you are?" KJ asked Adrienne.

"Not today." Adrienne wrinkled her nose. "Why do you say that?"

"Well, for one thing, because you always are." KJ tapped Adrienne's nose with the tip of her finger. "And for another, you looked like a little kid when your mom said it's Christmas time."

"I feel like a little kid. I love when we all get together at this time of year. I do wish Lawrence was here. He gets so stoked about the whole thing. It won't take as long to open the presents without him here. My parents have spoiled him, especially the past couple of years."

KJ enfolded Adrienne into a long hug. "I'm sorry he can't be here with us, but I'm glad I get to be."

"I'm glad too. Now how much longer does that water need? The longer we make them wait, the more grief we'll get."

"Then let's get out there. I don't want to give them any reasons to hate me."

"Silly woman." Adrienne pressed a kiss into the side of her neck. "You're doing so well already. Keep on doing what you've been doing. You'll be fine."

"If you say so." KJ let Adrienne go. "Lead the way." She touched the envelope in her pocket to make sure it was still there.

* * *

The pile of presents around the tree had dwindled to a remaining handful. Adrienne leaned against KJ, thankful that Carleton had seen fit to hand them a couple of cushions. As the last to arrive for the opening of presents, they'd had to pull up some floor. The chair and couch space was taken, with her ma reigning over them all from the overstuffed chair next to the fireplace. Her daddy perched on the arm next to her.

Adrienne picked up some scraps of wrapping paper and shoved them into the nearest bag of trash. Tamra passed her another handful, which she added to it.

"I have something for Justus, from Daddy," Carleton announced from the base of the tree.

"Don't throw it," their ma said, right as he let the package fly in his brother's general direction.

Justus snagged the underhand lob without issue, though the gaily-wrapped box was on the bulky side. "I got it, Ma," he said.

"Be careful," she said. "You don't want to break it before you even open it. Now, go on."

Everyone watched as he tore at the red and green paper, revealing a box with a picture of a small kitchen appliance on the front.

"It's a juicer!" Justus seemed truly delighted at the gift. "Thanks so much, Daddy."

"Justus is on a health kick," Adrienne murmured to KJ. "He was kinda pudgy as a teenager. He knocked about seventy pounds off when he was in college, and he's been working to keep it off since."

"Mm-hmm." KJ sighed.

"What's wrong? Too much background?"

"Not at all." KJ gestured to everyone sitting around the living room. "It's two hours later, and you're all still here opening presents. No one seems bored or ready to move on."

"Well, yeah." Adrienne twisted to look at KJ. "How else would we do it?"

"Christmas at my house was always a quick free-for-all. I would dive under the tree from one side, and Erik would go under from the other. We'd find what was ours and open it, then pass Dad his gifts. There weren't this many presents, either. It took about fifteen minutes, tops."

"That is not how we do things here."

"I can see that. It's really nice. How much longer does it usually last?"

"Longest we've ever gone is three hours, but that was a few years ago when Kaz and Lawrence were here. Mom dotes on her grandson." She pointed at a stack of unopened presents away from the tree. "I imagine those are for him."

"Holy crap."

Adrienne nodded. "Agreed. I'm not able to spoil him, so I don't mind if my family does."

"What did you get for KJ, Adrienne?" Tamra asked from the couch behind them.

"Oh, that's right." Adrienne scooted forward to pull the shoebox-sized package from where she'd tucked it next to the fireplace. KJ already had a few boxes around her. Despite not knowing her well at all, her parents had gone out of their way to get her some gifts also. They were thoughtful, if somewhat impersonal presents. No one could have too many pairs of black gloves, especially in this climate. The conical ice scraper had been something Levar had gotten all his children. He'd received a lot of grief for his choice but had stood firm in the face of their criticism, insisting they wouldn't be able to live without them.

As she picked up the box, she hesitated. *Will KJ like them?* It had seemed like such a great idea when she'd ordered them, but in front of the interested eyes of her family, she was starting to doubt herself.

"Well, don't tease her with it," Tamra said. "Hand it over."

"It's okay," KJ said. "She can tease me as much as she wants."

Carleton snickered and KJ's face turned bright red. The tips of her ears flamed so brightly, Adrienne couldn't stop herself from brushing one with her fingers.

"That's not what I–" KJ shot a guilty look at Moesha, who was sipping from her coffee cup, trying to conceal her own smirk. "I mean, teasing is fun. But not like that, I swear."

"Thanks, Tamra," Adrienne said. "Here, open this." She pressed the silver and red package into KJ's hands.

KJ stared at it for a moment, her ears still aflame, then hesitantly slid a finger under one of the seams. With care she hadn't shown for the other gifts from Adrienne's family, she peeled away the paper until she was looking at an orange Nike shoe box.

"Sorry about the presentation," Adrienne whispered.

"It's lovely," KJ murmured back.

"You haven't even opened it."

"It doesn't matter." She lifted the box lid to display six paperback books. Some of them had creases down the spines, and the pages were slightly yellowed. KJ picked up the first one.

"They're African science fiction books in French," Adrienne said. "None of them have been translated into English."

"French books?" Tamra asked.

"I was a French lit major in university," KJ said absently, her eyes glued to the book's back. She pulled out another one and read its back also. "These sound amazing. I took a course on literature in Haiti, but the African and Polynesian lit courses were all 400-level classes, and I hadn't gotten to those when I had to leave." She looked into Adrienne's eyes, suspicious shimmers forming along her bottom lids. "How did you find these?"

"You never know what you'll find on Amazon these days. I'm sorry most of them are used. All but a couple are out of print."

"I love them." KJ pulled her into a hard hug, then loosened her grip and let her go. "My present for you isn't nearly as thoughtful." She pushed an envelope into Adrienne's hands. It was a little creased on the edges.

Adrienne traced a finger over the inscription on the front: *To my Adrienne, from your KJ.* She popped open the reindeer sticker KJ had used to seal the envelope and pulled out a Christmas card that showed a brilliant red cardinal perched on snowy pine boughs. She opened the card and stared at the slip of paper inside. It was a gift certificate, an actual slip of paper instead of a gift card. The logo was two crossed sticks with a puck inside. Beneath that were the words Bob's Hockey Emporium, Harrisburg, P.A. Below that, the amount had been scribbled in with marker.

"KJ, this is too much." She hadn't spent nearly as much on KJ's present. Two hundred dollars was ridiculous. She tried to hand it back.

KJ held up her hands and refused to take it. "Your gear is on the wrong side of elderly. I know you can use some new shin guards, at least. One of yours is held together with safety pins and duct tape. New gear is expensive, especially the good stuff."

"Are you sure? How many extra shifts did you have to take to pay for this?"

"I'm sure." KJ took Adrienne's hands and pressed them gently back in her lap, closing her fingers over the gift certificate. "We'll go down after work one night. It's in Harrisburg, but their hours are weird on the weekend. It depends if the store staff have games or not. I thought Lawrence might like to come."

"Oh, KJ." A tear ran down the side of her nose and landed with a splat on the paper. All at once, she became aware of how quiet the living room was. All eyes were on them. She leaned over and pressed her lips against KJ's. "You're too good to me," she said after they separated.

"I'm nowhere near as good as you deserve, but I'm trying."

"Good answer." Adrienne snuggled into KJ's side, then looked back up to find the rest of her family watching in rapt silence. "Show's over, folks. Let's see what Cedric got for Jamal."

CHAPTER THIRTY-FOUR

Adrienne waited by the window listening to the ring of the phone at her ear. It was snowing, coating the mounded accumulation in her parents' yard with a fresh layer. Christmas had been wonderful. Not far from where she stood, KJ sat in a comfy chair with her feet tucked under her. She was deep into one of the books she'd gotten from Adrienne only an hour before. People were scattered throughout the house. Tamra had joined her parents at the movie theater. Her parents always spent part of Christmas Day at the movies. The kids were welcome to accompany them, but her parents got to pick the movie. It was a tradition they'd been doing for as long as the kids (or at least some of them) were old enough to be left home to watch their siblings. She and Kaz had developed their own traditions, before things had fallen apart. It would be nice to get back to some of those, when her life firmed back up underfoot again.

The smells of Christmas dinner were filling the house. Carleton was keeping a close eye on the turkey in their daddy's absence. This was about as perfect as it could get, save for one glaring absence.

"Hello?" Kaz's voice came through finally. Bits and pieces of conversations filtered through as well. It sounded like he was somewhere with a lot of people, probably her ex-in-laws' living room. It was a bit smaller than this one, but the tree would be as big. There would be way more children also. Kaz was a minority in his family for having only one kid. She winced as a piercing scream rattled down the line.

"Hi, Kaz, it's me." The caller ID would have given away her identity, but Kaz always answered his phone as if he had no idea who was on the other end.

"Oh, hey, Adrienne. Merry Christmas!"

"Is that Mom?" Lawrence's voice filtered through the phone to her.

"Merry Christmas to you too, Kaz. Can I speak with Lawrence?"

"Of course," Kaz said. "Don't hang up after you talk to him, though. I have a question for you."

"No problem." Adrienne waited as he passed his phone over to their son.

"Hi, Mom!" Lawrence was breathless. She had to strain to hear him over the ambient noise of Kaz's family. "It's Christmas!"

"It is!" Adrienne smiled. "Merry Christmas, baby."

"I'm not a baby, Mom. Merry Christmas to you too. I miss you."

"And I miss you, pumpkin bean. Are you having fun with your dad and grandparents?"

Lawrence let the bizarre pet name slide. "Yes! We did presents. I got a Fortress of Solitude! It's huge!"

"That's great." Adrienne made a note to ask her ma which superhero the Fortress went with. "Anything else?"

"Oh yeah." He grew even more breathless as he described all the gifts he'd opened that morning. It seemed he'd received a stack to rival the one that waited to go home with her. She made appropriate noises of interest as he described them to her. It sounded like it was mostly toys and superhero-related items. He was easy to shop for right now. Adrienne hoped that would continue for a while. When he moved out of the superhero phase, gift giving would become much more difficult.

"What did you get?" he asked after winding down the impressive recounting of his Christmas haul.

"Boring stuff," Adrienne said. "New gloves, some sweaters." The sweaters were gorgeous, but Lawrence wouldn't appreciate that they were cashmere.

"What did KJ get you?"

"That one's not so boring." Adrienne glanced over at KJ. She'd never noticed her habit of holding her chin while she read. Her fingers itched to ruffle KJ's hair. "It's a gift certificate to a hockey store in Harrisburg. I can get some new hockey pads."

"Harrisburg. That's where Dad lives!"

"Yes, I know." Trust Lawrence to be excited about that part and completely gloss over the important bits. If she was careful with the money, she could get two sets of pads. There was no doubt that her shin pads were in most dire need of replacement. After that, it was a tossup whether she needed new elbow pads or gloves more. Sure, the palms of her gloves had worn through in multiple places, but her elbow protection had an annoying tendency to twist throughout the game. She hadn't come down on the unprotected joint yet, but it was only a matter of time. "What else are you going to do today."

"Dad says we can go sledding this afternoon. Are you gonna go sledding?"

"No, I think we're all going to stay in and hang out. Gramma and Gramps are at the movies. Maybe I'll see if Carleton has any video games he wants to play with me." His Nintendo Switch had been a source of entertainment for the family for a while, and Carleton enjoyed getting the opportunity to beat the pants off his older siblings.

"Okay." Lawrence's voice faded a little at the end, like he was turning away to look at something his cousins were doing. She was about to lose his interest.

"Have a good day, Lawrence. Merry Christmas again. I'll talk to you tomorrow."

"Okay! Dad wants the phone back."

"I love you, Lawrence." He was already gone; all Adrienne heard was dead air.

She pulled the phone away from her head, and sure enough, he'd disconnected them. A moment later, the phone buzzed and Kaz's face appeared on the lock screen.

"Hi, Kaz."

"Hey. Sorry, I couldn't get the phone back from Lawrence before he hung up." The background was suddenly much quieter. If Adrienne really listened, she could make out some ambient noise, but it grew more faint as he moved through his parents' house.

"So what did you want to ask me?"

"Well, Lawrence has been talking a lot about a KJ."

"And?"

"Like, a lot. It sounds like you two have been spending a lot of time with her."

"So?"

Kaz sighed. "I'm not trying to give you a hard time. You're allowed to date whoever you want."

"You're damn right I am." She bit off the part where she thanked him for his permission. It wasn't that she felt the need to explain herself—he knew she'd dated women before him—but she needed him to understand that he had no right to an opinion on her life, not anymore. He'd squandered that opportunity, and she had every right to bestow the privilege on someone else, which she would damn well do, thank you very much.

From the chair, KJ looked up at her tone. She tilted her head in question.

Adrienne shook her head and took a deep breath.

"So you are dating her," Kaz said. It wasn't a question.

"I am, not that it's any business of yours." She smiled, trying to soften her voice, if only for KJ's benefit. "You no longer have a say, remember?"

"I do remember, but that doesn't mean I don't still care about you. And I want to make sure this is going to be all right for Lawrence, too."

"I also want what's best for our son, which is why I haven't told him." Adrienne started pacing back and forth in front of the window. "I'll tell him when the time is right. When I know what we have is solid. It's only been a month. I want his relationship with her to proceed naturally, to get on solid footing. If I find out that KJ and I aren't compatible or something, I don't want him to go through losing someone like that in his life again. He's had enough upheaval in his life the past few years."

"That's not fair."

"Maybe it is and maybe it isn't. Doesn't change the facts. We were a family, now we're not. I get to move on."

"Okay, okay." Kaz hesitated, then continued. "Maybe I shouldn't have brought it up. I only wanted to be sure Lawrence is being considered in all of this."

"Don't you ever assume I'm not considering my own son. He is my first consideration, before anything else. He always has been."

The other end of the call was quiet.

"Are you still there?" Adrienne asked.

"Yeah, I'm still here. I'm not sure what to say."

"Let's keep it that way then. Please don't tell Lawrence. I want to be the one to let him know when the time comes."

"I can do that."

"Good."

"Hey, more than anything else, if you're happy, then I'm happy." Despite the thorniness of their conversation, he sounded sincere.

Adrienne reminded herself that Kaz wasn't an asshole. She would never have married him if he was. While she didn't agree with his concerns, she also would have wanted some reassurance if she'd discovered he'd been seeing someone who was spending a lot of time around their son. Things were going well with her and KJ, and even if they ultimately ended up breaking up, she would be all right. Lawrence wasn't as resilient; he shouldn't have to get used to people coming and going from his life like that.

Her heart felt like it gave a little stutter at the notion of their relationship ending. She glanced over at KJ, who was doing her best to pretend she was engrossed in her book. Her eyes flicked over and caught Adrienne's. She raised an eyebrow.

"Are you still there?" It was Kaz's turn to ask the question.

"I am. Have a Merry Christmas, Kaz. Try not to let our son eat his weight in candy canes."

"I'll do my best. Merry Christmas, Adrienne." Kaz disconnected their call.

Adrienne stared at her phone for a second, then stuffed it into the pocket of her pajama pants.

KJ crossed the room and joined her in looking out at the snow. "Everything all right?"

"Kaz wanted to know if we're dating."

"Ah." She slid an arm around Adrienne's waist and snugged their bodies together. "And you told him?"

"Of course I did. I'm not ashamed of being with you. I didn't appreciate that he felt the need to pry or the insinuation that I might be doing something unseemly with you in front of Lawrence."

"I can see that. But we both know we've been perfect little angels around him, so why get bent out of shape with your ex?"

"Force of habit, I guess." Adrienne leaned her head on KJ's shoulder. "We argued a lot before we divorced. It's way better now that everything's out in the open, but we were both really touchy for a while. It's too easy for me to slip back into that frame of mind with him."

"Anything I can do to help?"

"Not really. I need to remind myself that I'm not in that situation anymore. That I have someone who loves to be with me in the ways he couldn't."

KJ's arm tightened around her. "You know it."

Adrienne heard the lascivious grin in her voice. Heat flared to life in her groin. She groaned and buried her face in KJ's shoulder.

"What is it?"

"When you talk to me like that, I want to take you upstairs and rip your clothes off."

"So why don't we? Everyone else is busy. They'll never notice if we nip off for a quick canoodle."

"This is my parents' house." Adrienne glanced over at the dining room. Everyone was focused on the puzzle.

"And they're not here."

"Yeah, but my siblings are."

"So we'll have to be quiet."

"Oh dear." Her belly tightened at the idea. "Are you sure you can manage that?"

"I can if you can." KJ grinned widely.

"All right, but we can't make a sound."

"What are we waiting for then?" KJ whispered in her ear.

"What indeed?" She slipped out of KJ's arms, then took her hand. Casually, they made their way out of the living room. No one took the least notice of them. They shared a smile that brimmed with anticipation, then made their way quietly up the stairs.

Which way? KJ mouthed at the top of the steps.

Adrienne pulled her toward her room. Best to be somewhere they wouldn't be interrupted. She locked the door behind them.

KJ turned toward her and Adrienne was already wrapping her arms around her. Their lips met, tongues entwining. Her arousal crested sharply, tightening within her. Adrienne moaned deep in her throat. She slid her hands up under KJ's top, then made a small sound of frustration when she discovered the bra impeding her progress. KJ let go of her hips to unsnap the offending article, then pulled Adrienne tight against her.

Adrienne bit her lower lip as the thrumming deep within increased. She needed to feel KJ's skin. She wormed her hands between them and up around KJ's breasts.

KJ tipped her head back toward the ceiling, her eyes unseeing as Adrienne's fingers closed on her nipples, rolling the sensitive flesh back and forth between her fingertips. Adrienne grinned, thrilled at the effect she had on her girlfriend. The pressure in her center twisted tighter still. She leaned forward and nibbled along the side of KJ's neck, heading toward earlobes that she knew through experimentation were very sensitive. KJ had to stay quiet, they both did, but oh, how Adrienne wanted to hear her scream.

KJ's whole body shuddered when Adrienne gently bit down on the soft flesh of her earlobe. Her fingers flexed on Adrienne's hips.

Adrienne walked KJ backward, through the room, never letting up on the assault on her breasts and neck, until they were stopped by the side of the bed. She pushed KJ down, then quickly straddled her hips. She slid her nails up KJ's belly, reveling in the feeling of her muscles and skin, in the ripple of gooseflesh.

KJ gasped. Adrienne's center was now a thrumming ball of tension. It wouldn't take much to undo it, but not before KJ came. She wanted, needed her girlfriend to share in her pleasure. She pushed up KJ's top and bent to lave one nipple with the flat of her tongue. KJ's hips jerked against hers, then Adrienne felt a hand slipping down the front of her pants. She lifted her hips in tacit permission, welcoming KJ's presence between her thighs, then stifled a sharp groan. It was a wonder she didn't burst into flames right there. KJ's fingers parted the lips around her most sensitive of places. They skated past the clit that ached to be touched, and yet direct stimulation would be too much, too sharp. Somehow, the act of skirting it was even more pleasurable than actual touch would have been, and it pushed at her with an urgency that couldn't be denied.

Adrienne leaned over, pulling KJ with her until they lay side by side, facing each other, the sound of their panting breaths heavy in her ears. She pulled at the elastic waistband of KJ's pajama pants, then gave a small pout of disappointment when she discovered a layer of boxer shorts in her way. She insinuated her fingers through the fly opening. Her fingertips brushed over tightly coiled hair wet with the evidence of KJ's arousal. KJ thrust her hips forward, seeking more pressure, more contact.

KJ's fingers slipped lower, grazing Adrienne's opening, but not entering. Adrienne clamped her mouth shut on the noises she yearned to make. The act of holding in the sounds of her satisfaction was sending her to greater heights. Illicit pleasures were so much sweeter when shared. She moved toward KJ, her own fingers stilled in their quest as she drew her girlfriend in. KJ's other hand clamped down on her thigh, holding her in place. The tips of her nails were hard points through the thin fabric of Adrienne's pants, adding to the crescendo of sensation that surged within her.

Adrienne shuddered, biting her lip on the cry that threatened to break free of her. This was no longer the time for subtlety, for teasing. She skimmed down the front of KJ's mound, taking her swiftly with two fingers. She pushed in as far as she could go, encouraged by the sharp intake of breath and the further tightening of KJ's hand on her leg. They paused, frozen on the edge of their respective orgasms, each poised, waiting for the other.

A breathy laugh escaped Adrienne's lips. So much for teasing being over. She thrust her hips against KJ's hand, while thrusting her fingers deep within her girlfriend. KJ rocked forward to meet her, her own hand mimicking the same movements within Adrienne. Her head swam with the sensations KJ awoke in her, the same pleasures she was bringing to her girlfriend. Adrienne gritted her teeth, not wanting to go over the rapidly looming precipice knowing that KJ hadn't yet made it there. KJ's eyes gleamed over a similar grimace.

She clamped her eyes shut as all sense of her body fell away, leaving behind only the pleasure that had been rising through her at KJ's hands. Her girlfriend released a deep gasp at the same time. Adrienne tried to resist the wave that was lifting her, determined that KJ should be brought to the same crest. She needn't have worried. KJ shuddered and writhed against her, caught in the same throes as Adrienne. They surged toward one another, wrapping each other up in a tangle of limbs and sensation. The moment expanded and she let go, surrendering to it. She was aware only of KJ within her and her fingers being squeezed by muscles deep within KJ.

Finally, her orgasm receded, leaving her panting and sweating within KJ's embrace. She relaxed, melting into the afterglow, secure in KJ's arms.

"Oh, Adrienne." KJ's voice rumbled deep in her chest, replete with satisfaction. "That was mind-blowing. You just…" Her voice trailed off.

"So did you." Adrienne sighed. "Let's stay like this forever."

"I'm happy to do that." KJ reached over and traced the curve of her cheekbone with her thumb.

"Deal." Adrienne looked up at KJ. She cupped her girlfriend's cheek. "I love you, do you know that?"

KJ's eyes glowed, and a slow smile suffused until her face radiated joy. "Really?"

"Really, really."

"I love you, too." She sighed and pulled Adrienne in for a hug.

Adrienne listened to KJ's heart tripping in her chest, only now starting to slow down. "That's so nice to hear."

"I didn't want to say anything. I was afraid you might think I was pressuring you to tell Lawrence or something like that. I've been wanting to say something for a week or more now."

Adrienne laughed. "You would have been fine, you big goof. I know you'd never use Lawrence as a bargaining chip. It's one of the many reasons I love you so much."

KJ's shoulders shifted against her in a shrug. "He's a great kid, and he's yours. Of course I want to spend time with him."

"That's good. We are a package deal, you know."

"And I wouldn't have it any other way." KJ's chest trembled with laughter. "Well, aren't we a couple of stereotypical queers. Not even a month, and we're professing our love for each other."

"Don't rent the U-Haul quite yet. I still want to do this right."

"And I'm okay with that. I'll take as much time as you need. I'm not going anywhere."

"I know." Or at least, so she hoped. It was starting to seem more likely. Adrienne snuggled down into KJ's arms, relaxing into the warmth and comfort they offered. When was the last time she'd felt this secure? It had been a while, that was for sure, and for the time being, she was prepared to believe it could last.

CHAPTER THIRTY-FIVE

The back door creaked open and Chester disappeared from his position at KJ's elbow. His supervision hadn't been as helpful as he'd seemed to think. KJ was still having no luck getting the feed from her laptop to run through the television.

At least there was no barking. It had been weeks since he stopped sounding the alarm when Adrienne and Lawrence came over. KJ continued to fiddle with her computer, hoping something might work if she simply refreshed this setting or rejigged that driver. Her rate of success was still zero, even though this was the third time she'd run through the troubleshooting steps she'd found online.

"Hi, KJ," Adrienne said as she walked into the living room. "What's up?"

"Ugh." KJ pushed the laptop into the center of the coffee table. "This piece of—" she glanced over to see if Lawrence was in the room. He was. "—poop isn't working for..."

KJ gritted her teeth. A good swearing session was exactly what she needed, but not in front of Adrienne's son. The last forty-five minutes of swearing hadn't done much anyway.

Frustrated, she stood, stabbing her hands through her hair. "I can't get the laptop to sync with the TV. I spent all my time trying to get this to work, so I don't even have dinner made." She blinked back tears of frustration before they could fall. "I'm so sorry, you two. It looks like tonight's plans are a bust."

"Aww." Lawrence's face fell. "Does that mean we have to go home?"

Adrienne glanced over at her.

"Of course not," KJ said. "I'm happy to have you over. It's more that Tuesday night hockey has been our thing, you know."

"We can do things that aren't hockey-related, you know," Adrienne said.

"What are these 'non-hockey-related things' you speak of?" KJ crooked her fingers into air quotes. "That doesn't compute."

"Neither does your laptop," Lawrence said.

"Someone is quick on the draw today." KJ flopped over onto the couch. "Since you both seem to want to abuse me, maybe you can come up with a better plan…"

"How about games and pizza?" Adrienne said.

"Pizza!" Lawrence grinned, his eyes bright. "Can we get pepperoni? But no Monopoly."

"Monopoly pizza?" KJ asked. "I don't think you have to worry about that. Little Sneezer's doesn't make that flavor."

"Not the pizza," Lawrence said. "The game!" He cast a glance over his shoulder at his mom. "We can't trust her with Monopoly."

"Another one?" KJ asked.

"Little Sneezer's?" Adrienne said. "That's a new one."

"It was one of Erik's favorite jokes growing up. Nice redirect, by the way."

"Oh, fine." Adrienne crossed her arms and affected a mock irritated look. "One or two of my siblings may have ratted me out to Lawrence that I used to cheat at Monopoly when we were kids. But I'm so much better than I used to be! I haven't cheated in years."

"Sure, Mom." Lawrence patted her on the arm. "We definitely believe you."

"Oh, yeah." KJ nodded. "We sure do."

"You two…" Adrienne tried to look annoyed, but she couldn't hide the amused sparkle in her eyes.

"So we've established pepperoni pizza," KJ said, trying to get the night's plans back on track. "I'm up for that. How about you, b-Adrienne?"

Her girlfriend raised an eyebrow at her near slip. "Let's do half cheese, half pepperoni. It gets a little too salty for me."

"I can live with that." She turned to Lawrence. "Do you want to pick out our game?"

His eyes lit up. "Sure!"

"You know where they are. Pick anything you want." She looked over at Adrienne. "If Monopoly is off the table, Risk probably should be too."

"Oh, yeah," Lawrence said. He squatted in front of the cabinet next to the TV stand and opened the door. Of the two dozen brightly colored boxes stuffed into the space, half were little kid games for KJ's nieces. The others were games that had been around since before her father died, some since she was young.

"I'll order the pizza," Adrienne said.

"Are you sure?"

"I am." Adrienne pulled out her phone. "You feed us multiple times a week without letting me chip in for groceries. I can manage pizza every now and again."

Lawrence was engrossed in the boxes, but KJ still lowered her voice. "I really don't mind. I know you're strapped by the end of the month."

The smile that crossed Adrienne's face was a little strained. "Things get tight, but we're not destitute. Besides, it's not like you have money rolling in."

KJ held up her hands. "Sorry, I didn't mean to imply…"

Adrienne sighed. "Please try not to jump to any conclusions. Yes, I'm a single mom, and yes, my cash flow isn't what I'd like it to be. All that means is that I need to be careful. It doesn't mean I need you to white-knight it for me."

"What do you mean?" KJ asked.

"I don't need to be rescued." She tipped her head. "My life isn't broken and in need of someone to fix it."

"Is that what I'm doing?" KJ cringed. "That's not what I meant, I swear." Adrienne didn't need anyone to come to her defense. She was stronger than anyone KJ knew, probably stronger than she was herself. "I was only trying to help."

"And you do, every day in so many ways. I'm not your damsel."

"Of course not." KJ snorted at the idea of Adrienne lolling about waiting to be saved from anything. She held up her hands. "I didn't mean to imply anything. If you want to get pizza, that's no problem. Let me know if I come on too strong again."

Before Adrienne could respond, Lawrence's voice interrupted them from behind.

"What about this one?" He held up a square box with a locomotive on the front.

"Ticket to Ride?" KJ said. "I haven't played that for a while. Yeah, of course it's okay. Have you played before?"

Lawrence shook his head as he brought the box over to her. From the kitchen, KJ could hear Adrienne talking to someone. A brief point of shame sparked in her head. She hadn't meant to be so over the top. And Adrienne was right, she wasn't exactly swimming in cash herself. The money she made from Carlos was decent since it was tax-free, but she had to put in more hours every year to cover expenses without asking Erik for extra cash. It was past time to figure that out. Of course that would mean figuring out what she wanted to do with her life. What did she want to be when she grew up?

"Are you okay, KJ?"

She shook her head. "Sorry, buddy, I got distracted." She looked down at the box in her hands. "This was one of my dad's favorite games."

"It looks fun."

"It is, though I'm going to have to remember how to play it. It's been years." So many years. Dad hadn't been in any shape to play anymore after she'd moved back home.

"If it makes you sad, we don't have to play," Lawrence said.

"Oh no, it's not making me sad. Or at least not bad sad. It's one of those things, you know? It reminds me of him and how he's not here anymore, but it also makes me happy to think about the fun we had playing." KJ smiled down at Lawrence. "You know in the basement, there's that area that's up on the wooden platform?"

"Yeah?"

"He used to have a huge model train setup down there. It covered the whole platformed area."

"Really? That's huge! What was it like?"

"It was amazing." KJ set the box down on the table and opened it up. If she remembered correctly, the board went like so, and the cards went down in a line to one side. "He was an electrician, so it was all wired up. He built most of the scenery from scratch, but the houses lit up and cars drove on the roads. The train looped through an area that looks a lot like this one."

Lawrence reached over for the game's instructions. "Do you still have it?"

"No." KJ looked down at the dozens of tiny plastic train cars still in their little plastic bags. "We sold it off after he died. Most of the pieces went to his buddies who were also big into model trains. It was kind of nice to see a lot of them again. They'd come over a lot when we were kids, but not so much after Dad got sick."

"Oh." Lawrence flipped through the booklet. "That's too bad."

"It is, I guess."

"But how great is it that you still have this to remember him by?" Adrienne slipped past her to join Lawrence at the table but not before resting a hand lightly on her shoulder for a moment.

"It is nice. I'm glad you picked out this game, Lawrence."

"Me too," Lawrence said.

"So pizza is on the way?" KJ raised an eyebrow inquiringly at Adrienne.

She nodded.

"And Lawrence has figured out how to play?" She turned her gaze to Adrienne's son.

"Maybe?"

"Good enough for me," KJ said. "Let's see if we can get a test game figured out before dinner gets here."

* * *

"Nice job, baby," Adrienne said, surveying the board in front of them. Lawrence had chosen to be green for their second game, after informing them it was Green Lantern's color. Her yellow pieces were scattered around the board, while KJ's black took up a good portion of the northeast on the map, but the green train was the only one that stretched from one coast to the other.

"I think you earned the longest route bonus," KJ said. "There's no doubt about that." She slid the little card over to a beaming Lawrence.

"How many points did I get?" he asked.

"It's pretty obvious you won," Adrienne said. "Do you really need us to count them out?"

"Yep!"

KJ grinned widely. "He's definitely your kid."

"He's my kid who is wearing half a pizza on his new T-shirt," Adrienne said.

Lawrence looked down. His face dropped when he realized how much pizza sauce and pepperoni juice decorated his front. "Oh no, Mom. It's all over Groot!" He plucked at the stained fabric and looked up at her. "What do I do?"

"You can soak it in the utility sink in the basement," KJ said. "I'll wash it after it sits for a bit. The stains won't even have time to set, I promise."

"Really?"

"Really."

"Go on, Lawrence," Adrienne said. "We'll get the score tallied while you take care of your shirt." He'd made the mess, and it was up to him to clean it up. They'd been operating under those rules for a few years now.

"Yeah, okay." He slid out of his chair but paused. "Make sure she's counting right."

"You got it," KJ said. "Do you want me to help him?" she asked after he'd left the room.

"No, he can manage it." Adrienne smiled. "Besides, now that he's going to be occupied for a bit, I can do this." She took KJ's hand and leaned forward.

KJ didn't hesitate. When she tasted her girlfriend, Adrienne had to close her eyes. Their evenings together were so much better than not being able to see each other at all, but it was the sweetest torture to be so close to KJ and not be able to show her all the affection Adrienne desperately yearned to.

Their breath mingled, their tongues greeting each other for the first time in a few days. The heat she was used to banking whenever KJ was near flared into flames that roiled inside her. She moaned into KJ's mouth.

Her girlfriend's lips moved into a smile against hers. KJ's hand slipped around her back and under her shirt. Adrienne was tugged forward, her body molding against KJ. They only had this brief moment, but Adrienne was going to take advantage of it.

"Should I put detergent in?" Lawrence's voice coming through the kitchen yanked her back to her senses. "Mom? What are you doing?"

The accusation in his tone bit deep. Adrienne stiffened against KJ, then extricated herself from their embrace.

"Hey, Lawrence," KJ said, trying to sound like he hadn't walked in on them kissing at the dining room table.

"Why were you kissing?" His eyes sparked with anger.

"Oh, Lawrence." Adrienne walked him over to the kitchen table and sat him down in a chair. She shot KJ a significant glance, trying to tell her to stay put. She returned her attention to her son, squatting down and looking him in the eyes. "This isn't how I wanted to tell you. I'm sorry for that."

"Tell me what?" He crossed his arms over his chest.

Adrienne put a hand on his arm. "KJ and I...We're girlfriends. We were kissing because that's what people who are dating do."

"But you and Dad!" Lawrence pulled his arm away from her. "You don't like girls. You like Dad."

"It's possible to like boys and girls," Adrienne said, her voice patient despite the pang in her chest as he turned away.

KJ stepped forward, her mouth opening to say something. Adrienne shook her head, and she hesitated, then stopped in the doorway.

"But Dad!" Lawrence's whole face had flushed an angry crimson and was getting redder.

"Lawrence, I love your dad," Adrienne said, "but we aren't married anymore, and for good reason. I know it's hard, but you need to understand that we're not getting back together. This is part of moving on. Your dad will always be your dad, and you will always be his son. KJ isn't going to change that."

The glare he shot in KJ's direction could have peeled paint. KJ winced, pain in her eyes at the strength of Lawrence's rejection. Adrienne cringed along with her. When she'd imagined what it would be like when they told him the truth about their relationship, she hadn't foreseen the depth of the anger he was projecting. Normally, Lawrence was so laidback, it was easy to forget that a temper lurked in there.

"I don't want her to be with you," Lawrence announced.

"That's not your decision to make," Adrienne said firmly. "I hear that you're mad about this, and I understand where you're coming from, but KJ is my girlfriend, which means you'll be seeing her with me."

Lawrence jumped up from his chair and stormed out through the kitchen, giving KJ as wide a berth as he could manage.

Adrienne closed her eyes and sagged forward, leaning against the chair Lawrence had vacated. KJ rushed over to her, squatting down next to the chair and taking Adrienne's hands.

"That could have gone better," Adrienne said without opening her eyes. She squeezed KJ's hands.

"I guess so," KJ said. "I wasn't expecting him to be so upset."

"I didn't want him to find out this way." Adrienne opened her eyes, then reached up and cupped KJ's cheek, her fingers warm and strangely reassuring on her skin. "I'm sure it would have gone better under different circumstances. He was completely blindsided. None of us would be very graceful in his place."

"Yeah." A tear escaped KJ's lower eyelid. She scrubbed it away.

"He'll come around. He really does like you. Even if you didn't have Chester, he'd still want to spend time with you."

KJ nodded, but her shoulders slumped.

"Oh, KJ." Adrienne wrapped her up in a hug. "We'll get through this. I promise. This is a little bump in the road, that's all." She rubbed the small of her girlfriend's back for a second, then reluctantly let go. "We should go."

"You'll be back?" KJ asked in a small voice.

"Absolutely. Lawrence needs a bit of space and time, but he's going to have to get used to this. To us."

KJ nodded, her head down. It snapped up as a thought occurred to her. "Hey, since Lawrence knows about us now, does that mean I can tell other people? Are you ready to take this public?"

"You know what?" Adrienne said. "I am."

CHAPTER THIRTY-SIX

KJ leaned against the headboard and stared at the print hanging on the wall on the other side of Adrienne's bedroom. The silhouettes of dark-skinned women with their heads swathed in large wraps of fabric faded into a red-brown background. Her brain tried to count the number of heads while refusing to dwell on what she was about to do. Below the print were wooden crates stuffed with CDs of bands she'd never heard of. An ancient CD player sat next to it, on its own crate.

What was the album with the bright green spine? KJ squinted at it, then realized what she was doing. Avoiding the discussion wasn't going to make it any easier.

She closed her eyes, then stabbed a finger down on the icon of her brother's face and lifted the phone to her ear. It was slippery, but only because her hand was so sweaty. She ran her other hand over the back of her head, reveling in the freshly shorn hair. The haircut had been past due, by about twelve months. It had been years since she'd let it get that long. It felt good to get it back to where she recognized herself in the mirror.

Adrienne's hand was a comforting warmth on her thigh as KJ waited. She hadn't spoken with Erik in three months, not since her blowup at him at Thanksgiving. Sure, there had been a text from him late Christmas Day, one she'd responded to, but aside from that, they'd had no contact.

On one hand, KJ would have been just as happy if he didn't pick up. They could go back to ignoring each other, and she wouldn't have to risk an awkward conversation with him. On the other hand, she missed her nieces. Watching Adrienne with her brothers and sister at Christmas had opened her eyes to how much she was missing. Maybe she and Erik wouldn't ever get to that level of comfort and enjoyment of each other's company, but she was willing to take the first step if they could get closer.

It didn't hurt that she'd been talking this plan over with Adrienne for the past week and a half.

"Hello?" Erik's voice finally came through the phone.

"Hi, Erik!" The excitement level was a little forced; KJ dialed it back. "Happy birthday."

"Um, yeah," he said. Here came the awkward. "Thanks."

And there the conversation sat, like a pile of cold dog vomit that everyone in the house was avoiding in case someone else decided to step forward and clean it up first. KJ waited for a moment to see if he would do any of the conversational heavy lifting, but Erik said nothing. Why should that change now?

"So you guys planning anything? Going out on the town?" It was only a little after four. Lawrence was in his bedroom working on a new piece of art, using the supplies she'd gotten him for the holiday. Watching his face light up when he opened it for the small celebration she'd had with him and his mom the weekend before Christmas had been wonderful. Of course things between them had taken a turn since then, but he was still using them, which was something. As chilly as he'd been since walking in on his mom and her, he hadn't thrown out her gifts to him. KJ held tightly to that small solace, checking to see if he was still using them every time he came over.

"Sophie and the girls are taking me out for dinner," Erik said. The tension in his voice eased a little. "We're going to the Capital Grille. Harper and Emma are looking forward to getting all dressed up."

"Are they really?"

"Well, Harper is. Emma…Emma is less excited."

"I don't think I've seen her willingly put on a dress since she was three."

Erik laughed. "She takes after her aunt on that one. How old were you when you laid down in the middle of the living room and refused to go to church if you had to wear that skirt?"

"Eight, I think. Mom wasn't thrilled."

"But she did talk you out of the house wearing it."

"Only because she let me wear my favorite jeans under them."

"Dad was fit to be tied. He thought that was so inappropriate."

"Inappropriate would have been him hauling me over his shoulder to Mass like he was threatening." KJ grinned at the memory. Her mom had been resigned, but her father had been willing to try her in a contest of wills. Mom had talked him out of it, but he'd never really let it go. He did forgive KJ, but not her mom. Not long after that their relationship deteriorated completely.

"I don't think we're going to go that route," Erik said dryly.

"Then maybe let her wear pants under. Or skip the dress altogether. There's no reason she can't look nice in things other than skirts. A nice pair of pants and a vest, for example."

"You don't think that's too…"

"Dykey?" KJ deliberately kept her voice light. This was supposed to be a call of reconciliation, not one where she found other reasons never to talk to her brother again. "What on earth is wrong with that?"

"I don't want her to get teased. Kids are cruel."

"Because they pick up on other people's discomfort." KJ sighed. "Look, maybe she'll decide dresses are something she likes when she's older. There are pictures of you running around in a tutu and cowboy boots when you were four, but I haven't seen you in that outfit lately. Unless there's something you're not telling me." Silence met her quip. "Let her be comfortable.

She'll be happier at dinner, you won't have to yell at her, she won't cry. Voila, birthday dinner is saved, all thanks to your wiser younger sister."

"You have a point."

"Of course I do."

"All right, let's not go overboard. Say…" Erik paused. "Can you give me a few minutes?" KJ heard him ask someone in the background.

"Of course," Sophie said back, her voice so faint in the phone that KJ almost couldn't hear it. There were a few rustling noises, then the sound of a door closing.

"About Thanksgiving," he finally said.

"Yeah?"

"I said some things I wish I hadn't."

"I'm not exactly proud of how that all went down, either."

"I'm sorry," Erik said quietly. "I'm sorry you ended up with the hardest job. I didn't know you felt so strongly about it. You were always so willing to help out, to get things done."

"What was I going to do? Tell you to drop your family and take it on?" Her voice sharpened. Adrienne took her hand and squeezed it. KJ smiled at her, her heart rate dropping back down closer to normal. "I know why things shook out the way they did. I know why I ended up being the one. I even agree, but that doesn't mean that I don't have some resentment. It was hard, Erik. The hardest thing I've ever done. It changed me. I'm not the kid I was when I left school."

"I see that now. It wasn't fair to you."

"It wasn't fair to anyone, least of all Dad. The situation sucked. We did the best we could."

"I guess that's why—" He stopped himself and exhaled sharply through his nose. KJ recognized the sound from the arguments they'd had as kids.

"Just say it, Erik." KJ took a deep breath, then exhaled slowly through her mouth. Adrienne had taught her the technique to keep from getting angry with him so quickly. "We both have things we need to say. Let's get it out there and over with, then we can move past it."

Adrienne nodded her approval. She let go of KJ's hand and shifted to rub her back in long, slow circles. KJ leaned into the contact.

"If you say so." He inhaled deeply. "I know you had to give up a lot and your life ended up on hold for five years. That's why I don't understand why you're wasting your time in that house. You should be ready to get out of there, to move on and get on with life. It's really frustrating, because I know you can be so much more than a small-town bartender."

"Maybe." KJ shook her head. "But I don't know anymore. I told you I'm not the same person I was. I don't know who I am. I need time to figure that out. Working for Carlos gives me space for that."

"If you didn't spend so much time on hockey—"

"Hockey isn't up for debate." *We are so not having this conversation today.* "It's the one thing I had to get me through. I know you see it as a money and time sink, but it kept me sane. It still does. It allowed me to be me and gave me a space where I could let go of the crap I'd been dealing with. If you're going to lecture me on the thing that kept me from going round the bend, then we should stop talking right now."

"But…No, you're right." Erik laughed. "Sophie gave me an earful after our argument, you know."

"Did she?"

"Oh, yes she did! She told me my line about the girls was asinine and insulting to your intelligence."

"She's not wrong."

"No, she isn't. I'm really sorry about that. Instead of trying to understand why you weren't moving on things with the house and Dad's stuff, I tried to find an argument that would persuade you to do what I wanted."

KJ blinked. Two apologies in one conversation? One had been a surprise, but two? "Apology accepted."

"Now that we have that cleared up, we do need to talk about Dad's estate. I haven't only been riding you about it because I'd decided you needed to move on with your life. I've already filed for an extension on the execution of the will, but we can't drag it out forever. The state isn't going to allow that."

"I know." KJ sat up straight. "Which is why I have a proposition for you."

"A proposition?"

"Yes. You don't have to say yes or no right away. In fact I wish you wouldn't. All I want is for you to listen, go away, and think about it. Do that lawyer brain thing you do, then let me know if it'll work. Legally, and for you."

"Okay." KJ could hear Erik holding back the judgment. It sounded like it was taking an almost physical effort. She smirked as she imagined what his face must look like as he did his best to combat his nature.

"Dad left us half the house each, right."

"Yes."

"You want to sell the house."

"Also, yes."

"I don't want to sell the house."

"I'm aware."

"Would you let me get through this?" KJ asked. "You don't have to rebut every line."

"Sorry. Please, go on."

"Good." Here's where things would get dicey. "You want to sell, I don't, and I can't afford to buy you out. I don't have that kind of money lying around." She paused for a breath to let that sink in. "What do you say to a rent-to-own kind of situation, but for your half of the house."

"I'm…not really sure what you mean?"

"So basically I pay you for your half of the house, but over time. Like I send you monthly rent and once I've paid back what you would have gotten if we sold it, then we're even."

"We'd have to get the house appraised. And there are going to be fees."

"I get that," KJ said. She knew her impatience was coming out in her voice. "I don't want you to run down the details right yet. I want you to think about it and let me know if you're all right with the concept. If it's a compromise that you can live with."

"Are you able to afford it? You haven't been paying anything to live there. I agreed to cover property taxes and utilities, but I'm not going to continue doing that going forward."

"I have some irons in the fire on that front." Adrienne had been such a big help in that regard. It remained to be seen if her plan to become an online French tutor would pan out, but it would definitely supplement the money she was getting from Carlos. She'd checked what the house might be assessed for, and it wasn't a huge amount, not with it being located in the back end of beyond. By the time Erik had thought things over and gotten back to her, KJ was confident she would know more.

"If you say so. Let me talk to Sophie, since we kind of have plans for that money."

"That's completely reasonable. And I'm up for paying fees or other costs we might run into doing things this way. I'm sure there's a bunch of stuff I'm not thinking about. I also know you'll want a contract. You are a lawyer, after all."

"A contract would protect both of us."

"I knew you'd say that."

"Yeah, well." Erik's smile came through in his voice.

"Are we good?"

"I feel like I should be asking you that."

"I'm good. It feels a lot better to have gotten that out. I wish I'd done it differently, but it's good that we both know."

"Agreed. On all parts of it." Erik sighed. "I need to get going. Thank you for the birthday wishes and the chat, but if I take much longer, we'll miss our reservation. I will for sure talk to my wife and I'll let you know what the answer will be soon."

"Thanks, Erik." KJ hesitated. They never said the words to each other, but maybe it was time to start. "Happy birthday, big brother. I love you."

"I love you too, pipsqueak. And thanks."

"You're welcome. " She let out a long breath. "Bye."

"Yep, goodbye."

The line went dead as Erik hung up.

"That seemed to go well from my side," Adrienne said quietly. "How are you holding up?"

"Good." KJ drew in a shuddering breath. "I didn't know how much I needed that."

"It's amazing how it sneaks up on you." Adrienne leaned forward and pressed a kiss into her cheek. "You're very brave for taking it on. A lot of people wouldn't have."

"It shouldn't be brave to talk to your family."

"Being your true self, talking about your deepest feelings to the people who have the capacity to hurt you the most, is always brave." Adrienne patted her on the back of the hand. "Accept the compliment, you dork."

"Dork, am I?" KJ rolled over on top of her girlfriend, bringing her fingers to bear and seeking out the most ticklish spot on Adrienne's body—her ribs.

Adrienne clamped her lips shut on a squeal. "Stop," she whispered through her attempt not to scream with laughter. "Lawrence."

KJ's hands froze. That was right. She'd forgotten he was around. It was a Saturday night, a time that Lawrence was usually with his dad, but Kaz hadn't been able to take him this weekend. It was a rare occurrence. Usually he was as regular as the postal service when it came to spending time with his son, but not this weekend. Adrienne had requested they call from here, where Lawrence could set up his art supplies while she and Erik talked. It was nice, the three of them in Adrienne's home together. The only thing that was missing was Chester.

It wasn't the first time she'd had that thought recently.

"Hey, if Erik says yes to me paying for the house on an installment plan, why don't you and Lawrence move in?"

CHAPTER THIRTY-SEVEN

Oh no! Adrienne froze. KJ watched her expectantly. Why had the suggestion thrown her so badly?

"So…" KJ said after the silence had stretched on a little too long. "What do you say?"

"I– I'm not sure."

KJ's face fell and Adrienne raced to cover her tracks.

"It's not no." That felt right. Whatever that reaction had been, putting off moving in together felt all right, but not right now. "It's only been a few months."

"I know. I also know that this place is hard on you, financially. I thought if you moved in with me, then you could save on rent, at the very least. Not to mention…" She waggled her eyebrows. It was meant to be suggestive, but Adrienne could tell KJ's heart wasn't in it.

"That's true, and I appreciate the offer, I really do." Adrienne took KJ's hand. "Look, Lawrence knows about us, but he's not happy about it."

"You said he'd get over it." The edge of KJ's mouth quivered.

"And he will." Adrienne looked into KJ's eyes, willing her to believe her. "I know he will, but it's going to take time. I don't know how long, but if we move in before he's made peace with the situation, it could push that off even longer. I want you and him to have a solid relationship, but moving too quickly might jeopardize that. He needs to know he's a priority for you, and I…"

And I need to know I'm a priority also. There it was. Adrienne shook her head. It was so obvious, why had it taken her so long to get there?

"It's fine," KJ said. "I jumped the gun. I've been trying to give you space and not push you on this, but that talk with Erik went so well." She cocked her head to one side. "Do you really think Lawrence would put up a fuss if it meant living in the same house as Chester?"

Adrienne laughed. "I'm sure he'd love that. The rest of it is unpredictable, though. He's pretty level-headed for his age, but you've seen him melt down."

"Yeah, like twice, I think. I mean aside from the other night."

"Even so. This has been hard on him. It helps that he likes you. He just has to remember that." She squeezed KJ's hand. "Let's give it more time."

KJ nodded. "If it's best for Lawrence, I can wait."

"It will be good for me too."

"What do you mean by that?"

"He's not the only one who needs time to adjust to all of this. I love you, KJ. I meant it when I first said it, and I've meant it every time since, but this is…"

"What is it?" KJ said when Adrienne went from pause to stop.

"It's a lot. I want it, but I need to be able to process it." She sighed. "I don't trust myself right now. The way it all went down with Kaz messed me up. I'm getting better, but I'm still raw in places. I want to believe that what we have is real and lasting, and most of the time I do, but I'm scared."

"Of me?"

Adrienne shook her head. "Of what it would mean if I were to get as close to you as I want to, then lost you."

"Oh, Adrienne." KJ pulled her into her arms, holding her tight. "I could never hurt you. It would kill me to see you in pain and know I was the cause."

Adrienne snugged her arms around KJ's rib cage and squeezed. Her eyes prickled with heat and she closed them before she could start crying. KJ's aroma surrounded her, grounding her and making her feel at home. She loved how her girlfriend smelled. She always seemed to carry something of the ice around with her, a clean scent that cut through everything that was bothering her.

"I know," Adrienne said finally. "But what if…" She tried not to dwell on all the things that could go wrong. That KJ could get into a car accident. That she could be diagnosed with terminal cancer. That she would find someone more exciting and decide they were a better match.

"I know I hurt you early on," KJ said, her voice barely above a whisper. "I didn't mean to, but I did. It still gnaws at me, and I've worked my ass off to keep from making that mistake again."

"I know, sweetness." Adrienne sniffled quietly so as not to alert KJ that she was crying. "I know. But none of us knows the future."

"No, we don't, but from where I'm standing, I think it'll be pretty great." KJ nuzzled her face into Adrienne's hair. "If you and Lawrence are in it, that is."

"I plan to be." She cleared her throat. "You've made it pretty obvious you want us around. I like that."

"Of course I do."

"I'm glad. I don't like it when I feel like I'm not welcome."

"You're definitely welcome here." KJ gave her a gentle squeeze. "And you're welcome in my home, whether it's the house I grew up in or anywhere else. It won't be home until you and Lawrence are there."

Tears welled up from under her eyelids and dripped off the tip of her nose onto KJ's sweatshirt. Adrienne had no words, only relief.

"Is that why you got so angry, back when you joined the team?" KJ asked a few minutes later. "Is it because I made it seem like you weren't wanted?"

Adrienne opened her eyes at the question. Her tears had tapered off and she'd been enjoying lying on the bed wrapped up in KJ's arms. Between the warmth of both their bodies and the steady rise and fall of KJ's chest, she'd been hovering on the edge of falling asleep.

"Yeah," she answered after taking a couple of moments to think about it. "That's pretty much it. I don't do well with that."

"Does anyone?"

"Probably not." Adrienne tried not to remember the overtures she'd made to other kids, only to have them rebuffed, but then she was talking. "Do you know how many teams I played on for half a season, where no one passed me the puck or the ball? The times people let doors swing shut in my face while looking right at me?" She pushed herself up, extricating herself from KJ's arms. "It happens a lot when you look like I do. When someone is being full-on racist, it's almost easier to deal with. It sucks, but you know what you're getting. When it's not so obvious, you start to wonder. Did that happen because they didn't see me? Or because they did and decided to be an asshole about it? It's easy to ascribe a racial motive to everything, but then part of you wonders if you're wrong."

"I think I get it, at least a little bit," KJ said. "Like, I wonder if I didn't get a job interview because they saw me and decided they didn't want someone so obviously queer working at their little coffee shop or was it the fact that my resume only has part-time bartender work on it."

"Yes, except you get the benefit of people not knowing for sure what your minority status is. Mine is right out in front for anyone to see. I couldn't change it, even if I wanted to. And I definitely do not want to."

Adrienne balled her fists in her lap. "It gets so tiring. I know what I'm capable of, but there are so many people who assume I won't be able to hack it, simply because of how I look." She laughed bitterly. "And then they find out I'm a single mom. A couple teachers at work have asked me if my 'baby daddy' is around. What the fuck kind of a question is that?"

"An ignorant one. As ignorant as 'which one of you is the man' when they find out I'm a lesbian."

"Exactly." Adrienne took a deep breath. "They don't think they're being racist or homophobic. To them it's a novel thing, but they have no idea how many times the question's been aimed at me."

"I can assure you that's not what I was doing when I was a jerk to you in October," KJ said. "It had nothing to do with your skin color, I promise."

"I know that now," Adrienne said, "but I had no way of knowing that then. I was exhausted then and ready to write you off. Thank god for Jamie. I'm glad we were able to move past it."

"Me too." KJ pulled her phone out of her pocket and checked the time. "We have time to pull dinner together before the Belles game. Do you want to get started?"

Adrienne pulled KJ back over to her. "We can have popcorn for dinner. I want to cuddle some more."

"Popcorn? It's not very nutritious."

"It won't kill us, and Lawrence will be thrilled." She wrapped KJ's arms around her midsection. "Now hush and snuggle me already."

"Yes, my love." KJ leaned back against the headboard, taking Adrienne with her.

Adrienne closed her eyes and allowed herself to drift. She could see them living with this woman. Their home would be filled with laughter and barking. Lots of barking. As soon as she knew this was it, that their relationship was on solid ground, she would consider moving in. But how would she know? Would she ever really know? They were good questions, neither of which she had any idea how to answer.

CHAPTER THIRTY-EIGHT

The phone at her elbow rang, startling Adrienne out of deep concentration. She blinked at the offending device, then sighed before picking it up.

"Ms. Pierce," she said. "How can I help you?"

"Adrienne, hi." It was Sylvia from the principal's office. "I'm sorry to be the bearer of bad news. I have Lawrence waiting here."

"What happened?"

"He's not in any trouble, but he is running a fever. Mr. Lancaster sent him down from class."

"Oh no." She saved the document she'd been working on. "I'll be there as soon as I can." It wouldn't take long; she was in the same general area as the principal's office.

"Thank you. Sorry again."

"It's not your fault." Adrienne quickly filed away the folders of the kids she'd planned on seeing that day, then locked the cabinet. "Kids are germ factories. They get sick when they get sick, no matter what our plans…" *Shoot. It's Friday.*

"All right then. I'll let him know you'll be here soon."

"Yeah. Okay." She hung up the phone, then stared at the monitor in front of her. "It's Friday," she said out loud to the tiny office. "Friday—the day before the most important game of our season."

No, it was too early to start freaking out. Maybe Lawrence would only be down with a twenty-four hour bug. She'd seen him bounce back in less than a day on more than one occasion.

First things first. She fired off a few quick emails, letting various teachers know her few individual sessions for the day weren't going to happen. Satisfied after a quick perusal of her office let her know that anything of a sensitive nature was locked away, Adrienne grabbed her purse and headed down the hall.

Lawrence was slumped in a chair opposite the main reception counter. Her heart dropped as she took him in. While his skin was lighter than hers, it usually didn't betray much heightened color. Today wasn't usual. Two red spots burned high up on his cheeks.

"Oh, baby." Adrienne crossed over to him. It was a testament to exactly how bad he must have been feeling that he didn't object to the pet name. He didn't move when she pressed the back of her hand to his forehead. He was very warm.

"I don't feel good, Mom," Lawrence whispered.

"I know, sweetie." Adrienne reached down and picked up his backpack. "Let's get you home and into bed."

"Okay."

Adrienne paused to sign him out at the register. It seemed a little ridiculous, given that she worked there, but the rules were the rules, even for employees. From her seat behind the counter, Sylvia smiled her thanks.

"Feel better, Lawrence," she said with a little wave.

Lawrence nodded listlessly. He didn't resist as Adrienne guided him out of the building. His usual energetic pace had dwindled to a shamble. She opened the car door for him, noting that the day was warmer than it had been for a while. Spring was threatening, though the sky was gray and heavy. Would they have rain or snow? Who knew? It might even be a wintry mix.

She slid into the driver's seat, aware that her preoccupation with the weather was more to distract herself from the very real possibility that she was going to have to bail on KJ and the team. The rest of the Bolts would probably forgive her, but would KJ? They were so close to qualifying for playoffs. If they could beat Saturday's opponents, they would clinch their spot. If they didn't win, they might still get in on points, but it would be a much longer shot. They *had* to win this game.

"When did you start feeling sick, baby?" Adrienne glanced through the rearview mirror at Lawrence.

"I dunno," he said. "A little bit ago, maybe."

"So you weren't feeling bad when you got up?"

He shook his head.

"Hmm." That was bad news. Something coming on this quickly usually meant the flu. "Does your head hurt? Sore throat? Muscles kind of achy?" At each confirmation, her heart dropped a little further. This wasn't looking good. The faster she got him home, the faster she'd know what the weekend would look like.

* * *

The thermometer read 103 degrees. Adrienne glared at the numbers on the digital readout as if that might change them. There was little doubt about it. Lawrence had the flu or something close enough that it made no difference.

"Here you go, sweetie." Adrienne handed her son a glass and a children's Tylenol.

"Will this make me better?" Lawrence asked in a much smaller voice than normal.

"It'll help." She smoothed a lock of hair back from his forehead, cringing at how warm he felt. "You're probably going to feel pretty crummy for a few days."

"Okay," he sighed, before putting the glass to his lips and taking a small drink of water to wash down the pill. "Can I stay home tomorrow?"

"Of course you can. I'll let Dad know."

Adrienne took the glass before he could spill it on the covers and put it on the small table at his bedside. His eyes had already drifted shut, so she pulled the blankets up around him. Satisfied that he would doze for a while, Adrienne let herself quietly out of the room.

She settled herself into the overstuffed chair in the living room and pulled out her phone.

Lawrence has the flu. I'll keep him this weekend.

Maybe she should have phrased the text as a question, but Kaz had never been good about taking care of Lawrence when he was sick.

Adrienne winced. That sounded a little judgy, even to her. *Not that you're wrong*, the voice of pettiness reminded her. No, she wasn't wrong. The mental accusation might be unfair, but it definitely wasn't unfounded. When was she going to be able to evict Kaz from her head?

Bad news, she texted to KJ. *Give me a call when you have a chance.* It was almost noon, so KJ was probably already at work or on her way.

She had just turned off her phone when it buzzed in her hands. KJ's face grinned cheekily at her from the lock screen.

"That was fast," Adrienne said into the phone.

"Is everything okay?" KJ asked. "Did something happen?"

"We're fine or will be. Lawrence is sick, probably with the flu."

"Oh no. The poor little guy. How's he holding up?"

"Pretty miserable, as you'd expect." Adrienne took a deep breath. "I won't be making our games this weekend." She let out her breath, then held it waiting for KJ's response.

Silence met her pronouncement.

"Well, yeah," KJ finally said. "That makes total sense."

"You're not mad?"

"What? No, of course not."

KJ was saying all the right things, and it even sounded like she meant it, but Adrienne wasn't sure she believed her. "Okay."

"You need to do what you need to do. Hopefully Lawrence bounces back quickly."

"So I can make next weekend." Adrienne struggled to keep her voice neutral.

"I'm not going to lie, I'd rather have you on the ice, but we'll get it figured out if you're not." KJ paused again. "Is everything all right?"

"Aside from my son being sick, you mean?" Adrienne nodded even though KJ couldn't see her. "Yeah, it is. I guess I expected you to be more pissed off about this."

"Hey, if it makes you feel better, I can whine and moan and carry on about how I don't want to play with one of the subs or babysit a center back there instead of you, but that won't change the fact that Lawrence is sick and he needs you more than I do."

Adrienne didn't try to stop the relieved laugh that KJ's response pulled from her. "Well, good."

"Let Connie know ASAP," KJ said. "That's all I ask. I'd rather have a sub back there than running two centers. Or I could let her know."

Adrienne hesitated. "Yeah, if you don't mind." While their relationship wasn't common knowledge with everyone yet, Connie could be trusted to be discreet. Plus it was one other thing she wouldn't have to take care of.

"I don't mind. Do you need me to get you guys anything?"

"I got groceries Wednesday night, so I'm pretty set."

"You don't need any Kleenex or meds or anything?"

"KJ, I work at an elementary school and it's still cold and flu season. This wasn't exactly unexpected."

KJ laughed. "Well, if you run out of anything, let me know. I'll hook you up."

"Thanks, sweetness." Adrienne smiled into the phone. It was nice knowing she had someone to lean on if she needed it. "I should get going. I want to be able to hear Lawrence."

"Of course. Tell him I hope he feels better soon."

"I will. Oh, and I want updates on our games this weekend. I may not be able to make it, but I still want to know how they go."

"Of course." KJ's voice softened. "I love you, Adrienne."

"I love you too." Adrienne pulled the phone from her ear and swiped her thumb over the face, ending their call. That had gone so much better than she'd expected. Hopefully tomorrow's game would go equally well.

CHAPTER THIRTY-NINE

For the fifteenth time in the past twenty minutes, Adrienne checked her phone. There was still nothing from KJ. She sighed in irritation. Where was her update? It was almost five o'clock. Their game had been over almost an hour.

What if we lost? She sat up straight on the couch. "Oh no," Adrienne whispered to the empty room. *KJ's going to hate me.* Losing the game didn't mean they were out of playoffs, but they were going to have to win the last three games of the season to have a chance to qualify.

She checked her phone again. Still nothing. Did she send another text asking for an update? No, KJ knew very well she was waiting to find out the final score. If she wasn't hearing anything, it was because KJ didn't want to tell her.

"She must be so mad," Adrienne said. Usually, when they were apart, KJ texted her regularly unless she was on the ice or in the middle of a work shift.

There's probably another explanation, her brain offered. *Maybe she got into an accident on the way back from the rink.*

That's not any better, Adrienne snarled at her anxiety. *All you've done is give me something worse to worry about.* But it was uncharacteristic for KJ to be radio silent for so long. *Great.*

She unwound the throw from her legs and stood, the living room's cool air doing nothing to improve her rapidly worsening mood. She left the phone on the arm of the couch. It was better that she got away from it before she sent KJ a shitty text.

Adrienne pushed open the door to look in on her son. The lamp on his bedside table was on, casting a small pool of warm light in the darkening room. He was asleep, a comic book open next to him on the comforter. It was close to his arm, so Adrienne rescued it. Wrinkled pages were something to be avoided at all costs. She knew how upset he'd be if he creased one of his comics by rolling over on it in his sleep. A quick glance at the cover confirmed that it was one of his favorites. He had certain go-tos when he was feeling down. It had been a few months since this issue of *Miles Morales* had come out of the box.

She was settling it on the nightstand when a soft sound grabbed her attention.

Was that a knock at the door? Adrienne stood still to see if she would hear it again. Yes, that was definitely a knock, though a quiet one.

She crossed Lawrence's room in a few steps, then closed the door carefully before hurrying down the hall to the apartment's front door. She hesitated at the door, suddenly aware that her pajamas were threadbare and stained. They were the ones she cared the least about, the ones she saved for period days or when she or Lawrence were ill.

The knock sounded again, a little louder this time.

She took a deep breath and opened it before the noise could wake her son.

"Hey," KJ said. She grinned widely, holding up arms laden with a few canvas tote bags. "A little help?"

Adrienne blinked at her girlfriend, then reached out for one of the bags. The unmistakable smell of freshly baked bread wafted from it.

"What did you do?"

"I thought you'd be able to use some comfort food," KJ said. "Both of you."

"Um. Yeah." Her plan for dinner had been store brand mac-n-cheese. The bread smelled so much better. Her stomach growled.

"Let's get this inside." KJ bustled through the door, heading for the kitchen and leaving a bemused Adrienne to take up the rear.

She closed the door and caught up with KJ in the kitchen, where her girlfriend was pulling tubs of something out of the other tote.

"Is that soup?"

"It is," KJ said. "Chicken noodle. I threw the makings in the crockpot and the ingredients in the bread maker this morning. Figured I'd bring them by after the game."

"That is…" Adrienne couldn't finish the sentence. Tears prickled her eyes.

"Are you crying?" KJ rushed over to her, grasping her hands and watching her with concerned eyes. "Are you okay?"

"No. Yes." Adrienne sniffled as she tried to bring her whipsawing emotions under control. Five minutes ago she'd been ready to rip KJ a new one, and now she was trying not to cry at the extent of her girlfriend's thoughtfulness. "This is amazing. I can't believe you did all this for us."

"It's not a big deal." KJ stepped back and surveyed the food she'd laid out. In addition to the soup, there were also crackers and a two-liter bottle of ginger ale. "I just wanted to help out how I could."

"It's a huge deal." Adrienne wrapped her arms around KJ and pulled her close. "You have no idea how massive a deal this is." She closed her eyes and tucked her head into the hollow of KJ's neck. It was warm and smelled of KJ, though her scent was somewhat diluted by the scent of soap. She'd showered since the game.

"Speaking of huge deals," KJ said.

"Yes!" Adrienne opened her eyes and leaned back so she could see KJ's face. "I've been waiting. Without any communication from you, I might add."

"Sorry about that." KJ grimaced. "I was running around getting all this together, then Erik called." Her cringe transformed into a beaming smile. "He agreed to our proposal on the house! It took him so long because he was looking into a few things. Then he had to talk to a lawyer buddy about getting some forms written up." Her arms crushed Adrienne to her. "I get to keep the house!"

"That is fantastic, sweetness!" Adrienne returned KJ's hug with interest. "You must be so happy."

"I am. Or I will be." KJ loosened her grip. "This is me not pressuring you, by the way."

"I get it. And I appreciate it so much." Adrienne leaned in for a kiss.

KJ met her halfway, her lips soft under Adrienne's as they tasted each other for the first time in a few days. It had been a while since they'd gone this long without being in physical proximity to each other. All she wanted was to stand there in the shelter of KJ's embrace, warm and protected.

"Mom?" Lawrence's small voice filtered over to her from the kitchen doorway. "Can I have a drink?"

Adrienne smiled ruefully at KJ, then extricated herself. "How about some ginger ale? KJ brought it over."

"Yeah, okay." He looked up at KJ, his face drawn. He seemed tired, but not cross about her presence.

"There's soup and bread too, if you're up to it," KJ said.

Lawrence shrugged.

"Let's get you back to bed, baby," Adrienne said. He shuffled out of the kitchen at her urging and allowed her to tuck him back in.

KJ appeared a moment later with a glass of ginger ale. "Here," she whispered from the doorway.

"Put it over there." Adrienne indicated the small bedside table.

"Thanks, KJ," Lawrence said sleepily.

"Of course, buddy." She smiled down at him, then disappeared back into the kitchen. From the sound of rummaging, she was getting things situated.

"Do you want a drink now?"

"Uh-huh."

"Okay." She held the glass out for him. He took a small sip, then set it back on the table. It wobbled a bit as he passed it over.

"Do you need anything else?"

"I might like some soup in a bit."

"I think we can manage that. Let me know when you're ready."

"Okay." His eyelids were drooping, so Adrienne tucked the comforter around him, then slipped out of the room.

She crept back to the kitchen, then stood in the doorway, watching while KJ bustled around. There was no sign of the bread or soup aside from the lingering aroma. KJ swept crumbs off the cutting board and into the sink, then pulled out the washcloth. She was running water to tackle the dirty dishes that had accumulated when Adrienne came up behind her and wrapped her arms around KJ's waist. She leaned her head against KJ's back and closed her eyes.

"When Lawrence is over being upset, I'll be happy for us to move in with you," Adrienne said quietly.

KJ stiffened. "Oh my god," she said. She turned around to stare at Adrienne. "For real?" Unshed tears shimmered on her lower eyelids.

Adrienne nodded, then smiled, the effect a little spoiled by the moisture in her own eyes. "Do you realize we've talked about all sorts of things on the same day as a really important game for the Bolts, and you still haven't told me the score?"

"I haven't?" KJ blinked. "Huh, I didn't."

Adrienne leaned forward and placed a gentle kiss on her forehead. "Nope. Now, would you please tell me how the game went?"

KJ's laughter burbled up in an awkward combination of surprise and tears. "Okay, okay. We won!"

"Thank god!" Adrienne relaxed. "I was so worried that you weren't saying anything because we lost."

"No, nothing like that! It was a close game, we definitely could have used you, and it could have gone either way a couple of times, but we pulled it out." KJ let out a heavy sigh. "We're going to playoffs."

"I'm so happy for you, sweetness!" Adrienne hugged KJ fiercely.

KJ laughed, her tone surprised. "So am I. It's funny, though…"

"What is?"

"I dunno, just that I'm way more excited that you and Lawrence are going to move in. The game is cool and all, but that's not what I'm thinking about. I'm trying to decide which bedroom will be for Lawrence and which side of the closet should be yours."

"Weird." Adrienne stretched up and kissed the tip of KJ's nose.

"Yeah. But I'm okay with it."

"Me too."

CHAPTER FORTY

The rink smelled the same as the many others KJ had been in: ice, propane, and the accumulated sweat of hundreds, if not thousands, of hockey players. It was one in a small complex on the outskirts of Philadelphia. Her bag slung over her shoulder, she turned in a circle as she walked to take it all in.

Playoffs were always exciting, but this year she felt like they were poised on the edge of greatness. They'd ended the season on a high note, winning their last four games, even if a couple had been close. The Bolts had only lost one game since their tie against the higher-ranked team, and that one had been close, even with half the team out with the flu. The tournament was theirs to lose.

KJ shook her head sharply. It was thoughts like those that jinxed things. None of their games were decided; she needed to be at the peak of her form.

A small group of players from another team waved to her as they passed by. KJ nodded back at them. One looked familiar, but not the other two. She was much better at recognizing people in their gear than out of it. Without helmets, she was crap at figuring out if she'd played against them before.

"Wait up," Adrienne called to her.

"Sorry." KJ shortened her stride. Their first game was in an hour. So much anticipatory energy sparkled in her veins that she was surprised she hadn't run through the rink's lobby.

"We'll get there with plenty of time to go." Adrienne paused to hike her bag up higher on her shoulder.

"I know, but I really need a warmup." KJ shook her hands out. "I'm going to explode if I don't get moving soon."

"You're lucky that's how your nerves go. Mine are butterflies. I feel like my belly is full of them."

"I bet a warmup would help them too."

"Or a good puke."

KJ looked over her shoulder at her girlfriend. "I've never seen you throw up before a game. Are you feeling all right?"

"I doubt I'll actually barf. It's been a long time since I did that before I played. Doesn't stop me feeling like I need to." She raised a hand when KJ was about to say something else. "I'll be fine once we hit the ice. A bit of anxiety is good. Makes me sharp."

"If you say so." KJ stopped in front of the locker room assignment screen. "Looks like we're in seven." She pointed to the left. "I think it's down that way."

The hallway was painted a royal blue which sucked the light out of the cheap fluorescent fixtures in the ceiling. They paused to let a group of women in gear past them. None of them were sweaty enough to have played a game yet.

"Good luck," KJ said.

"Thanks," came the muffled response from a few mouths. A couple held out their hands for fist bumps.

KJ grinned as she bounced her fist off their gloved knuckles. The competition was part of the draw of playoffs, but the other part was the camaraderie. Everyone was here for the same thing. They'd all put in the same work to make it to the top of their little corner of the hockey world, no matter which skill level they played at.

This was the year. She would finally get a league championship. She would make her dad proud, wherever he was. This one was for him, as it always had been. He'd been so proud when her various teams had made it to the final round over the years. Sure, there had been a number of tournament wins, and he'd been so tickled by them, beaming down at her for the drive back from whatever rink they'd been at. Her chest swelled at the memory of his approval. Heat prickled the back of her eyeballs, and she quickly blinked to keep from crying in the middle of the rink hall.

"Here we are," Adrienne said. She stuck her head in the locker room. "Looks like someone's on the ice right now."

"We can dump our bags over there." KJ pointed out a dark corner out of the way of women trooping through the corridor in full gear. "That game should be finishing up soon."

"We're a little early."

"Only a little." KJ let her bag slide from her shoulder, then propped all three of her sticks up next to it. She bounced on the tip of her toes, swinging her arms in front of her. "Want to go for a quick run?"

"A run?" Adrienne cocked one eyebrow at her. "When have you ever seen me run?"

"After Lawrence and Chester that one time."

"Any other time?"

"Nope!" KJ grinned down at her. "I thought I might be able to convince you this once."

"I'm going to go watch the end of the game." Adrienne flipped her hand at KJ in dismissal. "You go work off some extra energy."

"Got it!" KJ craned her neck to check down the hall. It was clear. She swooped in for a quick smooch. "See you in a few!"

KJ jogged back up the hall, through the lobby, and out the door. There was no surprise in Adrienne's refusal to accompany her on a jog. Her girlfriend hated to run, though she had professed an interest in cycling. Maybe once the weather improved, they could go for a bike ride somewhere.

The day was one of those that gave a body hope that winter would completely loosen its grip soon. It wasn't warm by the standards of summer, but it was warm enough that piles of snow had developed small trickles running from their bases. She could run outside, instead of up and down the bleachers. A wide smile split her face as the sun bathed it. She wanted to turn her face to the sky but had to keep an eye out for puddles. Her shoes weren't close to waterproof.

"KJ!" She knew that voice.

"Jamie!" KJ turned to behold the glory of her best friend maneuvering herself out of Joe's truck.

Jamie waited as her husband came scampering around to offer her a hand. It was a testament to how uncomfortable she must have gotten since she allowed him to help her down.

"How much longer is that truck going to last?" KJ called out as she jogged across the parking lot.

"It's in fine shape," Joe said. "No need to trade it in yet."

"Oh, really?" KJ met Jamie's eyes.

Jamie smiled sweetly, but there was some bite to it.

"You made it," KJ said. She held her arms open for a hug.

"You know I did." Jamie stepped in and held her tightly for a second. "I wouldn't miss this for the world."

"Are you sure you should be here? You look ready to pop."

"Four weeks until the due date yet." Jamie stood up straight and knuckled the small of her back. "I'm ready to be done. It's funny, I was worried about going through labor, but these days, I can't wait."

"Me either." KJ grinned down at Jamie's pregnant belly. "I'm going to be the best aunt your kid could ask for."

"I bet you are. I've seen you with your nieces. And with Lawrence. How is he?"

KJ shrugged. "Still not really talking to me." He'd thawed a bit since he got over the flu, but they still weren't where they had been. It had only been a couple of months, but she missed their easy rapport.

"He'll come around. Try not to worry too much about it."

"That's what everyone keeps saying. I'm trying to be the same old KJ with him, but it's hard."

"Keep at it, you two will be palling around in no time." Jamie glanced toward the rink. "I need to sit down. Get back to your run. I'll see you on the ice."

"For sure." KJ jogged backward a few steps, waved at Jamie, then turned to take a quick lap of the building. Her steps were light and easy. She hoped that translated to the game.

* * *

"One coming," Adrienne hollered. The opposing team's forward had powered past her right inside their zone, despite Adrienne's best efforts to slow her down. She transitioned into a forward stride, her head down, pushing to eat up the ice before the wing could make it to the hash marks and unload her shot on Vaughn. It was obvious in the first two strides that she wasn't going to catch up to her, but she kept going. At the very least, the sound of her skates carving up the ice might make her opponent nervous enough to rush the shot.

They were ahead by one halfway through the second period, but the Squirrels had come to play. This was a team they'd handled pretty well the only time they'd played them during the season. Adrienne didn't remember the woman at wing, though. The way she skated and handled the puck wasn't something Adrienne would have forgotten. Maybe they'd done so well because their best player hadn't been there. There had been some locker room chatter about where the Squirrels had placed in the regular season standings, but Adrienne hadn't paid much attention. Those speculations weren't particularly useful. She wanted to deal with what was happening in the moment, not how they'd done months ago.

"I got her," KJ yelled from across the rink and behind them, her blades biting deep and fast and moving far faster than Adrienne could manage. She was over the blue line in a flash and deep in their zone.

Vaughn was set, waiting for the shot as KJ drew abreast with the Squirrels player. She transitioned from forward to backward and glided between the opposing wing and her goalie. She slid her stick under the woman's blade, tapping it up hard enough that she lost her handle on the puck. A wide grin crossed KJ's face, visible through her cage as she took possession.

Adrienne knew what was coming next. A quick glance over her shoulder let her know that the forwards were barely into the neutral zone. Lou had taken the opportunity to get to the bench; Bailey was hopping over the boards in her stead. No one was in position. More importantly, the other team was also changing up, confident the puck was deep enough in the Bolts' zone to give them a bit of a breather.

Adrienne abandoned her pursuit and transitioned backward, heading to the boards and giving KJ the world's biggest target.

KJ didn't look to make sure she was there. Instead, she seemed to be gauging the opposing team's progress at their bench. She fired the puck at Adrienne; it thwacked solidly into the blade of her stick.

Adrienne's feet were already moving as her blue line passed beneath them. She'd crossed center ice before the Squirrels realized they no longer had possession. Adrienne skated as hard as she ever had, paying no attention to the bite of blades behind her. One pair of them would be KJ's. Her girlfriend would make sure she wasn't hassled. Blue jerseys filled the corner of her vision as the rest of her teammates filled the ice between the Squirrels' bench and their zone.

She bit her lip in concentration, barely noticing the other blue line going past, considering instead how the Squirrels' goalie was squaring up to her. The upper glove hand corner was wide open, but the goalie was quick on her glove side. The short side had a gap below the blocker. She pulled the puck back and waited, the goalie growing larger in her vision, obscuring more of the net. She was set and waiting. The gap on the short side disappeared, leaving the upper corner most easily visible.

She couldn't see the short side gap, but Adrienne knew it was there. She bore down on the stick, flexing it under her body weight, letting the puck fly at the spot she remembered but could no longer see.

A sharp "ping" rang out over the sounds of skate blades and her teammates' shouts of approval. The rink went quiet, but there was no whistle confirming a goal.

Adrienne kept going toward the net. The puck hadn't bounced out, so it was still there, but she couldn't see it past the goalie's bulk. There was still no whistle. Someone was hollering something, but Adrienne couldn't make it out; she couldn't even tell if the yelling was someone from her team. She took another stride, then spied the puck sitting behind the goalie's skate blade.

"Don't move," a Squirrels player shouted at her goalie. The puck was less than an inch from the goal line.

Blue and white jerseys descended on the net, Adrienne leading the charge. The goalie moved as if suspended in Jell-O, not knowing where the puck had ended up, but not daring to move too much for fear of knocking it into the net.

At the hash marks, Adrienne launched herself forward. Her jersey couldn't stop the snow on the ice in front of the net from penetrating to her skin, but she hardly noticed. She laid herself out completely, her stick heading for the puck that still sat on the goal line. It was practically gift wrapped. A Squirrels player tried to step between Adrienne and her goalie, but she was too late. The goalie swung her stick down to try and knock Adrienne's blade off trajectory, but all of Adrienne's weight was behind it. The stick wavered a bit, but Adrienne got it back under control. She tapped the puck with the toe. Time slowed down as the puck finally crossed the line.

The ref's whistle gave Adrienne the confirmation she'd been looking for, but it couldn't stop her momentum. She let go of her stick as she slid into the goalie, pulling her down and plowing them both into the net.

"Oof," was all Adrienne could say as the goalie landed on her. The net popped off its pegs and slid backward a few feet before the pile of people and steel stopped sliding.

"Shit," the goalie whispered in her ear.

"Sorry," Adrienne said.

Her only response was an irritated grunt. That was fair; Adrienne hadn't really meant it.

A hand grabbed her shoulder and hauled her out of the net. More reached down and pulled her to her feet.

"Are you all right?" KJ's cage pressed against hers, her girlfriend's face inches away. Her expression hovered between terrified and exultant.

"I'm fine."

KJ answered her reassurance by throwing both arms around her and hugging her tight. More arms added to hers. Adrienne found herself in the center of an intense group hug, women whooping in her ear and her hollering alongside them.

"I knew you'd be there," KJ shouted to her through the din. "You're always exactly where I need you to be."

"You know it," Adrienne said. "Thanks for having my back."

"Always." She squeezed Adrienne more tightly, only letting go when the ref's whistle sounded to get the game going again.

CHAPTER FORTY-ONE

The final horn had sounded on their first game and they'd made their way through the obligatory handshake line. KJ leaned over, resting her stick across her knees, and coasted toward their bench. Halfway there, Adrienne caught up to her.

"We definitely needed that goal of yours," KJ said.

"I don't mind getting on the score sheet." Adrienne grinned at her through the bars of her face cage. "Usually I'm only on if I get a penalty."

KJ's mouth dropped open in exaggerated shock. "And none of those this game either. There's hope for you yet."

"Very funny." Adrienne stuck her tongue out at her girlfriend.

"I'm glad you've finally realized my comedic genius."

"Comedic genius this." KJ allowed the boards to stop her slow progress, then pulled off her helmet, then waited for Adrienne to remove hers. She leaned in for a kiss as soon as the helmet allowed.

Adrienne returned the kiss briefly, but with interest. "That doesn't make any sense," she said when they parted. Smugly, KJ noted Adrienne was breathing faster.

"How do you two have the energy to keep on?" Vaughn asked from behind them. "I'm beat."

"But not beaten!" Adrienne said.

"I'm not surprised," KJ said at the same time.

Vaughn snorted. "Thanks for the vote of confidence."

"I know you're solid between the pipes, and you know it," KJ said. "But you have to admit that you didn't exactly face that many shots our last game." KJ snagged her water bottle from the edge of the boards, then pushed open the door so she could grab her extra sticks. She passed Adrienne hers.

"That's true." Vaughn maneuvered their pads through the bench door and around the bench itself before disappearing out the door behind the bench.

"You had a really good game," Adrienne said quietly. A gentle smile creased her face, not enough for her dimples to show through, but her eyes sparkled. "I enjoyed watching you."

KJ bumped her with her shoulder. "And I enjoyed playing with you. How about next game you watch less, though?" She raised her eyebrows to let Adrienne know she was joking.

"I don't know." Adrienne made a show of leaning back to scope out KJ's rump. "With that thing waggling around in front of me, how do you expect me not to watch?"

"You little…" KJ advanced toward Adrienne.

"Hey now." Adrienne darted toward the door off the rink. "Mind your manners."

"I'll mind your manners." KJ sprang after her girlfriend. They barreled through the door in the boards and almost ran Coach Aaron over on the other side.

"Sorry, Coach!" they chorused like guilty children.

He shook his head and stepped aside to let them pass.

KJ didn't try to stop the snicker that bubbled up from the back of her throat. Her heart still pounded from the aftereffects of all that adrenaline, but it felt light. There was no reason it shouldn't. She was there, in the open, with her girlfriend, and everyone knew it.

"I'm so glad," she said out loud.

"Glad about what?" Adrienne asked.

"That we don't have to hide anymore. Yeah, I wish Lawrence would come around, but it's great to be able to be affectionate toward you and not worry about who might see."

Adrienne smiled, her teeth flashing white, her eyes sparkling in the way KJ never failed to be entranced by. "It's pretty great. And don't worry, as long as you continue to give him access to Chester, Lawrence will find it in his heart to forgive you."

"I see. So it's your professional counseling opinion that I should gain your son's affection with my dog."

"You have the tool. Why not use it?" Adrienne shrugged.

"But I want him to like me for me." The idea that Adrienne's son might never get back to being comfortable with her struck a nerve.

"Oh, honey." Adrienne nudged KJ with her shoulder. "I'm totally kidding. All he needs is time."

"So I shouldn't get him a puppy?"

"Are you insane?" Adrienne whipped her head around to stare at KJ, who laughed out loud, a guffaw of delight that echoed down the hallway to the locker room.

"Okay, no puppies," she finally said when the fit of giggles left her enough air to speak again. "A pony?"

"I'm not talking to you."

"Walrus?"

Adrienne picked up her pace. KJ lengthened her stride to keep up.

"Musk ox? Guinea pig? Regular pig!" She grinned, though part of knew she would have gotten some of those animals if it meant Lawrence opened up to her again.

CHAPTER FORTY-TWO

The flutters in her stomach were an unwelcome reminder of KJ's early days playing hockey at a higher level. She glared at her skates as she willed the irritating sensation to go away. This wasn't Division I hockey. As much as she wanted a win, losing only meant she would be in the same place next season. And was that really a bad thing?

She stuck a finger under her laces to see if they were tight enough. They felt taut, but her feet still had too much room to move around. With a muttered curse, she pried open the double-knot at the top and loosened them in preparation for re-tying them.

Her life for the past seven years hadn't been what she'd expected. Not that she'd had a clear path in mind, but missing out on the end of college to take care of her dying father hadn't figured in her plans. He'd died almost exactly two years previous. She'd missed the championship game, and the Bolts had lost. Two years. It was time to move on. The relationship with Adrienne had come out of nowhere, but she wouldn't give it up for anything, even if her girlfriend's son wasn't yet on board with the idea.

Why am I going over all of this? KJ wasn't prone to introspection, especially not such deep thoughts before such an important game. She sighed. It was probably just the same bout of melancholy she'd gone through last year on the anniversary of her dad's death.

The noise of the crowded locker room washed back over her as she finished tying her skates. They still felt a little off, but that was probably all in her head. She strapped on her shin guards, then tugged her socks down to cover them. Tape went over the socks to hold everything in place.

"Listen up, everyone," Connie said from the door. "You have sixty seconds to get dressed before Coach comes in."

Only a minute until chalk talk? KJ yanked off her shirt and bra and replaced them with a ratty sports bra that had seen a few too many games and her undershirt. She stood and stepped into her breezers, then yanked on her elbow pads. She was getting her chest pad settled when Coach Aaron knocked at the door.

"Come in," chorused half a dozen women's voices. The other half were pulling shirts over their heads and getting themselves decent.

The door opened slowly, and Aaron stuck his head through the gap with caution, looking down at the floor. As usual, Mavis was only now getting her boobs covered, and she grinned as she took advantage of their coach's cautious nature.

"You good, Mavis?" Aaron asked.

"All covered, Coach," she responded cheerfully.

"Good." He entered the rest of the way.

Everyone stared at him expectantly. The tension hadn't been there for the previous night's game, or maybe KJ was projecting her nerves onto the rest of the team.

Aaron cleared his throat. KJ wasn't the only one who was anxious. "We haven't played this team before. They weren't available for many exhibition games. I watched last night's game, and they're good. Not as good as we are, of course." He paused to let confident murmurs pass between the seated women, his face serious. "But they can beat us if we're not on the top of things. Don't get cocky out there."

"Can't get cocky, Coach," Lou said.

"I know, I know," he said. It wasn't the first time she'd given him a hard time for his choice of words. "The point is, keep your heads on that swivel. Use your teammates. Be on the lookout for the outlet pass. Defense, hold that blue line. If we can keep the puck in their zone for the majority of the game, we'll have this one in the bag." He held up a white board covered in Xs and Os. "Remember the face-off setup in their zone. I'm going to leave this here for anyone who needs a refresher." Aaron looked around, pausing to lock eyes with each of them for a moment. "We can do this. I believe in us. Any questions?"

A few heads shook in the negative and quiet reigned. Energy buzzed below the silence. They were ready to get on the ice. KJ flexed the muscles in her thighs. She was ready.

"All right. Finish getting dressed and I'll see you on the bench." Coach Aaron paused in the doorway and cocked his head. "Sounds like the Zamboni is hitting the ice, so don't dally too long. Connie has the lines." The door eased shut behind him.

"You heard Coach," Connie said. "Let's make sure we're sticking together out there. Lines are," she glanced down at the list in her lap, "same as they always are when everyone's here. Do I need to read them out?"

"Nope," KJ said loudly, her response disappearing into a cacophony of similar responses. Some of them had been playing on the same line for years, same as KJ had before this season. She glanced over at Adrienne, who was leaning back against the wall, her eyes closed. She looked at peace.

KJ stood and crammed her helmet on over her skull cap. She settled the mouth guard around her teeth, pushing it into place with her tongue.

"Ready?" she asked Adrienne with somewhat mushy syllables.

Her girlfriend understood her nonetheless. A smile crossed her features before her eyes opened. "As ready as I'll get."

"You'll be great."

"You'll be better."

KJ shrugged. "We'll see about that." She picked up her water bottle with fingers rendered clumsier by her gloves, then made for the door. Her legs needed to move. She snatched up her sticks from the corner and went out to stand by the boards and watch the Zamboni go by.

Aaron nodded at her when she joined him.

"Anyone I need to keep an eye on, Coach?" KJ asked.

"One of their centers is pretty speedy, but you can handle her. She's a pretty potent combo with one of the left wings. When thirty-six and seven are both on the ice make sure you're on your toes. Otherwise, you'll be able to handle anyone else."

"Good to know." KJ shifted her feet, rocking from one to the other as the ice was cleared one long row at a time. Normally, she appreciated the time between when the resurfacer finished and they were allowed on the ice, but not today. The ice would be pristine when they stepped on it, but she was ready to go now.

"You all right?" Adrienne asked. "You're amped way up today. Even more than yesterday."

"Semifinal's a big deal." KJ hopped up and down. "I want to get out there, is all."

"If you say so. Don't kill your legs in warm-ups."

"I haven't done a rookie move like that in years."

"Glad to hear it." Adrienne sidled up next to her but didn't say anything.

After a few seconds, some of KJ's extra energy started to drain away. Adrienne was like a rock, and KJ was glad she had her.

As the home team for the game, they were able to get to their bench without going on the ice. The other team gathered on the far side of the rink, waiting for the referees to arrive. KJ stowed her extra sticks in a corner, where they were lost amid those of her teammates. She inspected the tape job on her stick. The white tape was full of black marks from the puck and a few cuts, but overall was holding up pretty well. That done, there was nothing to do but wait.

When the refs finally arrived, the home bench was full of women perched on the boards or standing around behind them. No one seemed to want to sit. KJ bounced the heels of her skates off the thick sheets of plastic that protected the bench. Adrienne, Vaughn, and the other line of defense were having a quiet discussion behind her. She avoided joining in, trying to calm her mind and get into game mode. The bleachers were filling up with spectators. Nothing like a pro or college game, of course, but they always had more fans for playoffs, which was nice.

A waving sign caught her attention. Large, multicolored block letters proudly proclaimed "Go Mom! Go KJ!" When Adrienne's son caught her looking, he waved vigorously, then held his sign higher. He was wearing a knit hat and mittens, KJ noticed with amusement. Lawrence hated being cold, but he was braving their game.

KJ reached over and tugged lightly on Adrienne's jersey. "Check out Lawrence."

"Oh good," Adrienne said. "He found something to draw on. I had a text from Kaz asking if I had any art supplies, like I tuck them away in my hockey bag." She sighed. "Of course, with a kid like Lawrence, it's not the worst idea."

"I think it's awesome." KJ waved back at Lawrence. "I love that he's here for us." *Both of us.* A grin tugged at the edges of her mouth.

The door opened along the far side of the boards, and two black and white-striped referees stepped out onto the ice, which gleamed smooth under the lights.

"Finally." KJ dropped onto the ice, bending her knees to absorb the shock as her skate blades hit the hard surface.

The other team streamed in behind the refs, gray and burgundy jerseys providing a welcome contrast to their blue and white. There would be no mistaking who was on which team.

KJ pushed forward, extending her leg behind her in a long lunge, then switching up her legs. With each stride, her nerves subsided and her body's tightness loosened, allowing her to move freely. By the time she was crossing one skate over the other in a long turn in front of her own crease, her confidence was back. The Royals didn't know it, but they were in her house. She grinned as the air whistled through the openings in her helmet.

The warm-up was over in a blur. KJ's skating had been crisp and powerful, her shot hard and low. Energy still ricocheted through her arms and up her spine, but she was turning it to good use. By the time her line went out to take the opening face-off, she was ready. Her heartbeat had settled, and she was seeing the ice well.

Adrienne lined up to her right, a couple of feet back from the center ice face-off circle. She always gave herself a little extra room. KJ knew she had the legs not to need it, but mentally, she always made sure there was that space. KJ shrugged. It worked for her partner; that was all that mattered.

Connie skated into the center of the circle, and KJ settled herself into a crouch. Jean and Michelle took up their positions next to the opposing team's forwards. A little curl of anticipation twisted in KJ's belly. She bit her lip, focusing on the puck in the ref's hand. He held it out for a second, then another, the centers tense in front of him, then let it drop.

Before the puck was halfway to the ice, Connie had tapped the other center's stick out of the way. She slapped the puck straight back to KJ, who skated up to meet it. Michelle was already taking an angle toward the boards and the other team's blue line, having beaten her opponent off the line. There was enough separation that KJ felt comfortable firing the puck her way, angling it to bounce off the boards and onto Michelle's stick as she streaked into the zone, a burgundy jersey on her tail. Connie busted her ass toward the net, with Jean crossing the blue line an instant later. The Royals' defense had dropped back, but they weren't getting much support from the forwards, not yet.

Michelle kept skating, carrying the puck deeper into the zone, toward the crease where the goalie was squaring up on her. She passed to Connie, who swiveled and pulled back as if to deliver the shot. The goalie threw herself across the crease, laying out to intercept the puck, but Connie was already dumping it back to Jean, who had entered the zone late, right between the hash marks. A defender stepped up on Connie but was too slow. The other had Michelle covered on the back door. No one was ready for Jean to pull back and fire the puck into the net's upper right corner.

The ref's whistle rang out but was almost drowned out by the whoops of jubilation from the three forwards who crashed together into a group bear hug in front of the net. The Royals goalie picked herself up and banged her stick on the post in frustration. One of her defenders swatted her leg pad in commiseration.

"Feeling better?" Adrienne asked as she skated up for a more sedate fist bump.

"Getting there." KJ grinned through her mouth guard. "I have a feeling that's the only easy one they're going to let us get past them, though."

"Either way, we're ready for them."

CHAPTER FORTY-THREE

Adrienne plopped down on the bench, her legs aching for the reprieve, no matter how brief it might end up being. Only a little way into the third period, there was still lots of game left to play. They'd gotten that first goal, but the Royals weren't allowing them anything more. It seemed like the game was taking place mostly in the neutral zone, neither team able to bury the puck at the far end for long enough to get any offensive momentum going. They hadn't yet resorted to icing the puck to get line changes in, but it had come close a couple of times. Their single goal lead held, but it felt tenuous at best and more often like disaster waiting to happen. If they tied with the Royals, there was no guarantee they'd make the next round of the tournament, and Adrienne knew how much the win meant to KJ.

A flash of red from across the ice caught her attention. Lawrence stood at the glass on the far side, his arms raised to pound on the clear Plexiglas. He smiled and waved when he caught her watching, then pressed his homemade sign to the glass.

She grabbed KJ's elbow and pointed. Her girlfriend's smile spread across her face, and she gave Lawrence an exaggerated nod, then her jaw dropped as two familiar little girls joined him at the glass.

"Is that—"

"Sure looks like it." Adrienne had only seen them once, but they sure looked like KJ's nieces. Beyond the glare of the glass, Erik and Sophia were sitting back next to Kaz. Her ex was deep in conversation with them.

"I don't think he's been to one of my games since…" KJ's voice trailed off.

"That long?"

"Yeah."

"Heads up!" Connie's shout pulled Adrienne's attention away from the stands and back toward the ice. She ducked as the puck flew past her head, then clattered around the back of the bench. A moment later, the ref's whistle shrilled, and her tired teammates streamed off the ice.

Her legs weren't back to normal, but she could do her part yet. Adrienne stepped back out onto the ice.

"Here we go," KJ said to Adrienne as she skated past her toward her spot at the bottom of the circle.

Adrienne was glad to see the slightly shell-shocked look in KJ's eyes being replaced with determination. There was less than a period to go, unless the Royals could get one past Vaughn. The Bolts offense joined them, Connie taking her place at the center of the circle. They were being matched up against the Royals' first line. That hadn't happened too often. Fast as that first line was, the Bolts had been managing to hold them in check with only their second and third lines.

The puck dropped, but Connie couldn't get her stick on it. The Royals' forwards scattered, heading for the boards as their defense cycled the puck, waiting for someone to break free of the Bolts' coverage.

Jean and Michelle skated back to put pressure on the defenders, and a Royals wing angled toward the center of the ice.

The puck came flying out of the Royals' zone at waist height. KJ slapped at it but couldn't make contact. She stopped and took a quick hop in the opposite direction to chase down the puck.

"Two on!" Adrienne and half the bench yelled. The Royals' power duo were breaking down the ice after the puck while the rest of their teammates made for the bench. The Bolts' forwards were too deep in the Royals' zone, so it was up to KJ and Adrienne to slow down the burgundy jerseys before they could get to Vaughn.

Adrienne pushed off toward her own crease. One of the Royals would post up in front of Vaughn while the other tried to get the puck away from KJ in the corner. She saw the play unfolding in her head, having experienced this scenario dozens of times.

The puck ringed its way around the boards, and the Royals' center shifted her trajectory. As Adrienne had predicted, the wing started to slow at the hash marks. Adrienne slid to a stop, interposing her body between her opponent and the puck. KJ took a wide turn around the net, following the path of the puck, which had finally come to rest in a pile of hardened snow at the Zamboni door. She extended her stick along the boards to pick up the puck before she had company.

It happened too quickly for Adrienne to make out the exact sequence of events, but suddenly KJ's stick was wedged in the boards at a ninety-degree angle. All the momentum she had built up in pursuit of the puck took KJ through her stick, which gave until it could bend no further, then snapped, the blade breaking off a little above the heel.

KJ went down, sliding forward on her belly, but still had the presence of mind to get a hand on the puck. She looked behind her. Adrienne knew exactly what to do. She abandoned the forward above the crease and headed for the opposite corner where the puck was already headed, propelled by the strength of KJ's arm. It wasn't as hard as she would have gotten from her stick, but it was moving. Adrienne picked up the puck, carrying it up the boards, the clash of blades carving the ice behind her.

She looked up and caught a glimpse of white and blue an instant before a burgundy jersey filled her vision. The forward bounced into the boards, her shoulder taking the brunt of the collision. Adrienne swiveled her shoulders, trying to force the puck between the Royals' player and the boards, but it stopped short when her opponent stuck her foot in the way.

"Dammit," Adrienne snarled at herself. She should have looked up to see if any Bolts were closer before trying to jam the puck through. There was nothing for it now. She lunged forward, trapping the puck against the boards and the opponent's skate. If the Royals' player shifted, the puck would pop free. It was a good plan, but the puck was stuck fast. She jabbed at the black rubber disk but couldn't break it loose. More players were arriving; she heard their skates, but didn't dare look up. Instead, she kept hacking at the puck. Her own harsh breaths filled her ears, drowning out what anyone might be trying to say to her.

More sticks joined hers along the boards, a couple seeming to help, but more trying to knock her out of the way.

"No!" The puck squirted out from behind the stick, robbing Adrienne of the chance the ref might whistle the play dead. She looked up and with sinking heart saw that the player who had made it out of the scrum with the puck wasn't on her team.

Rebecca had joined KJ in front of the net, but Adrienne's girlfriend still didn't have a stick. KJ was doing her best to cover the stubborn Royals' center, who refused to give up her prime spot while also screening the crap out of Vaughn. The goalie bobbed their head up and down, trying to track the puck as it was carried away from the boards and toward the center of the ice. Rebecca stepped forward to challenge the puck-carrier, giving Adrienne the chance to drop back and pick up another Royals' wing who was trying to set up on the opposite post.

"Not gonna happen," Adrienne muttered. She put her stick over her opponent's and leaned on it, pinning the blade down. She wasn't going to get a clean swing at the puck, not if Adrienne had anything to say about it. KJ should have been the one with the stick; she could do far more with it than Adrienne could. But if she let up, the forward would be open.

She lost her view of the puck as the Royals' player disappeared behind the bodies of KJ and the other center. She shifted to solidify her angle between the puck and the forward, just in time to see the wing pull back her stick and let the puck fly. KJ pushed off the center, creating some separation between them. She kicked out, catching the puck with the side of her skate. Her grunt at the impact echoed back to Adrienne, but KJ didn't let the pain stop her. The puck dropped in front of her and she skated forward, kicking the hard disk forward a bit, then kicking it again, dribbling the puck toward the boards as if it was a soccer ball.

It was an audacious move, one that seemed to take everyone by surprise, as KJ got a few strides in before anyone moved to counter her. She waited until the forward who had taken the shot made a move at her, then calmly gave the puck one last kick, sending it sliding toward the boards where Lou was able to corral it and finally move it out of their end.

"Aw, hell," the Royals' forward said in Adrienne's ear, then peeled off to clear the zone.

Adrienne grinned in relief. She skated in hard chopping strides toward KJ, her stick out-stretched, knob first. "Here!" she yelled.

KJ spared her a quick glance, then grabbed the offered stick and took off toward the neutral zone.

From across the ice, the bench was hollering Adrienne's name. She clocked where the puck had ended up and decided it was deep enough in the Royals' zone that she could grab a stick. Half a dozen were held out for her when she made it across the ice. Adrienne grabbed the first one she could reach, then sprinted out to the middle of the ice to await the next surge from the Royals.

CHAPTER FORTY-FOUR

Vaughn reached over and swatted KJ on the knee. "Nervous?"

KJ tried to muster up her cockiest grin, but feared it might slide off her face. "I guess so."

"Play it like you did this morning," Vaughn said. "You were a beast out there." Murmurs of assent from the rest of the team accompanied their assessment.

"Just doing what I can to help," KJ said. She busied herself pulling her pads out of her bag. Accolades from her teammates always made her uncomfortable.

"It's a good thing too," Connie said. "We barely squeaked that one out. Who would have thought that after scoring sixteen seconds into the game, we wouldn't manage to put at least one more past their goalie?"

"You'll do great, KJ," Adrienne said. She patted KJ's thigh.

"Thanks," KJ said. The encouragement from her girlfriend was what she really needed. The tips of her ears started to heat up. All she wanted was to give Adrienne a long, deep kiss. There were times when they played together that all KJ wanted to do was get her girlfriend home and get her naked. This was looking to be one of those games.

"Bring it down, KJ," Vaughn said. "This is the big one. Can't have you all worn out."

"Am I that obvious?" KJ's face was starting to heat up.

"You were looking at her like she's a glass of water and you're dying of thirst."

She shrugged. "I can't help it."

Vaughn rolled their eyes. "Pace yourself, that's all I ask."

"One step at a time." Adrienne smiled at KJ.

"This is the one I've been waiting for," KJ said. And now that they were here, she wasn't sure how she felt. Excited, yes, but not as much as she'd thought. Her chance to do it over, to get it right was here, and yet... Winning wouldn't bring her dad back. It wouldn't erase the years she spent caring for him. She wanted to win, but she always wanted that. The game felt important, but somewhere along the way, she'd lost her laser focus on it.

Adrienne's phone buzzed from the depths of her purse, pulling KJ out of her thoughts. Adrienne swiped open her messages.

"Oh."

"Oh, what?" KJ asked.

"Message from Kaz." Adrienne held up the phone. "He and Lawrence are out front. I guess Lawrence wants to see us."

"Us?"

Adrienne nodded. "Yeah. It specifically says to bring KJ."

"Oh." KJ swallowed, her mouth and throat suddenly dry. "Maybe I should stay here."

"Nonsense." Adrienne stood up. Already in her skates, she towered over KJ. "I'll be there to protect you from my tiny little ten-year-old son." She held out her hand.

KJ groaned, then reached out and allowed herself to be drawn up next to her girlfriend. "I'm not worried he's going to beat me up," she said quietly as they headed out the door. "I'm…"

"You're what?" Adrienne asked when KJ didn't continue.

"It's dumb," KJ grumbled.

"How you feel isn't dumb."

KJ sighed. "I'm not afraid he'll beat me up. I'm afraid he'll be mad at me."

"Ah." Adrienne didn't say anything for a few seconds. "You know, if we live together, he'll be mad at you again. It's part of living with somebody else, especially a kid."

"Yeah, but…" It was KJ's turn to pause as she tried to put her emotions into words that made sense and didn't make her sound like an asshole. "Well, I didn't think it would be this hard."

Adrienne chuckled, a deep laugh that made KJ's mouth twitch into an answering smile. "Put it this way: you've gotten the first one over with. It's going to happen again, but you'll get better at handling it, I promise. You're really good with kids, KJ. I don't see why it has to be any different with Lawrence."

"With other kids, their mom isn't going to decide not to be with me if I mess things up."

Adrienne stopped. "Is that what this is about?" She took KJ's hands.

"Maybe." KJ stared at the floor.

"KJ, I love you. More than that, I trust you, not only with my heart, but with my son. We're going to disagree about how to deal with him, but I know you won't do anything to hurt him any more than you'd do something to hurt me."

"That's true."

"Then I have nothing to worry about. And neither do you. Now come on, let's go see what Lawrence wants, then you can get back to obsessing over the final."

"Oh, well, if those are my options." KJ trotted ahead to catch up to Adrienne.

They made their way from the warren of the locker rooms and out to the lobby. Lawrence was standing to one side, talking to two very familiar little girls. Harper pointed at them over his shoulder, and he turned, waving energetically, a huge grin on his face. Next to him, chatting with her brother and his wife was a man KJ had seen a handful of times before. He'd always been accompanying Lawrence, and she'd assumed he was Kaz. It was nice to have some confirmation.

"This looks like quite the party," KJ said as they walked up to the little group.

"Auntie KJ, Auntie Adrienne!" Emma threw herself at KJ's legs. The hug was no less exuberant than normal, even with the added presence of a fair amount of padding.

"Hi, Emma." She reached down and ruffled her niece's hair. "Hi, Harper. You two," she said in Erik and Sophie direction.

"You two?" Erik asked. "We come down to watch you, and all you have for us is 'you two'?"

KJ grinned at him. It was nice to see him and the family. "Thanks for coming," she said.

"Wouldn't miss it," Sophie said. "This is a big one."

"We're so proud of you," Erik said. "You're playing great. Everyone is."

"They really are." KJ beamed at her brother. This was almost as good as having her dad there to watch.

"Well, good luck on the next one," he said, reaching forward to corral Emma, who still held on to her leg. "I want to see you hoisting that trophy."

"Watch for us," Harper said. "We have signs!" She held up a not-too-battered piece of poster board that was as much glitter as paper.

"I will," KJ said. "I'm so happy to have you here."

She smiled widely at her family as they trooped out of the lobby, Emma and Harper competing to see who could hold their sign up higher. With a contented sigh, she turned to Adrienne.

"KJ, have you officially met Kaz?" Adrienne asked.

KJ shook her head. "I mean, I know who he is, but that's it."

"Then, KJ this is Kaz." She pointed from KJ to the man, then back again. "Kaz, KJ."

"It's good to meet you." KJ offered her hand to Adrienne's ex-husband.

His face relaxed into an easy smile and he took her hand in his. "It's good to finally meet you too, KJ." His hands were callused, his handshake was firm but with no attempt at a crushing grip. "I've heard a lot about you from Lawrence and Adrienne."

"Likewise."

"We watched you win!" Lawrence announced.

"We did, at that," Kaz said. "Lawrence wanted to talk to you before your last game. He's very excited for it."

"I'm stoked to have fans in the stands," KJ said. "Our fan base doesn't travel well, so it's good to have people cheering us on." She looked down at Lawrence. "Thank you for that."

Lawrence met her eyes. The smile dropped from his face and he gazed up at her, his brows lowered slightly as they did when he was being serious. He opened his mouth, then closed it.

"Go ahead, buddy," Kaz said.

Lawrence took a deep breath.

KJ crouched down so she was eye level with Adrienne's son. "So what's up?"

"I was really mad at you," he said.

"I know," KJ said. "And I'm sorry about all that. It didn't happen how I wanted."

"Yeah." Lawrence sighed. He looked up at his dad, then over at his mom. "I told Dad about it. He said he's never going to be married to Mom again, but it's not fair to not let someone else get married to her just 'cuz he can't, you know?"

"Um. No." KJ was having problems wrapping her head around the sentence. She'd stopped processing about the time Lawrence had talked about his mom being married again.

"Well, I wanted Dad and Mom to be together," Lawrence said with slow deliberation as if talking to someone who wasn't too bright. "But they're not gonna be. Dad said."

Kaz smiled and nodded encouragingly. Adrienne laid her hand on KJ's shoulder. She couldn't feel it very well through her shoulder pads, but that didn't matter.

"I know that's something you wanted," KJ said slowly. "I'm sorry that's not going to happen. But I like your mom a lot. And I like you a lot too. I miss how we used to hang out before you found out."

Lawrence smiled wide, flashing the same dimple KJ saw on Adrienne's face when she was happy. "Well, Mom smiles a lot when you're around. And I like you and Chester." He shrugged. "So I'm okay if you and Mom are together, I guess."

Adrienne's hand tightened over her pads.

KJ blinked fast to keep the tears prickling at her eyes from spilling over her eyelids. "I see. I should've known Chester would factor into things." She grinned to show she was teasing. "I'm glad you're willing to let me date your mom." She lowered her voice. "I wouldn't say it to her like that, though. Your mom doesn't need anyone telling her who she can or can't see. Can you imagine that?"

Lawrence giggled and shook his head.

"I'm really glad we got to talk about this," KJ said. "You've made me very happy. Can I give you a hug?"

Lawrence threw his arms around her neck and held on. Even having asked for it, KJ was a little taken aback. He seemed to be a different kid than the one who'd been giving her the silent treatment for weeks. She held onto his wiry body and hugged him.

Her nose had developed a sudden sniffle. She gave Lawrence a last quick squeeze, then stood up before she could start bawling all over him.

"Good talk," she said.

"You too." They nodded at each other.

"Okay, I'm done," Lawrence announced to the lobby at large.

"Glad to hear it," Adrienne said. "You doing all right?" she asked KJ.

"I think I'll manage," KJ replied.

"Good game, you two," Kaz said. He sounded genuine.

KJ realized she could easily come to like this man, notwithstanding that he'd managed to hurt Adrienne pretty badly along the way. Still, her girlfriend had made her peace with it, so KJ supposed she should as well.

"Thanks," she said. "We'll see you after it all goes down."

"Go Bolts!" Lawrence said.

Adrienne held out her knuckles for a fist bump, then followed KJ back toward the corridor under the bleachers to the locker room. She should have been getting her head into game mode—there couldn't be that much time before they were to go on the ice—but KJ couldn't shake the feeling that she'd already won.

"That was a really positive development," Adrienne said. "For the record, I had no idea he was going to do that."

"It's cool," KJ said in an elaborate show of casualness. Her elation was impossible to hide, however. She beamed at her girlfriend. "Lawrence doesn't hate me!"

Adrienne stopped in her tracks. "Of course he doesn't. He never really did." She took KJ's hands. "Seriously, though, KJ. This is a huge deal, and I'm ready to call it. Yes, we'll move in with you."

KJ tried to contain her excitement, but it jangled through her body, demanding a demonstration. She leaped up and slapped her hands against the wall above the entrance to the tunnels. Her heart was full, her energy high.

Adrienne shook her head in amusement at KJ's exuberance. Her grin widened as KJ advanced on her. When KJ held out her arms, Adrienne stepped into them, meeting her halfway. She stared into Adrienne's eyes, with their thick lining of lashes. She could fall into them if she gazed long enough. Adrienne didn't give her the chance. She pulled KJ toward her and leaned in until their lips met. Her heart raced as she parted her lips and allowed the tip of Adrienne's tongue to slip inside her mouth, tasting her, breathing her deep. KJ savored the flavor of her girlfriend, remembering their first kiss. It had been in a rink too, albeit with a huge audience. Every kiss they'd shared had been the best one, and this was no exception.

When they eventually parted, KJ's cheeks were damp, but she couldn't stop smiling.

"This is it," she said. "This is everything I want."

"We haven't won yet," Adrienne said.

"We've already won."

With a championship game to go, and the rest of her life with the woman she loved stretching before her, KJ couldn't have been happier. There was no stopping them now.

EPILOGUE

"Does she wear that every day?" Jamie asked as she bounced up and down to soothe the baby held across her front in a sling.

Across the front lawn of KJ's—no, their—house, her girlfriend was supervising the removal of furniture from the U-Haul. Her gray T-shirt was very familiar to everyone in their life by now. Even Lawrence would occasionally give her a hard time about it.

"Technically, no," Adrienne said. "KJ bought six of them for herself. Five to wear almost constantly and one that she's packed away. And then there are the ones she bought for her family. For her friends. For the regulars at the bar. For Carlos. I hear he even wears his on occasion."

"Classic." Jamie laughed. "Do you think she'll get tired of wearing the League Champions shirt everywhere?"

"It's been three months, and she's not showing any sign."

"I'm surprised she didn't buy more, to be frank." Jamie pressed her cheek against the top of Adam's head.

"How are you doing with him?"

"It's a bit of a learning curve, isn't it?"

Adrienne laughed. "It sure is. Don't worry, you'll get a full night's sleep again one day, I promise."

"That's good to hear."

"Mom." Lawrence stuck his head out the front door. "Can I take Chester for a walk? He's getting antsy with everyone coming and going so much. He's starting to make breaks for the front door."

"Of course, baby," Adrienne said. "Once you get back, maybe take him in the backyard and wear your arm out throwing the ball for him."

"Okay," Lawrence said. "And I'm not a baby." He pulled back into the house.

"They never stop being your baby, do they?" Jamie said.

"No, they don't." Adrienne sighed. "I keep forgetting not to call him that." She looked up. "We should clear out of the way."

Joe and Lou had gotten her dresser maneuvered off the back of the truck and were trundling up the walk with it.

Adrienne pulled the screen door as wide as it would go. "That goes in the upstairs bedroom," she said when they were closer. "Just put it down anywhere. KJ and I will get it settled in place."

"Yup," Joe grunted.

After some maneuvering to get it past both doors, Lou and Joe disappeared into the house. Happy barking heralded Lawrence's arrival with a leashed Chester.

"Try to be back in twenty minutes, funky bean," Adrienne called to his back while he trotted down the stairs.

"Sure thing, Mom." He disappeared down the block at a run, Chester pulling him on.

"Is there anything I can do to help?" Jamie asked. "I feel bad standing around while everyone's working."

"If you don't mind being in charge of the door, I'll go help with the boxes."

"Perfect." Jamie smiled at her. Her eyes were bright, even with the faint shadows beneath them. Adrienne remembered those days well. Luckily, Joe had seemed pretty attentive.

Hopefully they wouldn't have the same problems she'd run into with Kaz.

It had been nice to be able to take a break before diving back in to unloading the truck. They'd been moving since early that morning, and though it was closer to evening than she'd hoped they'd be, Adrienne could see the back of the truck. The volume of stuff she and Lawrence had accumulated over the year since they moved to Sussburg had surprised her. Fortunately, many of their things had already been moved to the house. While today was their official moving day, they'd been mostly living with KJ for the past month.

"Hi, sweetness," KJ said. "All rested up for the final push?"

"You bet." Adrienne passed her girlfriend a bottle of water. Condensation dripped down the side in the stuffy heat of the back of the truck.

"You're a lifesaver." KJ took a long pull from the bottle, draining nearly half of it.

"All right, it's your turn to direct," Adrienne said. "I'll get the last of this moved out." She took KJ by the shoulders and directed her toward the front of the truck. "Keep drinking that water. We don't want you getting dehydrated."

"Yes'm." KJ grinned. She hopped down, leaving Adrienne alone with a couple of bookcases and a dozen or so boxes.

Hers were easy to tell. They were clearly labeled. She'd left Lawrence in charge of packing up his own stuff. His labeling system seemed to be based on a system of elaborately drawn superheroes. He would have to figure out what that meant as he unpacked.

Sweat prickled into existence along her upper lip and trickled down between her shoulder blades. The sooner the truck was unloaded, the sooner she'd be able to settle somewhere for a while. First things first. Time to load up the dolly with boxes. Adrienne got to work.

People came and went as they had been all day, each moving something or bringing her water and food. KJ did take a break, though not nearly as long as she should have. Soon, she was ferrying the last of the boxes through the front yard into the house, while Joe and Lou wrangled the rest of the bookshelves into the upstairs sitting area.

They were the last of a large group. Half the team, along with a good group of teachers and staff from the school, had descended on her place in the morning. She'd hoped for a handful of helpers but had gotten far more than that. Without all the hands who'd helped throughout the day, they would still be getting the apartment packed up. The year was coming full circle. If someone had told her this was where she'd be almost a year after moving to town, she would have told them to lay off the hallucinogens.

The back of the truck dipped a bit behind her as she settled the last two boxes on the dolly. One was hers and destined for the bedroom, the other belonged to Lawrence and the Incredible Hulk.

Warm arms insinuated themselves around her waist and snugged her back for a nice, if sweaty hug.

"I can't believe we're almost done," KJ said in her ear.

Adrienne smiled. "I'll never be done with you."

KJ's chest shifted with a quick chuckle. Teeth closed lightly around Adrienne's earlobe, sending a delicious shiver down her spine. "You know what I mean."

"I do. You're too much fun to tease."

"Mmm. Keep teasing, but we're both going to be too wiped to do much about it tonight."

"That's all right. We have so much time to make up for missing one opportunity."

"True." KJ sighed. "I hate to miss any chance, you know?"

Adrienne wormed her way around until she was facing KJ without breaking their embrace. "I love you so much, KJ Stennes," she said.

"And I love you, Adrienne Pierce." KJ's smile warmed her voice. "Last two boxes. Are you ready to go home?"

"With you, always."

Bella Books, Inc.

Women. Books. Even Better Together.

P.O. Box 10543
Tallahassee, FL 32302

Phone: 800-729-4992
www.bellabooks.com